I0665304

SHANE: MARSHAL OF TALLAV

SONS OF TALLAV #1

CAILIN BRISTE

Shane: Marshal of Tallav

Copyright © May 2016 by Cailin Briste

All rights reserved. This copy is intended for the original purchaser of this e-book ONLY. No part of this e-book may be reproduced, scanned, or distributed in any printed or electronic form without prior written permission from Hot Sauce Publishing. Please do not participate in or encourage piracy of copyrighted materials in violation of the author's rights. Purchase only authorized editions.

Image/art disclaimer: Licensed material is being used for illustrative purposes only. Any person depicted in the licensed material is a model.

Second Edition
eISBN 978-0-9989125-4-7
Published in the United States of America

Hot Sauce Publishing
514 Americas Way #12514
Box Elder, SD 57719-7600

This e-book is a work of fiction. While reference might be made to actual historical events or existing locations, the names, characters, places and incidents are either the product of the author's imagination or are used fictitiously, and any resemblance to actual persons, living or dead, business establishments, events, or locales is entirely coincidental.

Warning

This e-book contains sexually explicit scenes and adult language and may be considered offensive to some readers. Hot Sauce Publishing e-books are for sale to adults ONLY, as defined by the laws of the country in which you made your purchase. Please store your files wisely, where they cannot be accessed by under-aged readers.

Disclaimer

Please do not try any new sexual practice, especially those that might be found in our BDSM/fetish titles without the guidance of an experienced practitioner. Neither Hot Sauce Publishing nor its authors will be responsible for any loss, harm, injury or death resulting from use of the information contained in any of its titles.

Smashwords License:

This ebook is licensed for your personal enjoyment only. This ebook may not be re-sold or given away to other people. If you would like to share this book with another person, please purchase an additional copy for each recipient. If you're reading this book and did not purchase it, or it was not purchased for your use only, then please return to your favorite ebook retailer and purchase your own copy. Thank you for respecting the hard work of this author.

❧ Created with Vellum

For Dr. K, the love of my life.

ACKNOWLEDGMENT

This book was three years in the writing. The path was sometimes arduous, but also satisfying. The encouragement, knowledge, and support of many people were vital.

The editors, cover artist, and staff at Loose Id guided a first-time author through the maze of prepublication details. I'd like to thank my editor, Kierstin Cherry, for the elbow grease she expended to help polish the book.

Without developmental editor Lea Schafer, this book never would have made it to market. If you'd read the first or second draft, as some of my early beta readers did, you'd agree. Lea Schafer took all the pain out of what could have been the devastating process of refining my original story. She taught me more about writing a good romance novel than the pile of how-to-write books I'd read. She was worth every penny.

Lew Rubens doesn't just tie people up. His suspensions are works of art. He is a true rope bondage Master who teaches all over the world. Thank you, Lew, for reading the suspension scenes in this book and brainstorming with me about the future of bondage in a technologically advanced universe. You are my evil genius muse. Someday we'll meet in real life at a Lewbari weekend.

My husband, Dr. K, has encouraged me to tackle every new project I've undertaken. Writing a novel was no different. He reads every word I write, discusses the storyline and character motivations, and brings me tea and toast. He's my chief research assistant, helping me test in real life the ideas that have bloomed from my imagination.

1

Adrianna sat, the picture of training excellence: spine straight, hands folded neatly in her lap, knees clasped together, feet flat on the floor. A slight whiff of musk and leather overlaid with a hint of something metallic stung her nose. The Frau's personal fragrance was a scent memory that triggered a desire to scrunch into a tight ball and scream herself hoarse. It was a reaction Adrianna had not succumbed to since the first of many lessons with the Frau. The sweat inching its way down Adrianna's back was the only outward expression of her struggle to stay unruffled, poised, and confident. She hoped even that wasn't obvious to Frau Heinrich, who along with Adrianna's mentor, Master Trey, was conducting her exit interview.

Although the woman seemed to live on the scent of fear, Adrianna was damned if she'd let her visceral response oblige Frau Heinrich. No. Adrianna managed to breathe, projecting calm. She mentally checked the time on her Electronic Biological CoServer again. *Please make this brief.* This interview with the intimidating, polished blonde was the last item on Adrianna's required checklist before leaving the Opio Institute to meet her new employer.

"I don't know whether Master Trey"—the Frau made a tiny moue after spitting out the name—"has told you, but one of the offers you spurned was resubmitted. The terms would repay your Opio loans completely. If you like, I'd be happy to assist you in breaking your current contract and accepting this offer."

Master Trey bristled. He wasn't required to come to this meeting, but he'd insisted. He filled any room he entered with his presence, a phenomenon for which his bulk wasn't the sole cause. Frau Heinrich's last statement had elicited his heated stare and intensified his air of dominance.

"That is not appropriate." He shot a glance at Adrianna. "We eliminated that offer for reasons other than money."

Adrianna's eyes had widened despite her efforts to remain expressionless. The infighting between Master Trey and the Frau was often grist for the gossip mill at the Opio. Rumor had it Master Trey had pushed the board to rescind Heinrich's right to mentor students. With no desire to get between the two, Adrianna nodded, keeping her eyes on Master Trey, waiting for the icy viciousness that was Frau Heinrich's trademark to respond.

"Trying to be helpful, Trey—dear. Nothing sinister."

Frozen crystals filled Adrianna's veins when Frau Heinrich's attention turned to her. Everything about the Frau was sinister, especially offers of help.

Adrianna responded to Heinrich's offer with as neutral a tone as she could. "I have a signed contract. It would be unethical to break it." If the woman already hated Adrianna for being Master Trey's mentee, why worry about offending her now? The Frau couldn't stop her from graduating. Adrianna's paperwork and accounts were all in order. The supposed point of this interview was to confirm that fact. Why couldn't Heinrich just do her job?

The Frau's eyes narrowed. "You seem so very tense, my dear."

"Get on with it." Trey's voice was a guttural rumble.

The Frau's teeth clicked shut. She bared them and hissed her response through them. "Don't push me."

Her civilized veneer settled back into place. "Adrianna, you doubtless understand that the premium paid for your special service will not apply to future contracts. Therefore, it would be to your advantage to learn as much as you can from your new employer and return to test with the Masters for additional sexual certification."

"Yes, Mistress."

Frau Heinrich continued, her voice a steady acidic drip. "Since you are a true submissive with mild masochistic tendencies, you are fortunate a Tallavan marshal holds your contract. We are always pleased to place our students with a marshal from Tallav. They're such an exclusive club of men."

Not a club, but exclusive? Yes. Only a man from Tallav could be a marshal. Wasn't there a historical reason? If she was going to be contracted to a marshal, she should probably find out. And what was with the Frau's sarcasm? Another mind fuck?

The Frau's voice drew Adrianna back. "They take excellent care of all those under their control. You can expect him to be a forceful dominant but always mindful of your well-being. A marshal's calling is to serve and protect; he states he is not a...sadist."

The muscles in Adrianna's torso clamped down on a shudder. Despite the information she had been given about her future employer, he was still an unknown. Her potential Master had started as a dream with all the accompanying fancies of perfection. The closer he came to her reality, the more dark possibilities impinged on her fantasy. Today she would meet him. The Frau, true to her sadistic nature, was picking at Adrianna's aversion to sadists, hoping for a painful reaction.

Trey reached out and took Adrianna's hand, squeezing it. Adrianna squeezed back and then released it. It was time to stand on her own two feet again. Master Trey was protective, but he wouldn't always be available to fight her battles. She'd allowed him to coddle her because it made him happy. That respite had come to an end, and he needed to realize it as much as she did. She braced herself to turn her focus on Frau Heinrich, who pinned her with glacial eyes before continuing with a smirk.

"He will expect you to function as his assistant as well as his companion. Such a lot of responsibilities. The possibility for failure..." Heinrich waved a hand in the air, allowing Adrianna to finish the statement in her mind.

With effort, Adrianna kept from narrowing her eyes. "Yes, Mistress. I also completed studies in ship administration and supply, and basic maintenance and housekeeping for small space vehicles. Before coming to Beta Tau, I was already a certified low-orbit shuttle pilot and emergency med tech."

Frau Heinrich's voice scraped across Adrianna's nerves like the slender fillet knife she liked to drag along the skin of her bound students. "Yes, I'm sure all these extra abilities helped secure you the position. Nevertheless, you understand that you will be meeting his sexual needs also, and do not doubt that if you fail in that arena, you can expect to be released from your contract and dropped at the closest station. In that eventuality, please come see me. I'm certain I could help you find your…true calling."

Master Trey gave a soft growl.

Adrianna couldn't stop from checking the time again. She steeled herself by looking at the picture behind and to the right of the Frau. It was a painting of smiling children. How very odd. Silence stilled the room. *Did I miss a question?* When she looked, the Frau's sneer had faded, and she was businesslike once again.

"The paperwork for your debt repayment appears to be in order. I see you've opted to make quarterly payments. Hmmm." She smiled. Adrianna didn't trust that smile. "You've also made a substantial prepayment. If more girls came to us as unsullied"—her smile became a smirk, showing a glimmer of white teeth—"as you, my dear, they would benefit from paying down their loan by almost a full year. How lovely for you."

"Yes, Mistress." Adrianna was ready to leave and never see Frau Heinrich again.

"Will you be meeting the marshal on the space station?"

The question confused Adrianna. It was the kind of thing a friend might ask. Frau Heinrich was no friend. "No, I'm—"

"Don't answer that, Adrianna." Master Trey's interruption was accompanied by a heated glare at the Frau.

With pinched lips, the Frau ignored his comment, focusing on Adrianna. "Do you have any questions?"

"No, Mistress." Adrianna kept her face blank. *Please finish.* To her surprise, the Frau did. Perhaps because Master Trey was there. If he hadn't been, the Frau would have drawn out the interview for the pleasure of tormenting Adrianna.

Once outside the Frau's office, Master Trey asked her to come with him. He shut the door to his own office behind him and motioned her to sit. The room was a reflection of the man. Most of it was taken up by an arrangement of two oversize plush armchairs and a side table. The desk, standard in other instructors' offices, was missing. A vidscreen on one soft green wall was the only accommodation to the need for record keeping. Emotionally charged images of Masters and submissives hung in rows in the remaining space. In the corner stood a spanking bench.

Rather than sitting, he balanced on the edge of the table, looming large above her, arms crossed over his chest.

"Adrianna, you are probably the most trusting individual I know. You're submissive to the bone. It's something I like about you, but it also scares the hell out of me."

Adrianna attempted to digest that statement. The point of her studies at the Opio was to train her to become a professional submissive, able to adapt to any Master who held her contract. Part of that had been learning how to create a relationship of trust between Master and submissive. Wasn't that the ideal they were all supposed to achieve? Her confusion must have shown on her face.

"Let me give you an example from today's interview. You don't always keep personal information to yourself. You need to be better about not telling people things that don't concern them. Frau Heinrich had no valid reason to know your travel itinerary today. What the hell business was it of hers where you were meeting the marshal?"

He sighed and dropped his hands to his hips. "Trust needs to be earned. You offer it up to anyone you think is nice and some you hope will be nice."

Her lips pressed together, she struggled to figure out what Master Trey wanted from her. Wasn't it trusting him that had brought her to the Opio in the first place? Where would she be if she hadn't trusted him? "But..."

"You would have told the Frau where you were meeting the marshal. And although she has access to the record of the classes you took at the Opio, she didn't know you are a shuttle pilot and med tech. She's exactly someone you shouldn't trust. She may work for the Opio, but she has connections to some unsavory people."

Adrianna wrinkled her forehead.

"Does that surprise you? It shouldn't. You trusted her because she works for the Opio even though you're aware she's deeply twisted. Assume the worst until proven otherwise. Understand?"

"Yes, Sir." She bit her lip, worrying it while her mind chewed on Master Trey's advice. Trust the Frau? No, it wasn't trust that made her respond to the woman's questions. It was the combination of Heinrich's position at the Institute and her shrewd display of dominance.

Trey sighed and scooped her hand into his. "I'm going to worry about you no matter what. I want you to be careful. I fully expect your contract with the marshal to work out. But things happen. I'm here if you ever need me. Message me. Okay?"

"Yes. Thank you, Sir." Adrianna tightened her fingers around his.

"We haven't discussed how you'll use your empathic senses once you leave the Institute." He moved to squat in front of her. "Don't tell anyone about your abilities or that you were born on Preatiens. People will use you for their own ends. Even nice people." Trey placed a finger under her chin and stared intently into her eyes. "That means the marshal too. Don't tell him. You've lived here at the Opio, blocking your empathic gift. It's in your best interest to continue doing so. Promise me."

Adrianna felt the full force of his personality behind the concern of his words. "I understand what you've said, and for the most part I agree with you."

Master Trey's chin dipped, and his eyes narrowed.

She continued. "I appreciate you want to keep me safe, but it's time for me to make my own decisions. So far I think I've done pretty well."

After a moment of hesitation, Trey nodded. "You have—"

Adrianna held up a hand. "I'm making only one modification to your advice. I'm not going to block my empathic senses. At least not routinely. I won't disclose I have them and I will be careful how I use them, but they're a tool. They'll help me protect myself."

Trey sighed. "I can live with that change."

Adrianna smiled. "I'll comm you regularly."

"Good." He stood and pulled her up into a hug. "Be safe." He kissed her forehead, turned her, and with a hand on her bottom, pushed her toward the door.

When she opened it, Adrianna looked over her shoulder, blinking back the tears that threatened to fall. "Good-bye, Sir."

SHANE GRITTED his teeth in lieu of snapping at the clerk to hurry up. Filing his request to have his leave reinstated was supposed to be quicker in person, but the man's methodical attention to detail was edging close to burning through the time advantage. *Fuck.* The muscles in his neck were tightening; he needed to relax before he got a throbbing headache.

The air in the Beta Tau Marshals Service Office was tinged with the odors of burned café, sweat, and noxious food choices. Nevertheless, eyelids clamped shut and head tipped back, he filled his lungs to the brim. After a moment, he dropped his chin to his chest, releasing the deep breath with a whoosh.

"Hard day?"

Shane opened his eyes to find the man peering at him. "Something like that. We done here?"

The clerk gave a nod. "Yes, your leave status is reinstated. If there's anything else I can do for you, let me know."

"Thanks." When Shane turned to depart, he heard his name called.

"Tiernan. What the hell are you doing here?"

To Shane's right stood an old friend. "Riordan. I knew you were back with the service. I didn't realize you were stationed on Beta Tau."

Riordan shrugged. "Yeah… Not my first choice. You have time to talk?"

"Sure." Shane nodded, noticing how much weight his friend had lost since last seeing him.

"My office is at the end here."

Shane followed. If only he could say something that would make things better. Paul Riordan's wife had died six months ago, and the toll the loss was taking on him showed in his slumped shoulders.

Riordan's office was an orderly arrangement of leftovers from previous inhabitants. Shane sat, elbows on his knees, in a worn-out chair, twining his fingers together and gazing straight at Riordan. His friend slouched, dark smudges under his flat-brown eyes.

Shane asked, "How're you doing?"

Riordan didn't respond immediately, instead rubbing the heel of his palm across his chest, staring vacantly at a sector map on the wall.

Finally, he spoke. "Better, I guess. At least that's what the docs tell me. Told me I had to go on meds to get reinstated. Still can't sleep."

"I'm sorry." That simple statement was the best Shane could do. Well-intentioned people had nearly choked him with their platitudes when his brother died. He wouldn't do that to Riordan.

"Thanks. They say time heals all wounds. They must be idiots." Riordan huffed and shrugged a shoulder. "Enough about me. What are you doing on Beta Tau?"

"I was on my way here on vacation. I got waylaid to run courier duty since I was coming to Beta Tau anyway. But I'm officially back on leave. I'm actually..." Riordan was the first person Shane had considered telling, beyond his best friend, Maon, about hiring an assistant. *Fuck it... Tell him. It will be undeniable once the woman is with you.* "I'm picking up my new assistant." He ducked his head, waiting for what he'd said to register fully.

When it did, the sound of Riordan's low chuckle was followed by the obvious question. "A Beta Tau assistant?"

Shane sat back, lifted his chin, and glared at Riordan. "Not my idea. Maon's." The words *I am not a lecher* hung on his lips. But fuck if he felt he had to prove anything.

"That sounds like Maon, but are you sure he was serious? You know Maon."

"We've been friends a long time. So yeah, I do know Maon. And he was serious. He thinks I need someone a little more..." Shane grunted while *he* now focused on the sector map hanging on the wall. "Permanent...for my..." Shane's lips twitched when he returned his gaze to Riordan and held up his hand. "His words, not mine—'romantic needs.' She's a graduate of the Opio Institute."

"Hmmmpf. Rumor has you with Ceana Kendrith. I knew that couldn't be right. No one in their right mind would go anywhere near that Tallavan she-devil."

Shane scratched the back of his neck and looked away. The gossipmongers on Tallav must be having a heyday. "Actually, I've contracted with her for a child."

"That evil witch?" Riordan's question made Shane wince. "I appreciate that your mother needs a female heir, but isn't there someone else that could carry a baby for you?"

Shane returned his gaze to Riordan and shrugged. "We're a founding family. My mother expects me to marry a Tallavan aristocrat. This is my alternative. My dad would raise the baby." Marrying and raising a Tallavan aristocrat's babies was supposed to be the ideal all Tallavan men longed for. Shane didn't and never had, but Riordan was one of those husbands who'd found happiness in a Tallavan marriage. Shane's own dream of happiness involved collaring the right submissive. Any Tallavan woman he collared would be ostracized. No woman dared admit to being dominated, even in the bedroom. He'd never made a point of hiding his predilections, so the gossips would assume the worst of any lady he was connected to. The Tallavan worst, allowing a man control over her. Not his. For now, he endured Ceana.

Riordan looked like he'd swallowed something nasty. "But Ceana Kendrith?"

Memories of interminable hours spent attending society functions, courting, even bedding the cream of Tallavan—aristocratic, unmarried women—only to be spurned by all flashed through Shane's mind. "I got no other takers. Ceana needs the money. So yeah, that evil witch. She's working it for maximum torture."

"Talking to that bitch would be agony, but you don't have to live with her while she carries the child." Riordan shook his head while he fidgeted with a loose thread on the sleeve of his shirt.

"Oh, you don't know the half of her wickedness. She insisted on natural conception."

"Shite, that is evil." Riordan flicked his gaze up to Shane and rubbed his fingers over his chin.

"A fucking nightmare." Shane's fists clenched. Pounding something wouldn't be productive, but it would feel fucking good. He forced himself to relax, unclenching his hands.

"Okay. I officially pity you." A weak smile played along Riordan's lips.

"Four months, and even considering a fifth makes me sick to my stomach." The chair squeaked when Shane shifted his weight.

Riordan's head jerked back. "She isn't pregnant yet? You tested her, right?"

Shane glared despite his resolve to keep his turmoil below the surface. "Of course. I wouldn't go near that woman if she wasn't fertile."

"Fate sure screwed with us. Bollocks! I'd give anything to be back on Tallav, raising kids with my wife. And fate's forced you to have a child when all you want is to be a marshal."

The two men sat quietly for a while, absorbing that thought. Finally Riordan snorted. "So tell me about your new assistant. I can see why Maon suggested one."

Adrianna restrained her desire to pirouette. She was free. Free to live her life. And, damn it, free to twirl if she wanted to twirl. No one and nothing but her own sense of propriety was stopping her. So she twirled and then looked around her, a little light-headed at her own audacity. She'd probably not be able to twirl in public once she was with the marshal, but right now she could.

No more of the Institute's regimentation. She would miss Master Trey. He'd been so good to her after rescuing her from Furzine and the Benefactor's attempt to coerce her into marriage. Master Trey's help with her postgraduate contract negotiations had been immense.

She'd chosen a Tallavan marshal. His payment would cover half her debt, and if he extended for additional years, she'd be debt-free in three. She did a happy dance and giggled. Her EBC verified that she was still on the mapped path to the spaceport bar where she was meeting him. Marshal Shane Tiernan. She turned the corner of the pedestrian corridor onto the main access way that led to the shuttle concourses and ran smack into a man coming the opposite direction. The reek of body odor hit her nose when her face mashed against the dark shipsuit that covered his lean chest. With a startled sound, she began to apologize but found herself drawn backward into the corridor, the man's rough hands gouging into her upper arms.

"Please excuse me, miss. Allow me to make certain I haven't harmed you." His tone was unctuous, but his grip was brutal.

"I'm fine. Really quite fine," Adrianna bleated, struggling against his hold while he steered her toward a long, dim service alley. She really didn't want him touching her, and she needed to free herself before the encounter grew ugly.

"There's a bench down that hallway. Let me take you to it so you can rest and recover."

Ahead there was no bench, but neither was the service alley empty. Another larger man waited at the end. Broad as he was tall, solid but not fat, he looked like he'd spent a lot of time in a heavy-gravity gym. He had more muscle in one of his arms than in her entire body. Worse, he was looking at her as though she were the last piece of homemade apple pie. *Not good.*

Her shoes found no purchase on the polished floor. With a twist, she attempted to free herself. Pain lanced through her shoulder when her wiry captor yanked her back. Her heart was thudding a mantra of danger. *Escape.* She had to get away before they reached the bigger thug. *Think. You've had defense training. What are you supposed to do?* The man had given up politely propelling her and was outright pushing. With a flash of insight, she let her whole body go limp and cried, "Oh, maybe you're right. I am a little overwhelmed."

The man's fingers slipped while he struggled to keep her from sliding out of his grip. Adrianna smashed her palm into his chin, pain exploding in her wrist and down her arm. The blow staggered him, allowing her to wrench herself from his hold. He bellowed curses harmlessly after her while she scrambled away.

An adrenaline boost sped her on her way. The goal—head as quickly as possible to the bar and grill where she was meeting the marshal. The thudding footsteps of the second man sprinting to catch her sounded closer. *How can a guy that size run so fast?* While she ran along the concourse, people browsing in shops turned to stare. Six shop lengths had never seemed so long. At last, eyes focused on the interior of the bar and the patrons seated there, she barreled into it, narrowly avoiding the waist-high railing that separated the tables and chairs from the open concourse. *Please let the marshal be early!*

She frantically scanned the bar. None of the faces of the customers turning to her resembled the marshal even a little.

Oh gods. Her pursuer was nearly here. She grabbed hold of the edge of the polished wooden bar top. A quick flip and she was over, landing on her feet on the other side. A frantic search for a weapon amid the barware and liquor bottles led her to an ice chipper. The bartender charged toward her, demanding in loud, angry tones that he get out from behind his bar. When she snatched up the chipper, bolstered by the solid handle in her grip and sharp tines pointing up, he pulled to a stop and raised his hands in capitulation. His reaction surprised her. For an instant, she paused, blinked and shook her head then turned in time to see the man chasing her slide into the entrance. With the commotion and everyone staring at her, it didn't take long for him to move in her direction.

Adrianna settled into a stance, prepared to defend herself. Her focus rigidly set on her pursuer, she resisted the urge to lower her defensive posture when a voice rumbled, "What is going on in here?"

Every head but the assailant's turned to look while Adrianna continued to stare at her attacker, frozen in a motionless tableau. "Marshal Tiernan?" Adrianna blurted, her voice squeaky.

A change washed over the thug's body. He relaxed his stance and wheedled, "Miss, I think you dropped this, and I wanted to return it to you." He pulled a credit chip from his pocket and held it out to her.

"Thank you. Put it on the bar," she responded, watching him closely.

As he did, he gave the marshal a smarmy smile, then slid out the exit and was gone.

Adrianna slumped. The breath she didn't know she'd been holding whooshed from her lungs. "Here's your chipper." She stretched what she hoped was a disarming smile across her face when she handed the tool back to the bartender.

Mouth hanging open, the bartender took the chipper. "Thanks." He rotated, staring at her while she scooted past him and made her way through the swing-top entrance at the other end of the bar.

Oh shit. A darted glance informed her the marshal was standing, arms folded over his chest, waiting for her. The desire to run washed through her. She filled her lungs with a deep breath and resisted the impulse, resolutely walking toward him, opting to keep her eyes lowered. When his boots came in sight, she slowly lifted her gaze, soaking in the details of the man planted like a mountain in front of her. Her initial impression of well-muscled male was confirmed. More than confirmed. What she saw below his belt... Mmm, some things just couldn't be tucked away and hidden.

She felt her cheeks heating and continued her upward perusal. When her inspection reached his face, she met the brightest pair of blue eyes she had ever seen. Unable to put one rational thought behind another, she blinked and succumbed to drowning in fathomless azure pools until they filled her entire vision.

"I asked, are you all right?"

She blinked. *The blue eyes have a voice?* "Y-yes. Just a bit shaken. My wrist is a little sore." She wiggled it, puzzled.

"You must be Adrianna Pacquin."

He was staring down at her. *Pull. Yourself. Together.* "Yes, I am." She winced. "I'm so happy to meet you."

"Hmmm. Well, I don't think we should continue this conversation here," he said with a meaningful glance over her shoulder. The bar patrons were still watching them with interest. "Follow me."

The marshal spun toward the exit. "Don't forget your credit chip."

Adrianna scurried back to the bar top, snatched it up, and with a sheepish smile, plunked it into the bartender's tip jar. It was the least she could do. She rushed to catch up with the marshal, who was already heading down the concourse in the direction she'd come.

"Damn." Where was her satchel? She brought a hand to her brow when the realization hit her that it had dropped when the man grabbed her.

"Is there something else?" Shane sent a distracted look back at her.

Adrianna tensed. "I lost my satchel. It must be around the corner. I hope." When they neared the turn, she clenched her hands. Everything she had taken before she fled home was in that bag, including her identity card and the data cube with her official contract. What was she going to do if they were gone?

"Is this it?" He pointed to her dark leather satchel, sitting open and empty next to a messy pile of her extra clothes, toiletries, and keepsakes.

"Yes, that's it." She gave a wobbly laugh, flicking a pair of panties back into the bag. While she sorted through the items, she inventoried her belongings. The only thing missing was her mother's silver locket. It was irreplaceable. Her shoulders hunched, but at least her ID and contract weren't gone. With shaky fingers, she finished cramming everything inside, zipped the satchel closed, pulled the strap over her arm, and stood.

With his intense blue eyes concentrated on her, he scowled with toe-curling force. Composure, composure, composure, she chanted rhythmically to her favorite Bach Invention. Bach always steadied her. Time for her to be still and wait for Marshal Tiernan's direction.

"Come." The command was terse. Adrianna fell into a jog to keep up with him, not wanting to further his apparent frustration.

2

Mentally fuming, Shane rearranged his plans, sending a delay notice to the security clinic through his EBC. Ms. Pacquin wasn't coming aboard until he'd settled a few issues with her. First, she'd explain what happened to his satisfaction or else. The life of a marshal was full of twists, turns, and abrupt outbreaks of chaos; an assistant didn't need to add to his problems.

Fuck. He'd gone along with Maon's idea to hire the woman, and now it was blowing up in his face. *Admit it, Tiernan. It was never about her ability to manage your schedule, research, and do the laundry.*

No, the idea was to relieve his sexual frustration. Most of the submissives he'd played with were either too emotionally needy to suit him, couldn't handle the demands of his work, or wanted to play games. He didn't play "make me."

His tally list of the perfect assistant was short but essential. An insistent need for submission that equaled his own to dominate. Able to work independently and accept the risk that came with working with a Tallavan marshal. Most of all, prepared to sever the relationship without a lot of emotional turmoil when he decided it was time.

Ms. Pacquin had seemed to fill the bill. Trained submissive. Well educated, with training in the essential duties he required. And she was under contract with no illusions of permanence. He'd hesitated at hiring someone so young and a virgin to boot. But the idea of a fresh, pure, nubile woman appealed to him. The opposite of Ceana was perfect. That had been the plan.

Shane looked over his shoulder to see if Adrianna was following. She was several yards behind him, trotting to keep up. Mentally reprimanding himself, Shane slowed, allowing her to catch up, and then pulled her in front and to his left. With a hand placed on her back while he scanned for trouble, Shane steered her toward his hotel.

Calm down. It's not her fault she was attacked. It better not be. Since his brother's death, simmering anger always seemed ready to boil over. He released the tension in the muscles of his shoulders and breathed deeper. Whether she was innocent or not, he did not intend to abandon her if she was in trouble. Only if necessary would he void the contract. Besides, she handled herself pretty well. He'd spotted the girl at the other end of the access way running toward him, and his instinct had been to find out why she was in such a hurry. He'd closed most of the distance between himself and the bar just as she sailed over the bar top. The look on the bartender's face after she grabbed the ice chipper was priceless. The thug had been three times as big, but she'd made him pause when she waved her weapon at him. A lot of warrior spirit in her actions.

At the hotel, Shane ushered her into the lift. While they stood next to each other facing the doors, Shane moved his head slightly to examine Adrianna. *Pretty name.* Despite the images he'd seen and the personal descriptor he'd read, she wasn't as small as he'd imagined. At six foot seven, he dwarfed most women, but she came to right below his nose. Dark slacks snugly caressed her long, lithe legs, showing off fit calves and thighs that culminated in the perfect curvaceous swell of hips and ass. When she'd vaulted over the bar, her athleticism had been on full display. Athletic was good. It was possible to do so many things with an agile woman. A demure cream blouse with a drop yoke and a sweet bow at the keyhole neckline covered her upper torso. It, too, was close fitting enough to reveal the jut of rounded breasts. Her nipples didn't show. What would it be like to pull the string on her shirt and delve inside to discover them? That brown braid snaking down her back would be perfect for winding round his hand to hold her in place while taking that enticing bubble butt. Physically she was everything he could hope for.

His cock hardened, trapped painfully against the tight fabric of his pants. Shane shifted his stance and attempted an unobtrusive effort to reposition himself at the same time Adrianna turned to glance at him. An appealing red tint flushed her neck and face. He wanted to reach over and nip her neck to see if he could make that blush deepen.

If she'd caused the commotion at the bar, he could brighten her ass to a tempting erotic red with a spanking. Fuck, he could paddle her for the fun of it. No, they had to talk first, and then if satisfied, he could spank her. Perhaps give her a taste of punishment before the fact so she'd be less likely to stray. That was probably better than what his cock was demanding he do—tie her up and fuck her senseless. *Gods.* Why did she have to be so irresistible?

When they reached their floor and the doors opened, Adrianna made a quick exit, as though she were eager to escape his proximity. He chuckled under his breath. The suite might be bigger than the lift, but she'd be just as alone with him there.

ADRIANNA WAS MORTIFIED. She'd blushed when she'd caught him adjusting his cock. The presence of strong male that emanated from him was magnetic when ramped up with potent overtones of arousal. And she wasn't even using her empathic senses. Not that she intended to. Those would stay bottled up. Her secret. Master Trey's advice flashed through her mind. She shouldn't reveal those abilities.

Despite her agreement with Master Trey to give her trust gradually, Shane had an overpowering presence. He was a walking sex dream that had her nipples taut and her clit pulsing. The urge to kneel and offer herself to him suffused her. *Idiot.* She was already his. *Your first.* The thought of him. Over her. Filling her. Would he take her right away? Her insides went quivery. With her body a puddle of desire and her need to submit battering her, she was on the edge of losing herself.

When the lift doors opened, she mentally pulled her shoulders back and dipped into the imaginary icy pool at her core, reinforcing her control. She would take things slow, as they came and not before, placing her confidence in him only when he proved himself trustworthy. That was going to be difficult. Her naturally submissive, trusting nature screamed at her to fall into his arms and divulge every stray thought running through her mind.

When she darted from the lift, she heard him chuckle. Was that a good sign or a bad one?

Shane opened the door with his key code and ushered her inside. The lounge, kitchenette, and dining area were luxurious, a mixture of leather upholstery, *bastingue* wood tables and cabinets, bronze fixtures, and floating glass shelves with artisan crafts from Beta Tau displayed. The giant bed in the next room caught her eye, a huge expanse of cream, sienna, and gold coverlet and pillows. Her hands tingled when nerves got the better of her.

Now that she'd met him in real life, Marshal Tiernan was both less and more than expected. Less upright, austere lawman and more long, slow drink of scotch, a whiff letting you know the burn was coming. Would he take her in that bed? He'd seen her pictures, so he knew she wasn't the sultry, sexy type. Oh sure, the Institute photographer had worked to make the most of her skinny legs, bubble butt, and small chest, but the focus had been on creating images of purity and virginity. After her deflowering, would she have what it took to keep a man like the marshal attracted to her? Master Trey had told her she was one of the most captivating submissives he had ever mentored. But would Marshal Tiernan think so? The marshal was the embodiment of Adrianna's dream man—tall and muscular without being muscle-bound. Rugged and handsome, he had a presence that exuded controlled strength. His dark hair was pulled back in a ponytail at the nape of his neck like an ancient warrior. *Please let him want to keep me.*

SHANE MOVED FROM behind her and settled himself on the center of the couch. "Take your shoes off."

Adrianna complied with the terse command, placing her satchel on the floor near the door, swiftly removing her boots and putting them next to it.

"Sit on my lap. Straddle me, facing me." Watching Adrianna's face while she straddled his knees, Shane took her by the wrists to help her settle. When her weight sank onto him, it was all he could do to resist groaning and pulling her forward to rub against him. *Don't go there. Your cock's not in charge right now.* He placed both her hands on his chest. "Keep them here."

"Yes, Sir."

Her pulse throbbed against his left thumb. With his right hand, he stroked her shoulders. The need to pull off her shirt to let his fingertips glide across the smooth skin beneath whispered at him. Instead, he gradually strengthened his motions, massaging tense muscles around her shoulders to the back of her neck. The drumbeat of her heart slowed while she relaxed under his touch. "Look at me."

Adrianna raised hazy green eyes to him. Shane leisurely trailed his fingers up her neck to behind her ear. With her face cupped in his palm, he ran his thumb across her cheek, relishing the velvet skin. He dropped his thumb to trace her lips, soft, full, and plush as a fresh, ripe apricot. *Would the taste be as sweet and juicy?* The image of her mouth savoring his cock made his groin tighten further. *In due time.* He hadn't had a woman arouse him to this extent in…forever. He brought his hand back down to grasp her other wrist. *Focus.*

"Ms. Pacquin, we are beginning a new relationship without knowing more than the information contained in the paperwork we exchanged. To complicate matters, our connection will be both personal and professional. If we're to make a success of this new arrangement, we'll have to be open with each another. When I ask you a question, I expect the truth. Trust won't happen if lies pile up between us. I will always be honest with you, and I require the same from you. Do you understand?"

"Yes, Sir." Her pulse was steady, her eyes clear.

"Excellent. Explain what was happening when I came into the bar today to meet you. Tell me in whatever fashion you prefer, but you must answer several essential questions. Did you know the man chasing you? Has this happened before? Does someone have reason to abduct you? Who is that person and why? Look at me while you speak." The skin of her arm was smooth under his fingers. He resisted the urge to stroke it. *Concentrate on her words and body language, Tiernan.*

"Yes, Sir." Adrianna paused and, with a deep breath, began. "Today I came straight from the Opio Institute to the spaceport by tram. I guess I've gotten used to being in a safe environment at the Institute because I wasn't paying proper attention to the people around me. I'm from Furzine, and although I wasn't ever allowed out in public without my chaperone and bodyguard, still I know not to get so distracted that I don't see danger coming. My second governess always said, 'It's sensible to be prudent and wise to be cautious.' I wish I'd heeded her advice.

"I was paying more attention to the map on my EBC and the shops of the spaceport. That's why I didn't take a wider arc around the passage corner. I ran into a man, who grabbed my arms and started hauling me off. I would have noticed him before he could grab me if I hadn't been—"

"Stop a moment. Assume that I understand you were uncharacteristically distracted from keeping an eye out for trouble." Shane's cheek twitched, her dithering amusing him. "How did you manage to escape?"

Adrianna pressed her lips together and gave a tiny nod. "He was dragging me off to a service corridor where the man coming after me was waiting. When I saw that, I knew I needed to get away from him before he got me close enough for that brute to grab me. So I went limp. That almost always throws people. If you've been resisting and suddenly go rubbery. That's what my defense instructor told me, but it's actually the first time I got to try that. It really does work."

"He let go, and you ran?" Shane prodded.

Adrianna's eyes widened. "Oh no, Sir. He did loosen his grip, so I took that as the opportunity to give him a good palm thrust to the chin. Then he let go, and I ran. I was really hoping you'd already be at the bar when I dashed in, but I didn't see you." She shook her head and continued. "The big guy was running after me, so I knew I'd need something to protect myself." Her voice lowered. "Weapons can be found everywhere. That's what my defense instructor said." She paused and gave him a significant look. While Shane struggled to keep his face blank, she resumed her account. "The best place to find a sharp object seemed to be behind the bar, so I vaulted over it and grabbed an ice chipper. I think that's when you came in. You know the rest of the story."

Shane leaned in, taking up a fraction more of the space between them. "That's the play-by-play, but you haven't answered my questions yet."

"Yes, Sir." Adrianna looked at her wrist in his hand, appearing to collect her thoughts.

"Eyes, Adrianna."

Her gaze snapped back to his. "Yes, Sir. First, I have never seen those two men before. Second, on Furzine it's always possible to get kidnapped, but it hasn't happened to me." Her mouth twisted.

"There is a person on Furzine who might want to abduct me, but I didn't think he would continue to pursue me after I enrolled in the Opio Institute. It really doesn't make sense that he would. Do you know who the Benefactor of Furzine is?" Her eyebrows lifted.

Shane's brow furrowed in response. "Yes, I do. Why would he want you? Not that you're not a lovely girl, but why you in particular?"

Adrianna shifted her legs and rear, which caused his cock to flare. Shane realized her position was becoming uncomfortable for her. "Turn and sit sideways across my lap, Adrianna. Keep your eyes on mine." He helped her adjust, maintaining a thumb on her wrist. Her thigh pressed against his erection. When she glanced down, Shane murmured in her ear, "We'll get to that. Answer my question."

"Yes, Sir." Her voice had grown husky, her eyes shimmering the dark green of freshly cut grass. She cleared her throat before continuing. "Why still seems odd to me, but it's what my father led me to believe. The Benefactor wanted a virtuous wife to marry and bear his children. Not easy to find on Furzine. It was an image thing, I guess. He desired his family to be above reproach." She shook her head. "My parents were scholars studying deviant sexual behavior. He was sponsoring my parents' research. My bodyguard was one of his men. That's why I was never accosted on the city streets."

Shane's jaw clenched. He couldn't understand how any parent would put a child in such a position.

"When I turned sixteen, the Benefactor requested that I start attending parties with my parents. I had met him many times in private and have always been very well treated by him. He can be kind to children. He proved as considerate in public settings, but he also began dropping hints about marrying me. My mother told him he'd have to wait until I was twenty-one. I think she'd planned to have me off planet before he could try to claim me. However, she died, and my father couldn't take care of himself, much less deal with my needs. In the end, he did stand up to the Benefactor. My father informed the Benefactor he was sending me off Furzine to my grandmother. Two days later, he was killed in an accident at his office. A heavy partition fell and crushed him."

Shane narrowed his eyes. The timing of her father's death was grossly suspicious. Poor girl. Losing both her mother and father at such a young age. He stroked her wrist with his thumb. Adrianna bit her lip but didn't stop.

"I wasn't confident in my father's ability to protect me, so even before his death, I'd already been looking for my own way off planet. I didn't want to go to my grandmother. My parents had pretty much left me to be raised by nannies, chaperones, and instructors." Adrianna flicked her gaze down in a momentary look to where Shane had placed his hand lightly on her hip. "I'd lived a life under constant supervision; I wanted something… more adventurous. I'd previously met Master Trey from the Institute at a dinner party and spent several hours talking with him that night. Unlike the academics who frequented my parents' parties, Master Trey discussed an actual lifestyle rather than population statistics and psychological profiles and such. I really liked him." Adrianna's tongue swiped across her upper lip while her cheeks bloomed with a little more color.

Her chin lifted. "To leave Furzine I would need to show that where I was going, I wouldn't become a burden. I had to have a job waiting, a student slot, or family that could support me. I knew if I went to the Institute, I'd be classified a student, so the Benefactor couldn't stop me from leaving."

Amazing, this girl is rattling away on my lap as though she's talking about her latest shopping trip. She was very lucky her plan to evade the Benefactor had worked.

"I used my father's e-address to send Master Trey a message, hoping the Benefactor's snoops would dismiss it as work related. Master Trey came to Furzine a few days after my father's death. I slipped away to meet him, signed the Institute contract, and immediately went with him to the Furzine spaceport." Adrianna's hands curled into fists. Shane pressed his thumb under her closed fingers and rubbed her palm while Adrianna finished her story. "We'd gotten through customs control when a group of men including my bodyguard ran up and demanded that the Federation officials turn me over to them. Since I was now on Federation territory, Federation law applied. There were no criminal charges against me. I had a contract with and placement at the Institute waiting, so there were no immigration problems. The Feds refused to hand me over. I escaped just in time. I spent a year at the Institute, and I assumed I didn't have to worry about the Benefactor anymore. Although I'm still a virgin"—she paused to swallow—"my studies wouldn't be considered virtuous. I expected the Benefactor to have forgotten me."

Story finished, Adrianna sat, her muscles visibly tense. She latched unblinking eyes on Shane. He studied her. Desire had tightened its hold on him when her lips had spoken the word *virgin* and then pursed as she swallowed. Kissing her now was out of the question. Especially since she was anxious, worried about his response to her involvement with the Benefactor. If she thought Shane would cancel her contract, she didn't realize that dismissal was not an option. Not with what she'd told him about the Benefactor. No, the Benefactor and the criminal society he ran, wrapped in the camouflage of a federated planet, was one of the biggest problems in this sector of the Federation. As Furzian head of state, he was untouchable.

If the Benefactor wanted Adrianna, Shane would protect her. Would she give him an edge in the ongoing effort to unravel the Benefactor's machinations? He hoped so. Besides, he was beginning to like her. Maon was right. She did solve Shane's craving for a physical relationship on his terms with no strings attached, and she could think on her feet, although she'd need more training.

With gentle fingers, Shane grasped Adrianna's chin. His lips brushed across hers when he bent toward her. "Thank you. I appreciate that it was difficult for you to tell me some of this. Is there anything else you want to tell me?"

Adrianna gave a quick shake of her head. "No, sir."

Shane pulled back and stared long and hard at her until a blush stole over her cheeks. His cock pulsed. He resisted the urge to satisfy his physical desire.

"Good. We have a lot to do today. You'll be getting an upgrade to your EBC and a new wardrobe." He ran his finger along her shoulder. "First I want to establish the protocol for how we will address each another. When we are in public or working in an official capacity with others, you will call me Marshal or Marshal Tiernan. I will call you Ms. Pacquin or Pacquin. When I wish you to respond as my submissive, I will call you Adrianna. You will call me Master. I do not want a twenty-four-hour submissive relationship with you. It will be clear when I wish you to assume your submissive role. You will obey my commands promptly and fully. All other times you may call me Shane, and I will call you Dria. As Dria, you can freely express yourself to me, but I will expect you to be respectful. We will be spending a great deal of time alone together. The *Adrasteia* is a small ship, too cramped to allow an atmosphere of tension to intrude. I want it to be your home, a place you can be comfortable and relaxed. Can you do that, Dria?"

Shane's whole world narrowed to the woman on his lap. Her warmth and softness soothed him. How perfect it would be to wrap himself around her and soak in her comfort. With every small shift of her body, arousal lit up a living flame inside him. How had he gotten so needy?

Adrianna gave him a hesitant smile. "Yes, Sir. I mean, Shane. That sounds wonderful to me. I am used to interacting with only one or two people, and stayed home most of the time. I think I will adjust easily to shipboard life"—peering up at him through her lashes, she blushed—"and to you."

"That pleases me immensely." He paused and brushed his lips across hers again. "You please me very much." With his fingers, he grazed the side of her breast, letting them drop to caress the sweet curve that flared out below her waist, a spot designed for a man's hand to rest, to grasp, to control a woman while he pulled her body onto his cock. His erection twitched, urging him to bury himself inside her, but that would have to wait.

When Maon had suggested Shane hire a paid submissive, the notion had rubbed Shane wrong. It had seemed like hiring a glorified long-term prostitute. His friend had reminded him she'd also be his assistant and advised he romance her before indulging in any added benefits. Romancing or not, he didn't pay for sex. And he certainly didn't pay to claim a woman's virginity. He might push at the constraints of his Tallavan upbringing, but the objectification of women was a Tallavan thou-shalt-not he held to. Besides, if he wasn't able to seduce Adrianna into his bed, he was in more trouble than he thought. Her virginity was his to take, but he wouldn't until he knew money wasn't her only reason to consent.

"Your contract stipulates that you engage in sexual activity with me. That won't be happening."

Adrianna's face paled.

Her next breath came with a jerk.

"Shhh. Don't worry. What I mean to say is that I want to give you a choice. I am very much attracted to you." He pulled her lower lip down, his focus riveted on her open mouth. His nostrils flared. "Very attracted. But I'm giving you the option to decline. Right now, you can tell me no sex and that you just agree to be my assistant. I will honor that for the full term of the contract. Do you wish to alter the terms of our agreement?"

Adrianna's eyes widened. "No," she whispered around his finger on her lip.

Shane's cock greeted the news with a twitch. "Thank you. You may change your mind at any time, and as our relationship develops, I'll try to give you the choice of refusing before taking things further." The serious little furrow on her forehead begged to be kissed. She was wonderfully sweet, a sweetness he longed to taste and explore. First he would do what he'd been wanting to do since he'd caught sight of her sailing over the bar, her incredible ass on full display. "Adrianna?"

Adrianna's spine straightened. "Yes, Master?"

Shane's voice was calm and measured when he spoke. "When I address you as your Master and tell you to go somewhere and wait, I expect you to go there, remove your clothing, fold it neatly, and set it aside. Assume a kneeling position, legs wide, hands clasped behind your back. Do you understand?"

Adrianna's nostrils flared when she responded. "Yes, Master."

"Excellent, Adrianna. Please wait for me in the bedroom. You may take a pillow from the bed to place under your knees."

"Yes, Master." Adrianna climbed off Shane's lap and went. Shane sighed, enjoying the warmth spreading through him and the prospect of finding her kneeling in the bedroom.

3

When Shane entered the bedroom, he stopped midstride, allowing himself to bask in the pleasure of the sight of Adrianna, fully submitted and waiting for him.

"Stand, Adrianna."

With fluid grace she rose, long limbs straightening until she stood with the elegance of a marble caryatid. She was no stone column, but a living, breathing woman, a maiden to whom he would demonstrate the surging power of a man when he broke through her virginal barrier. A rumbling growl filled his throat while heat flooded through him. Gods, it would be so easy to let his control slip.

Slow down. You're not some rutting brute. First things first, Tiernan.

His words roughened by desire, he said, "If at any time you need me to stop what I'm doing, you will say the word *red*. I will not terminate your contract for using your safe word. Do you understand?"

"Yes, Master."

Fuck, he loved the sweet lilt of her voice. With deliberate steps, he eliminated the distance between them until he was bare inches from her. The heat from their bodies mingled. He held his breath, the better to hear her slightest response while he stroked her collarbone with his fingertips, moving them to circle under her breasts then spiral in toward her pale nipples.

No reaction. No sigh. Not even a tiny intake of air.

"Hmm." Hot need thrummed through him. Yet she was unmoved.

A tremor pulsed along his spine when he reached to clasp her nape, threading his fingers into the tight strands of hair held in place by her braid. With a tug, he pulled her against him and began a soft perusal of her lips. It was almost painful to brush against a mouth he wanted to plunder. He slowly drew the tip of his tongue across her plump bottom lip. When she opened to him, he kissed her deeply, tasting and teasing.

The sense of urgency that was hammering him found no equal response from Adrianna. He discerned no overt reaction from her, and yet he was drowning in the sweet lushness of her mouth. His pants had grown tighter while his erection hardened to a throbbing ache.

Gods, maybe he'd been right in comparing her to a caryatid. She was more like an android who could mimic the act of sexual desire without the passion that transcended the purely physical.

He stroked her breasts, pulling and tweaking her nipples until they were stiff and erect.

No other response from her.

Nothing audible.

Her breathing hadn't changed. *What the fuck?*

With two fingers, he reached and swabbed her pussy. She was wet, so her arousal was unmistakable. Her body wanted him, but her mind was somewhere else.

This wouldn't do. If her instruction at the Institute required her to become a sexual automaton, then he needed to reverse that training. He wanted more than just a pliable body.

"Where are you, Adrianna?"

Her brow wrinkled. "Where am I? I'm here with you, Master?"

"Are you?"

She nodded, but her eyebrows remained knitted together. "Yes, Master. How may I please you?"

Her face grasped between his hands, he demanded, "Look at me, Adrianna."

Eyes, a hazy green, any hint of sparkle muted, rose to meet his.

Was she in subspace? She couldn't be, but with her lack of reaction and those eyes... "When I am with you, I want all of you present. Even though your bio said you slide into subspace easily, I never imagined..."

He tapped her face with one finger. "Don't. I want you with me. No disconnecting. You will experience everything I do to you fully. Understood?"

She blinked. "Yes, Sir."

Shane watched the slow transformation while her body became more animated and her eyes brightened. Most submissives required a steady buildup of pain and endorphins before they found subspace. This ability to will herself there was something he had never encountered. He rubbed against her, pressing his chest into the cushion of her breasts, sliding his erection, hard and demanding, along her belly.

"I want to feel, hear, and see your response. Don't hide from me. I need your responses to make this right for both of us." With those words, he wrapped her braid around his hand and pulled her head back, taking her mouth in a devouring kiss.

This time, her tongue twining with his, Adrianna moaned, her body melting into him, her heat penetrating his skin. The insistent ache of his cock incited him to sink into her warm, wet depth. A groan rose from his gut in testimony to his rampant desire.

"Much better," he breathed, kissing his way up to her ear, biting, then sucking on the lobe. "Much, much better. Trust me not to harm you." He flicked his tongue along the shell of her ear. He had to stop. *Get back on track. You're taking this slow. Remember.*

"Mmmmm. Come." Shane drew Adrianna to the bed, sat, and then hauled her over his lap facedown, holding her in place with one hand across her shoulders and the other on her back. "Adrianna, you have a truly glorious ass." It was impossible not to appreciate the perfectly rounded shape or to smooth a palm over each firm half. "Plan on me spanking you regularly." He gave her a light slap and watched the jiggle. "Huh. Definitely gonna spank you often." Among other things. His cock twitched its agreement.

He returned to stroking, getting lost for a moment in the softness. Her skin was slightly cool to the touch, but that would soon change. He smirked, then caught himself. This wasn't going to be that kind of spanking, not erotic, not sensual. He'd always taken pride in his ability to remain in control, but it was fucking hard with this delectable woman pressed against his thighs.

"I don't enjoy punishing, but I will when it needs to be done. Punishment in whatever form it takes will always be painful."

He squeezed her shoulder. Spanking might not be the appropriate penalty for her, but it was his preferred corporal punishment. Time to find out her reaction before they were in a situation where it was needed. This would help him decide.

"Day to day you can expect me to discipline you, but the goal of that is not to cause you pain and will rarely be physical. Punishment is different. It's reserved for willful disobedience. If you refuse to obey me, without using your safe word, I will punish you. If you lie to me, I will punish you. If you do anything that reflects negatively on the Marshals Service, I will punish you. Are we clear?"

"Yes, Sir." The response was muffled since Adrianna had buried her face in the bedding. He bent and kissed her shoulder, his nose filling with her bright, tangy scent. She was sweet lemonade on a hot summer day. He controlled his desire to continue to nuzzle.

"I'm going to give you a sample of what to expect. I spank a lot in play. This will not be like that."

Adrianna's core tensed against his thighs.

"Five swats. No buildup. Expect them to be hard and to hurt. It would be better if you relaxed your muscles."

"Yes, Sir." The lilt was gone from her voice.

The tension in her body decreased slightly, but she was nowhere near at ease. He hadn't really expected her to be.

"Are you ready?"

"Yes, Master."

Shane raised his arm and brought his palm onto her right butt cheek. His hand flashed, and he struck her left butt cheek. He dealt two swift, forceful spanks to each of the sensitive areas where her ass and thighs met. His final blow smacked her right butt cheek with another brisk slap.

Adrianna had cried out with the first strike, and by the last she was sobbing. Shane pulled her up and into his arms, snuggling her against his chest. A shudder shook her frame. He'd limited the spanking to stinging blows and, despite what he'd told her, used a light hand. Her aversion to excessive pain was documented in the paperwork he'd received from the Institute. She clearly required pleasure to balance pain. Her high marks in composure still baffled him. To do well, she'd have had to endure physical and emotional duress. Her ability to drop into subspace might explain that, but how did she have such amazing control? She was intriguing.

"Hush. You're a good girl. Hush now." He stroked her back, her arms, her hair, comforting her until she quieted.

He brought her chin up, looking into her eyes for long seconds. "I'm proud of you. You took that spanking bravely." She sniffled and nodded. With his thumb, he wiped the damp trail from her cheek, kissed her forehead, and pulled her close. A slight judder ran through her, and he gave her a squeeze. Holding her was incredible. This was what he needed. Someone to hold, someone to bury himself in, a retreat from the misery that beleaguered him. He brought his lips to her forehead and kissed her again.

"You are such a beautiful submissive." He tweaked the nipple of one breast and then the other. She quivered slightly. Whether as a last remnant of her tears or in arousal, he couldn't tell. "I will always find pleasure in obedience and honesty even if the truth is unpalatable. Don't lie to me, Adrianna. It's the one thing I can't abide in a submissive."

"Yes, Sir. I understand."

"Good. You deserve a reward." His cock twitched.

"Yes, please. Thank you, Master." She trembled in response.

He dipped her back and touched the tip of her nipple with his tongue, then swirled it around before drawing the nipple into his mouth. *Mmmmm.* He could suck for hours, but he didn't have much time, and he wanted to give her a release for taking her sample punishment so well. His personal code as a Dom required he do so, but the need to experience her complete abandonment to pleasure was his truer motivation. He continued to tease her nipples, enjoying each taut peak, trailing his tongue over it before nipping and sucking. The little gasps Adrianna made while he played were an erotic counterpoint each time he grazed his teeth over her breasts. She was so responsive. What would it be like to get his rope on her? He would make her beg for the friction of hemp along her skin.

He drew his fingers featherlight down her side, spread her legs, and stroked her mound until she was bucking up, seeking him to press into her folds. Which he did, sinking one finger inside, exploring her moist heat. This time her gasp was louder, her back arching in a sharp jerk.

He smiled and flicked his tongue in teasing circles around her nipple, the flavor of her skin just the right combination of salty and sweet. What would her pussy taste like? He swiped through her wet arousal, bringing his fingers to his mouth to lave, licking up every tart drop. Her flavor was like sunshine, warm with a citrusy tang he could become addicted. He returned his fingers to her pussy, swirling to find the sensitive nub and caressing it with measured strokes. She was amazing. When he finally had the time to do things right, he would make her come and come and come.

Lips grazing her succulent mouth, he murmured, "You are so delectable, Adrianna. I could spend hours touching you, tasting you. I want to savor every inch of you." He drew two fingers over her clit to her entrance, rubbing up and down. The need to watch her tumble into orgasm was running counter to his desire to make this perfect for her. She moaned, her hips rocking on his lap in a gentle rhythm. "Does that feel good, Adrianna?"

"Mmmm, yes, Master."

"Would you like me to fuck you with my fingers?"

"Yes, please, Master." She bucked harder against his hand.

He bit her nipple lightly and moved his index finger inside her tight channel, curling and exploring to discover where his strokes gave her the most pleasure, while avoiding tearing her hymen. "Let me hear your desire, Adrianna."

The injunction had barely left Shane's lips when Adrianna's breathing hitched. She puffed out little breathy exclamations that touched off emotions inside Shane that he'd not experienced in a very long time. His deep-seated need to protect, to provide, and to possess, yes, even to cherish was awash in satisfaction when she conceded control of her body to him. It had been ages since he'd been with a submissive that brought out this response. That he felt it so soon was beyond crazy. Maon had said he was an emotional wreck. He must be if he was allowing thoughts of cherishing to infiltrate his brain. Domination. That was what he needed, a woman to dominate. And this one was as close to ideal as he had ever found.

"You are so perfect," he groaned, taking possession of her lips in a deep kiss, pushing his tongue into the warmth of her mouth while he thrust two digits into the snug moisture of her sheath. With his thumb stroking her clit, Shane urged, "Come for me Adrianna, come for me."

The blush that had stolen across her neck and upper chest deepened. A frenetic energy overtook her until her pussy clenched tight on his fingers, and her body jerked, rigidly arched. He breathed in the heady scent that rolled from her and found that he was panting too, watching the orgasm work its way through her.

When she stilled, he withdrew his hand and stroked her hip while he continued to murmur words of appreciation. With a half-lidded stare, she offered him a sweet smile that crept up her face from her lips to her eyes like a sunrise cresting over the horizon. He kissed the warmth of that smile.

With a heavy sigh, he pulled away. "*A mhuirnín*, sweetheart. We have much to do."

He scooped her in his arms and carried her into the bath, setting her on the counter. With a freshening cloth from the warmer, he wiped her clean and then rinsed his hands. When she was on her feet, he said, "Get dressed." A quick pop of his palm on her rear made her squeal. He grinned to himself. Maybe Maon was right. He'd needed something to brighten his life. Adrianna Pacquin was a blaze of sunshine that had already pushed back the gloom that overwhelmed him. *Fuck.* He was one lucky bastard.

He stepped into the bedroom and watched her pull on her panties. "We need to eat, shop for your shipboard wardrobe, and keep an appointment to upgrade your EBC and immunizations." Another drop of pleasure plopped into his heart when she looked up, eyes and mouth rounded in O's of surprise.

THE DAY HAD BEEN like her introductory low-orbit shuttle ride. Adrianna had struggled to maintain her equilibrium. That flight weeded out students who suffered from air or space sickness. It had been a yank-and-bank thrill that left her queasy and visually staggered. She wasn't nauseous today, but she was overwhelmed with all the stops they'd made and all the clothes Shane had bought her.

Now, she lay on an examination table at the Federation EBC Clinic. In the next room, Shane and an EBC doctor went over the changes and enhancements Shane wanted to make to Adrianna's nanite specifications and her EBC. While they were talking, a technician came in and placed her arm in a medical analysis unit attached to the side of the table. She noticed a slight sting when it took blood and tissue samples.

Upon entering the examination room, Dr. Shinjinta introduced himself. Shane grasped Adrianna's hand. "I'll be leaving you in Dr. Shinjinta's capable hands. He'll explain the particulars of what he'll be doing. I have errands I need to run. I'll be back before you're finished. Try to relax and rest if you can."

"Yes, Sir. Thank you." Adrianna's gaze turned to the doctor when Shane left.

Dr. Shinjinta, a short, kind-looking man gave her a perfunctory smile. "Ms. Pacquin, why don't you come with me so I can explain the procedures we'll be doing today?" He offered her a hand, which she took and then followed him to the next room.

The doctor sat in the standard-issue office chair behind his utilitarian desk. A variety of anatomical models cluttered shelves to his right. The opposite wall held a large cutaway image of the human brain. He gestured for Adrianna to take one of the chairs in front of him. "I'll be introducing several additional nanites to your system. One set will transform your current EBC into a military-grade hardened unit. We'll be injecting you with a cocktail of ingredients that the nanites will use as building blocks for the project. In addition, you'll receive a set of long-term military-grade replicating nanites that will make up the storage and information transport system of your upgraded EBC. You will have access to all files via tablet as you have in the past, but there will be an added layer of security access. Your internal access will work as usual. Faster, but you are unlikely to notice the increase in speed. Your civilian system is top quality. Its speed benchmark is close to the one we are giving you today."

Adrianna's eyebrows went from raised to furrowed when she grasped what the doctor was implying. Military grade. Hardened. That meant she'd be storing things that others weren't supposed to find out. She imagined someone had stamped TOP SECRET across her forehead. Adrianna, secret agent and nemesis of the evil forces plotting the downfall of the Federation. Thrilled, she also feared what would happen to all the bits and pieces of her life stored away in her current EBC. Would she lose the few comm messages from her mother and father she'd saved? What about her personal vids and images? And the texts and training manuals from her studies? She hadn't been able to afford backup storage, so her EBC was the only place most of her files existed. She was fast becoming someone else, someone new, someone she liked, but not someone who wanted to dump her past in the dustbin.

Dr. Shinjinta continued. "You will still have access to your current set of nanites and information stored there, but those nanites will not be able to access the new system. If you wish, we can have that information security validated and stored to the new system. Anything not passing the validation process would still be available on your old nanites."

"Yes, please. That would be very helpful." Adrianna exhaled slowly.

The doctor folded his hands across his stomach. "Very good. In addition, Marshal Tiernan has asked us to upload a variety of information modules to your system. These include a complete copy of Federation law, a number of language courses, and additional courseware in subjects chosen by the marshal. Duplicates have been sent to the marshal's shipboard account if you prefer to read or study from a vidscreen."

After a glance at his notes, the doctor said, "I'll also be surgically inserting a subvocal microphone and transmitter in your neck and attaching an audio receiver to your auditory nerve. The set you are receiving is modified to respond to the marshal's own transmitter and receiver alone. It will allow you to communicate in private even when others are present."

Adrianna nodded, the overwhelming sensations from earlier in the day crawling back up her spine. Secret agent indeed. "But won't my lips be moving?"

The doctor smiled. "No, most people do not realize that when they read they often subvocalize. Novice readers do move their lips. But the movements skilled readers make are not detectable by people. It takes a machine to register this type of subvocalization. With practice, it won't take long for you to stop moving your lips."

"Oh."

"You'll also receive a cocktail of immunonanites that expands the number and types of diseases and allergens covered by the standard immunization you've already had. Do you have any questions?" He gazed at her, awaiting a response.

"No, sir."

The doctor rose and moved to sit on the edge of the desk next to Adrianna. "You'll be able to rest or read through most of this if you like. It will take us about an hour to produce the new nanites, using your blood and tissue samples to ensure they will integrate properly with your body. Once they are ready, we'll place you in twilight sleep for the injections and subvocal insertions. After you wake, we'll monitor you before releasing you."

He patted her arm. "My tech, Ms. Jeffson, will take you to the surgical bay, prepare you for surgery, and get you settled into the surgical couch. We'll talk again before you receive the sleep medicine."

"Thank you, sir." Adrianna rose from the chair, acknowledging and then following the tech.

"You'll need to undress. Once you've been through the irradiation booth, I'll give you a gown to wear."

Adrianna soon found herself freshly irradiated, wearing a surgical johnny that stuck to her skin in odd places. When she squirmed, trying to pop loose the plastic, it sealed to larger swathes of her body. She had the uncomfortable impression she was being shrink-wrapped. The bed's medical analysis unit attached to her left arm constrained her movements, keeping her from using her free arm to loosen the clinging fabric. She lay still, deciding it was her only option to avoid looking like a delicacy preserved for later consumption.

Adrianna checked the time on her EBC. She'd been lying here fighting the gown all of five minutes. With a whoosh of air, she forced the constricted muscles of her diaphragm to loosen. *Calm yourself.* With the strains of Tasmanos's "3rd Concerto for Synth Violin" flowing through her mind, she began working her way through her breathing exercises. The concerto was a piece that was played to her in the crib, later becoming an integral part of the regimen used to train her empathic skills.

Centered again, she cataloged the day's experiences and considered the changes in her life. First was Master Marshal Shane Tiernan. Her interactions with him had shown him to be firm and clear about what he expected from her. His rules were unambiguous. His generosity was evident by the amount of money he had spent on her. Her new clothes were neither cheap nor shoddy. He'd bought enough for two girls. Since the moment she'd set eyes on him in the bar, he'd impressed her with his solid strength and self-control.

At first, she had been concerned about his offer to skip the sexual side of their contract. It was hard to believe that he would abstain from sex with her for an entire year. He'd said he would never lie to her. Per Master Trey's rules to trust slowly, she'd used her empathic abilities to help her discover what lay beneath Shane's words. When she'd opened her senses fully to him, she'd found it possible to know the underlying honesty of all he said. It had been to her advantage to take down her empathic barriers. It was true he could touch her deeper and gauge her reactions to him, but she could also determine his emotional state. She read his concern for her.

A tendril of guilt inserted itself into her thoughts. No, she hadn't really lied to him. Her idiotic nature made her feel guilty about not disclosing everything about herself. Master Trey would be proud of her. She wasn't sure how long she could or even should hold back from Shane. His emotional reactions were…perfect.

When he spanked her, her empathic ability provided clear, almost tactile evidence of his desire to protect her. The pain had brought on tears, but his effort to avoid truly harming her had increased their flow. She was aware in every cell of her body of the dominance that oozed from his pores. He'd taken her in hand in a way that was best described as masterful. Master. Her first exclusive dominant/submissive relationship. The thought fed a tiny pool of giddiness that threatened to bubble up in a giggle of delight. Her Master!

A wisp of hair had escaped her braid, and she fiddled with it, smiling to herself. What would they do when he returned? He wanted her. Desire had been a constant thread woven through his emotional state. His erection was also hard to miss. *Soon. Please. Soon.* Marshal Shane Tiernan. Tall, potent, scorching. Lying on the bed, she surrendered to her imagination and let her fantasy run wild.

That bonus of a fine physique walked toward her. A better-looking man didn't exist. When he engulfed her in his arms, she grabbed hold of his tapered waist, relishing how perfectly it fit in her hands. He moaned into her mouth while she clutched his gorgeous ass, digging into the firm flesh. With powerful arms, he pulled her up so she could wrap her legs around his rock-solid torso. Like electric-blue lasers, his gaze sliced through her, setting off explosions in her erogenous zones. Liquid strands of his dark hair flowed along the tops of his shoulders. She drew her fingers up his sculpted back, threading them through his hair and scraping his scalp with her fingernails. His immediate response was to pull her tight to his muscled body, giving her the opportunity to grind against his erection. She drowned in a flood of seductive sensations, trapped by his gaze that continued to lash her with smoldering looks. Gods, she loved his eyes.

Mmmmm. Somehow, she expected her little fantasy would pale in comparison to the reality. What would it be like to have his cock deep inside her? It was hard to imagine what she'd never experienced. He hadn't allowed her to touch his naked skin yet, but she hoped he would soon. Touch, stroke, lick, suck. What would he taste like? His smell? Sandalwood and male musk combined in a heady scent. He must exude lots of pheromones, because being near him kept her on the edge of arousal.

Master Trey had discussed dominance and the way it was projected differently by different men. Adrianna knew the type of dominant she most desired. Shane fit her preference in every possible way. Well, he seemed to. He wanted a relationship built on trust. No lying. Even punishment was tailored to her, not excessive as it might be with someone who punished in anger. Of course, she hadn't made him mad at her yet. Still, he exuded self-control.

As his contracted submissive, it was her place to satisfy him, and yet he hadn't found his release with her. Rather, his gratification had come from pleasuring her. It had radiated from him. His satisfaction, in turn, met her emotional need to please him. She loved that about him.

Damn. She did not just think the *L* word, did she? She was old enough to know that girlish fantasies about falling in love at first sight were foolish. Sexual attraction was not love. *He's no different than Master Trey.* She loved Master Trey, but she wasn't in love with him. She wouldn't be rattle-brained about this relationship. Friendship would be her emotional limit.

The contract was for one year. But could she stay detached that long with her empathic senses completely open to Shane? He demanded it during sex, but what about the rest of the time?

On Furzine, opportunities to work on maintaining her empathic shield while selectively opening it to another person hadn't come often. She'd spent most of her time fully blocked.

However, the parties and dinners she'd attended with her parents became the venue for her most interesting adventures. She'd used her empathic abilities to practice dipping into the emotional soup swirling around her. The gatherings were like a broth of fear, envy, greed, lust, and anger that bubbled away beneath the surface of beautiful faces and clothes. Dark emotions repulsed her, so she tried to find and focus on people whose passions were lighter. The ins and outs of lust were always a diverting educational pastime.

Thoughts of lust brought her right back to Shane. Keeping her feelings in check with him was problematic, but she realized that her bedroom duties, which had caused her the most anxiety before meeting Shane, were now the least of her worries. Her responsibilities as his assistant were not for show. She wasn't just going to be tending to laundry and making meals. Otherwise, she wouldn't need a military-grade EBC or a complete copy of Federation law. What courses did he want her to complete? More languages too. Standard was spoken pretty much throughout the Federation.

Whatever her new responsibilities would be, they would be challenging, but not top-secret spy challenging. Ha! Her eyes rolled at her own silliness. She'd need to absorb, learn, and develop the knowledge and skills to make Shane glad he'd hired her, to be pleased in and out of the bedroom. Her Master lover and her Master tutor. Her Master. The thrill of those words wrapped around her in a comforting embrace.

4

———

Shane pulled open the door of the Wild Rover Pub and ushered Adrianna inside. The pub was crowded with tourists in casual attire, but after a quick scan, he pointed Adrianna toward a free booth. "Wait for me there." When he approached the bar, a booming voice greeted him.

"Why look what the cat dragged in! Shane Tiernan, it's good to see you. What brings you to my humble pub?"

"Patrick O'Toole! You know I can't stop on Beta Tau without coming by. How are you? The wife and kids?"

"Mary's as pretty as ever. The kids are growing like weeds. Let's see. The littlest thinks she's a dog. Sean's decided to become a pro footballer and kicks balls at the side of the house all day. James has taken up drumming. With Molly, it's singing at the top of her lungs. I come to the Rover for peace and quiet." A wry grin made it clear Patrick wouldn't have his family any other way.

Shane laughed. Like Maon, Patrick was a happily married man. It wasn't something Shane had ever wanted for himself, but he enjoyed playing uncle to his friends' children.

"I've brought my new assistant." He gestured toward the booth where Adrianna was sitting. "I need to feed her and hear the latest rumors."

"I've got a fine Irish stew tonight. How about that and a pint of my new ale? I think I've perfected the recipe with this one."

"The stew sounds great. But Adrianna will need something light to drink. She's just come from surgery."

"I've just the thing. Go join the lady, and I'll bring your drinks and stew right out."

Adrianna scooted to the center of the curved booth, sliding across the forest-green leather with ease. Shane slipped in next to her.

"How are you doing?" He brushed the backs of his fingers over her forehead.

"I'm a little hungry, and my ear aches. It's a little noisy too."

"We won't be staying long. The doctor gave me some pain meds for you." He pulled a plastic pouch from his pocket, removed a pill, and handed it to her. "Take that when the food comes."

Adrianna nodded; then she subvocalized, her lips completely still, "Yes, sir."

Shane grinned at her. "Very nice."

"It's kind of fun to talk like this. Feels very clandestine, spy-like."

With one dark eyebrow raised slightly, Shane responded, "And it lets me say things like what a stunning ass you have."

Adrianna dropped her gaze to her lap, a blush blooming across her cheeks. It was so easy to make her blush. Blushing seemed at odds for a submissive who'd spent a year at the Opio Institute, but he wouldn't deny that he enjoyed it immensely.

Patrick approached their booth with a tray. Shane reached over, stroking Adrianna's hand with his finger. "Here comes supper."

"Here's the stew and ale I promised, Shane, and lingberry tea for you, miss." Patrick placed steaming bowls filled with vegetables, chunks of meat, and a thick broth in front of both of them, followed by their drinks and silverware. With one beefy hand, he passed the tray to a waiting server and stretched the other out to Adrianna, a smile beaming through his carefully groomed dark-copper beard. "Patrick O'Toole."

"Patrick, this is Adrianna Pacquin. She's my new assistant."

Adrianna shook Patrick's hand. "My pleasure, Mr. O'Toole."

"Oh, call me Patrick." He sat and asked Shane, "What brings you to Beta Tau? Personal or official business?"

"I'm on leave. I stopped to pick up Ms. Pacquin." Shane stared intently into Patrick's eyes. "I contracted with her through the Opio Institute. Maon's idea."

Patrick held Shane's gaze and gave him a slight nod. "Understood."

Relieved he wouldn't have to explain in front of her, Shane looked at Adrianna. "Patrick is an old friend and former marshal. He's an expat from Tallav." The significance of an expat male Tallavan was lost on her. Something he'd have to clarify later. "Go ahead, dig in." Shane returned his focus to Patrick. "What's new here on Beta Tau?" He set himself to listen, scooping tender chunks of meat and potatoes into his mouth.

Patrick grunted. "Beta Tau is Beta Tau. A Langian prince got himself into trouble a while back. Had some notion the companions provided at the Elysian were disposable. Came close to killing three of them. All quietly hushed up, but apparently he's no longer in the succession."

Shane nodded while he sipped his ale.

"We've a new sex school opened six months ago. Wellington School of Pleasure. Set up in its own private dome. It's endowed by an anonymous benefactor, providing free tuition to approved applicants. All young—of legal age, but young. Every week, a shuttle arrives with thirty new students who are taken straight to the dome. Three months ago, they started sending shuttleloads of these kids back up to space dock. Word is they take ship for the Cantile system."

Shane grimaced. "Runner's Hub?"

"That was my thought." Patrick frowned in response.

"That's a lot of fresh sex workers even for Runner's Hub. You're thinking slavers?"

Patrick nodded, gazing at the floor. "Most probably. Easy enough to register them in one of the Hub brothels and then ship them to their new owners. It's routine for people to go missing on Runner's Hub. Most of the Hub's business is illegal shipping. The right bribe will let anyone bypass the ident system."

Shane plunked his spoon into his empty bowl. "True, but I thought we'd convinced Marge Boleo that it was in her best interest to stay out of slaving."

Patrick shrugged. "Something changed her mind. She's always done what's best for the Hub and best for her."

"I assume that the powers that be know this already. I've been in the Bing Lon sector for weeks fixing a cluster fuck..." He raised his hands. "Let's just say, it shouldn't have happened. And it's left me playing catch-up." Shane grunted and downed the last of his ale. "Excellent brew. You bottling it? Can I get some?"

"Wild Rover Pale Ale. I've been bottling it for local consumption at the pleasure domes. I'll have Mary send some cases up to the *Adrasteia*."

"Thanks, I really appreciate it. I'd better get Ms. Pacquin back to the hotel. It looks like her pain pill has kicked in." Adrianna's eyelids were at half-mast. She jerked when he touched her shoulder, realizing that she'd been listening but not truly engaged in the conversation. "Time to go."

"Oh, yes, Sir."

"It was nice meeting you, Ms. Pacquin," Patrick said.

"You too, and please call me Dria."

"Will do. Until next time." Patrick slapped Shane on the upper arm when they both stood.

"Kiss Mary and the kids." Shane thumped him back.

Adrianna allowed him to steer her from the booth and out the door.

SHANE LOOKED at Adrianna as she caught her breath from running to catch the tram they were riding. Last night, when they'd arrived back at the hotel from Patrick's pub, he'd put her straight to bed. He'd slept next to her, keeping his hands to himself, a torment that ended this morning when she woke fully recovered from her minor surgery.

Today had been wonderful. They'd spent it wandering in the botanical and shopping domes, getting to know each. It felt good to talk with her, to touch her shoulder, and to hold her hand. She'd practiced her subvocalization skills. While they people watched, she provided a running subvocalized monologue on the various individuals and couples. Her descriptions turned into stories, becoming more and more absurd. At one point he'd laughed so hard tears came to his eyes. He hadn't laughed so much in a long time. If anyone had been watching them, they would have wondered what was so funny. A few curious glances darted their way, but no more hulking strangers intent on kidnapping.

Adrianna was perceptive about people. She seemed to break through the surface persona they showed others. What did she discern when she looked at him? He hoped it was good.

Their tram pulled up to a tourist lookout. Shane held Adrianna's hand, pulling her off the tram and toward a bench seat away from the row of viewing platforms. Once seated, he snuggled her close, her soft hip pressed into his side, his arm draping her shoulder, his fingers teasing the sleeve of her shirt. She sat quiet next to him while she took in the view.

"The spaceport is built on the edge of the desert flatlands. This viewing area faces the direction the sun will set. When conditions are right, you can see spectacular sunset mirages here. It's something I wanted to share with you."

Adrianna nestled into his side, resting her hand on his thigh. When the sun grew closer to the horizon, the temperature began to drop; but inside Shane, a warm glow expanded. He nuzzled his face into Adrianna's hair, enjoying the wafts of citrus, the scent he'd come to associate with her. The light this woman shed on those around her, on him, was marvelous. She was like a bright ray of sunshine, bursting into his life, clearing away the shadowy dimness he'd accepted as normal.

"Oh, look." Adrianna pointed. "There are two suns now. The one on the bottom looks like it's rising toward the one that is setting."

"Keep watching. It will slowly change, and we may catch a green flash." Shane looked at the sparkle of enthusiasm in Adrianna's emerald eyes, enjoying her delight.

Adrianna pulled his attention back to the sunset. "It's like an upside-down sack now, with the drawstring being gradually opened so all the light can pour out and drop below the horizon, out of sight."

"They call that the omega, when the mirage takes on the look of the Greek letter omega. Toward the end of the sunset, when the sun starts to look somewhat like an oval hanging over the desert, that's when you may see a green flash."

While the seconds ticked by, Adrianna gripped his thigh in anticipation. "Oh, I saw it." Her hand patted a rapid beat on his leg. "Did you see it?" Her excitement bubbled over in a huge smile. When she beamed up at him, her eyes provided him his own chartreuse spark.

"I did." Shane answered her with a grin of his own. Then grasping her behind the neck, he pulled her close to him and kissed her with gentle thoroughness. When he leaned back, Adrianna's lids rose, her expression soft.

"There it is again. In your eyes. They flash green too."

Tonight he intended to make those eyes flicker for an entirely different reason. His groin tightened. The need to return to the hotel growing, he urged her to her feet. "Come on, the next tram back should be here soon."

A few minutes later, they boarded the tram that took them back into the heart of the dome. They transferred from it to another tram on a route that would deposit them at their hotel. After what seemed like an endless amount of time, they were at last off the tram and walking through the hotel's entrance. The wait for the lift tacked on countless minutes. Finally, after the longest thirty-three and a half minutes of his life, they made it to their suite.

When he opened the hotel room door, Shane looked at Adrianna. It was time. All day, he'd felt the urge to sweep her back to the room and claim her. The temptation to do so had constantly assailed him. The touch of her long, slender fingers grazing his arm, resting on his thigh… Fuck, holding hands had kept him in a state of arousal. His body knew what it wanted from her. In the past, mindless coupling with a stranger would satisfy him. Mindless wasn't good enough anymore. He wanted a connection. A connection he hoped for with this budding relationship. A contracted relationship. Was it foolish to think that his contract with Adrianna would be different from the one he'd made with Ceana? Both involved sex. Both women were getting paid. Ceana had rebuffed his sensuous advances, controlling their encounters and turning them into sterile, emotionless acts. She'd even excluded lust. Was it any wonder a child had never resulted?

His best friend had convinced Shane that taking on a paid submissive was a valid option, not a sign of desperation. Yet, at this very moment, desperation overwhelmed him. As much as her touch aroused him, Adrianna's vibrancy was equally arousing. So full of life. Her ebullience poured out in excited exclamations and effervescing laughter. He wanted her. Needed her. Needed her to need him. This wasn't part of the plan, but it was where he found himself.

Adrianna looked up at him expectantly. Her face cupped in one hand, he searched her eyes, hoping to find an equally heart-thumping response to the press of desire to claim her.

"A mhuirnín, I want to make love to you. If it is too soon for you or you've changed your mind, tell me now."

Adrianna's eyes flicked back and forth, her expression solemn. With a barely detectable tremor, she lifted her hand to cup his face in return. "Please make love to me. I'm glad you will be my first."

Shane released the breath he'd been holding, and the floodgates restraining his desire opened. He swept Adrianna up.

"Wrap your legs around me."

Then he secured her mouth, kissing her thoroughly, passionately while he carried her into the bedroom. The sensation of her rounded curves sliding down his muscled torso was sublime while she dropped to stand between his legs. His pulse thundered like the drumbeat of a druid ritual while he continued to plunder her mouth, nibbling and licking her lips before sliding his tongue deep, tasting her sweetness. She responded by tangling her own tongue with his. Fuck, with a kiss she made the aching need inside him ratchet up another unbelievable notch.

He pulled both of her arms behind her and held them there, stroking her throat with his free hand. She had ceded complete control to him, adding fuel to the inferno that burned in his heart. *Fuck.* With one last bite to her lower lip, he drew away, hissing as though she'd scorched him. Adrianna shivered against him.

"Put your hands over your head."

When she complied, Shane lifted her shirt up and off, flicked open her bra, and peeled it away. *Fucking beautiful.*

"A mhuirnín, lower your arms."

With quick efficiency, he added single ties to her wrists, checking the ropes before releasing a pleased grunt. Wearing his rope, she was beyond perfection.

He clasped her ribs, drawing his thumbs under the bottom of each breast, appreciating the utterly feminine round curves. "You are so lovely." He stooped to kiss the nipple, taking it into his mouth, sucking and flicking the tip with his tongue. She made a mewling response. With his lips, he ravished his way down the slope, across, and up her other breast, repeating his attentions and ending with a featherlight bite to her nipple that elicited a groan from Adrianna.

Her body swayed, so he steadied her, then set to work removing her boots, socks, and pants. He took his time, running his hands up her legs, imagining them squeezing him tight while he pumped her to release.

Standing and stepping back, he resisted the pressure to rush, examining her while he moved around her. Once the fastener had been pulled from her braid, her hair unraveled and spread across her shoulders in long mocha tresses like a waterfall. The silky texture caressed his fingers when he combed through them. The golden highlights gave her a sun-kissed look.

His scrutiny continued until he had gone full circle. "Exquisite." Close enough to be aware of her heat, he reached his hand out to tease the dark curls slipping out from her lacy lavender thong. "I like curls here." He skimmed his hands up her sides, drawing her arms above her head and holding them there. With a smile playing about his lips, he nestled his nose into her bare armpit, and then he licked it from bottom to top. Her body writhed.

"Does that tickle?" He licked again and got the same reaction.

"Yes, it tickles."

He nuzzled her armpit again, chuckling when she squirmed.

"I like curls here too. Don't shave. Just trim."

While he continued his exploration, he pulled her body close to him, kissing her shoulders, neck, and lips while his hands roamed the silky softness of her torso. He yanked his shirt up over his head and off his arms and hurled it behind him, burning to be skin to skin with her.

"Touch me." The words were abrupt, harsh. Adrianna wound her arms around his neck, pressing her body against his.

"Yes." The single word hissed between his lips.

With a pull on the tie holding his hair, she freed the dark brown strands to float along his shoulders. Another hiss slipped out when she caressed and kneaded his back, her strong fingers digging into the rigid muscles, forcing them to loosen, for him to relax into her. She undulated against him, brushing her breasts across the wiry dark hair on his chest, pushing her belly against his straining crotch. He took a deep breath, overcoming the urge to fling her down and plunge his cock into her depths. He would do this right.

Thumbs in either side of her thong, he pulled the small bit of lace to her thighs, past her knees, and to her ankles, steadying her when she stepped out of it. He squatted and buried his face in her curls, breathing in her scent, a combination that included the slight odor of female sweat, the full-bodied musk of her arousal, and a hint of the citrus from the soap she used. Her fragrance was drawing him to take his first direct sample of her pussy. He drew her outer labia aside and ran his tongue from her center up, circling her clit. Adrianna leaned into him, sighing when he continued to swipe up and around. *So. Fucking. Good.*

He lost himself in her taste until her legs grew wobbly. After he rose, he lifted her in his arms, carried her to the bed, and placed her with tender restraint so her bottom was at the edge. On his knees before her, he drew her limbs over his shoulders. He smiled in satisfaction. She was his now. Completely. Unreservedly. His to do with as he pleased. He had a long list of things he intended to do with her.

He buried his face in her pussy, muttering his appreciation. "So good, a mhuirnín." He pushed her knees to her chest and continued the languid swirling of his tongue. She moaned and thrust her hips up, seeking more, but Shane clamped them down and denied her.

"Please, Sir!"

"Please what, Adrianna?"

"Please make me come."

He paused. Normally he would deny a sub's request this early on, but fuck, he wanted her to come probably more than she did. "My pleasure, Adrianna." Shane flattened his tongue and drew it across her clit, relishing the shudder that shook her body. While rubbing her labia with his thumbs, he sucked her clit into his mouth, fondling it with his tongue. He continued his assault while Adrianna's pleas for more turned guttural. Then he took her clit between his teeth, bit enough to cause a brief sting, and pulled away. Her torso taut, Adrianna cried out in an anguish of bliss while her release rippled through her. A tremor ran through him, hunger pummeling him. He needed to bury himself inside her.

In rapid succession, he pulled back, stood, and stripped off the rest of his clothing. He grasped Adrianna under her arms, moved her to the center of the bed, and attached the ropes dangling from her wrists to the tie-off points he'd devised on the frame. When he lowered himself between her thighs, he said, "Wrap your legs around me." Held up by one forearm, he nuzzled his face into her hair, dusting kisses across her eyelids, nose, and cheeks before tangling her tongue in a kiss, letting her savor the flavor that had already addicted him. After a quick bite to her lower lip, he moved to nibble his way up to her earlobe, nipping hard enough to make Adrianna squeal. "I need you, a mhuirnín," he whispered. The tension inside him was close to breaking wide open.

"I'm yours. All yours. Please take me now, Master."

He gazed into eyes glinting with green fire, reading in them what she was offering him. Her virginity, a once-in-a-lifetime gift, was an amazing thing. The trust she granted him by giving him total control gratified him. His cock would be the first inside her, and she was letting him choose how he would take care. She was presenting him with more than her body, more than sex. She was submitting her will to his. It left him thrilled, intimidated, proud, and above all determined to cherish her and never fail to appreciate what she offered him. His cock dripped with precum. His base side wanted to fuck her, fuck her hard until she begged him to stop. He wouldn't. This was not the time for rough sex. He slammed the lock closed on his self-restraint.

His cock positioned at her entrance, he fixed his eyes on hers, and then he thrust in one long, slow motion, breaking through the scrap of tissue that blocked his path, seating himself deeply inside her. Her tight warmth enveloped his erection. On the brink of release, he stopped as much for his sake as for hers. A brief narrowing of her eyes was the only sign she suffered any pain.

"More please." Adrianna hummed.

Fuck yeah. He pulled out, leaving the tip of his cock barely penetrating, and then thrust back in steady, protracted movements. The pace was driving him crazy, bringing him to the edge and no further. With Adrianna pushing her pussy up to meet his thrusts, murmuring unintelligible words, he wasn't sure how long he could maintain this tempo.

"Oh, faster. Please."

As the words burst from her, Shane threw off all constraints. He wanted her. He was taking her. The urge to imprint himself on her was foreign to him. His body gave him no opportunity to consider it. He shoved his hands beneath her, grabbing handfuls of plush ass. He thrust into her while pulling her onto his throbbing erection. *Feels. So. Fucking. Good.* Adrianna arched her back, giving him full access, panting with each thrust. He'd never been this hard. The sensations buffeting him had never been this intense. Never. Adrianna's spine grew rigid, and the walls of her pussy spasmed about his cock. Her orgasm coursed around him. His mind lost to all thought, overloaded on pleasure, he ground as deep as he could go, shooting long eruptions of cum. Their bodies still shuddering from release, Shane untied Adrianna's wrists, rolled, and clasped her tight to his chest. When their breathing slowed, he drifted into the sated sleep of a lover.

ADRIANNA DIDN'T KNOW if she'd be able to describe all the feelings and sensations she was experiencing. Making love with Shane had been better than anything she'd ever imagined. She was no longer a virgin. Funny. Before she'd thought of losing her virginity much like the act itself, a breaking through of a barrier into a new knowledge of herself and her body. But it hadn't been like that at all. It was as though she now lived on the opposite rim of a great chasm that had been so wide she hadn't been able to see the far side. The only way to cross required another person and the profound body and soul connection that had blossomed between them as Shane moved inside her. The pain had been sharp but of little consequence compared to the ecstasy of their union. Something special had happened between Shane and her. It must not be like this for every woman. Otherwise how could they move from partner to partner? If it was like this every time, she didn't think she'd want to move on after a year of such incredible bliss.

Resting in his arms, surrounded by his strength, the waves of contentment rolling from him reinforced her desire to meet his every need. Was it possible to fall in love in a matter of days? *Merde!* Lust had flooded her from the first time she'd looked at him, the fantasy fulfillment of all her dreams.

Indolence suffused her, and she realized happiness did too. Happiness was something she'd learned to make for herself, but this was something he had given her. There was safety in his arms, security to release her control and to trust that someone else had her well-being at heart. Shane was safe because he exercised an amazing restraint over himself—he'd never take her too far from her comfort zone. *Wherever he takes me, I want to go.* She placed a brief kiss amid the wiry dark-brown hair on his chest, closed her eyes, and drifted to sleep.

5

A drianna woke to Shane spooned against her backside, radiating heat and something more. He was awake, his hand stroking her bottom where it met her thigh. Any lighter and the touch would have tickled. His palm drifted up her back, sending a tingle down her spine. With a brush of his fingers, he pulled her hair away from her neck and then braced himself up on his arm. His breath warmed her before he planted a series of brief kisses, moving up to her ear.

His lips brought back memories of the night before. She'd known her first time would hurt. And it had. But a gift wasn't worth much if it didn't cost you anything. Her virginity had been a commodity peddled to the right bidder. She'd sold that to Shane, but last night she'd given him something else. She'd surrendered her will to his. Master Trey would have told her to hold back, to protect herself. But there was no need with Shane. He was now her protector. And it felt right. It felt good. Felt more than good.

Waking up next to him was a part of her contracted life she'd never imagined. Life with Shane wasn't going to be a series of scenes added to a schedule of sleeping, eating, and attending to shipboard duties. His presence was a continual force. It was as though he was a cloak that could wrap tight around her, surrounding her with hot desire or lying loose along her shoulders, brushing against her with touches that kept her at a slow simmer.

"Good morning, a mhuirnín."

Feather-soft lips continued kissing her jawline toward her smile.

"Mmmmm." If she could purr, she would.

He nibbled her earlobe, flicking it with the tip of his tongue. When she wriggled in response, he asked, "Are you sore?"

"No, I'm fine." *Better than fine.*

He eased his way down the side of her face and neck to stroke her breast. His fingers tweaked her nipple, sending a pulse of heat thrumming through her body. Her desire was awake now, an ache building. The hand trailing along her hip and back to the crease in her bottom was tender, excruciating. Finally, he nudged between her thighs and up to her cleft. She bucked against his intrusion.

"A mhuirnín, I think you need something."

"Oh yes. Yes, I do."

Shane's body heat was burning through her. His raspy morning beard matched the hoarse quality of his voice. It took all her self-control to keep from grinding her ass into his erection. Her body wanted, but the craving for his control was greater.

"Tell me?"

She bit her lip. "I need you thrusting into me, taking me, making me come. Please."

He huffed a laugh. "And I need to do that."

When he pulled his cock between her cheeks, Adrianna wriggled to give him better access. She fluttered her eyes closed when he pushed inside her partway, repositioned his hips, pulled out, and then thrust his erection deep. Within her, he found a spot that extinguished her ability to speak. Hot, rigid man filled her, his thrusts punctuated by her moans when he slammed into her apex. He owned her, and in these moments of unaffected carnal expression, she owned him. Lost in the surplus of sensation, she tipped over the edge into a roiling orgasm when Shane's steel-hard erection released his warm semen.

She was drenched in the emotions flowing from Shane, his hungry desire, the pure physicality of his passion, and his intense elation. The connection she'd felt when they first made love strengthened. She laughed, joy bubbling out of her soul and along the link to Shane. When he chuckled too, she turned in his arms, catching the smile curling his lips and beaming from his sparkling sea-blue eyes. She basked in their mutual enjoyment of the moment.

"Time to get up." He gave her a quick peck and smack on her hip.

She sighed. *So that's a quickie.* Well, she'd gotten her cuddles in the night. The man was type A. When he had something to do, he was going to do it.

With boyish expectation, he said, "I've got a ship to introduce to you." He nudged her. "Go"

She quirked an eyebrow in response. "Introduce? Don't you mean show me?"

"Introduce I said. Introduce I meant. *Adrasteia* is a beautiful woman. Her name means inescapable. It's an epithet of the Greek goddess Nemesis. She defends the righteous. You must always treat her with respect." Humor continued to glimmer in his eyes, but Adrianna could tell he was half-serious.

She responded to the earnest part with a resolute nod. "I shall."

He kissed her again, the smile returning to his lips. "Good."

It had taken them longer to get to the ship than Shane had planned. Part of that was his fault. He hadn't been able to keep his hands off Adrianna in the shower, demanding she supply him an appetizer before breakfast. He'd given her two orgasms while he plundered her pussy with his mouth. Maybe he could work in a quickie over lunch. They'd also run into a delay when Adrianna's new wardrobe hadn't been delivered yet. He'd had to contact the merchant and arrange delivery on station.

As he reached the end of the ship's access tube, Shane palmed the door open, ushered Adrianna inside the air lock and then on through to a small foyer.

"Welcome to the *Adrasteia*."

Adrianna walked in, seeming to try to soak up every detail. Attractive wood-paneled cupboards lined a foyer that led to a lounge with dark-brown seating, and on the other end of the room stood a sleek, rectangular ebony table surrounded by eight matching chairs. A light, crisp cinnamon scent hung in the air. A landscape picture covered one wall, while opposite it, a partition displayed a view of space. The *Adrasteia* was magnificent. Adrianna trailed her fingers along the back of a chair, noticing that the scene on the partition had changed. It was still space, but now a structure was visible. "Is that the station? Outside?"

"Yes, that view panel can be switched to display any of the fixed cams on the *Adrasteia*. Right now, it's set to rotate through the external cams. There are internal ones too. You can also watch vids on it. The image above the table is a picture of my family estate on Tallav. It's called Gleann Milis, 'Sweet Glen.'"

Adrianna scrutinized the picture. Rolling hills with copses of trees surrounded an enormous white stone building that was part castle and part mansion. In the distance, other buildings, farmland, and orchards spread. That explained the luxurious fittings of the *Adrasteia*. Shane was wealthy, or at least his family had money. She turned to find him watching her.

"What do you think?" Shane asked.

"It's amazing. You grew up there?"

Shane's gaze fixed on the picture. "Yes. It belongs to my mother. I haven't been home in years. Mother and I are not on good terms." He waved a hand in an encompassing gesture. "Don't let the luxury fool you. She outfitted the *Adrasteia* before we had our falling out. I don't have access to my mother's money and probably never will."

He rubbed his palm on his chest, his eyes dark, narrowing while he continued to stare at the picture. The separation made him deeply unhappy. What had caused it? What would Shane find important enough to quarrel with his mother?

As quickly as the glum mood had struck, he snapped from his reverie with a flicker of a smile. "Let's finish the tour."

He took up the role of tour guide, showing his obvious love for the *Adrasteia* while he pointed out the little niceties that made this his home. The thoughtful arrangement of the rooms and their furnishings impressed Adrianna, the ease of moving through the ship apparent in the layout. No sharp corners or low tables angled to catch the unwary.

Of the three levels, she realized she would spend most of her time on the middle level. The top level contained the bridge and the armory. The bottom level was primarily storage and engineering, although there were also two prison cells, a gym, and a cargo access lock. The main level was divided into three sections: crew quarters, a services section with the main lounge, and guest quarters. The captain's quarters took up most of the crew section and comprised an office with an auxiliary command station, a sitting room, and a bedroom. One of the two additional crew quarters would belong to Adrianna. The guest quarters section included three guest bedrooms.

All bedrooms included en suite bathrooms. *My own bathroom.* She wasn't sure why this pleased her so much—she'd never minded sharing a bathroom—but it did even though the bathroom was microscopic, just a shower tube, sink, and toilet. Her quarters were equally small with not much room for more than a bunk, nightstand with drawers, and a wall of cabinets and drawers on the entry-panel wall. The bathroom took its chunk of space out of the corner of the room opposite the bunk. Definitely cozy.

The galley, med clinic, and housekeeping could be accessed from the main lounge and a passage that ran behind. That corridor running from the crew to the guest section also offered access to a long narrow room that stretched the length of the services section. Labeled ADMIN, anything that hadn't fit into any other section on board was found there, including Adrianna's workstation.

Living on the *Adrasteia* would require adjustments. The automatic panel doors made her jump. The touch security on the door to her quarters was a welcome addition. She had nothing to hide from Shane, but it was obvious if there were guest rooms, they wouldn't always travel alone.

Housekeeping, the galley, and med bed in the med clinic were standard and in line with the equipment she had used in training.

She'd grown used to living a clutter-free life at the Institute. Order was a necessity on any spaceship, but the *Adrasteia* wasn't coldly utilitarian like the space liner she'd taken to Beta Tau. Someone with excellent design skills had made the *Adrasteia* an inviting, warm place to live.

The tour completed, Shane guided her back to the main lounge. A giant *lodan* moth set to flapping in her stomach. *What now? Will he explain my duties?*

A doorbell interrupted. *A doorbell?*

Shane grimaced. "Just a minute, Dria." He strode into the foyer, and Adrianna could hear him talking with someone through an intercom system. Adrianna let her senses extend out toward the dock to whoever was at the other end of the access tube. She didn't like what she perceived. It didn't set right with her.

When Shane reappeared, he said, "Dria, you need to go to your quarters and stay. A confidential informant wants to speak with me, and she won't if I'm not alone. You should remain there until I come and get you."

Adrianna's brow puckered. "Yes, Sir, but are you sure?" Something was wrong. She could sense it. How could she get Shane to believe her without letting him know about her empathic abilities?

Shane held her shoulders. "Dria, she's a CI. Talking to me is dangerous for her. She's been a longtime confidential informant. Coming here to the *Adrasteia* is an even bigger risk. Someone could recognize her, and certain elements would consider her being here reason enough to kill her. What she has to tell me must be very important."

Not wanting to argue with Shane, Adrianna nodded in acquiescence, but she believed there was something more going on than anxiety over being discovered boarding the *Adrasteia*. "Okay, Sir," she said and turned to go to her quarters. She bit her lip and looked back over her shoulder. She needed to do something. The emotions coming from the CI weren't right.

"It'll be fine. Now scoot," Shane said.

While Adrianna moved along the passageway to her quarters, she reached out with her senses. Fear, fear of—yes, fear of Shane and being caught was rolling off the informant in waves sufficient to force an adrenaline rush in Adrianna. But entwined with the woman's fear were other emotions—desperation, self-loathing, and a thread of defensive anger. Adrianna couldn't put her finger on why, but her gut was telling her something bad was about to happen. There was no way she was going sit in her quarters while it did.

Caught between two options—obey Shane or do what she thought was best—Adrianna considered the ramifications. Then it occurred to her. Shane had called her *Dria*. Not *Adrianna* or *Pacquin*. He hadn't been in Master mode or official mode, but in the relaxed position somewhere in between. Thus, she reasoned, she could take initiative and do something to assure Shane's safety while keeping herself hidden from the CI.

Instead of entering her quarters, Adrianna strode past and made her way to housekeeping via the back passage. Once inside, she located the room's vidscreen and set it to monitor the entryway and main lounge. She watched while Shane showed the woman in and offered her a seat in an armchair midway between the foyer and the lounge entrance to housekeeping. When he sat next to her, the woman turned toward him, her back toward the screen Adrianna was watching.

With a stab of anxiety, Adrianna realized she needed a weapon. She'd forgotten to arm herself; and she didn't have the code to the locked armory. *Make do, Dria. Think. Think. Yes!* The solution came to her in a flash. She looked through storage cabinets until she found what she was looking for —a long metal cylinder with a fitting at the end that made a perfect handgrip, a replacement tube for the ship's vacuum system. Armed with the tube, Adrianna took up station near the door, but not close enough to trigger it open, and watched the vidscreen.

SHANE WALKED to the ship's entrance. He was pleased that Adrianna seemed eager to start work as his personal assistant immediately. But a meeting with a CI wasn't the place to begin. He opened the air lock, allowing his guest entrance to the ship. "Hello, Concordia. I haven't seen you in a long time."

"I've been around." She followed him through the foyer into the lounge. His backward glances caught her eyes flicking back and forth as though she expected someone to leap out at her.

"You seem nervous. Everything okay?" Concordia had never been jumpy like this, but this was the first time she'd come to the *Adrasteia*. She'd always avoided being spotted with him. "Have a seat." He gestured to a chair that would allow him to sit between her and the foyer.

Concordia nodded. "Yeah, sure. What I have to tell you is scary crap. You have to promise to protect me 'cause this will really stir the big shits up."

Shane reached out and covered her hand. "I'll do everything in my power to keep you safe."

Concordia gave a bitter laugh. "Sure." Then she placed her other hand over Shane's.

A sting like an insect bite pricked his skin. "What the—" His mouth dropped open, and he jerked away. Initial surprise turned into a hiss of anger when Shane realized she'd doped him with something. Already going woozy, he attempted to grab her arm, but Concordia moved out of the chair and backed up from him. Her arms squeezed around her stomach. "Sorry. It was you or me. I chose me."

A buzz of white noise filled Shane's ears while he slumped toward the deck. Was that Adrianna? His vision was blurry. He strained to say her name, but his tongue refused to work. Darkness claimed him.

ADRIANNA PERCEIVED A flare of triumph from the woman. Surprised anger burst from Shane but muddied into a confused jumble of fear and panic. Shane tried to grab the CI, missed her, and crashed to the deck. Not waiting an instant longer, Adrianna rushed through the door as soon as it swished open, covering the space between the CI and herself faster than she'd ever moved. Vacuum tube held ready while she sprinted, Adrianna brought it up, smashing it down as hard as possible just as the woman turned. The tube connected with the side of the woman's head in a blow that knocked her out. Adrianna threw the tube aside and fell to her knees beside Shane, rolling him over.

Shane's skin was a grayish white and clammy to her touch. His lips were colorless, his breathing shallow, and pulse weak. Hands shaking, she was on the verge of panic. Whatever he'd been injected with, it hadn't just knocked him out but was also killing him. She had to get him to the med bed. With strength she would later attribute to adrenaline, Adrianna grabbed Shane beneath his arms and dragged him toward the med-bay door panel, kicking the unconscious CI out of her way. After barely managing to pull Shane onto the med bed and then only because it was in the fully lowered position, Adrianna slapped his arm into the analysis unit. With it activated, she waited, arms curled over her head, while the machine analyzed Shane's body fluids.

Analysis completed, a *ping* sounded, making her jump even though she expected it. A warning in bright red screamed its dire message into her brain. Ten minutes. He only had ten minutes. Adrianna scrambled to the med cupboard to locate the prescribed remedy. While she fumbled to find the correct bottle, she lost precious seconds. *Why is everything moving so fast?* Once she located the antidote, she thrust it with trembling fingers into the portal on the machine. It had to be in time. What would she do if Shane died now? Her heart was gripped by a fist of suffocating fear.

What else should she do? *Scanner. Turn the scanner on.* She toggled the foot pedal to raise the bed to waist height and engaged the scanner. The machine would now monitor Shane's body and, along with the analysis unit, notify her with an alarm whenever action on her part was needed.

Up to this point, she had been running on adrenaline, responding as the situation dictated. Now that there was nothing further she could do for Shane, she shook, her breathing rapid and on the verge of hyperventilation. *Get a grip, Dria.* She purposely slowed her inhalations and focused her mind on a soothing concerto. Calmer, but still feeling shaky, she forced herself to think.

Shane's CI was still a potential threat. However much damage the knock on the head had caused the woman, Adrianna didn't want to give her a second chance at Shane. A quick glance out the door told Adrianna that the woman remained out cold on the floor. Surgical tape and med scissors in hand, Adrianna hurried into the lounge and made quick work of taping the CI's hands behind her back, strapping her feet together, and then pulling them up to hog-tie her. It didn't matter how badly hurt the woman was. No way would Adrianna displace Shane in the med bed to help this murderer.

That accomplished, she checked on Shane before heading to the comm station and contacting the local Marshals Service Office. Relieved that assistance was on the way, she hurried back to the med bay. A quick scan of the readout of Shane's vitals showed he was stabilizing. Color was returning to his skin, but he remained paler than usual. She stroked her hand across his forehead and ran her fingers through his hair. "You're going to be all right. I saved you."

Shane's eyes fluttered open. "Dria?" he slurred.

"Hush, I'm here. Everything's going to be all right. I saved you." While she continued to stroke him, Shane sighed and lost consciousness.

"Ms. Pacquin, let's go over a few things one more time. I want to be sure I have the facts straight." Marshal Riordan watched Adrianna, intensity radiating off him like banked coals.

Adrianna was an inch taller than Riordan, but she felt much smaller. Throughout his interview, he had been considerate yet direct.

She sighed, steeling herself for another round of questioning. "Of course." When the medics took Shane to the station clinic, she hadn't been allowed to go. The cup of tea sitting before her on the *Adrasteia's* ebony dining table had grown cold. Despite that, she continued to sip it.

"You yourself are not acquainted with Concordia Demont? And Marshal Tiernan never expressed to you any concern about her?" Riordan looked at the notes on his tablet and then peered directly up at her again.

"No, Sir. I've never met her. Marshal Tiernan told me she was a long-time informant and must have something important to tell him, otherwise she wouldn't have come to the ship." Adrianna inspected her cup, brow furrowed. How many times did they need to go over this?

"But you were still concerned enough to take up a post behind the door to housekeeping to watch and intervene. What caused you such concern?"

A small sigh escaped her lips before she could hold it back. "It was just a feeling. I can't really explain it. I just...felt like I needed to make sure

Marshal Tiernan was safe." No way would she tell Marshal Riordan she had empathically sensed danger.

Riordan didn't interrupt the silence that fell after her last statement.

Adrianna forced herself to maintain eye contact, her gaze pleading for him to end his inquisition and let her go to Shane.

The empty moments eating away at her, she broke and said, "Really. It was only a feeling. When I saw Marshal Tiernan slump, I needed to act."

Riordan nodded. Relief flooded Adrianna when he turned from that line of questioning.

"The likeliest theory is that this attack was focused solely on Marshal Tiernan and had nothing to do with you. However, on the outside chance it did, do you have enemies? Is someone opposed to you working for the marshal? Anything from the past that might be the root of this assault?"

Adrianna hadn't considered that she might have brought danger to Shane's door. What if she had? What if whoever had been behind the attempt to kidnap her was also behind this? How stupid of her not to even consider the possibility. How could she go on working for Shane, knowing she'd nearly caused his death? Her thoughts a muddle, Adrianna stared at her hands, clasped unmoving in her lap.

"Ms. Pacquin." Riordan's sympathy touched her almost as though he'd reached out and placed his hand on her arm. "I realize this has been distressing. We're just about finished. Is there anything else you need to tell me?"

When she looked up at Riordan, Adrianna said, "Yes, sir. On the day Marshal Tiernan and I met down planet for the first time, just a couple of days ago, I was attacked on my way to meet with him. I managed to escape from one thug, and the other was scared off by Marshal Tiernan."

"Was the crime reported?" Riordan straightened and tapped on his tablet. If he'd been a hunting dog, his ears would have perked up.

"I don't know. If it was, Marshal Tiernan made the report," Adrianna responded, moving her hands from her lap to cover her stomach.

"Are you aware of the reason behind the attack, or was it random?"

She closed her eyes briefly when she shifted, the wooden chair an unforgiving slab against her back. "As I told Marshal Tiernan, it could have been chance. But it also might have been because I ran away to Beta Tau to escape a man trying to coerce me into marriage."

"Who? Does he have the resources to mount an interplanetary pursuit?"

"He's the Benefactor of Furzine," Adrianna said, looking down at her hands.

"I see." The patter of Riordan's fingers on the tablet filled the silence.

When the tapping stopped, she looked up.

Riordan was observing her, one finger over his lips. "I've already placed a guard on Marshal Tiernan at the med clinic. It's my understanding they will keep him overnight. I'm sure you are eager to go check on him. If he's up to it, I need to talk with him. I'll escort you there, but I do not want you going anywhere without a guard. Once we get to the clinic, I need you to stay with Marshal Tiernan and his guard." He attempted a smile. "With you around, he'll have a double guard, won't he?"

Adrianna lips quirked. "If there's a vacuum tube handy."

Riordan grunted at her attempt at humor.

Her face heated. Why was she making jokes? "Thank you, sir. I do want to see the marshal as soon as possible."

"Right then. Collect anything you'll need, and we'll head out. The forensic unit should finish up here shortly. I'm placing a guard on the passenger and cargo locks." Riordan stood and went to talk with the marshal overseeing the crime scene.

Adrianna hadn't even had time to take the few things from her satchel before calamity had struck. She grabbed it and the necessity bag Shane had given her with the few new clothes she'd carried with her and her toiletries. When she returned to the lounge, the techs were putting away their equipment, preparing to leave. She approached Marshal Riordan and, when he had finished speaking with the other marshal, told him, "I'm ready to go. One thing though. We were expecting a number of deliveries today."

Riordan asked, "What kind of deliveries?"

"Mostly clothes and such for me. I don't know if Marshal Tiernan made any other purchases."

Riordan turned to the other marshal, asking him to brief the guards and to use full precautions on any items delivered to the ship. His hand on her elbow, he guided Adrianna to the foyer, through the access tube, to the cart he had waiting outside. She sank into the seat, glad to be off her wobbly legs and on her way to see Shane.

SHANE SHIFTED IN THE BED, unable to contain his restlessness. The doctor had said it would take another twelve hours to determine if there would be any residual effects from the poison. Adrianna had somehow gotten him the antidote in time. The first ten minutes after the poison had been administered were crucial. He might have lived even if the delay between antidote and poison had been up to thirty minutes, but the physical consequences would have been ever more catastrophic. Somehow, she'd beaten that ten-minute deadline. Like magic, she had appeared almost the instant he was poisoned, hurtling through the door, brandishing something. He rubbed his hand across his face. Details were difficult to remember, but without a doubt, Adrianna had saved him. If he could just get up to deal with whatever was happening... His eyes closed, and the next thing he knew, a nurse was bustling around his bed, straightening the sheet that covered him and checking his water pitcher.

"You're awake. You need to drink more fluids. When I return, I'd like to see this pitcher empty. Okay?"

"I'll try." Shane's voice was raspy, the dry cracks in his throat making speech painful. He reached for his cup and drained it.

The nurse refilled it and said, "Good start. You have visitors. A Marshal Riordan and a Ms. Pacquin are here. Do you feel up to seeing them?"

"Yes. Send them in, please. I've been waiting for someone to get here."

Hand holding the door open, the nurse looked out of the room. "You can come in now. Keep it brief. He needs his rest."

Riordan entered first, but Shane focused on Adrianna. No sign of her sunny personality was evident despite the broad smile she wore. When the two came toward his bed, he lifted up on his hands and raked his eyes up and down Adrianna. "Are you okay?"

"I'm fine," she said.

"She didn't hurt you?"

"No, not at all." Adrianna moved to the opposite side of the bed, placing her bags in a corner, and returned to stand next to Shane. He continued to scan her, hoping she was as emotionally okay as she was physically. *She's just tired.*

Marshal Riordan cleared his throat.

Shane pushed those thoughts to the back of his mind, relaxing to lie back down. "Riordan, they've put you in charge? What happened to Longaxe? Wouldn't this be something he'd handle?"

"Yes, I'll be overseeing things. Longaxe is on special assignment where his *special* skills can be put to best use."

"He doesn't have any... Oh." Shane grunted. "Couldn't happen to a better man."

"I need to get your statement, but after interviewing Ms. Pacquin, I believe this incident is part of something bigger."

Shane nodded, his expression hard. "We'll have to discuss this further in a secure location, but yes, something more significant is going on. As to my statement, it's brief. Concordia Demont, a CI of mine for six years, came to the *Adrasteia* and requested to speak with me. I asked Ms. Pacquin to go to her quarters so I could talk to Concordia alone. Concordia seemed jumpy. She told me she had scary news that would, as she put it, 'stir up the big shits.' I remember placing my hand on hers, which she then covered with her other hand. I felt a sting, and then everything slid out from under me. I tried to grab her, and the last thing I remember was falling and seeing Dria, Ms. Pacquin."

Riordan rubbed his finger along the bed rail. "Was that normal? For the CI to approach you on your ship?"

"No, she never did." Shane raked his fingers through his hair. It hadn't been like her at all. "If I was on station, I'd get a message with a date and time to visit her at the brothel she ran."

"Why would she try to kill you?" Riordan asked.

That was the question, wasn't it? One that Shane'd been rolling around in his head and coming up empty. "I can't think of any reason." He scrunched his face while he thought. "Oh, I remember her saying it was her or me." His lips pursed. "She must have been coerced. She was careful to stay on the right side of the law. Most of the info she passed on was insignificant stuff about the spacers that visited her establishment. I forwarded it along to the local guardian. You know how it is. There's always a hope she'd discover something of greater interest. For her, the information was a trade-off for quick police intervention if her bouncers couldn't handle a problem at the brothel. Attempted murder is way out of her scope."

Riordan's mouth twisted. "Hmmpf. Well, I'm on my way to question her next. Looks like you'll be getting out of here sometime tomorrow. When you feel up to it, we'll talk again."

Shane pushed his water cup from one hand to the other on the tray table in front of him. "The sooner the better. I'd like protection for Ms. Pacquin in the meanwhile."

"Already done. She'll be staying here with you. A guard's on the door. You'll be escorted back to the *Adrasteia* tomorrow. I've also placed guards on both air locks on the ship." With a nod, Riordan turned his attention to Adrianna. "You've found yourself a top-notch assistant. I don't think a trained agent could have reacted better."

Adrianna blushed when Shane settled his eyes on her. "She's turning out to be more than I ever expected. Although we'll have to have a discussion about ignoring my orders and doing her own thing."

Riordan tapped a finger on Shane's tray table. "Yeah, well, remember she was right. Right and saved your butt."

Shane didn't respond. Instead, he continued looking at Adrianna, a corner of his mouth lifting.

"I'll let you get some rest now, Tiernan. If you need anything before tomorrow or remember anything else, give me a call, Ms. Pacquin."

Adrianna pulled her focus from Shane to look at Riordan. "Yes, Marshal, I will. Thank you for everything."

"You're welcome. Until later, Tiernan."

Once Riordan had left the room, Adrianna dragged a chair up next to the bed. She took hold of Shane's hand and laid her face against it, rubbing it with her cheek. "I was so afraid."

Despite her whisper, the words fell harshly on Shane's ears. Tension gripped his chest. He didn't like to see her upset. "I'm sorry, a mhuirnín. It goes with the job that I'll be in danger from time to time."

"I understand that. It's hard being three people. Adrianna wants to do whatever you tell her to do. Ms. Pacquin wants to be all gung-ho crime fighter."

"And Dria?" he asked.

"Dria was afraid you were dying."

Shane stroked her cheek. "Dria, I didn't die. Trust me to take care of you."

"That's the thing. I did trust you to take care of me. But now, I don't know."

Shane took a deep breath and slowly released it. "You're much stronger than you realize. You haven't known me long enough to truly need me."

She lifted her head, her eyes blinking rapidly, and then she stared at him wide-eyed. "But you want me to trust you. Well then, I want the same from you. You need to believe I will always have your best interests at heart."

Fuck. How did she flip this conversation around on me? He conceded that she desired to please him. But have his best interests at heart? Always? That was a different matter, and something he'd never considered. This relationship was more confusing and complex than he had expected. His goal was to find someone for shipboard duties, help with research, and to meet his needs in bed. He realized he'd envisioned some kind of automaton without feelings or personality. The reality was quite different. The reality was Adrianna. Reality light-years better than anything he could have imagined. So much more.

"I'll try. I've never had a long-term relationship like this. At this point, I can't promise to do more than try. Will that do for now?"

Adrianna gave a quick nod.

Shane's brow furrowed when the tightness in his chest refused to ease. He dropped his hand to the sheet beside him.

In a quiet voice, she said, "I don't think you should punish me for not going to my room."

Her eyes held his, a steady lush green that soothed the churning inside him. He still thought she should be punished, but pronouncing judgment was beyond him with those eyes on him. *Fuck, what the hell is going on with me?*

Adrianna's soft smile plucked at him. "Rest now," she said, laying her head back on his hand, letting her eyelids drift shut.

She was so beautiful. If he could trust any woman, it would be Adrianna. She was sweetness and light with a staggering punch. Such a contrast. A total submissive to him and a tenacious fighter. But he couldn't afford to place all his expectations on her. Adrianna was his for one year. His savings could cover another year, but once that was gone, he didn't have the funds. After that, no matter how much she might want to stay or he might want her to stay, she couldn't. She had debts. The Opio Institute wasn't cheap. The payments he was already making should knock off a chunk of her loan, but it would probably take an additional two to three years of compensation to pay off the rest.

At the time he'd taken out the contract with her, he hadn't thought doing so would really work for him. That was part of why he'd chosen a paid sub, to be able to walk away without drama. In the past, he'd had to detach himself from club subs who had expressed unacceptable expectations of him. He would have to be less personal with Adrianna outside the bedroom. If he wasn't, the inevitable separation would be hard on her.

When he turned his head from her, he sighed and shut his eyes.

A drianna laid her head down on her desk. It had been a long day, and it was only half over. When they'd returned to the ship after Shane was released, he'd wanted to dig into the case. His system was still recovering from the effects of the poison, leaving him tired and with the disposition of a large, angry lion. Startled twice, he'd growled at her about not sneaking up on him. Rather than growl in response, she'd knuckled back her own cranky retort.

His frustration level had ratcheted up when he couldn't get through to Riordan. After losing his temper and slamming the comm set down on the desk, Shane had finally agreed that perhaps he could use some rest. It was probably best he hadn't learned that Concordia Demont had committed suicide; he would be unhappy. He was in bed now, which was where he should have gone the minute they got back. Adrianna had promised to have all the information she could get ahold of ready and collated for him when he woke up.

She'd finally connected with Marshal Riordan, and he'd agreed to forward all information on the poisoning case to her. When he'd asked how Shane was doing, she'd hedged around the truth. Riordan wanted Shane to come in as soon as possible so they could talk. Adrianna warned Riordan that would not happen until the next day. She'd gotten Shane into bed, and she would not wake him.

If only she could close her eyes and rest too. After a difficult night sleeping in Shane's med room, she was flirting with exhaustion. The chair had pulled out into a bed, but it still hadn't been comfortable. That, and the onslaught of Shane's emotions was abrading her nerves. Everything frustrated him, which made him angry. He was aggravated that he couldn't work, that he wasn't controlling his anger well, and that Adrianna was enduring the worst of his temper. All of which made him feel guilty.

Control was an issue for him, which only made sense considering his dominant nature. A good Master controlled himself before he sought to control someone else. His testiness under the circumstances didn't surprise her. The Masters at the Opio got testy all the time. Somehow it was a bigger deal for Shane. It was almost as though he'd built a dike to hold back deeper long-term frustration and anger. Normal everyday irritation poked pinholes in the dike, threatening to break the whole construct wide open if he didn't reassert his self-discipline and patch the hole.

Beneath his surface emotions, she had sensed a gray tumult that was always with him. He was an unhappy man. The only hint at what caused his unhappiness was his reaction to the picture of his home. His estrangement from his mother. What had happened between them? Adrianna sighed and rubbed her eyes. For now, rest was the best thing for him.

On the desk, the locket, stolen during the abduction attempt on her at the Beta Tau spaceport, glinted up at her. The guard at the cargo lock had given her a note and the necklace when she'd gone down to check on deliveries. He'd said a blonde woman had brought it and asked that it be placed in Adrianna's hands. A glance at the note told her Frau Heinrich was the delivery person. Adrianna picked it up and reread it.

Little Girl,

I'm returning the locket you left behind. It's never wise to throw away the past. It will catch hold of you when you least expect it. But what fun!

Frau Heinrich

Adrianna hadn't left the locket at the Institute. She knew that for a fact, having checked and double-checked that she'd packed it. Master Trey had been right. Frau Heinrich wasn't her friend. It looked as though she had connections to the Benefactor. Adrianna would show Shane the note tomorrow, but it didn't really change anything. Meanwhile, she'd fight her exhaustion and get the work done that she'd promised him. His trust in her was important.

~

SHANE WOKE to the aroma of fresh-baked…something. He inhaled the fragrant scent deep into his lungs. No, he couldn't tell what it was, but it was definitely baked goods. It reminded him of the boiled fruitcake, spices blending with sweet sultanas, that he'd eaten as a child at home. He kicked back the sheets and climbed out of bed, stretching his arms above his head and arching his spine to loosen the kinks. Another smell, pungent and rank, assailed his nose. Body odor. Fuck, he was ripe. Once he peeled his clothes off, he stepped into his bathroom and made quick work of his morning routine: piss, tube shower, teeth. In his bedroom, he picked up his dirty laundry and shoved it into the bin. Then he selected his usual work attire, accenting the white button-down shirt with a bolo tie.

The tie, a symbol of the Marshals Service, was an anachronism he never quite understood for a service based on an ethnically Irish planet. Faux ethnically Irish at that. Every child of the founding families on Tallav learned about the roots of their Irish ancestry. But the truth was most had only a smidgen of Irish blood in them. And the Irish customs they sought to copy had been cherry-picked. St. Patrick was never mentioned. No one seemed to know why the marshals wore bolo ties from Earth's American West. Every marshal endured jibes, asking when they'd last kissed their horse. At least they hadn't decided to call the Marshals Service the Tallavan Rangers.

He wiggled his toes and decided to wait until after breakfast to put on his boots, preferring to go barefoot. He'd been an ogre, and he wanted to make it up to Adrianna.

He followed the luscious smells emanating from the galley and found Adrianna placing hot muffins on a platter.

When she looked up, she said, "I was just coming to wake you up. You slept all yesterday and through the night."

Shane hated the time lost, but he'd needed the rest and Riordan could do the footwork on the case. "You can cook! The smell is heavenly."

Her hands fluttered over the muffins. "It was on my resume."

"I thought that meant you could use a flash cook."

"I can, but it didn't look to me like your oven had seen much use, so I baked you a treat." She finished arranging the muffins on a plate. "Our housekeeper taught me when I was twelve. I nagged her until she broke down and gave me baking and cooking lessons. She was a genius at making do with whatever was on hand, so I learned by the some-of-this and some-of-that method. Your pantry doesn't have many baking ingredients, but I was able to mix these muffins up. I hope they're not awful. Sometimes my creations don't turn out very edible."

Shane embraced her from behind, nuzzling his nose by her ear and murmured, "If they're not, I know something else that is incredibly edible."

Her breathing hitched, and he relished the swell of her rib cage against his arm. Then she pulled his arms away from her waist. "You need to eat real food. You have a busy schedule."

With a muffin in her fingers, she turned to face him and placed it to his lips. "Bite."

Shane opened and took a big mouthful.

Adrianna brushed the crumbs from his lips. "You like?" she asked.

Inflamed by how seductive the domestic Adrianna looked, his mind grew numb, all cerebral functions heading south when her tongue swept out and licked her bottom lip while removing the last bit of muffin from his mouth. He swallowed with difficulty. "Yeah."

Adrianna's lips pricked into a quick smile, and she gave him a tiny push backward. "Café, tea, cocoa? You have cases of café in stock, so I assume you prefer it."

"Yeah, café. Can't afford real coffee." He stared at her, not moving.

She popped his muffin onto a plate and said, "Sit. Eat," pointing at a stool. "Black? Cream? Sugar?"

"Black." Shane shook himself back to awareness. In obedience to her commands, he sat, picked up the muffin, and ate another crumbly bite. Adrianna placed a steaming mug of café in front of him.

"I'm sorry for taking my frustration out on you yesterday," Shane said.

"That's okay. You were tired."

"Still, it's not the way I should treat you."

"You were recovering from a near-death experience," she said drily.

"Yeah."

Adrianna leaned on the counter. The position accentuated her breasts, but he didn't think she knew that. He grinned and took another bite of muffin. Even outside the bedroom, he enjoyed having her around. Then a thought slapped him like a wet rag. Was it only two nights ago he'd decided to keep things impersonal outside the bedroom? So far, he'd been nothing but personal. If he didn't start now, he never would.

"You don't need to do that," he said.

"Do what?" Adrianna poured herself a cup of café and added large doses of sugar and cream to it.

"Bake. I'm used to packaged meals. I don't need you to do that kind of thing. We're not a couple like that." His voice grew harsher with each statement. He fixed his eyes on Adrianna when he looked up from his mug.

Adrianna's cheeks went pink. "I wanted to take care of you. After all, you were sick. I like to bake. It's fun. If it bothers you, I won't." The words tumbling out of her mouth began soft and placating, but the more she said, the angrier her voice became. "But let's get something straight. Ever since the attack, you've been a pain in the ass. When it was the fatigue talking, I could live with it. This morning, however, you've sent nothing but mixed signals. You cozy up behind me and start seducing me. Then minutes later, you're mad because I baked you a muffin, saying we're not a couple like that. Like what?"

Shane tried to interrupt, but Adrianna barreled on after a quick breath. "As your employee, I'm good enough for sex but not good enough to be a friend who bakes you a damn muffin. Well, let me tell you, Tiernan, I'm a professional. But if it weren't for our contract, I'd have been packed and gone already. What the hell do you want from me?" With that, she inhaled deeply and dropped her head. She took a muffin from the platter and began shredding it with her fingers.

Shane stared at Adrianna, a muscle in his jaw twitching, his chest tight. Fuck, he was such a jerk, but it was for her own good.

"You're right. You are my employee. I didn't realize you enjoyed baking. By all means, bake if it pleases you, but don't try to worm your way into my affections. Once the contractual period is over, I will pack you off to your next assignment. You are two things to me. You are my contracted sexual submissive and my associate. I apologize if my actions have led you to believe our relationship could be more than that."

Adrianna threw the last chunk of her muffin onto the pile of crumbs she'd created. She brought her head up, her eyes a cold, glittering green. "Fine. I understand. Thank you for making that clear."

"Thank you for baking muffins. It was very considerate of you."

"You're welcome. Sir." Adrianna brushed the fragments from her fingers and began cleaning up. Her voice rigidly formal, she said, "I've added the current info on Concordia Demont and her attack on you to your tablet. Marshal Riordan has been busy interviewing her known associates. Nothing of much use so far. That's the good news. The bad news is that she died in custody, a suicidal overdose of meds, which she got her hands on even though they were in a locked medicine cabinet in a secured medical supply room."

"What?" The surprise dropped all thoughts of Adrianna from his mind. "Where did this happen? The station med clinic?"

Adrianna shook her head. "No, the Guardia infirmary. Someone decided she wasn't injured badly enough to take to the station clinic. She was being monitored for a concussion. The official story is she evaded the staff, broke into the locked med room, and smashed open the medicine cabinet. When the staff realized she was no longer in her observation bed, they found her dead on the floor in the med room."

Shane frowned. What the fuck was going on with the Guardia? "That's not possible without help. The monitors on the observation bed would have alerted the staff the minute she got up. Everyone in that infirmary had to be deaf and blind for that scenario to happen."

"Pretty much," Adrianna said. "Riordan doesn't believe it was suicide. He's certain that one or more 'someones' inside the Guardia arranged her premature death."

"Fuck, I'm positive she'd have talked. But I guess the ones that sent her recognized that too." Shane grimaced, then smacked the counter with his palm. "Okay. I need to get my boots on and scan the info you prepped for me. Call Riordan and arrange a meeting with him."

"Already arranged. With the Guardia compromised, he asked us to meet him down planet at the Marshals Service Office on Beta Tau. I'll send him a heads-up that we're headed his way."

Shane watched Adrianna for a few seconds. His chest tightened. "Thank you. You've been a great help. I should have hired you a long time ago. Can you be ready in fifteen minutes? Plan to return to the *Adrasteia* tonight. I'm fairly sure we'll be traveling to Tallav before the day is over."

"Fifteen minutes. I'll be ready."

ADRIANNA TOOK sips from the oversize cup of cream tea Marshal Riordan had brought her. Hot, sweet, and spicy, it warmed her insides while she contemplated the two marshals seated at the conference table with her. They were alike in that they both had intense eyes and potent masculinity. Shane emanated unruffled steadiness with a gentleness hidden by his size and the power of his physical presence. Riordan, though physically smaller than Shane, had a similar formidable demeanor, but unlike Shane, Riordan's control masked something much darker, a miasma of anger, self-hatred, and deep loneliness. Adrianna had seen his office, perfectly ordered despite the eclectic mix of furnishings. It was an island amid the clutter of stained mugs and instant-food detritus overlaying a frayed decor that made up the rest of the Marshals Service Office on Beta Tau.

Riordan seemed to want to control himself, everything, and everyone about him. The loneliness she sensed in him probably meant he had no wife or girlfriend. She'd met similar controlling men. Generally, those in long-term stable relationships were softened around the edges. Not Marshal Riordan.

"Pacquin?" Shane said.

Adrianna snapped from her meandering thoughts. "Yes, Sir."

"Pay attention."

"Yes, Sir."

Shane tipped his head toward Riordan. "Go ahead."

Riordan raised his eyebrows before continuing. "As I was saying, we've connected Concordia Demont with the new Wellington School. Apparently her house bouncer was her longtime lover. We caught him at the right moment, crying his eyes out, and he told us she'd had a private meeting with a guy from the Wellington. She'd come back afraid but wouldn't talk to her boyfriend about it. Claimed it was better if he didn't know. She dolled herself up and left the brothel. That's the last anyone there saw or heard from her."

"Who's behind the Wellington?" Shane leaned toward Riordan.

"That took quite some digging to ferret out. It's held by layers of multiple entities, but they all lead back to a private corporation on Furzine."

"Which means the Benefactor of Furzine." Shane frowned and turned to face Adrianna. "A man also very interested in you."

Adrianna blinked rapidly under the intense stare of two sets of eyes— one blue and one brown.

"Are you a plant, Ms. Pacquin?" Riordan spit out the question, lowering his chin.

"N-no. I'm trying to stay as far away from him as possible." Adrianna jerked her gaze between the men before focusing on Shane, waiting to hear what he would say.

"She's telling the truth. I trust her, beyond the fact that she saved my life." Shane voiced his protest, leaning back in his chair. Adrianna was grateful for the conviction she sensed coming from Shane. The suspicion she felt from Riordan was daunting.

"She could have staged it to secure your confidence."

Shane dismissed the statement with a wave of his hand. "No, the method was way too risky to stage an attempted murder. I could have easily died or been incapacitated. Then what? No, Dria's been truthful from the start. She's been out of the Benefactor's reach at the Opio Institute for a year. He sought to grab her between the Institute and her first meeting with me. When that failed, he tried eliminating me."

"Sir?" Adrianna tentatively interrupted the two men.

"Yes?"

"I meant to tell you before we left the *Adrasteia*, but I forgot." From the pocket of her jacket, she pulled the locket and the note. "This was left with the cargo-lock guard for me. It's the locket that was taken when I was attacked at the spaceport and a note."

Shane reached for the note, read it, and handed it to Riordan. When Riordan had scanned it, he asked, "Who is Frau Heinrich?"

"She's an instructor at the Opio Institute. She's one of the staff sadists.

Before I left the Institute, Master Trey, my mentor, told me she had connections to unsavory people."

Shane scowled. "It's an obvious threat. This Frau Heinrich must be connected to the Benefactor. And he's the past that will catch hold of Ms. Pacquin."

Riordan's brow furrowed, but he nodded in agreement.

Shane reached out and placed his hand over Adrianna's. "The question is why. There's something about you that is essential to whatever enterprise the Benefactor is launching."

Adrianna couldn't believe she was vital to the Benefactor. No, it wasn't possible. "I'm no one important. I have only a couple of friends. All my close relatives except for my *mémé* are dead. I just…"

"Your mémé? Who is that?" Shane asked. "I ran your name when I was considering hiring you. The report listed your parents and paternal grandparents as deceased. It didn't mention maternal grandparents."

Adrianna glanced at Riordan and then returned her gaze to Shane. *Damn.* If she told them about her grandmother, she'd have to tell them she was from Preatiens. She'd promised Master Trey not to do that, but surely under the circumstances, she should. She'd leave out the Preatiens part. Maybe they wouldn't ask which planet her parents had come from. Besides, her mémé couldn't have anything to do with this.

"Mémé is my grandmother on my mother's side. My mother was disowned when she and Father moved to Furzine. I was supposed to stay with Mémé when I turned twenty-one, so she could bring me into society and find me a suitable husband. I think she hired all my nannies with the idea that if I was raised in a proper fashion, she would accept me back into the family."

"What is your mémé's name?" Shane's question, spoken in a soothing tone, helped calm the jangling thoughts in her head.

"Mémé Sauveterre. Her first name is Élise."

"Élise Sauveterre of Preatiens?"

Adrianna's eyes widened. How had he known that? She worried her bottom lip between her teeth, trying to think of some way to deny it.

Shane's lips flattened. His voice sliced through her. "You are the granddaughter of Élise Sauveterre, born on Preatiens. When were you going to tell me you are an empath?"

"I-I wasn't." Adrianna dropped her gaze to her lap. Her whole body jumped when Shane's hand slapped down on the conference table. When she looked up, Shane was angled away from the table. His jaw was working. No need to use her empathic senses to discern how deeply angry he was with her. If his previous frustration had poked pinholes in his self-control, she'd just slammed a fist through it.

After what seemed like a long time, Shane swiveled to face Riordan, away from Adrianna. "It would appear whatever the Benefactor is up to, it involves Adrianna and Preatiens. If he intended to use Adrianna to manipulate Élise Sauveterre, he didn't need to wait until she turned twenty-one, much less marry her. That makes no sense."

Adrianna didn't understand. Her grandmother was important? She'd been told that women on Preatiens didn't run things. The men did. Women were secluded at home. Adrianna was certain Shane was wrong about her connection to the Benefactor being more than his marital interest in her. It had to be the only reason, but there was no way she'd interrupt him. When Riordan asked the question for her, she was grateful.

"Who is Élise Sauveterre?"

"She's the grand dame of Preatien society, very powerful. She can and has made or broken individuals, families, and even companies. Nothing happens on Preatien that doesn't receive her scrutiny or approval," Shane said. "Unlike on Tallav where women formally control everything, on Preatiens it's only the older women that move in society. They are the arbiters of public opinion."

Adrianna was dumbfounded. Her mémé was the most influential woman on Preatiens. Why had her parents never told her these things?

Shane's fingers drummed on the table. "We've got more dots, but how they might connect is still not clear. The Benefactor is pumping out a steady supply of young, trained sex workers on Beta Tau and shipping them off to Runner's Hub. He's also trying to get his hands on Élise Sauveterre's granddaughter. I think he's hoping to acquire a foothold on Preatiens using Ms. Pacquin to manipulate Sauveterre."

"Possibly, but Preatiens doesn't have brothels, so I don't see how sex trafficking figures in," Riordan said.

Shane pursed his lips in thought. "If he could set up brothels, offering services that Preatien males could only find off planet, he'd be making money at the same time he manipulated and blackmailed his way to become a behind-the-scenes power broker." Shane grimaced. "No, I can't see that happening. Sequestering women of childbearing age is too integral a part of Preatien society. Preatiens is a closed planet for that very reason. They would never bring in young women from other planets. However, if he could get Élise Sauveterre to invite him to be her guest on Preatiens, he'd have the stamp of approval for Preatien businessmen and politicians to associate with him. They've long denied Furzine an embassy on Preatiens, but this could be his in."

Riordan leaned back in his chair, frowning. "I don't doubt the Benefactor is itching to expand his power to Preatiens. He has his fingers in so many quasilegal pies; I can imagine what a prize Preatien goodwill would be to him. Surely, he can't think marrying Ms. Pacquin will gain him access to her grandmother. Sauveterre cut off her own daughter, after all. Wouldn't she disown Ms. Pacquin?"

"Good question." Shane sat back in his chair, fingers laced behind his head, staring at the ceiling. "Maybe he intended to threaten to harm Ms. Pacquin once he had her in his hands. Although as I said, he's waited until she was twenty-one to attempt to kidnap her. He could have threatened to harm her at any time while she was on Furzine. Ms. Pacquin told me he also provided her bodyguard on Furzine. It's definitely worth exploring."

"For that matter, why not marry her earlier?" Riordan asked.

"Females must be twenty-one to marry on Preatiens."

"That only matters if he's trying to obtain Élise Sauveterre's goodwill." Riordan shook his head, scratching the side of his neck. "We don't really have enough information, but it's clear the Benefactor is willing to kill a marshal."

Shane righted himself, slapping his fingers on the edge of the conference table. "Okay, here's what I suggest. Riordan, you continue to pursue matters from your end on the attacks on Ms. Pacquin and me. I also want you to nail down numbers and names of the kids coming into and out of the Wellington School. We can't ignore the possibility that the school is part of an illegal human trafficking pipeline. I'm surprised the corporate directors of Beta Tau allowed the school. They've always been careful to avoid even the hint of anything illegal. Reputation matters to them. The school itself may be completely legal, but what happens to its students may not—

Fuck, probably isn't. Someone must not have done their due diligence, or credits crossed palms."

"Will do," Riordan said.

"I'm going to head back to Tallav to request a marshal higher up the chain of command to connect with Élise Sauveterre. But before I leave, I want to send a message to the Benefactor."

"Message?" Riordan asked.

"I'm thinking Ms. Pacquin and I should show him we're not running scared." Focused on Adrianna, Shane deepened his voice and asked, "Are you up for it, Adrianna?"

Like a blue flame, his eyes kindled a heated response inside Adrianna's chest.

"Yes, Sir."

Her thoughts splintering, Adrianna tuned out their conversation, wishing she could spend time alone to recover from the emotional ride she'd been on since she'd first decided to bake muffins this morning. The definition of her relationship with Shane wasn't stable. They weren't friends. No. Definitely not. They were associates who had sex. Hurt and angry at his rebuff, she'd played the role of personal assistant to perfection. Colleagues didn't tell each other their deepest, darkest secrets. Yet, it had felt like Shane was furious enough to end their contract because she hadn't told him she was an empath. Which meant she was more than an associate to him no matter what he said. And now he'd gone all Dom on her, at work no less, with that panty-melting look and voice that made her stomach drop. What kind of message was Shane planning to send that required Adrianna, not Dria or Ms. Pacquin?

She'd been listening carefully, hoping to make sense of all the information about the case she had yet to digest. Until he said her name, *Adrianna*. After that it was an effort to give half her attention to the two men's conversation. She refocused her attention on them. Shane was saying something about Patrick O'Toole and going to the Wild Rover Pub. He stood and gripped her elbow to assist her from her chair, causing her to squeak out a quick good-bye. The pressure of his fingers made it clear he was still livid. Well, damn it, she was mad too.

8

Ten years ago when he'd been stationed on Beta Tau, Shane had eaten at an automat down the street from the Marshals Service's local station. It should be relatively empty this time of day. Hand still gripping Adrianna's elbow, he guided her there and to a two-seat table in one corner away from the food dispensers.

"Sit." He pointed a finger at one of the chairs. Instead of taking the other seat, he paced alongside the red-checkered plasti-form table, seething. If he vented now, the automat might not survive. He curled his fingers, wanting to grab hold of a chair and fling it the length of the shop. No one else had been inside when they entered, but he heard the scrape of the door when his back was turned. He spun sharply around and glared at the man coming through the door. The man froze, blinked rapidly, and exited.

The man's response was like a bucket of cold water that Shane desperately needed. Why was he so close to allowing his self-control to shatter? He shut his eyes, took several long, deep breaths, and consciously relaxed his core muscles, which had tensed nearly rigid. Calmer, he sat in the chair opposite Adrianna.

"Explain why you didn't tell me you were from Preatiens and an empath, please." His voice was gruff, but his emotional meltdown must have been far scarier to an empath.

Adrianna stared past him, her eyes unfocused and her words scarcely audible. "I'm sorry I didn't tell you I was from Preatiens during our negotiations."

Shane tried to ameliorate the harshness of his tone. He didn't want to continue to frighten her. He knew the attempt was a failure when she jumped at his question. "Why didn't you?"

Adrianna's gaze dropped to Shane's chest. "Master Trey, my Institute mentor, told me never to reveal I was from Preatiens. He thought my abilities made me vulnerable. He was afraid I might fall into the hands of someone who would exploit me for nefarious purposes. I promised him not to tell you."

Adrianna stopped speaking. She flicked a glance up at him and then back down.

Shane studied her. "Did you promise him anything else?"

Adrianna gave a slight nod.

"Words, Adrianna. Look at me."

When she met his gaze, Shane didn't see apprehension any longer. A spark of green fire had kindled. Her empathic skills no doubt told her he was cooling off.

"Yes."

"Will you tell me what that was?"

"No."

Shane placed his hand on the table, tapping his index finger while looking at her. "Why not?"

"We haven't reached a level of trust in our relationship for me to tell you. We are associates, after all. Associates don't share their life stories."

Shane stopped tapping and dragged his hand over his face. "Yes, we are associates, but we are also Master and submissive. You don't suppose you should have told your Master about your empathic skills?"

"No. I'm trained to protect myself from empathic overload. Are you worried I would somehow use them against you? Because your emotions are your emotions. If you're as honest with me as you want me to be with you, then you wouldn't want to hide your feelings from me. Which you are. At least the deep ones. But you'll note I haven't gotten mad about that.

I haven't expected you to tell me your deepest, darkest secrets. Come to think of it, I don't know much about you, Marshal Shane Tiernan. Hell, you could be waiting to spring some bizarre fetish on me like an unnatural love of cabbage and the desire to make love in a vat of coleslaw."

Shane blinked. *Fuck.* She'd done it again. Turned the argument back on him and made sense while doing it. She was right. He was making demands of her he had no intention of reciprocating. Truth be told, he agreed with Master Trey. Adrianna's empathic skills were best kept a secret.

Adrianna was tracing patterns on the checkered tabletop.

"Dria. Eyes up." When she complied, he said, "I understand why you didn't tell me about your Preatiens background. Thank you for sharing that with me. I promise never to use your skills for"—he raised his eyebrows—"nefarious purposes."

Adrianna responded with a curt nod. "Yes, Sir."

Shane reached out and covered her hand with his. "I'm sorry for expecting...pushing you faster to trust me than you're comfortable with. It's obvious we need to spend more time getting to know each another. Gods. There's a lot we should talk about, but right now isn't good."

With a tug, he pulled her around the table by her hand and said, "Come here. Sit." He hauled her onto his lap, squeezing her in his arms, lips nuzzling her temple. "I'm sorry I lost control and scared you. I would never physically lay a hand on you to hurt you. As long as we're together, you're mine to protect. The emotional stuff... I don't want to harm you that way either."

Adrianna pulled back and looked into his eyes. "I trust you not to want to hurt me. Relationships take time. My interpersonal relationships instructor at the Opio said that conflict is the sign of a growing relation-ship. That makes today a growth spurt for us. When we talk and get every-thing resolved, that's like getting bigger size clothes."

Shane chuckled. "Dria, you have such an imaginative way of looking at things. As long as I don't have to pay credits for the clothes. I've already spent more than enough on new clothes for you."

"Hmmm." Adrianna snuggled up against Shane again.

"Oh, and I don't have an unnatural love of cabbage. No vats of coleslaw in our future."

Adrianna giggled. "That's a relief."

"Hmpf. We're going to do some playacting this evening. I haven't gotten it all figured out yet, but our first stop is a visit to Patrick at his pub." He lifted her chin and kissed her lips with smooth tenderness. "Tonight will require a lot of trust. Can you handle that after what's happened today?"

"If this is about the case, then yes. Absolutely I can."

"Okay. I can delay a day if you need it."

"No, I trust you."

Shane brought his mouth to hers again, kissing her deeper. Adrianna Pacquin was pretty fucking amazing. Reluctantly, he broke the kiss. "Let's go."

ADRIANNA PERCHED on a stool at the far end of the bar in the Wild Rover Pub. Shane had instructed her to stay put and eat a high-carb meal with no alcohol. He'd conferred with Patrick and then departed after admonishing him not to take his eyes off her. Patrick brought her a big plate of pasta with a cheesy white sauce and a large glass of iced lingberry tea.

"How about some tea cakes for a sweet to top that off?" he asked.

"That's sounds wonderful. Thank you." Her first bite of the tender, creamy pasta hit the spot, and she soon found her plate empty. She selected a cake from the dish Patrick had brought her, biting into it and groaning at the buttery goodness. Patrick looked at her from the other end of the bar, smiled, and strolled back to stand in front of her, hands supporting him while he leaned on the bar.

"These are amazing," she said.

"My wife, Mary, bakes those for the pub. She's a right one in the kitchen."

"That she is." Adrianna didn't want to impose, but she was burning with curiosity. "May I ask you a personal question?"

"Ask. I'll answer if I can."

"Marshal Tiernan has told me you are a Tallavan expat. What made you decide to live away from Tallav?"

A shadow crossed over Patrick's eyes, and Adrianna wished she hadn't spoken. "Mary and the children are my home. I wasn't planning to marry an off worlder. I was posted to Colt IV and fully intended to serve my four-year stint and return to find a wife on Tallav. That changed when I met Mary. Within six months, I knew she was the woman I wanted to be with the rest of my life. I made the official request to have the marriage sanctioned by my mother, but that was pointless. The mere idea that I'd consider marrying an off worlder was scandalous. O'Tooles didn't do that." He gave a humorless laugh. "It delayed the wedding two years while I earned enough as a marshal to start this pub, but we've done well and been blessed with beautiful children."

Adrianna's brow furrowed. "Your mother had to sanction your marriage?"

Patrick sniffed, and his left cheek ticked up. "Tallavan men, the sons of landowners, that is to say, have to get their mother's permission to marry a non-Tallavan woman. They can't bring her home to live, but they can work as a marshal off world if their mother sanctions the marriage. Otherwise, they're completely on their own, cut off."

Adrianna's mouth was hanging open. "Wow. That's…"

"That's Tallav," Patrick said. "Mind you, marrying Mary was the right decision, and one I've never regretted."

"Love conquers all," Adrianna mused.

"I wouldn't say love conquers all, but it certainly bears all." His smile was kind. "Have another cake." He took one from the plate and consumed it in two bites. Adrianna rolled her eyes and helped herself to another.

Patrick gave her a keen look. "Now Shane, he's not like me. I don't think he could leave the Marshals. It's who he was meant to be. The way things stand in his family, he'll not be allowed a sanctioned off world marriage either. It's a pity. He's a man that needs marriage. He's tried hard to do without. He's got a reputation in kink clubs on several worlds. No dearth of women falling all over themselves to be taken on as his submissive. If sex was all he was after, he'd never lack a partner. Speak of the devil, here he is." Patrick winked at her.

Adrianna turned on her stool. Shane was headed her way, carrying a black duffel bag. "O'Toole, may we borrow your office?"

"Sure."

"Come, Adrianna." Shane strode past Adrianna to the doorway that entered the kitchen. Adrianna followed him through, beyond the cleaning stations to another door and on to a small office complete with baby crib. Definitely a family business.

"Strip and put these on." Shane handed her a black leather harness with red studs, a see-through red chemise with opaque panels across the breasts and hips, a matching thong, and red heels. While Adrianna removed her clothing and pulled on the thong, she wondered what Shane was planning and where they were going. She began puzzling out the harness, a little confused about which strap went where.

"Here." Shane turned to her. He'd shed his clothes and put on a pair of leather pants. They weren't formfitting, but they didn't have to be. When he moved, different parts of his muscular body were outlined against the leather. His upper torso was bare, and he was delectable. Adrianna cast her gaze to the floor, a deep need for her Master flushing through her.

Shane helped her into the harness, adjusting it to fit her. "This is a suspension harness. Do you have much experience with suspension?"

"Yes, Sir. Master Trey used me as his rope model for exhibitions and classes at the Institute."

"Excellent. Nothing would please me better than to spend hours tying you up, but tonight I'm opting for the harness. We're going to the Whip Hand. Randolph Meryon, the owner, is an old friend of mine."

He helped her draw the chemise over her head, pulling the hem down until it rested several inches below her ass. "Perfect. You are beautiful, Adrianna. Turn and let me do your hair." With a yank, he removed the band from the end of her braid and then smoothed her mane into a long ponytail. The skin at her temples tugged tight enough to hurt, but it would soon loosen. With red leather strips he'd taken from the duffel, Shane spent several more minutes working with her hair. "There. I should corset your hair often, Adrianna." He held on to the caged ponytail while he turned her and bent her back, kissing her, plundering her mouth with deep thrusts of his tongue. She responded, sucking him in with each urgent, heated jab. His right hand skimmed up her abdomen to seize her breast. She relished the security of his hold, his powerful torso pulled close to her, his muscles moving against her while he ground his pelvis and hard erection into her. When he ended the kiss, he bit her earlobe. "You are such a tempting vixen." Adrianna trembled, her fingers tingling with the desire to caress Shane.

He reached into the duffel, pulling out a packet. "Black eyeliner. I want dramatic." He pointed her to a small mirror hung on the back of the door. While she deftly added the black eyeliner to her minimalist makeup, she watched Shane from the mirror. His torso was now covered in a flowing white shirt, and he was snapping the six-inch cuffs. The hem was stuffed into his pants, and the collar was open three buttons, leaving a gap with a tantalizing glimpse of his chest and the dark hair nestled there. When she turned, he glanced up. "Just right. They won't be able to stop looking at you."

"Thank you, Master. Everyone will want to *touch* you," she said.

Shane reached out and held her at arm's length. "Do I detect a hint of jealousy in that remark? Claws in, little cat." He stared, letting the time stretch uncomfortably. "This is serious tonight, Adrianna. Keep your eyes on me. No one else. I am your world, your focus. React only to me. No thoughts but for me. Burn with fire for me. No one else. I will display you, and they will covet you. But you are mine. Mine alone. Do not offer them even a glance. Do you understand?"

"Yes, Master." Adrianna returned his stare, willing him to see she craved to give him all he asked, as much as he required it from her.

"This is for you," he said when he picked up a box from the desk. He opened the lid and pulled out a shiny silver collar. Holding it in front of her, he read her the inscription. *Master Shane Tiernan.* Then he placed it around her throat, locking it in place with a small key strung from a black cord. He hung the cord around his neck. "You are mine. No one else belongs to me as you do. I want no one else the way I want you. You have no need for jealousy. As you are mine, I am yours. Do you understand?"

"Yes, thank you, Master." Adrianna's eyes pricked with unshed tears. This was what she wanted to hear, but was it real? He'd said they were playacting this evening.

Shane hugged her, holding her for one long minute, reinforcing his words with the strength of his embrace. He pulled back and ran his thumb down the side of her face. "I need you to lock that understanding deep inside you. Tonight will be difficult for us both. We'll have an audience, and I want to leave a false impression. I will say and do things. Things that would hurt you if they were real, but they won't be real. That collar will remind you of the truth. It will help you remember I cherish and respect you. I will call you *Pet* as another reminder of what is and isn't genuine. Adrianna is my reality. Pet is my undercover plaything. Do you understand?"

Her pulse had quickened. It was hard to stop herself from bouncing on her feet. She knew exactly who she was when Shane addressed her as Adrianna. She was his sub. The relationship between Dria and Shane may be a mess, but as Master and submissive they were still on track.

"Yes, Master. Tonight, I am Pet. I will focus on you and respond as your enthralled plaything even when you act out of character. I am honored that you allow me to play this role with you, and I treasure the opportunity to serve you. I will hide you, my true Master, in my heart."

Shane gently kissed her. "As I have hidden you in my heart." With his thumb rubbing across her cheek, he said, "Shoes." He knelt, reached behind Adrianna, and pulled the heels to him. Each foot lifted in turn, he massaged her insoles before slipping the stilettos on her feet. He stood, put on his own boots, and added her discarded clothes to the pile of his on the desk. "We'll get those later." Duffel in his hand, he ushered Adrianna out of the office.

9

Shane held Adrianna's face in a tight grip. "We're here. Keep fixed on me. Do not respond to anyone unless I give you permission to do so. The club has a damper, so we won't be able to communicate subvocally. Trust me. If you need to block emotions, do." He caressed her cheek, turned, and strode toward the entrance to the Whip Hand. Adrianna walked beside him, matching his strides, fire and ice personified. Shane couldn't help the pride that flared inside him when he opened the door for Adrianna to enter. They were a striking couple, and he expected eyes to turn and follow them.

"William," Shane greeted the maître d' while approaching the understated steel podium.

William, a slender silver-haired gentleman, beamed. "Master Shane. It's so good to see you again. Will you be dining with us, or do you wish to go straight to the club?"

Shane rapped the stand with a finger. William had not changed since they'd first met. "It's good to be back, William. We'll dine." He scanned the club restaurant. "Please give us a table that will display my pet well. I'll need access to the private and the public club venues later." He slipped fifty credits into William's hand. "I've asked Randolph to arrange time for me on the main stage and procure an assistant with suspension experience and my usual equipment."

"Indeed, sir. I have just the table. Randolph informed me of your arrival. We are all very pleased. It's been too long since we enjoyed one of your presentations." William eyed Adrianna up and down. "She is quite delectable. You will be envied tonight. Follow me."

Shane noted that the dining room had been updated since he'd last visited. Slate-gray walls were decorated with fine-art images of bound men and women, displaying the agony and ecstasy a whip in the right hands created. Modulated lighting fashioned brighter and darker areas. One could be private or fully public. Black leather and steel tables and chairs stood at various levels from the floor to a tier of seating built into a peninsula that extended out from the wall. In the center, a column rose higher than the rest, supporting a single table. It was to this pinnacle that William led Shane and Adrianna. While they climbed the stairs that wrapped the column, the murmuring of the diners hushed. The attention of the room focused on them. Good.

As they reached the top, Shane advised William, "My pet will sit next to me. One place setting. We'll have water to drink since we'll be playing tonight. And an order of Chocolate Seduction."

"As you wish, sir." William left after moving a chair as Shane asked.

Shane seated Adrianna, placing her corseted ponytail behind her chair. After sitting, he leaned back in his chair, studying her. As he had requested, she was fixated on him. She was graceful and captivating. Later he would have to thank Master Trey for nurturing Adrianna into the spectacular woman who sat before him. She was self-possessed but undeniably submissive; her strength and intelligence was his to use. She did not sublimate her personality but gave herself as she was, not assuming a persona. And she was his. "Do not move. You are perfection itself right now. It pleases me to sit here and consume you." The smooth column of her neck encircled by his collar. The green lightning in her eyes. The rise and fall of her breasts, nipples outlined against the chemise, curves constricted by the leather harness visible through the transparent yoke of the dress. She was flawless, and she made him hard just looking at her.

A waiter arrived carrying their water and a plate of chocolates. Shane thanked him and waited for him to leave, never letting his gaze stray from Adrianna. She waited, hands in her lap, her attention glued to him.

"This is a treat for you, Pet. You've been such an obedient girl. I know you want to please me this evening. This is to remind you that when you are very good, I will pamper you. You will be very good tonight, won't you, Pet?"

"Yes, Master. I will be very good tonight."

"Excellent because I will punish you severely if you are not. You know how much I like to chasten you."

"If it pleases you, I will be naughty so you can spank me."

A slow smirk spread across Shane's lips. "Oh, you won't have to be naughty on purpose. I'm sure I'll find a reason to correct you tonight, Pet." The five chocolates on the plate rested in a half circle with a dollop and drizzles of milky brown sweetness offsetting the confections. Shane selected the vanilla cream. "We'll start with something pure with a kiss of flavor. Open."

With her teeth, Adrianna accepted the candy from his fingers, her eyes rapt on him. The muscles in her throat and jaw moved, and he wanted nothing more than to nuzzle the spot above the juncture of her collarbones that rose and fell when she swallowed. When she'd finished, she licked her lips with the tip of her tongue.

Shane restrained himself from brushing a finger across her mouth. He offered her the second sweet, a chocolate-dipped slice of pear.

"Now something juicy. Careful, it may drip." With a half smile, he wished for just such an occurrence.

Adrianna ate the treat from his fingers in two bites. The last, a little large, forced a trickle of juice to escape the corner of her mouth. When she swiped it up with her tongue, Shane copied her action. Adrianna smiled sweetly at him.

"You're such a minx, Pet. You're definitely ready for something with a little nip to it." He plucked the chocolate-covered raspberry from the plate, holding it before her lips and then pulling it back when she leaned in to accept it. "Tart." When her eyes widened, he chuckled and then allowed her to take the chocolate.

"I hope that got your juices flowing, because it's time for something hard." He took the dark chocolate-covered almond and pressed it into her mouth, pushing it all the way in with his finger. While she chewed, he fixed his attention on her and then put his finger into his mouth and sucked it clean.

"You make me so hot, Pet. I'd like to bend you over this table and take you right now." When he placed the final confection to her lips, he stared at her while she bit down. She let out a gasp when the heat of the chili-flavored center flooded her mouth. A dark pink flushed her face while she swallowed several times in a row, the muscles in her throat moving, her eyes widening. Shane waited, experiencing her reaction. "Very good, Pet. No water yet. Soon."

He swiped a dollop of chocolate sauce off the plate. "Suck," he commanded when he offered it to her. She swept her tongue out to catch the drop threatening to fall and then engulfed his finger with her mouth. Shane withheld the moan that rose inside him when her tongue swirled around his finger. He pulled it halfway out and penetrated her again, imagining her lips around his cock while he thrust in and out.

Fuck, she was such a challenge to his control. Under other circumstances, he would have taken her to the private area of the club and had her on her knees as fast as he could. There were other considerations tonight. While Adrianna waited, he rinsed his finger in the water glass and wiped it on the napkin. He offered her a drink of water. After she'd drunk her fill, he wet a corner of the napkin and cleaned her mouth, patting it dry with the opposite end of the napkin.

"It's time, Pet." He rose, assisted her, and said, "Follow me." Once again, every eye not already inspecting them turned and followed them while they descended the steps and wound their way to the club's public play entrance.

MAINTAINING A TIGHT focus on Shane had been easy for Adrianna. He was magnificent, pure sex and dominance. Every female in the dining room had lusted after him. Now, as they entered the public play area, she could sense the hunger of the people, but she relegated it to the background. Her world was Shane, her Master. He was obviously planning a suspension exhibition, and he must be good to command the main stage on short notice. Anticipation curled its way through her core, throbbing deep inside, making her ache to be filled. Shane's own expectancy fed hers, but he also radiated an authority that left her no doubt who was in control.

"Master Shane. William said you had arrived. It is so good to have you back with us." An average-sized man approached, average build, average looks, average in every way but one. He evinced a charisma that made him stand out. Perhaps it was his chocolate-brown eyes that utterly focused on whomever he spoke to. Or his elegant bearing. Or something dark and naughty that shimmered through his veneer of civility. Adrianna had thought no one could distract her from Shane tonight, but the moment this man had neared, she hadn't been able to keep her eyes from turning to him. The man's energy screamed, *Look at me, adore me, follow me.*

"Randolph." Shane reached out and clasped arms with the man. "It is good to be back. I've missed the energy here."

"I've missed you too." Randolph clapped him on the arm. "It's you that brings the energy tonight, brother. The news that you'll be presenting one of your suspension exhibitions has spread, as has word of your sub. The descriptions do not do her justice. She is exquisite. Have you had her long?"

Adrianna pulled her attention back to Shane.

Shane grunted and smirked. "She is a pleasure. I've only recently collared her. I'm still conforming her to my ideals, but she is already well trained. This will be my first opportunity to suspend her, although she has experience as a rope sub. Don't you, Pet?" Lust gleamed in Shane's eyes when he looked straight at her while discussing her with Randolph. Although she was no longer looking at him, Randolph's intense speculation buffeted her empathic senses.

"Perfect! I have made all the arrangements we discussed. The stage will be yours in about thirty minutes. Master Trey from the Opio has agreed to act as your assistant. He's a top rope suspension Master. He has his own kit that should have everything you require in it. If you find you need anything, don't hesitate to ask one of the club staff to assist you. Why don't you make yourselves more comfortable? I'll send Master Trey to fetch you."

Shane's eyebrow rose slightly at hearing that Master Trey would second him. "Thank you, Randolph. As always, you are the perfect host." Shane shifted, began to move away, but then stopped and said, "Tonight is business. We'll get together to talk soon."

"Call me. Anytime."

"Will do."

Adrianna was puzzled. Shane had acted like he was surprised but emotionally he was satisfied when Randolph had told him Master Trey would assist him. The same little chink of feeling he got when his plans fell into place. *What did Master Trey have to do with his plans?*

Shane motioned her toward the changing rooms. Once inside, he removed his shirt, folded it, and placed it in his duffel bag. Finished, he drew her out and onto the main floor of the play area. *He must intend to have me strip onstage.*

With quick peripheral glances, Adrianna tried to find Master Trey. She hadn't expected to see him this soon after leaving the Institute. Manjii's "Vibrations of Lust" throbbed through the room. Her stolen looks revealed small platforms around the edge and a much larger one against the far wall. That must be the main stage where they would perform soon. She didn't spot Master Trey. Shane led her to a group of sofas and chairs at the center and sat in a large armchair. "Stand here." Shane pointed to a spot in front and to the right of him. Adrianna complied. "Take off your shoes and remove your dress—slowly, please." He settled back to scrutinize her.

While she slipped her heels from her feet, Adrianna fused her gaze to Shane's. A show was what he wanted, so she smoothed her hands languidly down the sides of her body to the hem of her dress. The interest of others in her little performance tingled along her empathic senses. She inched the sheath up, pausing, taking her time. After she'd bunched it up to her armpits so that her breasts were exposed, she flipped the whole dress inside out and over her head, pulling it away from her caged pony-tail at the last. She held the dress, turned it right side out, and folded it, awaiting further instructions.

She pursed her lips to avoid the smile quivering below the surface. For now, she narrowed her empathic senses to focus on Shane. Her sensory perception was under barrage from the lust aimed at her from all directions. Shane's arousal was more than enough and what she desired most.

"Put it in the duffel, Pet. Show me your ass while you do it."

The bag was lying on the floor next to Shane's chair. Adrianna turned so that her bottom would be in front of Shane when she bent to place the dress in the duffel. Before she could straighten, he pulled her over his knees. Her clit pulsed when he gave her cheeks several slaps, then rubbed lightly. "You have such a tempting ass, Pet. Get your leash now." Adrianna rose from his lap and searched through the bag, finding a red lead hiding in the bottom. After positioning it across both her palms, she brought it to him. "A little slow, Pet. That's one punishment for later. Kneel." Shane attached the leash to the ring on her collar, giving it a gentle tug. He leaned toward her, his musky sandalwood scent teasing her nose. "There. You're ready for the night now, Pet. Sit at my feet." Adrianna scooted in next to him facing his legs on his right side and sat with her rear on her heels. Shane stroked the top of her head.

A pixie of a girl dressed in black leather with a tiny skirt and vest, STAFF emblazoned at the top of her left breast in silver letters, approached Shane. "Sir, would you like a refreshing drink? We have a variety of fruit and veggie juices, café, and sodas. Anything nonalcoholic you can imagine."

Shane extended a finger, almost touching the small whip fastened to the top of her skirt. "Do you ever use that whip?" he asked.

The girl giggled, a sound peculiarly grating to Adrianna's ears. "Oh no, Sir. That's just for decoration. I'd much rather the whip was used on me."

Shane responded with a low, rumbling laugh. "I'll bet you do, little one. I don't require anything right now, but I will need three glasses of water available onstage for me in a bit. Would you also verify a private room reservation for me, Master Shane, and two guests? Something with a variety of restraining methods. It should be available following my scheduled suspension."

"Certainly, Sir. I'd do anything for you." The girl winked and swished her hips.

Adrianna was glad when the girl moved off. Damn, he was flirting in front of her. She hadn't expected that. Or her reaction. More jealousy. She wanted to reach out and trip the girl.

It's part of the act, not real. At least she hoped it wasn't. She remained properly submissive, focusing her gaze on Shane. A tiny rush washed through her when a familiar voice spoke to him. "Master Shane, may I introduce myself. I'm Master Trey. I believe we have a mutual interest in your sub."

"I've been looking forward to meeting you. Please, Trey, sit next to me. Let's chat a moment before we go to the stage."

Oh crap. He did not just tell Master Trey what to do.

Since she was facing Shane, Master Trey was out of her direct line of sight, but the tone of his voice when he responded sounded strained. He reeked of tension. "Thank you. It looks as though things are going well for the two of you."

"Yes. Adrianna and I are a good fit. I'm tolerably pleased with her initial training. I'm hoping to refine that here tonight."

Adrianna couldn't believe how officious Shane was acting. She wanted the men to like each other.

"Please understand, Trey, I appreciate your assistance tonight, but I must make it clear that I will be in charge. Follow my instructions to the letter and do not interfere with how I choose to use my pet."

Adrianna sensed the anger that lashed out from Master Trey toward Shane. It sounded like Master Trey was gritting his teeth while he spoke. "Naturally. That's understood. Shall we head to the stage?"

She couldn't believe the rudeness Shane had leveled at Master Trey. Common courtesy dictated that no one interferes between a Master and sub. To imply that Master Trey would do such was a blatant insult. She clamped down on her spinning thoughts. Not knowing what was real or false made it difficult to understand what Shane did. Trust. It was a matter of trust.

"Up, Pet. Follow." Shane pulled on her leash and led her.

Her gaze focused on the men while they walked to the steps leading up to the stage, Adrianna expanded her empathic senses to encompass the room. Curiosity, lust, jealousy all swirled around her, and then she picked up a virulent note of hate. Ahead and to the right. She swept a glance over that area without turning her head. When she drew closer, she pinpointed the person but was quickly past him and moving up the stairs.

Onstage, Shane took her hand, led her to the center of the platform, and turned her to face the audience. The chairs and sofas in the room could rotate into positions that allowed guests to concentrate on one of the small stages or the main stage. Activity had quieted. The largest platform was now the center of the audience's attention, and she was standing smack dab in the middle of it. From behind, Shane swept an arm around her shoulders and clasped her to his chest. He nuzzled her hair, his voice gently filling her ear. "Remember you will focus on me alone. I'm going to display your perfection. Enjoy yourself."

"Yes, Master. Shane, there's a man at the foot of the stairs, small, wiry, not a tourist, by himself. He hates you—not jealousy, extreme hatred." While she spoke to him, Adrianna leaned into Shane, writhing against his chest.

Shane brought his other hand up to caress her breast. "I see him. I will watch him." He kissed her shoulder, removed her leash, and pulled away. "Wait here, Pet. Standing."

Adrianna assumed the appropriate position, arms behind her back, hands clasped, breasts pushing forward, legs spread, head up, eyes down. Behind her, she heard the sounds of equipment moving into place and the murmur of Shane's voice when he explained to Master Trey what he intended to do. Shane must have persisted in his rude behavior because Master Trey's anger continued unabated. People were noticing the animosity between the Masters.

Shane had told her to keep her focus on him. That meant ignoring Master Trey. *Immerse yourself in the suspension.* She had always loved the sensations that bondage created, the exhilaration, especially when rope was involved. Anticipation suffused her body, a longing to be touched in whatever way Shane desired to touch her.

A moan slipped from her lips when Shane came from behind her to begin the binding process. He slapped her upper thigh hard enough to leave the reddened shape of his hand. "Quiet, Pet. No sound." He snaked a loop of rope across her stomach, winding upward until he snared her nipple and jerked the rope down and away.

Yessss! Do it again.

As though he'd heard her inner plea, Shane obliged, lassoing her other nipple and letting it experience the rough pull of the hemp. Damn, she wished he hadn't used a suspension harness. She yearned for his hands guiding the rope around her breasts and between her thighs. Instead, he stroked her shoulders, arms, and wrists while he worked to tie cuffs that would bind her to the suspension ring. He assisted her to sit on the stage floor to secure cuffs on her ankles and feet. She leaned, supporting herself with her arms and arching her back so her breasts thrust upward when he lifted each foot.

After testing each of his ties, Shane helped her to her feet. Master Trey lowered a large silver suspension hoop. It had rings along the inside edge and two more with rotating anchors lined up on the outside at top and bottom. Shane attached a rope to the bottom and secured it to a mooring point in the floor. After assuring both ropes were taut, Shane spun the hoop. Adrianna squeezed her hands against her legs. He was going to spin her.

"Stand in front of the ring, face forward, Pet."

Adrianna did as he asked. Grabbing her by her ears, he kissed her long and deep while simultaneously inserting small Stop-Dizz earplugs. She went breathless because it meant he planned to do extreme movements that would leave her, without the earplugs, overwhelmed from vertigo. Stunts that could make her throw up.

Shane released her and walked out of her line of sight. Her harness tugged when rope was attached to its rings. He tied her with meticulous care so her torso was held rigid in the center of the hoop. She wasn't sure what the pattern looked like, but it was evident by glancing down, the ropes zigged and zagged across the hoop behind her. A hard squeeze on her right butt cheek made her jump. She would have jerked, but she really hadn't moved except for her arms. Her restraints were snug.

Shane walked around to face her and asked, "How does that feel, Pet?"

"Wonderful, Master." A smile twitched her lips, and a giggle escaped. Damn, she was positively giddy.

Although Shane seemed to have in mind another end for this performance than their enjoyment, he gave her a wicked grin in response. He pulled one arm up with the rope tail from its wrist cuff and then the other, attaching each to the hoop. Adrianna flexed her arms, giving the bondage tie a test. Just right. Shane stroked each arm, slipping a finger between wrist and rope to assess the rope's constriction.

With an evil chuckle, he wrapped her caged ponytail around his fist and pulled her head to the side. While he spoke in loud, harsh tones, he glared over Adrianna's shoulders in the direction Master Trey stood. "You're mine and no one else's. You've got my collar. Now you need my mark." He latched on to her neck above the collar, biting and sucking her skin. The prickle of blood vessels breaking stung, and then Shane flattened his tongue and licked over the area several times. "Lovely." He dragged his palm up her torso, stopping to give her breast a fierce squeeze before twisting her nipple. His hand rose to cage her mouth, two fingers poised over her lips. "Suck, Pet." When Adrianna complied, swirling her tongue along the calloused pads of his fingers, Shane resumed his sensual assault on her neck.

When he released her, Adrianna reveled in the pride that emanated from Shane. Her Master's pride in her was an immeasurable gift, one she returned in equal measure, for she was proud of his skills. It was easy to want to please him. Some might consider she had granted her trust too quickly. Sure, Master Trey hadn't responded to Shane as she hoped, but he couldn't experience the sincerity of emotions that bolstered Shane's words and actions. Well, that and Shane seemed bent on making Master Trey dislike him. Still, she trusted Shane, and she was right to believe in him. While he attached the ropes from her ankle cuffs to the hoop, securing her in a full spread eagle, she realized that Shane would take that confidence to send her flying tonight. When he was satisfied with his ties, Shane stepped back so the audience could view the finished result.

When the smattering of applause died, he rotated the hoop so her profile was toward the audience. A push on the center of her back demonstrated the binding had no give. Turned to face the crowd, Adrianna was stationery for a moment and then the crowd became a blur when Shane spun the hoop, batting it faster with each revolution. Her awareness contracted, focusing on her pounding heart and her body's struggle to resist the spinning while her mind reveled in her lack of control.

At some point, Shane had stopped his efforts to spin her. The rotation slowed until he forced it to stop, throwing his other arm out in a measure of showmanship. The spectators ate it up.

His hands slid from her wrists to her ankles. Crouched before her, he released the tie on the hoop at the bottom. Master Trey moved up to bracket her, jerkily grabbing on and holding one side while Shane held the other. Animosity poured from Master Trey toward Shane. She sneaked a peek at Master Trey. His face was livid. Shane grasped her chin and yanked her to look at him.

"Eyes on me! Not him!"

With an involuntary gasp and a nod, Adrianna signaled her compliance.

The pull of gravity lightened when Shane activated the device he'd attached to her harness earlier. He released the upper rope over her head. The moment he did so, she went from vertical to horizontal, eyes fastened on Shane looming above her. This was the point where both men would have to be careful how they handled the hoop. She hoped their tense interaction didn't distract them. She was like a helium balloon without a string. Where she went depended on where they guided the hoop. How high she went depended on Shane's use of the field controller.

At their mercy, the floating sensation of the gravity field was soon accompanied by another enchantment that beckoned her to immerse herself. Subspace sang its siren song. Adrianna was barely aware when the men moved her away from the suspension rig, released her, and stood back. While she floated up between them, she drifted, immersing herself in the physical sensations of the harness, the rope, and the glory of ascending. Shane used the gravity controller like an invisible string, pulling her down and then releasing more until she hovered a foot below the ceiling. Adrianna was barely aware of Shane returning her to the floor. When they moved in and recaptured the hoop, she was jolted to awareness. She felt their hands checking the rope and harness. Once her eyes refocused, she saw Shane looking down at her.

"Doing okay, Pet?"

"Yes, Master." She was. She could have remained floating high in the air for hours.

"Time to let the audience get a closer look at you."

A chill shivered down Adrianna's spine. What did that mean? Her heart leaped, and she gasped when a quick flip left her facing the floor. Nothing was visible but the faux wood of the stage below her. Shane and Master Trey thumped and shuffled. The hoop wobbled as though someone had grabbed hold of it. The men were talking, but she couldn't distinguish what they were saying. Shane had to be continuing to taunt Master Trey. Her concern must have been evident because Shane's next words were barked at her.

"You're going flying, Pet. Keep your eyes open and smile."

The floor shifted forward and backward underneath her, and then she was soaring higher, out over the audience. Her body went rigid. The faces of the crowd below went by so quickly it was impossible to focus on any one individual. How would he stop her from running into a wall? Or for that matter, how would he return her to the platform? *Stop worrying. Shane has that all figured out.*

More than halfway across the room, she slowed, the harness and bindings biting her skin sharply when she came to a full stop. Drawn back along the same path, she was soon over the stage. Shane must have attached a rope to the hoop. The smarting smack of Shane's palm on her thigh regained her attention.

"I told you to smile."

She'd forgotten. He sent her repeatedly over the crowd, angling his throws to cover different sections of the room. Her hands were free, so she waved them the way she'd say bye-bye to a small child.

After she'd been returned to the stage for the last time, Shane and Master Trey flipped her faceup once again and walked the hoop to the suspension rig. Adrianna studied their faces. *Thunderous* was the word that best applied to Master Trey, as though he were Zeus about to let loose lightning bolts. Shane was the clear target. Shane focused on Master Trey with a sneer of derision. Blows looked likely at any moment.

Instead, they stiffly continued the suspension Shane had planned, turning her upside down and attaching the upper rope alone. Shane crouched and stroked her cheek. "One more pose, Pet, and we'll be done. Then we'll go where I can prove to this jerk who your real Master is."

Shane had deactivated the field device, so now the full effect of gravity pulled her downward. Master Trey must have moved back to the rope controls, because she rose in the air. Shane altered the suspension safety field on the floor below her and moved his arm through it in a sweep up as though he was commanding her to rise. He was really checking the field density. Her ascent continued until she was close to the connection point for the rig at the top of the ceiling.

It was a substantial drop to the floor below. If she were to fall, she stood a considerable risk of face-planting or falling so the back of her head hit and cracked her skull. *Stop the gory possibilities.* She released her tension, mentally playing the Romanze from Mozart's "Eine Kleine Nachtmusik," allowing the slow, steady pulse of the strings to move her into a serenity that would help her remain suspended in this position as long as Shane needed.

She wasn't sure how many minutes she'd been drifting in her own world, eyes shut, empathic senses stretching out to touch individuals here and there. Tastes of excitement, a little awe, some fear. Overall, the audience was enjoying themselves. If only she could share this experience with Shane. Her senses narrowed to him, and the heat of his desire for her enveloped her, igniting a response that flamed through her.

As she reveled in Shane's ardent feelings, she was jarred back to full awareness. She was falling. She'd never fallen. *Shane!* The sudden plunge slowed when she hit the stasis field. Rather than a jarring impact, she realized Shane had rigged the field in layers of ever more solidifying stasis. The pain was from clenching her muscles tight in panic. Once she unclenched her fists and relaxed, she began to shake from an adrenaline rush.

The audience, collectively holding their breath, broke into cheers when she came to a stop inches above the floor. Shane waved his hand to signal the crowd to applaud. He'd planned the drop. How had he hidden that from her? He reeked of undisguised self-satisfaction now.

As the crowd applauded, Master Trey raised her higher with the rope he had once again drawn taut until her head was at the same height as Shane's. Shane held her by the hair and kissed her with fierce passion, pillaging her mouth with deep thrusts of his tongue, biting her lower lip when he pulled away. "Surprised, Pet?"

"You enjoyed that."

"I did." The grin he'd been trying to hold back finally escaped, matching the amusement that made his eyes sparkle like sapphires.

Shane liked to pull pranks. That should make playing with him especially interesting. She was on to him now. Hiding what he was doing by thinking lustful thoughts wasn't going to work again. Who was she kidding? It probably would. She was so damn susceptible to his passion-filled emotions.

He pushed away from her, and Master Trey lowered the hoop to the ground. Shane held her in place until Master Trey arrived to steady her. After removing the upper rope from the hoop, Shane helped Trey rotate her upright and began the process of untying her legs so she could stand. By the time the ropes were removed and Shane had checked her over, the shakiness had passed. He commanded her to kneel and sit on the platform.

After a wave and thanks to the audience, Shane turned and stood with a hand on his hip, an eye on Master Trey securing the equipment they had used.

Most of the room had returned its attention to the smaller stages, which were once again in use. Several people, however, remained, waiting for an opportunity to approach Shane when he left the stage.

10

W hile Trey finished cleaning up from the suspension, Shane
drank one of the glasses of water set along the side of the
stage and then picked up another, bringing it to Adrianna.
His thoughts were going in a myriad of directions—different priorities
clamoring for his attention. The man in the audience had disappeared once
the demonstration was over. He'd been right at the bottom of the stairs to
the stage. He hadn't been a normal club goer. His clothes were neither
those of a tourist nor a kink aficionado. If he showed up in the private area,
Shane could ask Randolph who the man was.

The events onstage were echoing through Shane's mind. Each time he
looked back at the memory of Adrianna spinning or the last drop, he
marveled at her grace and beauty. His ass clenched at ideas of what he
could do with her in the *Adrasteia's* gym with the gravity off. She'd need to
be fully trained to handle the effects of null gravity. Fully trained... He
allowed a leer to linger on his lips for a moment.

Those thoughts moved to the side for later consideration; he concentrated on the next step in his plan for the evening. Time to set the hook and
reel Trey in. Trey couldn't have been a more fortuitous if unsuspecting
addition to tonight's activities. Shane regretted using Trey like this, but if

Trey had been told about Shane's plan, the Opio Instructor's sincerity of response might have been affected.

When Trey approached him, Shane handed him a glass of water. "Here."

Trey took it with a grunt.

Shane narrowed his eyes and stared at Trey. "I've always heard the Opio Institute's trained subs were the best money could buy. It surprised me she was less than I hoped for."

"Less?"

Shane sneered. "Yes, less. Do you teach all your submissives to lie to their Masters?"

Trey's voice deadened into calm control. "What the fuck are you talking about?"

"I know where Adrianna was born, and I know you told her to conceal that fact from me. If she hadn't been attacked on her way to meet me, she probably wouldn't have told me about the Benefactor either. Did you really think lying would keep her safe?"

Trey's face flushed red, his gaze fastening on Adrianna. "You told him?"

"Don't answer him, Adrianna."

Trey brought his glare back to Shane. "I advised her to offer her trust slowly."

"Fucking stupid advice."

Trey pointed a thick finger at Shane. "Listen, ass wipe. I don't need to take this shit from you."

The crowd milling about busily watching or engaging in a variety of fetish and kink activities began to take notice of the quarrel between the two Doms. Shane glared at those who gazed in their direction. More and more people turned to look at them, some pausing to stare, others glancing away.

Shane snarled at Trey. "Fuck you. It's my collar she's wearing, not yours. You can keep your fucking dicked-up advice to yourself." He glared at Adrianna still kneeling naked on the floor. "Get up, Pet. We're leaving." He threw the strap of the duffel over his shoulder.

When he turned, Randolph was striding toward them.

"Master Shane, how was your evening?" Randolph greeted him with a smile that quickly turned down, his brows knitting when he noted the tension between Shane and Trey.

Shane laughed, a bitter edge adding bite. "Couldn't have been better."

"I didn't see the finale, but I heard it was spectacular." Randolph looked at Adrianna. "Are you all right?"

Shane looked back at her, frowned, pulled her dress from the duffel, and threw it at her. "Put that on." To Randolph, he said, "She's perfectly fine." He eyed Randolph, who gave him the slightest of nods.

When Randolph was about to speak, Trey dropped on his haunches beside Adrianna. "You don't have to go with him. Come with me. You're still in the trial period of your contract. You can break it without penalty."

Adrianna jerked her head up to Shane, eyes wide and mouth dropped open.

Shane shoved Trey back from Adrianna, causing him to sprawl backward. Glaring down at him, Shane said, "Keep away from her. She's mine to protect. Spend your concern on the Opio staff. The Benefactor's got at least one stooge planted there. And you're too fucking blind to notice."

Trey rose to his feet and moved to get in Shane's face.

"Gentlemen," Randolph said. Four burly staff members surrounded the group and insinuated their way between Trey and Shane. "Let's take this to my office."

"No need." His mouth curled in a sneer, Shane grabbed Adrianna's leash and dragged her from the room, not bothering with his shirt or her shoes. Charging ahead, he thrust anyone in his path aside and ignored William when Shane passed him on his way out of the club. After scrambling aboard the first tram that came by, Shane pulled his shirt and Adrianna's heels from the duffel. He handed Adrianna the shoes and then slumped forward, burying his face in the shirt in his hands.

"Are you okay, Shane?" Adrianna rubbed his back and shoulder.

Shane straightened. "Am I okay? I should ask you that. Come here." He engulfed Adrianna in his arms, pulling her onto his lap, her head snuggled under his chin. "That was harder than you'll ever know. I don't like doing things I know will hurt you, Dria."

Adrianna raised her hand to his cheek and brushed her fingers back into his hair. "You didn't hurt me, Shane."

Shane's throat was thick when he spoke. "Be honest. I attacked your mentor."

She lifted her head and pulled him down for a kiss, brushing her lips against his. "I held on to what you said. It wasn't real."

Shane eased back and gazed deep into her eyes. "Thank you." Then he brought his mouth to hers and kissed her until the tenderness flamed into something more. When he broke away, he groaned. "I don't even know where this tram is headed."

Adrianna laughed, nudging him with her shoulder. "And here I thought you were super marshal getting us on a tram that's heading to the spaceport."

"Yeah?"

Adrianna nodded. "Yeah. Put your shirt on, or I may decide to have my wicked way with you. Even on Beta Tau I don't think sex in public is acceptable."

"I'd have to arrest myself. And you."

"Hmmph." Adrianna's smile faded.

"You're thinking about Master Trey," he said.

"Yes."

Shane held her, waiting to see if Adrianna would share her thoughts.

"He truly cares about me and has my best interests at heart. He's upset with me for telling you where I'm from. I have to explain to him."

Shane stroked Adrianna's hair. This was his fault. His plan. He'd make it right for her. Trey wouldn't make it easy. Not after everything Shane had said. "I'll make sure he understands. Besides, I think he'll approve once I explain what we're doing."

"Sometime you'll have to tell me what we're doing. You're the marshal, and you've got a plan, but I'll be honest that I haven't figured out where this is headed."

"As soon as we're on the *Adrasteia*, I'll explain everything." Adrianna nodded and snuggled into Shane to rest against him for the remainder of the ride to the spaceport. He'd have to find time to account for his actions to Randolph too. They were longtime friends, but even Randolph must be scratching his head, wondering if Shane had lost his mind.

11

Refreshed after a quick shower, Adrianna searched for Shane and found him in his office. When she entered the room, he glanced up.

"You look a lot better cleaned up. I've been talking to Marshal Riordan. Master Trey is a fast worker. He's filed a complaint against me with the Marshal Service."

Adrianna stiffened, her eyebrows knitting. "A complaint?"

"He wants the service to force me to end our contract."

"Oh."

"Riordan is sending it on to Tallav without explanation. He said he'd let me do that when I got there. I figure that will encourage more gossip, which is what I want. Our little dustup is already making the news on Beta Tau. Riordan's had to fend off one journalist."

Adrianna scowled at Shane. "I don't get why you're doing this."

Shane rose and drew her into his embrace. "Don't worry, Dria. It will all work out. Let's go to the main comm station. I'm going to call Master Trey now and explain things to him. You'll get a better understanding when I talk to him. Plus, he'll need to talk to you too."

Adrianna followed Shane through the corridors to admin. The bench in front of the comm equipment allowed two people to appear in the vid at the same time. She moved to sit next to Shane, but he waved her away. It took several minutes to get a secure connection through to Master Trey. The system located him at the Opio Institute. Adrianna recognized his private quarters when he came on-screen to answer the call.

Before Shane could speak, Trey launched a verbal attack against him. "What do you want? If you think I'm going to rescind my complaint against you, you are seriously mistaken."

"Not at all. I'm calling to explain things to you."

Trey bared his teeth and thrust a finger at Shane. "I don't need your explanations. It's clear to me who and what you are."

Adrianna winced but remained out of the comm's vid pickup range.

"Trey, Adrianna's here and wants to talk with you too. Please listen. Dria, join me on vid." Adrianna sat next to Shane with a sheepish smile and a brief wave to Trey.

Trey gave a curt nod but showed no signs of softening.

Adrianna felt the warmth of Shane's body through her shirt when he put his arm around her shoulders.

"First, I want to apologize to both of you for the way I acted tonight and the things I said. I have nothing but the highest regard for you, Trey. I can't find any fault in Adrianna's training or your advice to her. You were absolutely right to ask her to make her safety of primary importance."

Trey's anger didn't dissipate. He wordlessly continued to stare at Shane through the vidscreen.

Shane placed both hands on Adrianna's shoulders. "I need your help, Trey. The Benefactor is still pursuing Adrianna. We don't know his endgame, but it's my intention to stop him."

"Shit!" Trey, his jaw working, dropped his gaze to Adrianna for a moment before returning it to Shane. "He'll never let you close to him. Take her to Tallav. She'll be safer there."

Shane shook his head. "I can't do that. Not for very long. There's more."

Trey gave a quick, disgusted snort. "Of course there is."

Shane said, "It's a little convoluted..."

Trey huffed. "In what way?"

Shane's lips pinched together before he responded. "First, Adrianna should be safe as long as she's with me, and I'll be keeping her close."

"Should be?" Trey paused and drew in several slow, steady breaths. With a carefully controlled tone, he said, "That's not good enough."

"It has to be. Unless you want Adrianna to spend her life hiding from the Benefactor?"

Trey moved back. "No. I don't. But you'd better not be playing games with her life."

Shane kept his gaze steady on Trey. "No game. This is serious. Your part was vital tonight. You know Adrianna's history with the Benefactor of Furzine?" Shane grimaced. "We're pretty sure it has something to do with Preatiens and possibly illegal human trafficking. She was safe while she was inside the Institute. The day she left to come to me, he sent men to kidnap her." The corner of Shane's mouth lifted. "She foiled them rather handily."

With her cheeks flushing, Adrianna looked down at her hands.

"We're not sure how he intends to use her."

Adrianna caught herself scraping at a rough spot on the comm chair seat with her fingernail. The urge to continue scratching nagged at her. Instead, she folded her hands in her lap to focus on what Shane was saying. Although nothing he'd said so far was new. She still couldn't put anything sensible together from the jumble of facts he found important. Even if she didn't understand, Master Trey had to, or he might repeat his insistence that she leave Shane. Choosing between them would be heartrending. She struggled to quiet her interior monologue to listen to Shane.

"It's possible that his latest venture here on Beta Tau ties in to his plans for Adrianna. You've heard of the new sex training school, the Wellington? Opened in the last year here."

"I have. Not a lot. Secretive place. Graduates placed on Beta Tau seem well trained." The hardness had left Master Trey's voice, but it still held more than a note of wariness.

"Interesting," Shane said. "I didn't realize they were placing students on Beta Tau. Adds to their legitimacy." Shane's eyes unfocused. He nodded. "They're funded out of Furzine by the Benefactor. The young kids that are run through their program are shipped off to Runner's Hub and from there, who knows where. The Marshals Service believes they are being sold as slaves or forced to work in the Benefactor's brothels, including his private clubs. His workers are treated like a commodity. They tend to disappear. Killed by clients or by management when they're no longer of use. We believe the Benefactor is also trying to infiltrate Preatiens, a market and system he has never managed to break into, supplying the men there with nonempathic women."

Shane clasped Adrianna's hand. "Dria is Élise Sauveterre's grand-daughter. The Benefactor wants access to Preatiens, something Sauveterre has the power to promote or hinder. The Benefactor intends to use Adri-anna somehow to assure Sauveterre's stamp of approval. My plan is to create the perception he can manipulate me and, through me, Adrianna. That's where our act came in this evening. I wanted to send a clear message to the Benefactor that Adrianna is mine. Your reaction tonight and the complaint you lodged will assure that message gets broadcast by the gossip newsies. I apologize for putting you through that."

Trey's face went through a range of subtle expressions. "It looks to me like you're exploiting Adrianna. Did you plan this from the start? Is that why you sought Adrianna's contract?" The finger was once again jabbing at Shane from the comm screen. "Because if you let her get hurt, you lying son of a—"

"He's not taking advantage of me." Adrianna sat forward, interrupting with a rush of words. "He knew nothing about the Benefactor wanting me until after the kidnapping attempt. Even then, Shane wasn't aware it was the Benefactor. Shane and Marshal Riordan only put things together after the Benefactor tried to kill Shane. Please, Master Trey, this is what he hired me for. To be his assistant. It's what I want to do. I understand it's danger-ous, but I trust Shane." Adrianna gave Trey a beseeching look. "Please believe him."

"We've discussed this, Adrianna. Remember?" Trey's remonstrating stare leaped through the vidscreen, making Adrianna flinch.

"Yes, Sir. But my empathic senses have assured me Shane is trustworthy."

"Gods, Adrianna. Why did you tell him you're an empath?"

Adrianna had seen Master Trey this angry only once before when a student had pretended not to hear another student's safe word during a caning session.

"I didn't tell him. He figured it out when he learned who my grandmother was. I didn't realize she was such an important woman on Preatiens, or I wouldn't have given him her name." Adrianna flinched again, this time at the flash of anger coming from Shane. With a slump, Adrianna dropped her gaze. She didn't really know what else to say.

Shane straightened his shoulders and chest, expanding into a solid wall of strength. "Trey, I will not let the Benefactor abduct Adrianna. She won't get hurt. You have my word on that."

Trey's lips pursed, but he didn't hesitate more than a second before responding. "I guess I'll have to accept that." Then, with a posture that mimicked Shane's, Trey said, "But I warn you, if anything happens to Adrianna, you and I are going to have more than words."

"Understood," Shane said. "I have one further request. If you hear anything of interest about the Wellington or slaving, please go to the Wild Rover Pub and tell the owner, Patrick O'Toole. He'll contact the Marshals Service. Don't do anything overt. Definitely don't ask questions. These people are playing for keeps and have already murdered one person, maybe more."

"I can do that. You'll let me know how things work out?"

Shane held up his hands, palm facing the vidscreen. "Absolutely. When we resolve this and the Benefactor is no longer a threat to Adrianna, I will contact you. I'm sorry for putting you in an uncomfortable position. You've helped a lot of innocent kids and Adrianna as well."

"A little more than uncomfortable, but I grasp why you did it. I'm not happy about it." Trey's eyes narrowed to razor-sharp slits. "Keep Adrianna safe. She's—she's special."

Shane glanced at Adrianna. "She is that." He returned his focus to the vidscreen. "One of us will call when we're free to do so. Until then."

"Just a minute. You said the Benefactor had someone on staff at the Opio? Who?"

Shane grimaced. "Thanks for reminding me. When Adrianna was accosted at the spaceport, her mother's locket was stolen. It was returned to her by Frau Heinrich. She had to have gotten it from the Benefactor's thugs, even though she claimed different."

Trey grunted.

"That doesn't surprise you." Shane's words were a statement rather than a question.

"No. I've been trying for years to get her removed from the Opio faculty."

"Best of luck."

"Yeah."

"We'll be in touch."

"Right."

Shane closed the connection, turned, and embraced Adrianna, snuggling her head under his chin. "Do you understand what happened tonight?"

Adrianna's hand brushed Shane's chest in a back-and-forth pattern. "I think I do. The Benefactor won't stop. He always gets what he wants."

"Hmmm. Not this time. I won't let him take you. He may try to take you again. But he'll fail. If we could tie a kidnapping attempt directly to him, his diplomatic immunity wouldn't save him."

It was almost too much to hope that the Benefactor would end up in jail. That would be the perfect ending to her dealings with him. When she squeezed Shane, he placed a kiss on top of her head.

"We're heading to Tallav. This operation requires resources above my authority to approve, so I need to brief my superiors. They'll decide what direction we take."

"Mmm." Adrianna remained in his embrace, not yet ready to leave the warmth of his arms.

Shane kissed the top of her head again and said, "Time to head out. I'm going to get started with getting our clearance to undock and leave. Do a run-through of the ship to ensure everything is secured. I'm especially concerned with the deliveries that were made while we weren't here. Don't unpack anything; just get it all strapped down."

"Sure. And thanks for explaining to Master Trey. I feel better now."

"Hmmm. Okay, let's get going." Shane released Adrianna and scooted her off the bench. "When you're done, meet me on the bridge."

～

As SHANE CLIMBED the ladder to the bridge, he mulled over the events of the past days. Adrianna seemed to handle the turmoil they'd been through without difficulty. She adapted to change, which was good. So far, the plan he was executing was proceeding well. Once they arrived at Tallav, they'd have a lot to do. Before then, he intended to use the travel time to improve Adrianna's self-defense skills and familiarize her with the weapon he planned to give her. That and the talk they needed to have. It was necessary, but not something he looked forward to. He had to tell her about Ceana. His next rendezvous with that god-awful woman approached him as inexorably as death. Yeah, revealing his relationship with Ceana would be a fun chat.

For thirty minutes, he focused on setting up and obtaining clearance for a hyperpulse route to Tallav. Just before he began undocking procedures, Adrianna popped her head into the bridge.

"Sit in that seat." He waved her over to the flight chair on his left, reached across, and flicked on the workstation. "You'll be able to watch things from here. Don't touch anything on the panel."

"Yes, Sir."

Shane turned to Adrianna. "We'll be releasing from dock in about ten minutes. Right now, I'm running the checklist. Once we're undocked, a station controller will take over guiding us into the queue and out to the hyperpulse point. It will take about eighteen hours to get there. The trip to Tallav is about two days. Time varies in hyperspace, depending on the hyperstrand we connect with." He grinned at her. "I'm sure you're already aware of that. You'll notice one big difference from your previous flights. The effects from the Stanislaus field seem stronger in a small craft. I'm not up on the physics. It will feel like you are pulling G's in a surface aircraft. We'll be strapped in for that. Once we arrive in the Tallavan system, it's about another twenty-four hours to arrive at the Tallavan space station."

"Sounds good."

The sense of lightness from when he and Adrianna had spent the day on Beta Tau returned while he watched her. Her eyes were shining with alert anticipation. So much was new to her. He hadn't been able to sit still his first time on the bridge of a ship heading into hyperspace. He had lost that excitement during the many trips he had made since. Adrianna allowed him to taste that sensation again.

"Once we're in the queue, we can head to bed."

Adrianna returned his smile, the shine still sparkling in her eyes. "That will be good. It's been a long day."

"That it has," Shane responded.

The handoff to the Beta Tau controller was seamless. Shane sat back with a sigh, ready for rest. If problems cropped up, he'd be notified. He transferred bridge control to the auxiliary system in his cabin. He turned, offered a hand to Adrianna, and said, "Let's go to bed. Sleep with me tonight, Dria."

Adrianna placed her fingers in his palm and let him pull her out of her seat. His gaze heated while he watched her climb down the ladder. She waited at the foot for him to lead the way. When they entered his bedroom, he pointed to the wall of cupboards and drawers. "Use the bottom left drawer to store your things. From now on, everything must be stowed when not in use."

"Yes, Sir."

Shane dropped his clothes into the laundry bin and climbed into the oversize bed, his muscles crying with relief when he sank into the mattress and the cool sheet slid across his exposed skin. After Adrianna joined him, he reached toward the panel in the headboard and pressed a button. "I turned on the safety field. While we're moving, always use it when you're in bed."

"Yes, Sir."

"Come here." Shane pulled Adrianna to him and pushed the hair from her face, entwining his fingers in it. He paused to gaze deeply into her eyes. "You amaze me, Dria. At first, I thought of you as young and inexperienced, but you grew up on Furzine. That alone must have been an education. You've been through so much, but you haven't become cynical. You're so fresh and unsullied. So...amazing."

"You're pretty awesome yourself. Tonight, I felt like a kite, soaring and floating." She punched a finger into his chest. "But what's with that sudden drop? I could have messed my pants. No. Wait. I wasn't wearing any pants."

Shane chuckled. "I didn't think I could fool you. I was sure you knew something was coming."

She pouted. "I didn't."

Shane thumbed her lips. "Such a sweet little pout." He let his finger slip into her mouth. His cock, already hard, grew harder still when she began to suck, her eyes locked onto his. He didn't need to be empathic to apprehend that his amazing Dria was filled with passion. It struck him— he'd just thought of her as his Dria. That was true. For the next year. Dria was his as much as Adrianna. A package deal. A captivating package.

He rolled her to her back, covering her with his body and capturing her lips with a tender caress. "So amazing." When he deepened the kiss, Adrianna's thighs opened wider, and he plunged his cock into her pussy, her warmth enveloping him.

If sinking into the mattress had been a relief, plunging into Adrianna was more so. Regret for the way he'd yelled at her at the automat had pummeled him ever since. That she could be a willing, active participant in tonight's melodrama after such a brief acquaintance was a testament to her strength. And to her trust in him. He ached for her, but not with raw craving. The ache was in his chest, not his groin. With the gentleness she deserved, he moved in slow, even thrusts so the pleasure increased gradually and inexorably. With a shuddering cry, he came. Adrianna clutched him, her fingers anchored in his back muscles, sighing her own release. For languorous moments, he lay still, finding respite in the softness of wrapped legs and cushioning breasts. He brushed his lips over her smooth forehead, eyelids, and flushed cheeks. "You are so sweet, Dria. A mhuirnín."

Adrianna responded with her own murmurs of appreciation, her hands lightly stroking his sides down to his hips. With her clasped against him, he rolled so her head rested on his arm, her body nestled in tight against him, and her thigh over his hip. Satisfaction and something deeper, an emotion he didn't care to analyze, radiated through his body, soothing him while he drifted off to sleep.

～

After assuring herself that the housekeeping programming was functioning properly, Adrianna was sorting through Shane's dirty clothes, separating out items that would need more than the normal fresher cycle.

She'd been replaying Shane's lovemaking the night before. He'd called her Dria. Not Adrianna.

His voice came through her subvocal receiver. "Would you join me in the lounge, Dria?"

"Yes. Give me a minute."

With a flick of her hand, she opened the latch on the machine. After adding the clothes needing normal freshening, she shut the door and started the cycle. The remaining laundry she stuffed into a storage bin. She dusted her hands off and went to find Shane.

Shane sat at one end of the dark brown sofa, his arm draped along the back, fingers drumming. He was ready for the talk. Adrianna inhaled deeply through her nose and then exhaled through her mouth. So much had happened since she'd accused him of running hot, then cold with her. Most of the anger had bled away. The need to understand was still strong, but she didn't want to push him. Didn't really believe she could. Successfully at least. What Patrick O'Toole had told her about Tallav, the Marshals Service, and Shane helped her adjust her perceptions. Shane was caught between family pressures and his own dreams.

"Sit, please." Shane gestured with the hand on top of the sofa.

Adrianna settled into the other end of the sofa, one leg bent at the knee so she could face him. With her empathic senses wide open to him, his anxious determination was plain, as well as the thread of appreciation she'd come to expect whenever he first caught sight of her. Fingers laced, she placed her hands in her lap and waited for him to speak.

Shane cleared his throat before he said, "Yesterday, we both found reason to be frustrated and mad at each other. My own anger was out of line, and I apologize again for frightening you."

Adrianna reached a hand out and rubbed his knee. "You didn't scare me the way you think you did."

His eyes narrowed. Words didn't make it past his open mouth.

"All you really did was glower, pace, clench your fists, and raise your voice. Minus the pacing, that's pretty much what I did over the muffins. I'm just not as big as you. Or as intimidating. You're not used to the fact that I can sense your emotions. There is a difference between controlled anger and violent rage. Feeling furious doesn't mean you are out of control. My mother told me feelings by their nature are often instantaneous. It's not what you feel that condemns you, but how you act upon those feelings."

"That's...good to know."

"I wasn't worried about you physically hurting me. I was afraid you were going to void our contract." Adrianna pressed her lips together, clasped her hands in her lap, and lowered her gaze. "Then we need to get one thing straight. I will never precipitously end your contract. If I've given you the impression I would, I apologize."

Adrianna peeked at him from under her lashes.

"I guess it's this ambivalence I have about you," he said.

She dropped her eyes and rubbed her thumbs against each other.

"Fuck, that came out wrong." He clenched the hand on the top of the sofa. "I'm not ambivalent about you. I like you very much. More than I ever expected. I'd been telling myself to make things less personal with you because I'm afraid the more intimate our relationship gets, the more likely you are to get hurt when your contract ends."

Adrianna flicked her gaze at him for a moment, lifting a questioning eyebrow.

"Gods, you won't even let me lie to myself." Shane raised his hands and said, "Okay. That's only part of the truth. I can see myself becoming very attached to you." He dragged a hand across his face, then stared across the lounge.

"I didn't put a lot of thought into why I hired you. Maon suggested it, and I went along with it." Shane sighed.

"Who's Maon?"

"Hmpf. Maon's my best friend. We met at boarding school and went to the Marshals Academy together. Spent time stationed on Beta Tau. He and Randolph at the Whip Hand are the two people who always have my back. You'll meet him when we get to Tallav."

Shane's fingers traced a line along the sofa. The left side of his mouth curled up. "I did spend a great deal of consideration into *who* I wanted."

Adrianna's body softened, both at the words and the feelings he sent her way to accompany them.

"Maybe I'm thickheaded. I knew that there'd be three parts to our relationship. The Master-submissive part and the assistant part, I had all figured out."

His fingers drummed on the top of the sofa. Adrianna wanted to reach out and hold his hand but didn't want to make it harder for him.

"I have few friends. Lots of acquaintances and colleagues, but few close friends. I unconsciously put the third part of our relationship in the acquaintance category, but I've realized that isn't ever going to be a reality. We're together too much for that to be true. I told myself I could pull us back from the direction we were heading if I acted as impersonally as possible to you outside the bedroom." He winced and grunted. "That turned out well."

All of Adrianna's residual anger melted away at the remorse she sensed accompanying his words. She'd known intellectually that Doms were as likely as submissives to have issues when a relationship developed. Now she had firsthand experience of that truth. She scooted along the sofa to sit next to him and patted his thigh. "I forgive you for all your past beastly behavior, if you'll forgive me for…" Face upturned, she batted her eyes at him. "Well, you don't really have anything to forgive me for. Do you?"

A grin split Shane's face. He wrapped his arms around her and let his fingers fly, searching for ticklish spots. When Adrianna collapsed in a pile of panting laughter, he pulled her on his lap and kissed her until her laughing lips responded to his.

ADRIANNA GRINNED, her thoughts bouncing in a mental happy dance. After two days of practice in *Adrasteia's* gym, she'd finally dumped Shane on his ass. Her hand-to-hand training was going well, but she'd never best Shane. He was bigger and stronger than she was. She'd made up that difference by outsmarting him with a trick she didn't expect to get away with more than once. With him, anyway. No, vamping him wouldn't work again. She was surprised it had worked in the first place, but it had proven that Marshal Shane Tiernan was male and susceptible to certain male foibles. Foibles she'd enjoyed during the days they'd spent traveling to Tallav. Every time he said *Adrianna* in that hungry, deep voice, arousal wound a heated path from her nipples to her clit.

She'd finished her housekeeping duties for the day and had already secured the lower and main deck for transition from hyperspace. There was still time to grab her tablet and settle herself into her bridge seat to study while Shane prepared for their transition back to normal space.

When she reached the top of the ladder, he glanced up. "Hey. Glad you're here. Buckle in. The ship's computer will automatically activate your safety field when we exit hyperspace." Secured in her flight chair, she looked up at the main screen. "When we transition and the Stanislaus field engages to slow the ship, you'll sense it more than you did when you arrived at Beta Tau. The large space liner you were on was designed for maximum comfort for the passengers. The *Adrasteia* doesn't have the extensive buffers. I'll turn on your station again, so you can watch the readouts while we go through transition."

"Why is the main screen off?" She'd enjoyed the light show that hyperspace provided.

"Most people find viewing the transition from hyperspace to normal space disconcerting. The human brain doesn't deal well with the overload of visual change and interprets it in confusing, often disturbing, ways. Most feel like they're about to slam into something. Others get intense vertigo. It's better to leave it off."

"I guess so." Adrianna turned on her tablet and switched to the section of the Federation Codex pertaining to human trafficking. She wanted to be familiar with it. Immersed in her reading, she was abruptly brought back to the bridge when the computer sounded the five-minute alarm before transition. After she stowed her tablet, the slight change in air pressure when the safety field was engaged made her ears plug. She looked over at Shane to find him smiling at her.

"Ready?" he asked.

"Yep," she responded. She watched the readouts in front of her. The speed they were now traveling was multiple times faster than when they first entered hyperspace. If the Stanislaus field failed, they wouldn't be able to stop before flying into the Tallavan sun. All hyperstrands ended with a star as the ultimate terminus so that failures affected only the ship coming out of hyperspace.

This is taking for—The G-forces climbed, crushing her back in her seat. Immobilized by the force, she was glad the chair was padded. The intensity faded, as did the uncomfortable sensation of added weight. The computer pinged, and the safety field disengaged.

Shane immersed himself in determining their specific location and contacting the controllers at the Tallavan space station. Adrianna listened to the back and forth while they were advised of the course heading and trajectory that would link them up with the incoming queue. An hour later, a station controller took over guidance of the ship. In a little less than twenty-four hours, they would be docking. Tallav, Shane's home planet, awaited.

12

Adrianna settled into a comfortable chair, canvassing the director's reception area with its sleek, utilitarian furnishings, waiting while Shane met with the head of the Marshals. He was eager to explain his actions and to get the okay to proceed with his plans. She and Shane had come straight from the spaceport after taking a shuttle down world from the station. The receptionist, a well-built, sandy-haired young man had been eyeing her, looking away whenever she glanced in his direction. News of the scene between Master Trey and Shane on Beta Tau had spread. What portion of "the story" circulating on Tallav was true? How many embellishments had been added? Time to do a little investigating of her own.

When she approached the desk, she allowed a tentative smile to form on her lips, widening her eyes just enough and dropping her chin so she looked sweet and guileless. "Is he in trouble? People keep staring at us."

The receptionist hesitated before answering her. "Well…he could be. It depends. If the rumors are true…?"

"Oh!" Adrianna raised her eyebrows, her response breathy. "Rumors?"

"Well, I really shouldn't be talking about this." He glanced down the hallway leading to the executive offices. "It's all gossip at this point, but you, being part of it all, would know what's true or not."

Her voice grew plaintive. "Yes, I would. I don't want people lying about me. My name is Adrianna, by the way." She stuck her hand out toward him. "Glad to meet you…"

"Derek. It's Derek. Pleased to meet you too." He took her hand, dropping his gaze to her chest where Adrianna had opened one button more than propriety required. With a quick squeeze of his fingers and a saccharine smile, she drew his attention from her breasts. When he realized he hadn't released her hand, he quickly let loose.

"Do they say bad things about me?" Adrianna asked.

"No, no. Not at all. The way I heard it, Marshal Tiernan hired you to be his assistant and has been using you as his"—he lowered his voice—"as his sexual slave." He waved as though to negate his words. "I'm sure now you're here on Tallav, you'll get the help you need to break your contract and leave him."

Adrianna blinked with a rapid flutter of eyelashes, trying hard not to laugh at the young man whose cheeks had tinged red when he'd said *"sexual slave."* "But my contract includes serving as his sexual submissive. It's what I'm trained to do." She ladled on so much puzzled innocence that Derek stalled into a frozen stare.

With breezy insouciance, Adrianna explained her life as a submissive. Before she finished, Derek had blanched. She smiled and brushed her fingers over her hair.

Derek scowled, shifted in his chair, and asked, "You don't want to leave him?"

"Oh no. He's really not that bad. I could do worse. I'm not just a submissive by training." She leaned in and said in a stage whisper, "I really do like being dominated by a strong, handsome man."

Derek swallowed hard. His pupils dilated.

"What else are they saying?" she asked.

He again looked down the hallway. After clearing his throat, he said, "Well, I think you should know, and I'm telling you this only to help you. I've heard that Marshal Tiernan hates all women. That he insists on committing unnatural acts with the woman he's contracted to bear his child."

Adrianna's eyes widened and her breath caught. A child?

"That she can barely stand him but puts up with it because she needs the money that having his baby would bring her."

Derek nodded and gave Adrianna a look of admonition, implying his words ought to change her mind about remaining with Shane. "Even though he's one of the top marshals in the Service and has won all kinds of awards and medals, they are probably going to fire him. He'll have to go back to his mother's estate in disgrace or leave Tallav for good. I've heard other things, but none of that is believable."

"Goodness." Her investigating had turned up more than she'd expected, but in this moment she needed to focus on ending the conversation without breaking her froth-for-brains submissive pretense. "It was just a couple of Doms squaring off." She waved a hand. "Happens more often than you might think."

"That's just the *thark* that broke the hyperstrand. The other things…"

Adrianna crossed her arms over her chest, pushing her breasts up, and pouted at Derek. "I don't think he hates all women. He only punishes me when I've been bad. He's never done anything unnatural with me. I'm almost afraid to ask what an unnatural act is on Tallav." She waved her hand at him. "No, don't tell me. I don't want to know."

Derek looked close to swallowing his tongue when Adrianna reached into her shirt and adjusted each of her breasts in her bra. "That's better."

She continued chatting, since he seemed incapable of speech. "I sure hope they don't fire him. I'd have to start the contracting process all over again, and I was just getting to know Marshal Tiernan." She gave a long, dejected sigh. "Well, I better go sit. If he catches me talking to you, there'll be hell to pay." She winked at him and turned to resume her seat.

Once she pulled her tablet from her purse, she attempted to read the engineering manual Shane had assigned her. She lost track of the words she was reading. It was no use. The proper parameters for the *faeron* regulator were beyond her.

Why hadn't Shane told her about a woman contracted to bear him a child? What did that mean? Who was she, and why was she spreading rumors about Shane? Whoever she was, she didn't recognize a good man when she saw him.

Well, that was too bad, because Shane was now taken. No one else would be in his bed if Adrianna had anything to say about it. Images flashed through her mind of holding down this nameless, faceless woman with a knee in the middle of her back, hands lashed into her hair, lifting and slamming the woman's face into the ground.

Damn. Violent much? She wouldn't really act out on the desires despite how viscerally appealing hurting the woman felt. Would she? No matter. It was the rumors that were important. Unnatural acts indeed! She didn't know what the woman's problem was, but she'd better not be messing with Shane. Something had to be done. What that would be, Adrianna wasn't sure, but she'd figure it out.

Down the hall past the receptionist's desk, a door opened. The sound of angry voices reverberated into the reception area. Shane strode out, glaring at Derek when he passed. "Let's go, Pet." The guilty glance Derek had flashed at Shane and then at Adrianna must have registered with Shane, because he turned to face Derek. "You haven't been breaking the rules again? Have you, Pet?"

Derek flushed.

Adrianna rose and took a submissive stance. "No, Sir. I do not speak to someone unless you give me permission."

"That's right. You don't. Let's go." Shane took her by the upper arm and pushed her toward the lift. He continued to glare at Derek until the doors closed.

"Were you messing with that young man?"

Adrianna smirked. "Yes. I was."

"And?"

"He filled me in on the rumors about you. Thought you might get fired."

"I didn't."

"Didn't think so."

They didn't speak again until Shane had retrieved his car from the auto park.

"Wow. You have your own car!"

"Yes, Tallav isn't suited to public transportation. Most of the population lives on the estates and rarely travels between them. Cahernamon is the only large city."

Adrianna climbed into the passenger side of the vehicle. After he engaged the car's interior safety field, he drove away. "We're heading to Ettington, the estate of Selina Shirley. It's accessible by road," he said.

"Isn't that Selina the fashion designer?"

"Yes. Her family has always been involved in textiles. They raise sheep, although wool production is really more a hobby. Most of their income is derived off planet. Selina married my best friend, Maon. He lives on the estate, raising their three children. I've been officially suspended for a week, so we'll be staying with them. I'll continue to work from there. Maon's a data dink, so he's completely wired and then some.

"We might talk him into taking us on a ride over the estate. They have horses." He grinned at Adrianna and reached over to give her braid a tug. "Can you contain yourself?"

She enjoyed Shane's playfulness. "I'll try, but it's going to be hard. Will Selena be home?"

"I'm not sure. She does travel quite a bit. Maon didn't say when I talked to him." Shane began humming. Even off-key, the sound was a welcome addition to the contentment that flowed from him along her empathic senses. He obviously enjoyed being with her, and whatever his connection with this other woman, Adrianna had no right to expect more than that. She would have to wrap up the jealousy and anger she felt and bury it. If and when he told her, that bundle would probably explode brighter and sharper than if she questioned him now. But if there was more to the relationship, surely he wouldn't have mentioned being close to only two people. If that were true—and at the time, it had registered as true—then he wasn't emotionally involved with this woman, the baby pod. Yes. She would think of her as the baby pod.

The drive took two hours, during which Shane answered Adrianna's questions about Tallav and the countryside they were driving through. She was enamored of the rolling hills covered in woods that gave way to meadows with livestock and fields with a variety of crops. Along the road, wildflowers bloomed in a riot of vivid colors. The sky overhead was a soft blue with white, puffy clouds. She'd read books that spoke of idyllic settings, but she'd never seen one until she arrived at Tallav. If she were Shane, she wouldn't want to live off world. The Tallav she was experiencing was preserved by strict immigration rules that denied almost all off worlders residency. It was a place she could visit but never stay. She realized the charming life she'd created in her head, all rosy perfection of a home, kids, and Shane to love and care for her into old age, was nothing but a pipe dream. For her dreams to come true, he had to give up Tallav, which wasn't fair. Besides, she couldn't ask that of him. He evidently had other ideas about children too.

Staying as his assistant wouldn't be easy. Her loan had to be paid in full by the end of four years. She didn't have the money and wasn't sure Shane did either. Maybe Master Trey could help her get an extension. She released a pensive sigh, telling herself to live for now and let the future take care of itself. The difficulty with that wasn't in the deciding to do so but in making that decision a reality.

"What's the big sigh for?" Shane's gaze moved between her and the road.

"Oh, nothing really. I was wondering what it was like to grow up on Tallav. It must have been marvelous."

"It was. I spent as much time as I could outdoors. My brother and I spent one summer building a fort in the trees. We each had our own tree-house turret. The main tree house and our smaller tree houses connected by swinging ropes, so we could go from one to the other without ever descending to the ground. Once the rope ladders were up, we thought we were impregnable. It's still there. My mom wanted to tear it down, but my dad said we could keep it."

A pleasant image of Shane as a boy, climbing and swinging through the trees, filled her mind. "I didn't know you had a brother."

Shane rubbed his hand over his mouth. "He was my older brother, Thomas. He died almost four years ago. He was a marshal too. Have you heard of the Ilsandrian Riots?"

Adrianna nodded.

"Thomas was assigned to Ilsandria. The government was overwhelmed by an attack on the banking system. All credit was frozen, and the paper voucher system they tried as a temporary workaround exploded in their faces when counterfeiters took advantage of it. Thomas was delegated to design the reboot. A protest march turned violent. He was helping pull families with children through a window to safety. Rioters grabbed him, pulled him out, and beat him to death."

"I'm so sorry." She reached over and stroked his arm, wishing now she had said nothing about his brother.

"Yeah. I miss him." Shane gave her a lopsided grin and dropped his hand onto Adrianna's thigh, giving it a quick rub. "But we're here to enjoy ourselves."

"And work. Don't forget the work." Adrianna gratefully pushed the conversation away from the painful memory.

"And work. That's why we're going to Ettington. Maon will be running intel for us. He's the best at gathering and analyzing it. You'll be impressed. Plus, he's a lot of fun. He makes everyone around him feel at ease."

"I can't wait. Is he a marshal too?"

"Officially, no. He works for the Marshals. Eight years ago, Audrina Shirley, Selina's mother and the Director of the Marshals Service at the time, made a contractual arrangement. It allows Maon to work as a data analyst for the Marshals without being on their payroll. The Marshals pay the House of Shirley to provide them a data analyst—Maon."

"Oh. Does that kind of thing happen often?"

"No, not with the Marshals. But Maon's situation is a little unique. His wife wanted him to work part-time, but not in the family business. If male aristocrats get a job, it's almost always with their own families. The female heads of conservative matriarchist families don't allow even that possibility. They keep their menfolk home on their estates."

"It seems so archaic." Adrianna wrinkled her nose and shook her head back and forth in tiny movements. She could say more but didn't want to be impolite.

"Archaic, reactionary, idiotic…I could go on, but I won't spoil our trip. Besides, we're almost there." Shane slowed and turned down a narrow road. "The estate is a mile along this road."

WHEN SHANE CLIMBED from the car, he let his eyes roam over the expanse of the main house at Ettington. It was a low, single-story stone building that rambled with no recognizable logic for the placement of extensions off the central structure or the location of windows. The rationale for the architecture was an interior one. Every part of the house was built to bring the best of Ettington inside through sweeping vistas and intimate nooks. Shane sighed. It wasn't home, but it was as close as he'd get. Not that he wanted to be seduced into the life of a househusband trapped in an idyllic prison.

He helped Adrianna out of the car. "We'll bring our stuff in later. I want you to meet Maon and his family first." He held her hand while they climbed the spacious stairs leading up to an open, granite-paved court-yard. A raised central pond offered seating around its edge for watching the multicolor fish swimming in its blue-green water. Enormous pots of flowers and sun-soaked wooden benches were scattered throughout the courtyard. Childish screams and giggles moved in their direction. Three children came dashing in from the far side, laughing and crying out.

"Uncle Shane! Save us!" The oldest, a brown-haired boy of seven years, bawled, running straight for Shane. His younger sister squealed nonstop while she pumped her legs as fast as she could, pigtails flying. A toddler trailed them on chubby legs, his T-shirt and shorts covered in dirt. He waved grubby fists while he hollered over and over, "Shay, Shay."

As the older pair reached Shane, he scooped each up in an arm. "Devon! Annie! What am I saving you from?"

"Uncle Shane, Daddy's going to eat us!" Devon thumped a hand on Shane's chest. Annie shrieked and covered her face. The toddler arrived, clamped himself onto Shane's leg, and held on for dear life.

Shane laughed, but before he could respond, Maon came clomping toward them from the same direction the children had come. His eyes rolled. His arms flailed. He paused to growl and produce an enormous belch. "Must eat children!" he roared, stomping his way ever closer.

With Devon and Annie shifted under each of his arms, their heads aimed forward, Shane stomped toward Maon, toddler still clamped to one leg. "Once more into the fray! I shall use my trusty battering rams to bring down this menace."

As he got to Maon, he rammed first one giggling child and then the other forward, pretending to strike. Maon feigned as if he had been sorely wounded, clutching his stomach and falling to the ground.

"Get him, Petey."

At Shane's shouted command, Petey detached himself from Shane's leg and fell on his father. Shane let the other children drop so they could run squealing to jump on top of Maon. Maon pretended to die, ignoring the tickling and poking until Petey placed his hand on his father's cheek. "Daddy okay?"

Maon opened his navy-blue eyes. "Daddy okay, buddy. Hey, Uncle Shane is here." With a struggle, he got to his feet to grasp Shane in a bear hug. "How are you, old man?"

"Better now I'm here. The wild animals are getting bigger."

Devon and Annie had claimed Shane's hands. Petey had reached up until Maon lifted him into his arms.

"That they are. And dirtier too." Maon patted Petey on the stomach.

Adrianna had held back to watch the two men playing with the children. Maon glanced in her direction. "Shane, are you going to prove you're an ill-mannered lout, or are you going to introduce me to the angel who seems to be following you?"

Shane grinned and turned, pulling Devon and Annie around with him. "The angel is Ms. Adrianna Pacquin, my new assistant. Dria, this is Maon Shirley and his pack of wild animals, Devon, Annie, and the littlest cub, Petey."

Maon extended a hand toward her. "I'm delighted to meet you. Shane has needed someone to keep him in line for a long time. I'd be happy to share everything I know about him to help you corral him."

Adrianna gave him a warm smile and shook his hand. "Thank you, I'd love to hear stories about Shane. I'm glad to meet you." She stroked Petey's arm with her finger. "You too, Petey." Dropping to one knee, she offered a hand to Devon and then Annie, who each, now bashful, said hello and hesitantly shook it.

Maon gestured them toward the main doors, bellowing when he entered. "Maureen, our guests are here. Tell Raymond to get their bags. Come on in, you two. I'll show you to your bedrooms so you can get settled. Shane, you're in your usual room. Adrianna will be in the connecting one."

"Dria, why don't you go on ahead? I'm going to talk to Maon first," Shane said.

"Sure. Call me when you need me."

A plump woman in floral blouse and skirt arrived and, having overheard Shane, suggested she take Adrianna to her room. Before she escorted

Adrianna, the woman told the children there were cookies waiting in the kitchen.

When they were gone, Shane turned to Maon, who was bouncing on his toes, curiosity leaking from his pores. "What's she like?" Maon asked. "She seems nice."

"She is nice. She's perfect actually." Shane stared somberly at the hall down which Adrianna had gone.

With a gloating grin, Maon said, "Didn't I tell you it was a good idea?"

Shane grunted. "Repeatedly."

Maon dropped into a broad leather armchair and pointed. "Sit. I want details."

Shane sprawled across a matching sofa, pulling the decorative lamb's wool pillow from behind his back. "Details. Hmmm. Well, she might be able to take you in a fight."

He smirked at Maon and threw the pillow at him. "I am not giving you details."

Maon snatched the pillow out of the air. "After all I did to bring you two together?" He aimed the pillow at Shane's head.

Shane ducked, and the pillow sailed over the back of the sofa. He laughed. "Yeah."

Maon's expression became pensive. "It looks like you've stirred up the fire crickets. Again. Nearly murdered. Fighting in public."

Shane rubbed his neck. "Yeah. Let's talk fire crickets."

ADRIANNA SAT ON THE BED, looking at but not really seeing the painting of a bucolic scene of an apple harvest that hung on the wall. So many revelations today. Shane's plans to become a father. The loss of his brother. The way he played with Maon's children. The way they adored him. How many layers were there to this man? She shook her head. She really ought to get to her unpacking. This break from seeing new sights and meeting new people was a relief. A tiny knock sounded, and a small head peeked in the door.

"Hi, may I come in?" Annie's light brown eyes were overflowing with entreaty.

"Sure." Adrianna sent her a welcoming smile and gestured for the little girl to enter.

Annie plopped on the bed next to her. "You're very pretty."

"Why, thank you."

Annie tilted her head to the side and asked, "Are you going to marry Uncle Shane?"

Adrianna gave a small laugh. "No, I'm not going to marry Uncle Shane."

"Why not?" Annie awaited an answer with bright eyes.

"He's my boss."

Annie's eyes narrowed. "He's your boss? You don't look like a servant."

"No, I'm not a servant." It amused Adrianna to see the child wrestling to place Adrianna in her paradigm.

"But only servants work for men." Annie gave Adrianna a look that said *I might be little, but even I know that.*

Adrianna suppressed a laugh. "I'm not from Tallav. I come from Preatiens."

"Oh, you're an off worlder. Don't you want to be a boss?" Annie reached out to finger Adrianna's braid.

"No, I like working for your Uncle Shane."

"My mom says that Uncle Shane will never get married if he doesn't give up wanting to be the boss. Men are not s'posed to be the boss of women." Annie intoned this truth with a solemn voice.

"Where I'm from, the men are the bosses of women."

Annie dropped the braid, wrinkled her forehead, and shook her head, her sympathy overflowing Adrianna's empathic senses. "You and Uncle Shane sure have problems." She brightened. "But if you married each other, you'd both get what you want. That would be nice. I'm going to marry someone just like my dad."

"Well, we can't all have what we want, but I hope you do marry someone exactly like him. He seems really terrific."

Annie grasped Adrianna's braid and began painting her other hand with the end. "Oh, he is. He lets us have cake for breakfast sometimes even though Mommy says he shouldn't." She lowered her voice, sharing a private detail. "He doesn't always listen to her like he's s'posed to, but she lets him misbehave 'cause he makes her laugh. Least that's what she says."

Adrianna appreciated the direct, honest statement of the facts of life as Annie knew them.

Annie dropped the braid again and covered her mouth. "Oh, I almost forgot. You're s'posed to go meet Uncle Shane and Daddy in the library. Want me to take you there?"

"Sure. Let me grab my tablet." Adrianna held out her other hand and accepted Annie's return clasp. They wound their way through the halls to the library, Adrianna enjoying the soft skin and firm hold of the small hand in hers. When they entered the room, Shane looked up, breaking off what he was saying to Maon.

"Hi."

"Hi."

Annie pulled on Adrianna's arm and stood on tiptoe to whisper. "See, I think he really likes you."

Adrianna blushed when Annie's whisper carried to both men.

Maon's eyes twinkled. "Of course he likes her. Who'd hire an assistant they didn't like."

13

***

S hane gruffly turned all business, but Adrianna's empathic senses left her little doubt he was flustered.

"Dria, Maon's prepared a profile of the Benefactor. I wanted to go over it with you and have you add any insights of your own. You've spent time with him, so you might know something useful."

"Annie, go see what your brothers are up to," Maon said. A stern look aborted the plea Annie seemed on the verge of making.

With slumped shoulders, she altered her response. "Okay. See you later, Dria."

Maon motioned Shane and Adrianna over to several chairs facing a large vidscreen on the wall. Shane directed her to the center chair.

Maon stood facing them. "Can you clarify for me the objectives of this operation? I'm a little confused on why you felt the need to get into a tiff at the Whip Hand and how that's tied into illegal human trafficking through the Hub and a possible expansion by the Benefactor into Preatiens."

Shane pushed forward in his chair, perching on the edge. Using his hands to punctuate his words, he said, "Right. Right. First, we know the Benefactor coerced Marge Boleo into allowing illegal human trafficking through the Hub again. If we figure out how, we can neutralize the hold he has on her while making it look like I'm personally responsible. If he wants to get the Hub back in his pocket, he'll need to deal with me. In person. On the Hub."

Maon shoved his hands in his pockets and studied the floor while Shane spoke. He broke in on Shane's explanation with a raised eyebrow. "Why do you want him to come to the Hub? And what if he doesn't?"

"He will. He'll have the added incentive of something he really wants waiting for him at the Hub. Adrianna."

Maon pursed his lips. "Okay."

"He needs her—in what way, we're not clear on—for his move on Preatiens. My hope is he tries to kidnap her, and we catch him at it."

"And the director went for this?"

"I didn't tell him the kidnapping part."

Both Maon's eyebrows raised and his mouth opened. "Then what plan did you sell him?"

"The director is on board for stopping the trafficking through the Hub and blocking the Benefactor's move on to Preatiens. He approved Adrianna's role on the condition I was with her throughout the operation. The only way that happens is if the Benefactor sees me as a potential associate."

"I'm not sure…"

"Hold that thought because that part of the plan is moot until we figure out what he's holding over Marge Boleo and the Hub and how we can subvert it."

Maon nodded. "We'll have to back burner that for today. I've been working on a possibility involving the Hub's fuel supply, but I don't have all the data back to be able to say for sure. Why don't we look at what I do have on the Benefactor and get Adrianna's input?"

"Sure," Shane said.

Maon went to the vidscreen. "I've created a sector map showing the Benefactor's legitimate business interests. The lines between Furzine and each planet represent a particular industry or resource. Since these are aboveboard dealings, they can easily be traced back to Furzine."

"You've got the Wellington listed here?" asked Shane.

"No, that would be the next map."

A second map appeared on the vidscreen. "This map encompasses his operations through shell entities and under-the-table deals with other governments. I've simplified some of this, so it shows the primary connections. This is information anyone with enough money can discover. It's most useful for determining the Benefactor's political and business machinations. But it also has obvious connections to his illegal trade. The Wellington is legitimate, but what happens to its graduates may not be. You said some of them end up on Beta Tau?"

Shane nodded. "Yeah. Trey Johansson told me he knew of some. The Benefactor covers his bases, always has. Took what he learned from Cosmo Bonilla and expanded on it."

"Bonilla. What a friggin' mess that turned out to be. He played both the Marshals and the Feds when he brought the Benefactor on to take charge of the bliss bead trade eight years ago."

Adrianna broke in. "Who's Bonilla?"

Maon grimaced. "One of the biggest drug lords in the Federation. Eight years ago he took over the bliss bead trade from the local cartels. The sectors beyond the Sympallan Drift were put into the Benefactor's hands to run. The Benefactor's the first Furzian dictator to expand his illegal activities off planet, and he's done it in a big way. He's like Bonilla, but worse. Bonilla was found guilty of bribing an official and has actually served time, but he's never been indicted on drug trafficking. The Benefactor uses diplomatic immunity as an even better shield than Bonilla's business tactics, and he's involved in other illegal activities beyond drug smuggling."

Shane frowned. "The Benefactor's smart, and he plans his every move. He's leveraged ownership of the *sturnilium* mines in the sector to maintain his control over the bliss bead trade."

"Right." Maon pointed at the map. "If you look here and here, you see where he's tied up all the sturnilium in the sector. Not a big deal for most of the sector, except that it's a necessity on Gallarda. Gallarda happens to be the only source of *pyantha* this side of the Sympallan Drift. It requires sturnilium to process raw pyantha seeds into the extract that is the basis for bliss beads."

Maon switched to another map. "This third map shows that connection. Most of this map's data is extrapolated from the previous information, crime statistics, and evidence provided via criminal investigation."

Shane broke in. "As you can see, Dria, the Benefactor is involved in drugs, stolen artifacts, arm sales, counterfeiting, and what we're interested in, illegal human trafficking. Even more interesting, if you overlay all three maps, it shows that one planet has no ties to him at all, Preatiens. Preatiens's closed society makes getting as much as a toehold difficult. Impossible until now. He's planning something and has been willing to play a long game to achieve his goal. That is if his plan to marry you, which started years ago, is part of a scheme to infiltrate Preatiens."

Shane paused and looked at her, his lips twisted to the side while he studied her. The strongest emotion coming from both men was confusion. She was about to break into the silence when Shane spoke again.

"The Benefactor always looks for a weakness to exploit in individuals or societies. What do you think is the greatest vulnerability of Preatiens society?"

Dria looked at Maon, who was watching her closely, then slewed her gaze to Shane. They were asking her opinion, although it seemed more like a test. "I've been reading up on Preatiens, Sir. Their greatest vulnerability is sex. Interaction with females is rigidly structured. Women do not leave their homes, and they do not receive guests except in the presence of their father, brothers, or husband until they are past childbearing years. Preatiens has brothels, but even the women in them are safeguarded against men who want more than oral or vaginal sex. Evading the grandmothers, who are highly skilled empaths and who can and do move in society, is impossible. So sex is a weakness that could be exploited if given the opportunity."

"My thoughts exactly," Shane said.

Shane cocked an eyebrow, looking at Maon with an I-told-you-so expression. A quick turn of her head caught Maon shrugging his shoulders, a lopsided grin on his face.

"If we assume the Benefactor wants to use you as a way of gaining entrée to Preatiens, he will continue to try to kidnap you. If we give him what he believes is a clear shot, he'll take it."

Adrianna's eyes widened. A lead ball dropped into her stomach.

"Don't worry. I intend to be with you every step of the way. We'll take every precaution, but it will mean continuing our little game of Master and pet."

With a hesitant nod, Adrianna said, "Yes, Sir."

Shane leaned back in his chair. "Before we discuss the particulars, tell us your perceptions of the Benefactor. We're looking for a weakness we can exploit."

Adrianna pursed her lips and considered her response. "I always met the Benefactor in social settings. He's charming on the surface, but underneath he has the mind of a predator. No, not a predator, a demon. Predators kill for a reason. The Benefactor kills for no better reason than that he can. It's just as dangerous to be no longer necessary to him as it is to make a mistake. He never does his own dirty work, just flicks his finger and orders it done. But that power feeds something dank and sludgy inside him. I witnessed him giving a kill order in front of an entire room of guests who had no idea he'd ordered one of their number taken from the room and executed. The darkness in him slithered with pleasure." Adrianna shuddered.

"That sounds like what we'd expect of him," Shane said. "He's a sociopath. What I want to know is anything about him that is unexpected."

"Hmmmm. Well, I'm sure you've heard of his charity work with children. That's not a front to help his reputation. He really does like to help children in need. That's one reason he's called the Benefactor. He always treated me with respect, and I always felt I was one of the few people at his parties he saw differently. You'll find this strange, but his feelings toward me always seemed similar to his emotions when he showed off his ancient porcelain collection." She paused before adding, "Not many know it, but he has a girl living with him. She's his adopted daughter. She has physical problems and requires motor assistance to get around. Whatever is wrong with her can't be fixed. When I was younger, I was brought to play with her. She's very sweet. He genuinely loves her and is quite tender to her. I've heard him tell her she was his greatest treasure."

Shane tapped his index finger against his lips. "Interesting. Maon, do a breakdown by age of his human trafficking stats."

"Sure. Just a second." Maon walked to his desk, entered parameters, and brought the information up on the vidscreen. "Well, look at that." He raised his eyebrows. "No child trafficking."

"We'll have to figure out if we can use that angle," Shane said. He sat motionless, eyes unfocused for several minutes. Breaking from his reverie, he said to Maon, "I need you to find out if any of the Benefactor's known associates dabble in child trafficking and if any of them also supply his brothels or the Wellington. We'll need forged documentation if you can't find a link we can exploit."

"That shouldn't be too difficult to work up," Maon said. He walked back and leaned against the wall by the vidscreen, crossing his arms over his chest. "Your determination to dangle Dria as bait is a bad idea. How do you plan to do that without him taking her? He's already tried kidnapping her and murdering you. That man in the audience at the club on Beta Tau could have been someone sent by him and not just one of your many admiring fans."

Adrianna shrank back in her chair when the discussion took a heated turn, swiveling her head while they hurled statements at each other.

"I know you think it's foolhardy. Wherever she is. Runner's Hub or Tallav. He's not going to stop trying to grab her. Whatever his intentions are, I don't believe that includes harming her."

Maon's voice hardened. "She's not a trained agent, and Runner's Hub is dangerous at the best of times. At least wait and give me time to put undercover teams in place."

Shane shook his head. "No, that would take months. The sooner we move on this the better. The longer we wait, the more likely the Benefactor will think we're setting him up. He's going to suspect that anyway, but to a lesser degree if he doesn't believe we've had the time to put in teams as you suggested. Whatever he's planned for Dria and Preatiens, he's spent years in a holding pattern. He could have kidnapped Dria and threatened her with harm to gain Élise Sauveterre's cooperation. He didn't. He was waiting on something. Dria's twenty-first birthday. His plan has always been to marry her. He killed her father to keep Dria on Furzine. She barely escaped Furzine with Master Trey. This is more than Preatiens. It's personal for the Benefactor. We can get him to Runner's Hub."

Maon peered at Shane through narrowed eyes. "I don't know. He's always worked through intermediaries. He's got his own people on the Hub, besides the place crawling with people who will do anything he asks for the right pay."

Shane nodded. "Exactly. We're not trying to get him to Tallav. He'll feel he has the upper hand on the Hub if he thinks I'm flying solo. Dria and I will head to the Hub after my last week off is up. He should jump at the opportunity to get his hands on Dria. I intend to approach Marge Boleo with a demand to be included in the payoff from the illegal human trafficking going through her station. Whether the Benefactor believes I'm dirty or not won't matter. Dealing with me will give him added incentive to come to the Hub in person. If we can lure him to Runner's Hub, we might even get him on vid incriminating himself. It's a long shot, but it's too good to pass up."

"Fuck's sake, Shane, I don't like it. Your closest backup will be days away. If I were the Benefactor, I'd have you killed and grab Dria. I don't see how you can keep that from happening."

"We'll have a team hyperjump in short of the station and take cover in the Hub's asteroid field. Smugglers hide in there all the time. One of our supply ships could easily pretend it's a common freighter and act as our backup."

"That's still a twelve-hour wait for help. You'll be dead and Dria gone before they can respond."

"It's a risk. I understand, but you're forgetting Marge Boleo. Somehow, the Benefactor forced her to renege on the deal she made with the Federation to stop illegal human trafficking through the Hub. He's found a way to pressure her. If we find out what that is and eliminate it, I'll be in a much better position. I admit I don't have a lot of specifics yet. If it helps, I promise I'll abort if things don't line up. I don't want to argue go/no go until we know more. Ultimately, how I play it depends on what we discover. You said it might be the fuel supply?"

"Yeah. It's the most likely scenario I've come up with. But I can't guarantee I'll find anything we can use."

"We can call in more data analysts if you need the help. This is too important. If we accomplish nothing else, closing Runner's Hub as a transshipping point for illegal human trafficking will make the trade five times more difficult. That's a big win." Shane thumped a fist on his thigh, punctuating his final statement.

"I get it." Maon rubbed a hand across his face. "Give me a few days. If I don't find something, I'll call in and request additional help. I'm not sure that the Benefactor will react as you expect even if you get that far."

Shane leaned toward Maon. "The stakes are worth it. The possibility of bringing him down... I can't walk away from that."

"You'd still be risking Dria." Maon glared at Shane as though he wanted to say more but thought better of it.

"She's already at risk. Besides, I think he's truly infatuated with her and believes he'll gain admittance to Preatien society by making her his wife. If worse comes to worst and he does take Adrianna, we have a plan in place. The director has initiated discussions with Preatiens and will speak with Élise Sauveterre personally. He'll ask her to secure clearance for the Benefactor to bring Dria to Preatiens. The Benefactor is not an idiot. If he thought blackmailing Sauveterre would work, he'd have already done it. He won't turn down the opportunity to meet with Sauveterre in person. She's his in on Preatiens. He won't leave negotiations with her to underlings. If she wants to see Dria, he'll bring her. My chief worry in that scenario is what he'll do to Dria to make her cooperate with him. I'm not going to let it come to that. Once Dria's on Preatiens, her safety can be assured. He won't be leaving with her. He'd be risking his diplomatic immunity." Shane's jaw set, his gaze drilling into Maon's.

Adrianna decided it was time to break into the discussion and cleared her throat. "Gentleman, the lady in question is sitting here." She raised her eyebrows, looking first at Shane and then Maon. "I'll be going with Shane, and if it becomes necessary, I will go with the Benefactor. I am not the girl who ran from Furzine. You might think because I'm a submissive, I'm weak. Submissives are trained to discern their Master's needs. That discernment accompanied by my empathic abilities is my weapon. I don't consider myself at a disadvantage." With an abrupt nod of her head, she placed her hands in her lap and waited for a response.

A satisfied smile tweaked the corner of Shane's mouth.

"Fuck's sake, I think Shane's met his match in you, Dria," Maon said. "I can see there's no stopping you two, especially since Shane has the director in his pocket." With a big sigh, he rubbed his stomach. "Let's get some lunch, and then it's nap time around here."

Shane's lips curved into a smirk. "You take naps?"

Maon pulled his shoulders back, stiffening with overdone defensiveness, hand to his chest. "It's a habit from my younger days that I've taken up again." He dropped the pretense. "I don't know why I ever quit. The children and I take our nap together. You could join us." He waggled his eyebrows at Adrianna. "But I'll warn you. Petey kicks."

Shane's response was dry. "Maybe we'll stick to our own beds."

"I figured you would." Maon winked at Adrianna.

ADRIANNA FINISHED UNPACKING the clothes she'd brought with her, including a swimsuit. The pool was a luxury she was looking forward to. Lunch had been excellent, a cold soup made with vegetables grown in the estate garden and tender rolls with a creamy spread that Maon said was butter made from real cow's cream. The glass of milk he let her try had an interesting flavor, but she wasn't sure she would want to drink it regularly. She'd stick to the synthetic milk she'd drunk all her life, although the butter was much better than synthetic.

After slipping her shoes off her feet, she removed her slacks and blouse, ready to lie down and take a nap when Shane called to her from the other room. With the door shut, she hadn't heard him clearly. Rather than enter his room, she opened it a crack and said, "Yes, did you need me?"

"Yes, Adrianna. Come here."

Adrianna's stomach dropped. His voice, dark and low, reached inside her and plucked a taut fiber, sending a resonating note vibrating along every nerve in her body. Light-headed with instant desire, she moved into the room, shutting the door behind her. Her knees were the slightest bit wobbly as she walked toward him. His eyes were stormy with the lust that rolled in waves, breaking against her empathic senses. He'd removed his clothes and stood fully aroused, his hands on his hips.

"Kneel."

She dropped to the floor.

"Eyes closed."

The brush of his feet sounded as he moved across the carpet. He was there. Beside her. She knew it. But he said nothing. He made no move to touch her.

Please.

The weight of his hand landed atop her head. She leaned into it, savoring each stroke. He skimmed his palm down her braid. The distinctive smell of fresh male sweat filled her nostrils.

They were in sync. He knew what she needed. Knew what she desired. And knew how and when to give it to her.

Over the short time they'd had to grow accustomed to each other, they had achieved an amazing rapport in the sexual part of their relationship. It wasn't the norm. Her interpersonal relationship classes had taught her that deep and total trust between Master and submissive took time while layers of vulnerability were slowly shed. She felt vulnerable to Shane, but it was an astounding openness that had no tension except that brought by the excitement of waiting to find out what he would do and where he would take them. More time wouldn't make it any clearer that she had found her perfect Master.

Adrianna strove to stay alert, wanting to share each second with Shane. To commune with him, mind and body. To touch his soul. To climb under his skin and know him, fully know him.

He moved behind her, but she could still smell that musky scent that was pure Shane. He must have squatted, because his voice sounded near her ear.

"Keep your eyes shut, *a ghrá.*"

She gasped when he skimmed his hands down her arms and gripped her wrists. His grasp was firm, powerful, and yet never rough unless the moment called for it. He drew her wrists together behind her back. The slide of rope and his calloused fingers sent delicious shocks to her nipples while he tied her arms together.

When he was finished, firm hands clasped both sides of her waist, helping her rise after the single word command, "Up." Desire melted her insides, and her pussy, already wet, went damper still. A steady daily diet of Shane's light touches and quick caresses kept Adrianna in constant yearning for the moment when his fingers would linger on all the intimate places of her body, encouraging her into an upward spiral of arousal. He was taking her there now.

He turned her and propelled her toward the bed, where he bent her over its edge, stomach down, spreading her legs wide and taking the same measured approach to tying her ankles to the bed. The dark brown satin cover was slippery, so the ties were welcome if for no other reason than they would keep them from sliding off the bed from Shane's forceful love-making. The slick coolness of the fabric soon warmed beneath her. With her eyes still shut, the sounds of Shane moving and the fresh smell of the cover enhanced the sensations of each contact with her skin.

Her swirling need increased at the touch of his fingers to her thighs. He continued immobilizing her. The rope dragged and pulled with each loop and tug. His warm breath cascaded over her. Her inner thigh muscles stretched when he pulled the cord ends taut and tied them to someplace higher on the bed.

"Anything too tight?"

She shook her head. "No, Master."

"You are so lovely, Adrianna. And that ass. You know I love your ass."

His hand came down in a stinging blow.

"I'm going to make it a pretty pink."

With that comment, he began spanking her, varying the tempo and placement, never letting the stings build past the pleasure they brought. Her clit reacted with prickles of appreciation.

He finished all too quickly. The skin of his palm soothed each cheek.

His voice gruff, he said, "Perfect. Fucking perfect."

Her sense of his arousal mated with the heat building inside her. He took the time to check that the ropes hadn't tightened unexpectedly.

She loved to be tied, involuntary reactions made impossible by the rope. It was an ideal position to be in, her body open and available for her Master's use, allowing his talented fingers, tongue and cock to wring ecstatic response after ecstatic response from her.

His breath warmed her ear, his chest brushing against her back. "Maon had this room outfitted for me." A puff of air escaped from her when he wrapped her braid around his hand, pulled the skin of her face taut, and lifted her head to the side, placing his face in front of hers. "Open your eyes." His blue stare speared deep into her. "You're the first woman I've ever brought here." She was caught, unable to look away, held by his intense implacability.

"Shut your eyes."

She did, and he released her, the discomfort evaporating from her scalp. The breath she'd been holding burst from her lungs. Eyelids sealed, she was brimming with the desire to shout, exultant that she had captured a piece of him no one else had.

Metal skimmed cold across her flesh, up her thigh, accompanied by snipping sounds while Shane cut through the fabric of her panties. He pressed his hand under her chest to flick open the front of her bra. When he'd severed its straps, he slid the pieces out from under her. Her body and soul bare, her will in complete capitulation to his mastery, she became lost in a sea of vulnerability where time disappeared under his hands.

When he latched a set of palm clamps on her nipples, pain lanced through them, diminishing to an ache that served as a counterpoint to the throbbing need in her pussy. He proved himself a virtuoso at playing her body, making her ascend until she was one note from the peak of a crescendo, only to let the melody his fingers plucked and stroked diminish. With a series of light caresses, he frustrated her need for a little less pianissimo and more fortissimo. She felt the delicious stretch of a dildo next. He rolled it inside her, stroking that spot, that heavenly spot, in languorous motions. Her body reached and reached to hit the high note. *Damn it all to hell. Let me come.*

In a moment of clarity, she realized. *He feels it too.* She nearly bleated a vindictive laugh. As much as he was tormenting her, he was torturing himself as well. His need was swelling to the point it was a wonder he didn't explode. *Desire* was too weak a word to describe Shane's emotions curling around her. *Lust* was too coarse for the craving for bodily release and emotional connection that washed through him. He wanted her. Needed her.

In the moment before she resorted to begging, he removed the dildo, covered her with his body, and thrust his erection deep inside her, groaning her name. "Adrianna, *a ghrá geal*." He stroked rapidly, his chest and stomach rubbing across her bound arms. The steely control he'd maintained was converted into an inflexible drive to propel them to a higher plane where passion fused them into one. A harmony of unleashed fervor soared from their joined bodies, minor key changing to major in bright chords of bliss. Adrianna's empathic senses reveled in their mutual longing to reach the peak he'd held in abeyance.

The sensation of his taut abdominal muscles sliding over her while his arms clamped her to him made her toes curl. He was rigid everywhere, grinding in circles. Her need spiraled ever higher. The sounds of his harsh breathing when he gasped her name and showered her shoulders with kisses and love bites made Adrianna's own panting grow heavy. Deep satisfaction at totally surrendering to her Master rolled up from her depths. Little peals of ecstasy burst from her each time Shane drove himself into her.

Memories rushed through her mind of Shane pushing into her as far as he could go and holding himself stiff while he filled her with cum. Those thoughts sent her careening. With a hitch in her breathing, an orgasm barreled through her, more intense than she'd ever experienced. Her vaginal walls clamped tight on Shane until he too exploded with a fervor that made him cry with agonizing joy.

For long moments, Shane lay over her, gasping, before he eased his sweat-slicked body up from her. She sucked enormous drafts of air into her lungs while the rest of her body lolled, limp and utterly replete.

He freed her from the restraints and drew her up into the middle of the bed, engulfing her in his arms. "I don't want to let you go, Dria. I never knew someone like you could exist. I hoped, but I couldn't find you. And now you're here."

With her brain still muzzy, she managed a content smile.

He kissed the top of her head. "It's not the sex. I've had good sex before."

Wait. What did he just say? She gave a muffled protest and rapped his ribs with her fist.

Shane laughed. "Not as good as this." He kissed the crown of her head again. "You're strong, Dria, but you let me be stronger. You don't bully or manipulate me. You're strong but not domineering. I always believed the two went together in women."

She kissed his chest, appreciating the stroke of his fingers along her back.

"I'll do my best to take care of you and help you become the woman you're meant to be. I need you to help me be the man I'm meant to be."

Adrianna stretched her neck up and kissed him gently. "Deal."

14

Adrianna enjoyed the warmth of the sun's rays and the sound of children laughing and splashing in the pool. Maon emerged from the pool, carrying Petey. He placed the toddler into the wading pool, strode to the chaise lounge next to Adrianna, and sat down sideways. Water dripped from his light brown hair and ran down his tanned shoulders and chest. After a quick toweling off, he pulled Adrianna's tablet to him. "The engine manual for the *Adrasteia*? This is what you do on your downtime?"

Adrianna peered up at him through her sunshades with a wry smile. "Someone needs to know this stuff. Shane is an excellent pilot, but he's not really mechanically minded."

Maon shuddered. "Better you than me." His gaze turned to the children. Devon and Annie were diving for rocks in the deep end of the swimming pool. Petey was pouring water from his wading pool into containers lined up around its edge. The chaise lounge creaked when Maon swiveled and stretched his legs out. Hands clasped behind his head, he relaxed with a sigh. "You enjoy working with Shane?"

"Yes, I do."

"Mmmm. He can be intense."

"I like intense."

"So I've heard." Adrianna detected the smile in his voice.

They sat there for a while, soaking up the heat of the sun, listening to the children's chattering.

"You're good for him," Maon said.

Adrianna turned her head toward him.

"Shane's been a little adrift since his brother died."

"He told me about Thomas."

"Yeah, that was hard for him. They were close. It changed a lot for him."

"It would." Adrianna's chest ached. She recalled the moments when Shane told her about his brother.

"Yeah." Maon raised his voice. "Petey, you're getting too close to the big pool. Get back, buddy." He reached and picked up the towel he'd dropped, forming it into a ball he continued to jumble with his hands. "He didn't just lose his brother; he lost his future. Shane's always been an aggressive, get-it-done kind of guy. The Marshal Service was perfect for him. He was going to be a marshal forever. Maybe marry one day. Some off worlder that his mother could accept. Let Thomas do the family stuff. He was better suited for it anyway." Maon paused and brought the balled-up towel to his chest. "Shane's trying to be the dutiful son."

He fluffed the towel in his hands and set it back down. "The thing is, he might not be the kind of family man the Tallavan matriarchs consider proper, but he does love his family and his mom. He wants to make his mom happy."

"I often see him stare at the picture of Gleann Milis on the *Adrasteia*," Adrianna said.

Maon shrugged. "Yeah, he loves that place. I think he'd settle there if it meant he could do it with the right woman."

"He seems to think no Tallavan woman could be right for him." Adrianna still didn't understand why Shane felt that way.

Maon took a deep breath and let the air whoosh from his lungs. "He's not wrong. Women on Tallav do one of two things when they get older. They turn into even more rigidly domineering bitches, or they learn to appreciate a man sharing their load. Shane tried courting for a while, but most of the younger women are hyped-up on securing their own dominance. They can be bitchy, and Shane doesn't like bitchy." He snorted, shaking his head. "They nicknamed him the Beast. A group of them made a game of letting him bed them once so they could claim they survived the Beast."

Adrianna frowned, wanting to slap every one of those conniving bitches.

"After a year trying to find a suitable woman to marry, he refused to continue. His mother cut him off."

"I knew he'd fallen out with his mother."

"Yeah." Maon sat up and reached out to pat Adrianna's arm. "That's why I'm glad you're in his life now. You do him a lot of good."

Adrianna gave him a wistful smile. "I hope so."

"You do." He stood up, turning to holler at the children. "Offspring, time to get out of the water. Head indoors."

"Five more minutes, please, Dad, please," Devon said.

"No whining. Out now."

The children complained while they dragged themselves from the pool. Maon snatched up Petey and wrapped him in a towel. "Last one in's a snoot fish!" That got the kids moving. "Petey, say bye-bye to Dria."

Petey waved a chubby hand. "Bye."

Adrianna waved back. "Bye, Petey."

When the pool deck was quiet again, Adrianna closed her eyes. Most of what Maon had told her she'd known in general, but he'd certainly fleshed out her understanding. The contract with the baby pod began to make sense to her. At least Adrianna hoped that was all it was. Maybe she should dial back her jealousy. She'd stop thinking of Ceana as the baby pod. It still angered her that he hadn't told her even though he knew her deepest secret.

She'd heard a lot about Shane's mother but not his father. How did he figure in Shane's life? That was something she'd need to ask him. Not for the first time, she wished she had the wherewithal to set things right for Shane.

She should get out of the sun too. With a big sigh, she got up and headed indoors.

When she entered the hall leading to the library, Shane's voice was loud and explosive. "We'll be there." He paused then said, "Yes, I'm bringing her. She's my assistant, and I expect you to treat her with respect."

Adrianna decided it was best to step inside so Shane would know she'd heard him. With his back to the door, he didn't notice her.

"You will not put her in the servant's quarters. She'll be sleeping in my room with me."

Adrianna couldn't quite hear the response, but the woman on the other end of the conversation sounded equally heated.

"I don't care whether you approve. This is the setup you arranged, so deal with it. Expect us later this evening." He disconnected abruptly, shaking his head, his jaw rigid.

Adrianna cleared her throat. Shane spun about, glowering with eyes that had gone fierce. "Dria. I have an appointment to keep. You're coming with me. Pack for a three-day stay at another estate. I'll explain on the way there."

"Of course." Her attempt to hide her concern must have failed, because Shane came to her and wrapped her in his arms. Something was different. The prelude to being engulfed in Shane's embrace was usually a hungry stare, like a predator with eyes fixed on prey. Once he'd turned and recognized her, Shane had avoided looking at her. He kissed her, his tongue sliding hot between her lips. With a groan, he pulled back, eyes shut, leaning his forehead on hers.

"I'd like nothing more than to take you to bed and ravish you, but I have to do this. I'm sorry."

"I understand."

With a grunt, Shane spun her and gave her a push with his hand on her rear toward the library door. Adrianna barely heard the words he said under his breath. "I hope so."

WHEN SHANE TURNED onto the main road, he ran out of time. The car seemed smaller, and the scent of the leather seats, which normally brought a frisson of excitement at being behind the wheel, was oppressive. Adrianna sat in silence in the passenger seat. He had to tell her about Ceana. Maybe if he started with a little background. With his eyes fixed on the road ahead, he began. "When Tallav was colonized, it was with the specific intent to create a world where women were in charge. A consortium of wealthy women wanted to build a pastoral idyll based on a quasi-Celtic mythos."

Adrianna inserted a noncommittal hum into his pause. He gave her a quick glance. Her eyebrow had quirked slightly. This wasn't working. He sounded like he was reading from a textbook. The history of Tallav was drilled into every schoolboy. Still if she understood the problem…

"Reality didn't match the paradise they planned. Their sons and grandsons didn't accept the domestic role they'd been assigned. The Marshals were created to provide one entirely male enterprise to serve as an outlet for unwed males. Older men whose children were raised could return to the Marshals. Otherwise, marshals are always unmarried men, with one loophole."

"So if you marry, you lose your career in the Marshals."

The road ahead was a straight line with hay fields on either side. Shane risked another glance at Adrianna. The risk wasn't in removing his gaze from the road, but in what he would see in Adrianna's face. Her forehead was furrowed. He could tell her mind was racing. "Yes. It gets more ridiculous," he said. "At the time Tallav was settled, the Federation was going through a massive expansion besides the growth into the Tallavan sector of space. It was pretty lawless here because the Feds didn't have the manpower to really make a dent. The Marshals were delegated to fulfill the Feds role. Because the Service is an extension of the Federation Security Police, marshals serve on all the planets in the three sectors on this end of the Sympallan Drift. The matriarchy worried that their sons would come home with non-Tallavan wives. Ultimately, this is about keeping their men down on the farm."

He paused and shook his head again. "As a Tallavan aristocrat, I can remain unmarried and serve in the Marshals, marry a Tallavan and live on my wife's estate, or marry off Tallav and leave the Marshals. There is a loophole. Dispensation can be made to remain a marshal and marry off world if the man's mother sanctions the marriage. If an off world marriage is unsanctioned, the man is completely cut off. Either way, he can't return to Tallav with his wife."

"Patrick explained that to me. What does this have to do with where we're going?" Adrianna asked.

"I'm getting to that. My mother needs a granddaughter." Shane sighed.

"A full-blood Tallavan granddaughter." His hands clenched the steering wheel. "I'm her only remaining child. When she dies, the family estate and its holdings will go to her sister or her sister's heirs. My mother hasn't spoken to her sister in over thirty years. I don't know what they fell out over. No one discusses it. But whatever it was, my mother is adamantly opposed to her sister getting one blade of grass from Gleann Milis. Males can't inherit, but the bloodline can run through them. My daughter would become my mother's heir."

"Oh, I see."

Adrianna's response sounded flat to Shane's ears. Gods, he needed to touch her. To let her know that she was far more important than Ceana. He pulled off the road and shut the engine off. A flock of cowbirds burst from the field alongside the car, escaping their perceived danger with a flapping of wings.

"Dria..." He reached out and took her hand, his eyes focused on his thumb rubbing circles on the back. *Just tell her.* "I contracted with a Tallavan woman, Ceana Kendrith, to carry my child with the idea that if the child is a girl, she'll inherit from my mother. So far, Ceana hasn't become pregnant. She refuses to use artificial means, so I've been visiting her each month during her fertile period to... Well. You understand the mechanics. We've been trying for four months, and so far no baby." Shane paused, waiting for Adrianna to speak. When she didn't, he looked up. "What are you thinking?"

Adrianna's face was blank. Impossible to read. "Well, it sounds like a solution for having a daughter, but I can't comprehend why you are going about it like this. You could have married a Tallavan woman long ago."

Shane grimaced. "I've never found a Tallavan woman ready to accept me for who I am. I'd also have to leave the Marshals Service once I married a Tallavan woman."

"Oh, right." Adrianna's voice was muffled by her fist pressed to her lips.

"Tallavan fathers are expected to stay home and raise the children. I'm not good house-husband material."

"Really!" A hint of a smile played around her lips.

"No. Although the idea of someone else raising a child of mine is repugnant to me, even if it is my father. I haven't found another solution that will please both my mother and me."

Adrianna responded, "I understand, but I have to admit I'm not crazy about your solution or the method. I'm also sure I'd like to smack this woman—repeatedly. Maybe pull out her hair. Damn. I'm not kidding." Her chin jutted up when she frowned. "I don't think I want to share you. I accept that's not up to me. You're the Master. You're in charge, and you can have as many women as you want. If that pleases you, I'd come to terms with it." She shook her head, but the scowl remained.

"You have nothing to be jealous about. I can't stand her. She's a typical, emasculating, domineering Tallavan female. I'd never be happy married to that type of woman. She's doing it for the money. She'll get a stipend as long as our child is under the age of eighteen. Apparently, Ceana's mother left her estate in a mess when she died, and Ceana needs income to set things right." Shane looked out the window. The cowbirds were settling back into the recently mowed field, searching for insects.

"This is really none of my business. Thank you for telling me. It would have been awkward to meet her without understanding the circumstances."

Adrianna's voice had turned cool. Shane pulled his gaze from the birds out the window to find her face had gone smooth and impassive. *Fuck.* She was mad. Justifiably. He should have told her when they'd had their chat. He'd planned to. Today was inevitable, but he'd put it off, unable to expose his problems to Adrianna. Unable to risk her anger right when they were making up. He hit the steering wheel with his fist hard enough to hurt. Adrianna jumped in her seat.

"Sorry. I hate my life. It's a screwed-up mess. I wish I could make you understand that you're the only bright thing to come my way since my brother died." He stretched his hand across the gap between their seats, pausing just before touching her cheek, looking into her eyes, seeking permission to proceed before he caressed her tentatively. "I'm sorry. I should have told you sooner than this. It was unfair to you."

"I'll get over it, but you'll have to give me a little time."

Shane brought his hand down, holding back the sigh that would ease some of his tension. "Sure."

Her gaze drilled into him. "Is this the last big surprise? I know *I* don't have any more."

Shane's lips pressed into a line. "I'm certain there are more dark things hiding in my past, but nothing like this. Nothing this significant."

"Okay." Adrianna squared her shoulders. "Let's get going. The sooner you get this baby-making party over, the better."

"Yes, ma'am." Shane pulled back out onto the road, sending the cowbirds winging off again. His thoughts were a stew bubbling with all the ingredients that had made up the mess he called his life. They combined into a pottage of frustration, anger, and grief. *Gods.* Why wasn't Ceana pregnant already? He felt like pounding the steering wheel again but didn't want to startle Adrianna.

Sometime during the remaining journey, Adrianna reached out and took his hand, holding it in hers. No words. She just held his hand. His stomach settled, but the mild ache in his chest became more noticeable. He ignored it. Thoughts of how wonderful Adrianna was occupied him.

By the time they arrived at the Kendrith estate, Shane was much more relaxed. That changed when they drove up the long hedge-lined drive to the elegant manor house with its peaked roofs, towers, and expanse of lawn.

"We're here. Dria, do not let the staff treat you with disrespect. You are a guest in this house. You will accompany me to meals and at any other time I need you. When not with me, you can remain in our room if you prefer, but the common areas of the estate are open to guests. If someone gives you trouble, refer them to me. If you're assertive, most of the staff will defer to you. We won't be here long. Three days. I'll return to my room for sleeping after I've"—he looked aside—"done my duty."

"I understand. I'll do my best to make this an easy stay for everyone."

Shane looked at her and grasped her hand. "I know you will. Come, let's go in."

He helped her from the car, took her by the elbow, and escorted her up the steps to the oversize front door, striking the doorplate with the knocker. An older gentleman answered the door. "Good evening, Tucker," Shane said.

"Marshal Tiernan." Tucker's face looked like he'd been taste-testing lemons for lemonade and had found one both bitter and sour.

"This is Ms. Pacquin, my assistant. She'll be staying in my suite."

Tucker ignored Adrianna. "The mistress has placed your companion in her own room."

"I'm sorry, Tucker. That won't do. I've already explained to your mistress that Ms. Pacquin will be staying in my suite. She is a guest here with me. Do you understand?"

Tucker frowned. "Yes, sir. As you say, sir. If you'll leave the car key code with me, I'll have your luggage brought up and the car garaged."

"Thank you, Tucker. Much obliged. Where is the mistress?"

"You'll find her in the blue sitting room. She's expecting you." He made a pointed effort to infer that he meant Shane and not Adrianna.

"Thank you, Tucker. We'll see our way there." Shane steered Adrianna by her elbow past Tucker and to the right.

Adrianna was grateful for Shane's nearness after that frosty welcome. She was impressed with the grand staircase that split and went to either side of the two-story foyer. The dark golden brown of the stair treads and banisters gleamed under a huge chandelier. Enormous paintings of what she assumed were ancestors of the estate covered the walls, austere women who looked on her with disapproval. She was glad to walk through the wide doorway into the adjoining room. Shane didn't linger but worked his way through the room with its small gilt chairs, chintz sofa, and floral bric-a-brac. Through a white door in the back wall, he led her into what was obviously the blue sitting room. Enthroned in an ornate deep-blue wing chair, Ceana sat with an expression of repugnance on her face.

This was also a feminine room. The blue tones were soothing, and the ornaments were not as frilly or gilded. *Feminine* wasn't the word one would use to describe the chair's occupant. She didn't look demure, soft, or delicate. *Femme fatale* was a better descriptor, and at the moment, *bitchy femme fatale*. Ceana was dressed in black slacks and white button-up blouse. The expression of disgust on her face didn't harmonize with the generous breasts and hips that the simple, elegant clothing highlighted. A riot of honey-blonde curls fell past her shoulders, highlighting a perfect, sun-kissed complexion. If an artist was looking for a model to pose for a painting of Venus, Ceana would more than fill the bill. Adrianna's throat tightened painfully. Shane would be taking this woman to bed soon. *This is about getting an heir for Shane's mother. He doesn't want to be here. He doesn't even like her.* Still, she did have such a lot of hair to pull.

Damn it. There was that jealous streak again.

"So you've brought your little whore even though I told you not to." Ceana's sneer was directed straight at Adrianna.

"She is not a whore, and you will not speak of her like that. She is my assistant." Shane glared back. "Be civil, Ceana."

Ceana turned her sneer on Shane. "You have one hour to settle yourself in your suite. Then I expect you to be in my room, clothes off and waiting for me. Do you understand? I am at peak fertility for the next sixty hours."

"As you wish, Ceana." Shane motioned for Adrianna to precede him out the door through which they'd entered. Outside, Tucker stood expectantly.

"You've been placed in your usual suite, sir. I'll send up a maid to unpack and to assist the lady in preparing for bed."

"Thank you, Tucker."

The butler nodded, looked down his nose at Adrianna, and left. Shane led Adrianna back through to the foyer and up the stairs to the second floor where their suite was located on the left side.

Adrianna gave a small gasp. "This is lovely."

Shane scanned the room before agreeing. "Yes, it's designed for the male sensibilities."

"Well, I guess I have male sensibilities." The deep-green color acted like a foundation for the airy greens and creams that lightened the room, keeping the luxurious decor from seeming ostentatious. A sitting area occupied the left side of the large room with a deep brown burled sleigh bed on the right side. When she explored, she found that the doors on either end of the wall with the bed led to a bathroom and closet.

"I'm going to shower and shave," Shane said. "Make yourself at home. The maid should be here soon to unpack."

"I can unpack."

"Of course you can, but why not enjoy letting someone else do it?" Shane winked at her.

"Hmmm." Adrianna bounced onto the bed when Shane entered the bathroom.

Arms spread wide, Adrianna laid back. Why had Shane brought her?

Three days of absolute hell knowing that Shane was... Damn, she didn't want to think about Shane naked with that woman. Adrianna almost wished he'd not told her and left her at Maon's house.

Almost. A knock sounded at the door. She got up and opened it. A young woman stared at her expectantly.

"I'm the maid, miss."

"Yes. Come in." Adrianna moved out of the maid's way so she could enter the room. "I've never had a maid."

"Oh, well, miss, you let me take care of things." She gave Adrianna an efficient nod.

Unpacking aside, the maid was a godsend. It was the perfect opportunity to find out more about how things worked here. "Can I ask you some questions?"

"Certainly, miss. I'll do my best to answer." The maid focused on Adrianna.

"The only estate I've visited on Tallav has been Ettington. It's much more casual than here." She hesitated, not wanting to give offense.

The maid clasped her hands. "The mistress is very exacting."

While Adrianna considered that remark, it came to her that she'd been rude. With her hand to her chest, she rushed out an apology. "Pardon my manners, my name is Dria."

"Yes, miss." The maid's voice was full of deference.

"And you are..." Adrianna raised her eyebrows, hoping her smile would bridge the gap the maid seemed to perceive between them.

The maid's shoulders relaxed when she returned Adrianna's smile. "You may call me Georgie, miss."

Adrianna felt better at the maid's response. "Well, Georgie, can you tell me what kind of schedule to expect here? When's breakfast and so on."

Georgie began an animated rundown for Adrianna. "Breakfast is a buffet from six until nine in the morning, served in the small dining room. You can come down anytime during those hours. Cook will make you pancakes or an omelet fresh if you prefer. We don't serve luncheon, but offer tea and refreshments at twelve and fifteen in the afternoon. You can have that served wherever you please and is up to you to request. Dinner is served at twenty in the evening in the main dining room. The mistress doesn't dress for dinner, so nicer slacks will do. Except for meals, you really won't have much to worry about."

Adrianna set her hand lightly on Georgie's arm. "Thank you, Georgie. I hope everyone will bear with me while I learn my way around."

"Oh, miss, we're ever so glad to have you with us. Don't let Tucker throw you off. He's that way with everyone but the mistress. Your marshal is the kindest of men. He treats us all so well and never makes extra work for us."

"Yes, he is kind." That was one of the many things Adrianna loved about Shane.

Georgie brought a hand to her cheek. "Look at me talking away. I'd best get started on your luggage."

"Here, let me help you."

Georgie shook her head. "Oh no, miss. That wouldn't be right."

Adrianna clasped her hands together to keep from reaching out to Georgie. "Please allow me. I have nothing to do but read while the marshal is gone."

"Well, all right, but don't tell anyone." Georgie looked down and then back up at Adrianna.

With a friendly smile and wink, Adrianna acknowledged the conspiracy. "Our secret."

While watching Georgie begin to pull clothes from the luggage, Adrianna was glad she'd brought some of her nicer pieces. Georgie hung her blouses, skirts, and slacks in the closet, and Adrianna transferred all her lingerie to a drawer in the dresser.

"Oh, miss, you have such pretty things."

"Thank you, Georgie. Marshal Tiernan purchased them for me. When I came to work for him, I had no wardrobe. He took me shopping and bought me more clothes than I've ever had."

"That sounds like the marshal to me. He always leaves a bonus for the staff when he stays."

Adrianna opened Shane's suitcase, pulled out his underwear and socks, and put them into the draw below hers. When she laid his shirts and slacks on the bed and got farther into the suitcase, she found a canvas bag. Curiosity overcame her. A quick peek showed her he'd packed a few toys. They were an overoptimistic inclusion. She stored the bag in the drawer with his underwear. There was no way she'd be with Shane after he'd had sex with that woman. *Ceana. Her name is Ceana. You can do this.*

The moment they finished unpacking, Shane stepped out of the bathroom, wrapped in a dark blue silk bathrobe that covered him to his knees. Adrianna and Georgie looked up at the same time. Georgie blushed brightly, looked down, and murmured something about returning to help Adrianna prepare for bed. Then she flew to the door and was gone.

"I think you embarrassed her." Adrianna walked toward Shane.

Shane reached out and pinned her hands behind her back. He looked at her. "You're a little pink too. Do I embarrass you?"

"No. Don't you have something tattered and old and nasty you can wear?" Adrianna both hated and loved seeing Shane's muscular lower legs and the V of chest the robe exposed. She flicked her tongue across her lips, craving a taste of Shane's mouth. Why did he have to be so hot? She'd posted the no-sex sign and already regretted it, regretted that this sexy display was all for Ceana.

Shane wrapped his free hand around Adrianna's neck and pulled her tight against him. His hand held her in place, keeping her from turning her face away. His mouth covered hers, searing her lips and making her melt when his tongue thrust into her mouth. Adrianna slid her own tongue against his, enjoying the intensity with which Shane always kissed her. He came up for air and placed his forehead against hers. "That's all yours. I give nothing that's yours to her."

"Good. Just be sure to avoid her fangs." Adrianna didn't care if she sounded snarky.

Shane pulled back and smirked. "Did you just say she had fangs? My Dria who's nice to everyone she meets?"

"Well, she looks rabid. Besides, she's mean to you, and I don't have to be nice to people that are mean to you." She looked directly into his eyes to let him know she meant it.

"No, you don't." He gave her a quick, sweet kiss. "I'll be back later."

"Wake me if I'm asleep." She accompanied her words with an obey-me-or-else look.

"Yes, ma'am. Anything you say, ma'am."

She rapped him on the arm with her fist.

He grinned broadly and kissed her. "Bye."

Adrianna put on the best false smile she could manage when he released her and left the room. Tablet in hand, she sat to read, but after only a few minutes threw it aside to stand and pace. She hated this. Shane had tried to make her feel better before he left, but how could she deal with his feelings of pleasure while he was with Ceana? *Damn.* She couldn't. Time to close down her empathic senses.

15

T he door to Ceana's suite was cracked open, so Shane entered with a short rap. After shutting the door behind him, he scanned the room, but Ceana wasn't there. He removed his robe, slinging it over the back of a red leather side chair. She'd redecorated. Where had she found the funds? The ultrafeminine decor that had matched her mother's cloying style was replaced with sleek black, red, and steel-gray furnishings. When he slid under the soft sheet, he noticed that the wrought-iron headboard had multiple tie-off points in its design. A quick glance at the footboard showed the same thing. Did she know she'd gotten herself the perfect bed for dominating a partner?

What was he doing here? Riordan had called Ceana an evil witch. That only half described her. She was a fucking sex goddess. Every man's dream of perfect physical beauty, but inside she was perverted. Her fierce hatred of all things male was legendary among Tallav's aristocracy. But like a Siren, she still managed to lure the unsuspecting or unbelieving into her bedroom. The woman could use words like a whip, and here he was settling himself in for another round of slice and dice.

His reverie was interrupted by Ceana's appearance. Not saying a word, she approached him, her voluptuous body wrapped in a red silk robe. A sneer marring her face, she wasn't an erotic sight. *More a failed succubus.*

Shane watched while she climbed onto the bed and moved on top of him, straddling him with the sheet between them. She slid her hands into the pockets of her robe and bared her teeth at him. "Ready, lover?" Shane made no response, so she pulled her hands out, put them on either side of his head, and leaned down, bringing her mouth close to his. The spicy musk of her perfume filled his nose. Shane gritted his teeth when she stroked his neck. "So tense. You should really learn to relax."

A slight sting tingled on the right side of his neck. Shane brought his hand up to investigate when the first wisps of wooziness took him. Fuck, she'd doped him. What was it with women spiking him? An attempt to grab her and toss her off was short-circuited by the lethargy taking over his body. In seconds, he found himself unable to move.

Ceana snickered. "Don't worry, darling. It'll wear off in about eight hours. Meanwhile, you and I are going to have a little fun." She slid off him. The mattress moved beneath him when she pulled a duffel bag onto the bed. "Let me show you some of the toys I've bought just for our time together. I've heard you like to beat on women." Her hand slapped his face hard enough to mark him. The blow rocked his head to the side. His guts roiled. Her fingers dug into his cheeks when she turned his face back up. "Not nice!"

Fuck. He wanted to throw the bitch across the room.

With a snigger, she pulled items from the bag, waving them in front of him. A set of cuffs dangled over his nose. "I don't really need to restrain you, but then I wouldn't have the fun of using these delightful things." Cuffs set aside, she waved several more sex toys in his face. "Which of these would you like best? The flogger? The cat? Maybe this crop?"

When she slashed it down on the bed next to his head, the sound reverberated in his ears. Shane fought the paralysis that held him prisoner. Sensations that might have escaped his notice now clamored for his attention. The wrinkles in the sheet beneath him. Ceana's weight pressing down on him. The sweat beading up on his skin. But he couldn't move. He heard the harsh panting sound of Ceana's breathing as though she were working herself into a frenzy. Her overpowering musky scent rankled rather than enthralled. He was running on overdrive, his mind screaming at him to get up, but he couldn't escape.

"No? Why don't we start with these?" She pulled and twisted his nipple and snapped on a clamp. Shane's breathing hitched and froze when the sharp pain hit him. "Did that hurt? Try another." Ready for it this time, Shane breathed through the abrupt bite, his eyes fierce, staring at Ceana. "Not afraid yet? You should be. We're just starting, and we have all night."

ADRIANNA ROLLED OVER IN BED. She'd lain down when she grew tired of pacing and sitting. Despite sinking into luxurious plush comfort, she hadn't slept, spending the hours fermenting a wine of anger and jealousy she'd uncork on Shane when he got back to the room. The clock on the nightstand said it was five in the morning. Why wasn't Shane back? He hadn't planned to stay the night. He damn well better not be cuddling with Ceana.

What are you thinking? Shane is as unhappy with the situation as you are. Her animosity should be directed at the system that made this farce necessary. His mother. And Ceana. She kicked away the covers, preparing to pace again. Her stomach growled.

The staff should be up, making breakfast. Maybe she could go and beg a cup of hot chocolate. After a quick change, she opted to remain barefoot and found her way to the back stairs. The sounds of activity guiding her, she padded along the cool tile hall toward the kitchen. When she approached the door, she heard a loud female voice speaking. "I don't care how many times he comes here, there's not going to be any baby."

Adrianna stopped in her tracks.

"You're letting your jealousy overcome your common sense, Fi. The man has tested fertile, as has the mistress." That sounded like Georgie to Adrianna. Fi must be another servant.

"Perhaps, but the mistress is nobody's fool. She'll run the contract out, take his money, and there will be no baby."

A male voice spoke. "You seem certain."

"I am."

"Why?" he asked.

The woman's response was quieter, but Adrianna could still hear it. "She's got a bottle of those after pills."

"She's swindling the man." Georgie sounded appalled.

"She is. But it wasn't me that told you."

The words of an older-sounding woman routed them from their gossiping. "What are the three of you doing gabbing away? Get to work."

Adrianna took that moment to resume walking and entered the hallway that ran past the pantry. Georgie noticed her. "Do you need something, miss?"

"Yes, Shane hasn't gotten back to the suite, so I thought I'd come down for some hot chocolate. I know I'm early..."

"Let me tell Cook." Georgie turned and walked into the kitchen. Adrianna tagged after her, glancing at the woman and man who'd been speaking. When Georgie realized she'd been followed, she said, "I can bring it up to you when it's ready."

"May I sit here and wait for it? Is there an out-of-the-way spot?"

The cook bustled over. "Certainly you may, miss. Sit right here." She pulled out a stool and patted the seat. "It won't be a minute to heat the milk for your cocoa."

Soon the cook had prepared a tray with a pot of hot chocolate, two cups, and a plate of breakfast pastries. "The extra cup is for the marshal if he's up."

"Thank you." Adrianna reached for the tray.

"Oh! No, miss. Allow me," Georgie said

"I can carry it up."

"I'm sure you can, but it's my job."

Adrianna acquiesced and led Georgie up the main staircase this time. In the suite, Georgie set the tray on a side table by the sofa and chairs. "I'll leave this here. The marshal isn't back yet?" Georgie raised her eyebrows.

"No." Adrianna worried her lower lip.

"Well, I'm sure he'll be back shortly. He's an early riser."

"Hmmm. Yes. Thank you, Georgie." Adrianna gave Georgie a wan smile.

Georgie's forehead furrowed. "Not at all, miss. Remember you can ring me on the pad by the door anytime."

"Yes, thank you." Adrianna watched Georgie open the door and leave. She wandered over and sat on the sofa, curling and uncurling her toes in the carpet beneath her feet. The aroma of warm chocolate pulled her from her thoughts. After pouring herself a cup, she settled to resume waiting.

Half a cup later, a sound at the door got her attention, and she turned to see Shane hobbling into the room.

"What happened?" In an instant, she was at his side. She opened her empathic senses and was nearly knocked over by the onrush of pain, rage, and shame that poured out of Shane.

"Ceana happened." With each step, he muttered an oath under his breath. "Just let me sit for a minute."

Adrianna put her arm around his back to assist him and pulled away, startled when Shane gasped in response. "The bitch hurt you."

"It's nothing. But my feet and legs are killing me." Shane let out a sigh of relief when he sank onto the bed. His head bowed between slumped shoulders, his face covered by his long dark hair. A tremor ran through him. All of Adrianna's anger at Shane was now redirected at Ceana. That bitch would pay for this. Adrianna bent over to examine his feet, gently lifting one, then the other to check the soles. Although a reddish color, they weren't marked.

"Careful. She beat them, and they still hurt like fuck."

"Why didn't you stop her?" Adrianna couldn't believe that while she sat unaware, Shane had been enduring such pain. She should never have shut down her empathic senses. She would have sensed what was happening and stopped it.

Shane shrugged, a muscle twitching in his jaw. "She drugged me so I couldn't move but remained fully aware."

"Damn her." Adrianna rose, her fists clenching.

Shane halted her with a touch.

"No, Adrianna. Don't. It's over. We're leaving. She's breached the contract with this. Let's get out of here. I need to leave. Please don't do anything. Just help me leave."

Adrianna gazed at him, brushing away tears that burned with righteous anger. "All right, but first you need to clean up. Let me run you a bath."

While Shane soaked in the tub, Adrianna made short work of packing their suitcases. After returning to the bathroom, she picked up a cloth and wiped the seeping cuts on his back and chest, trying to be gentle when he flinched with each touch. "Where else did she hurt you?" She was worried about his delicate bits but was afraid to look.

"Butt and thighs, but at least she left my cock and balls alone. Something about them still being necessary." Shane croaked out a mocking laugh.

Adrianna sighed with relief. "Get on your hands and knees, and I'll do your backside."

Shane shifted and rolled over, moving in slow motion like the battered man he was. Adrianna fumed while she cleaned him. When she finished, she helped him up and out of the tub, patting him dry with a soft towel.

"Thanks," Shane said. "Ceana ground some kind of powder into the cuts on my back. It felt like she had doused me with fuel and lit it. It's still burning."

Adrianna muttered curses under her breath, culminating in an exclamation of murderous intent. "I could kill her!" With a mental slap, she reminded herself that ranting took second place to helping Shane. "Here. Let me help you into these clothes. They're the softest I could find." Adrianna helped him don shirt and pants and held his arm while he walked out and sat on the couch. "Georgie brought us some breakfast. Would you like a cup of hot chocolate and a pastry?"

"Not right now." Shane sat with his elbows on his knees, head bent, keeping his tender skin away from the couch.

"Are you going to report this?" Adrianna asked while carefully pulling socks and slippers on his feet.

Shane slumped. "No."

"Why not? What she did is criminal." Adrianna tried to soften her voice from its demanding tone, but when Shane looked at her, his eyes ablaze, she knew she hadn't succeeded.

"Gods. She would just love for me to humiliate myself publicly. It's bad enough she'll be trumpeting the story to all her friends. There's no fucking way I'd give her the satisfaction after what she..." He swallowed hard.

Adrianna winced and turned the conversation in a less painful direction. "Perhaps you can use what I learned this morning against her."

"Mmm?" Shane's head lifted, his face exhausted.

Finished putting on his slippers, she sat on her heels. "I overheard some of the staff talking when I went down for the chocolate. Ceana has been making certain she won't carry your baby by taking after-sex pills."

"What?" Shane straightened. His beaten demeanor was erased by this revelation. Adrianna scrambled back. "That bitch!" He stood up, a wince hitching his face. "Come on."

Adrianna followed behind Shane as he slammed open the door and walked the length of the hall toward Ceana's suite. "Ceana! Get the fuck out here!" When he reached her door, he found it locked and pounded on it. "We need to talk." There was no response, so he pounded again. "The game is over. I know you've been taking morning-after pills. Don't bother to deny it. Get your ass down to the med bed and get your blood tested right now, or I'm filing suit against you." More pounding. "Did you hear me?" He turned, strode past Adrianna, and went down the stairs, continuing to bellow for Ceana.

When he reached the small dining room, he found her seated at the table, sipping a cup of something hot. "I know what you've been up to."

"Stop yelling. The whole house has heard you. Really, darling, did our little session distress you so much you're willing to lie to get out of our contract?" She gave him a cutting pout of a smile.

"Lie! Last night alone is enough to release me from the contract. But morning-after pills! That's fraud."

"Really, darling." She drew a hand around the curve of one ear, making sure her hair was still artfully tousled.

"Cut the crap and get to the med bed." Shane's fists balled at his sides, his fingers flexing open and closed.

Ceana's shoulders tensed, a crack in the nonchalance she'd been affecting. "I will not be forced to defend myself from lies. Lies propagated by that whore of yours, no doubt." Ceana cast a sneering glance at Adrianna.

"I told you not to call her that." Shane's voice was like gravel. "Will you or will you not test your blood for possible drugs? Right now."

Ceana's face went pale. She stood, slamming her hands on the table, and stared him down. "I will not!"

"Fine. We're leaving. You'll hear from my attorney."

"File suit. I'm the aggrieved party. I'll countersue and take you for all you've got." Her shoulders were rigid with self-righteous contempt, her lips a slash of crimson. Hair that had looked golden last night now shone brassy. Thins lines etched her mouth and eyes. "Leave! And don't come back!"

Adrianna wanted to spit her animosity at Ceana. Instead, in the most businesslike manner she could summon, she said, "Your services are no longer required. If word of this incident spreads, we will seek recompense in kind."

Ceana sneered at her and said, "A whore like you doesn't worry me."

"Be that as it may, you should be aware that I've trained under one of the sector's top sadists. I've learned things you've never even dreamed of. And I'd be happy to demonstrate my expertise on that aging carcass of yours." Adrianna turned her back on Ceana, ignoring the spate of curses and threats that spewed from her, welcoming the spark of confidence she felt ignite in Shane.

Shane addressed Tucker, who had come into the room after Shane and placed himself in a position to defend his mistress. "Our bags are ready in our suite. Please see that the car is brought around and our luggage loaded. We'll wait on the front steps." He took Adrianna's hand. "Come, Dria. I'm sorry you had to be subjected to this finer side of matriarchal society."

SHANE DIDN'T REMEMBER the drive to Ettington, but he did it at a speed that shaved off an hour's worth of travel time. Adrianna hadn't batted an eye. They hadn't talked. Shane had no desire to rehash the events. Thinking about it was humiliating enough. Adrianna's words with Ceana had sparked a need to act instead of huddling in misery.

When they arrived at the estate, Maon met them on the front drive, an expression of concern on his face while he watched Shane walk with slow, careful steps across the courtyard to the front entrance. "I've called your dad. He wants to speak with you as soon as you get here."

Shane made his way inside to a chair in the living room before he responded. "I suppose it is time to get Dad and Mother involved."

Adrianna moved an ottoman to the chair so he could raise his feet. "I'm going to the kitchen and make ice packs for your feet."

"Thanks, Dria."

After she left the room, Maon asked, "What happened to your feet?"

Shane's arms dropped down the sides of the chair. If he kept it brief, maybe the telling wouldn't shatter him again. "Ceana beat the soles. She drugged me and then brought out her bag of sex toys. I think nearly every part of my body hurts. As soon as I finish with my dad, I need to visit your med bed."

Maon crossed his arms. "I can't believe her arrogance. Does she really think she can get away with treating you like that?"

"She must."

"What are you going to do about it?"

"I'm going to get the contract voided and get my money back."

"You're not having her charged?"

"Gods, no. Besides, Dria discovered Ceana's been taking morning-after pills to avoid getting pregnant."

Maon's jaw dropped. "That makes no sense."

Baffled, Shane rubbed his index finger on his forehead, unable to think of a reason for Ceana's actions other than outright animosity. Was fucking up his life more important to Ceana than the money? "This morning she had the temerity to accuse Dria of lying and refused to submit to a med test, which is practically an admission of guilt. I don't think she has a clue about how the legal system actually works."

Maon shook his head, voicing Shane's confusion. "I don't get why she'd take the contract and then make certain she didn't fulfill it. She needed the money, but with no baby, she makes far less money. It's not logical."

"No, it's not logical. She's closed off parts of the house because she doesn't have the staff to keep it up, and it's still decorated in her mother's taste for nouveau gewgaw, all frills and ornamentation. She's farmed her father out to live with his sister and sold all of his racehorses because she can't afford their upkeep." He paused, frowning. "But you know; she had her bedroom redecorated this time. I wonder where she got the money for that. The bed itself had to have put her back quite a bit, and the chairs were all done in red leather. Expensive stuff."

"Something's going on. You'll be requesting a fraud investigation, won't you?"

"Absolutely."

Maon paced the width of the room. "Let me get started on that. I'll look into her bank accounts and see where she's been getting her money. Go ahead and call your dad. You remember where the med bed is when you're finished."

"Thanks." Shane waited while Maon left and Adrianna returned with two bags of ice and towels to wrap them in.

He reached to take off his boots, but Adrianna shooed him away. She carefully removed his boots and socks and placed a bag against the sole of each foot. "Is that too cold?"

The ice was an instant relief to the swollen heat of his feet. "No, it's perfect." He clasped her forearm. "Thank you, Dria. And thank you for standing up for me back there."

"I should have known what she was doing to you." Adrianna's lips were curled down; her shoulders slumped.

"No. It's not your fault." He stroked her hair, saddened that she felt in any way responsible.

"I shut down my empathic senses because I was jealous. I didn't want to sense it if you were enjoying yourself."

"Dria." He lifted her chin. "If I'd thought of it, I'd have told you to do just that. I never want you to be hurt by anything I do. It wasn't your fault."

Adrianna bit her lip. "It wasn't your fault either."

Shane grimaced. "I know. It's taking my guts longer to realize that." After a long sigh, he said, "Would you get me my tablet, please?"

Adrianna nodded, bending over him to give him a gentle kiss before handing it to him.

"Thanks, Dria."

"My pleasure." She sat on the floor next to the chair and ottoman, leaning so she didn't touch any of the sore places scattered over his body.

When the tablet made the connection to his dad's comm line, Shane switched the audio from speaker to his internal receiver. "Hi, Dad."

"It's good to hear your voice, Son. Maon told me you've had a spot of trouble. Are you okay?"

"Yes, I'm fine. How are you and Mother?"

"We're both doing well," his father said.

"That's good. I miss you both."

"It's been a while. How are things with you?"

"Well, as Maon would say, I've been stirring up the fire crickets."

"No one's better at stirring up fire crickets."

Shane chuckled at his father's response. "Yeah, I guess I am good at that. I've run into a problem."

Shane explained the circumstances and trouble he was having with Ceana. "I didn't tell Mother because I wanted it to be a surprise. A baby, I mean, not this mess.

"There's more, Dad." His body tensed, and he shut his eyes while he detailed Ceana's attack.

He was grateful that his father just listened, and when Shane finished, his father quietly said, "I'm sorry, Son. That was a terrible experience. That it happened says nothing about you and everything about her. Don't let this affect who you are inside."

"Yes, sir. Thank you. I won't." Exhaustion beat at Shane.

Shane listened while his father told him he would talk to his mother and asked him to plan to visit them in Cahernamon the next day.

"If you think she'll have us, I'd be glad to come to the city. My new assistant is with me. I've got a couple of days left before I need to resume the investigation I'm working on."

"It's time you and your mother worked out your problems."

Shane took a deep breath. "All right, we'll be there."

"Take care."

"Yes. I will. Love you, Dad. Bye."

Shane closed out the call while stroking Adrianna's hair. "We're going to Cahernamon."

"So I heard. Not Gleann Milis?"

Shane pressed his lips together briefly. "No, my parents aren't at the estate. They're in the city."

"Hmm. Let's get you into the med bed and see if it can dose you with something that will get you on your feet faster."

Shane grunted in the affirmative.

SHANE HAD FALLEN asleep within minutes of taking the meds prescribed by the med bed. He'd stripped, climbed in bed, and snuggled up to Adrianna after demanding she join him. When he woke, she wasn't beside him any longer. He sat up and found her sitting across the room, reading her tablet. He ran a hand through his hair. "What time is it?"

She looked up and smiled. "It's just eight. You slept the rest of yesterday away. You have plenty of time before we leave. How do you feel?"

He moved to sit on the side of the bed and tested putting pressure on his feet. *No pain.* With a groan ending in a whoosh of air, he arched his back in a full stretch.

"I'm ready to go."

"Excellent." Adrianna rose and walked toward him. "I've packed our bags. Let's get you in the shower. There are biscuits and gravy available for breakfast."

When she neared him, Shane reached out, grabbed her, and tossed her onto the bed. Just what he needed. He pinned beneath him. "Getting bossy, aren't you, Adrianna?"

A smile quivering at the corner of her lips, she responded, "Yes, Sir. Forgive me, Sir."

"Clothes off. Shower. Now." He moved off her so she could comply. His growling commands hadn't seemed to worry her.

His initial reaction to Ceana's attack had been humiliation. He'd mired himself in a mantra of verbal abuse. *Helpless. Weak. Pathetic.* But he'd be damned if that woman's trick would define who he was. He wasn't powerless. Or toothless like she'd taunted. Right now, he would remind himself of his own natural dominance and that women existed who appreciated it.

Adrianna dropped her clothes on the floor as she took each item off on the way to the shower, looking over her shoulder to give him a cheeky grin.

He leered back, enjoying Adrianna's mischievous side. "Oh, don't worry. I'm already planning to punish you." He rummaged through his toy bag until he found the set of cuffs he was searching for. Waterproof with a chain long enough to allow Adrianna to plant her hands on the side of the shower, they were the perfect implement for today.

When he entered the bathroom, Adrianna was on her knees. *Fuck Ceana! This is a real woman.* He was free of the bitch, and his own sweet submissive was here, ready to offer herself completely to him. Her hair streamed loose around her shoulders, waves framing her breasts. Her nipples were tipped up at a delectable angle. His semierection took notice, growing longer and harder.

"Stand, Adrianna."

In moments, the cuffs were on her wrists and the spray set to the right temperature. He gathered the cascade of her hair, letting the dark strands slide through his fingers. With a tug, he brought her torso against his, kissing her silky shoulder. Everything about her was flawless, from her citrusy scent to the supple lines of her body.

After nipping his favorite spot at the juncture of her neck and shoulder, he pulled back. "Look at me, Adrianna." When her eyes met his, he grinned and chuckled. "We're celebrating, a mhuirnín. Well, I'm celebrating. You're being punished." He paused, smirking at her before taking her lips in a brutal kiss. Her arms flew around his neck in a tight embrace. She welcomed his rough demand with equal intensity, tangling her tongue with his.

He broke the kiss, allowing the satisfaction that flowed from deep in his heart to saturate her, knowing she experienced every emotion he felt. He chuckled again at her dazed expression. "My baby makers are all mine again. And I intend to distribute them soon. You, however, are not allowed to come. Do you understand? Not at all."

"Yes, Master." A look of chagrin crossed her face. She hadn't expected this, he could tell. But she didn't fight him. She wouldn't.

"Into the shower." He turned her away from him, pulled her cuffed wrists overhead, and attached the chain connecting the cuffs to a hook on the shower wall. The warm water streamed down his back while he ran his hands along her sides, briefly stopping to reach around and squeeze her breasts before moving to stroke her bottom. He loved her ass. "Your ass was one of the first things I noticed about you. Round and soft and full." He squeezed roughly.

"Oh." The exclamation popped out of Adrianna.

"Don't hold back, Adrianna. You know I love to listen to you respond to me."

"Yes, Master." She sighed long and slow, the sound zinging straight to his cock.

He reached up and changed the chain length on the cuffs, allowing Adrianna's hands to lower enough to let her bend over at the waist. The sight of her, water spraying across her backside, sent his arousal into over-drive. With one hand, he pulled her back against his groin while he swept the other between her legs, massaging her mound. The moan that slid past Adrianna's lips when he delved, seeking and finding her clit, was the perfect encouragement. Her hips began to roll, rubbing against his cock. Damn, if she kept that up, this would be over much too quick.

"Hold still."

With a groan, she ceased the delicious motion, momentarily stiffening before she relaxed, losing herself again in his sensual assault.

"That's right, Adrianna. Enjoy this, but remember, no coming."

She trembled against him. He brushed his smiling lips along her back before he planted kisses and long strokes of his tongue along her spine. Her skin was the perfect combination of sweet and salty. With the tip of his tongue he traced a line along the back edge of her armpit, nipping and sucking at the spot where her arm began.

"Oh, *mon dieu!*"

He nuzzled her shoulder. "You like that?"

"Yes," she said with a hiss.

He trailed his fingers from her hip to her breast and tweaked her nipple. The shudder that ran through her body caressed the muscles of his torso. He pulled his hand away. "Too much, sweetling? Will this help?" With his thumb and forefinger, he pinched her below the swell of her butt cheek.

Adrianna jumped and bleated. "Ack!"

He chuckled and then soothed the sting with a few soft strokes, staring at her bottom the whole time. Unable to resist, he smacked her right cheek. She gasped.

"It's too bad you can't see how perfectly your ass jiggles when I spank you."

He smacked her left cheek, water spattering from under his hand. A groan welled up from his gut. "Just like that."

Adrianna's voice was low and breathy. "Thank you, Master."

While he continued spanking her, alternating sides, a rosy blush bloomed beneath the rivulets of water spilling over her bottom. He loved taking her from behind, hips slapping against that gorgeous rear end. If he fucked her now, it wouldn't be long before she came around his cock.

Wasn't happening. This wasn't about how good her body felt when she shattered with him deep inside her. His dominant nature was demanding primacy. He would show Adrianna—and more importantly, reassert for himself—the sexual control he wielded with his bedmates.

"Time to get fucked, Adrianna."

"Yes, please, Master. Please fuck me."

Voice stern, he reminded her. "Remember. You do not have permission to come."

Her panting mewl was music to his ears. "My orgasms belong to you alone. Use me, please."

"I intend to. Use your safe word if you need to. I won't be holding back."

He gripped her hips tight, pulling her up, his cock rubbing her slit until he found her opening. He surged forward and impaled her with one push. Snug, wet heat engulfed him, the sensation adding to his overwhelming need to fuck her and fuck her hard. He ground his hips, plunging into her, taking her, smacking splashes of water marking the rhythm of his forceful thrusts. Tight friction urged him inexorably toward climax.

Through gritted teeth, he asked, "Who am I, Adrianna?"

Adrianna panted her response, one word bursting from her lips in a mantra. "Master. Master. Master."

The point of no return arrived in moments.

"Take it, Adrianna. Take it now."

His mind froze. His body lit off like a firework in frenzied explosions of sensation. His hot cum spurted deep inside her three times and then a fourth. He clasped her tight in his arms, savoring her sensuous grace while his body continued to shudder even after his cock stopped spasming. When he regained the ability to move, he straightened, keeping one arm around her while he undid the chain and removed the cuffs.

Adrianna turned. He closed his eyes, steeped in afterglow. The woodsy smell of his favorite shower gel wafted up. Her dexterous hands lathered his body, sliding over him in a soothing rhythm. Most of the cuts Ceana had inflicted with her metal-tipped cat didn't hurt now. Once done rinsing him, Adrianna asked, "May I wash your hair, Master?"

He didn't respond but got to his knees, holding her so her belly brushed his nose. Despite the steam beading up and dribbling down the walls of the shower, her scent was clear and strong. He leaned his head back to let her shampoo and rinse his hair. Then he returned to nuzzling her stomach. Approval thrummed through him. Could there be a submissive more suited to him? Not possible. Adrianna was everything he needed. Her body trembled at his next rumbled command.

"Back up and brace yourself."

He moved her backward out of the water flowing over her abdomen. With one arm, he reached between her legs and lifted her thigh over his shoulder.

He found the path between her lower lips with his tongue, alternating long, slow slides with quick little flicks. She tasted like nothing else, intoxicating, addicting. He switched to pulses against her clit while working his fingers into her vagina, pumping and curling them to stroke the sensitive spot inside her. He pulled back, his eyes feasting on her. Leaned against the wall with her eyelids closed, Adrianna's chest was flush with the bloom of passion. His breath caught at the wonder of how exquisite she was. Fuck, he was glad she was his.

"You may come now, Adrianna."

She lifted her lids to look at him, her breasts moving in a mesmerizing up-and-down jiggle, keeping time with her panting. "Thank you, Master."

Shane returned to his ministrations, fingers pumping into her while his tongue rubbed back and forth across her engorged clit. Her muscles tightened, her mumblings and cries sharpening his need to bring her to release. Each gasp, each sigh, was like a salve to his brutalized pride. At last, her inner muscles clasped tight around his fingers when she crested the peak and plunged deep into pleasure, every part of her quivering.

He pulled his fingers free and lapped her slit with long swipes, letting his tongue slide into her and pull up to stroke her clit. When her orgasm diminished and she was quiet, he stopped and stood, enveloping her in his arms, kissing her with a ruthless efficiency. Adrianna sucked his tongue in hard and reached to clasp his erection, which was extended firm and hot against her stomach.

"You must be a witch. You're the only woman I want to fuck right after fucking you."

With a mysterious smile, she knelt and her mouth closed over the head of his cock, sucking him in deeper while her tongue massaged the underside.

"Oh fuck, that's good, Adrianna. Yes, just like that." Her tongue swirled around the tip each time she slid his cock from her mouth, only to plunge his erection to the back of her throat. Shane thrust his hips in rhythm with her and then faster, urging her to speed up when the wave of his own orgasm flooded toward release. He clasped her head tight, his balls drawing up while he resisted as long as he could. When she scraped her teeth along the top of his cock while fluttering her tongue along the bottom, he couldn't hold back. He groaned, his cum shooting down her throat. He flinched when she sucked dry his now tender cock and gave him one last swirl with her tongue.

"You might kill me, but I hope not before we do a lot more of that." Shane pulled her up and kissed her. He turned and rinsed his cock and balls off. "Clean yourself up. If I don't get out of this shower now, we might never leave for Cahernamon."

"Yes, Master. Maybe you should lie down to recover." Adrianna looked at him, all innocence.

Shane growled and said, "You liked your punishment? Huh?" With a smack to her butt, he exited the shower. The humiliation he'd been feeling had eased into the background. He would let the anger that still churned inside him focus his determination to make Ceana pay for what she'd done to him.

ince they were headed to Cahernamon, Shane decided not to rehash their plans with Maon, happy to leave the preoperation details to him so Shane could focus on personal matters with his parents. Maon would come into the city for the final briefings.

As Shane watched the numbers change over the doors of the lift while they sped upward, he wrestled with a case of nerves he hadn't expected. The closer they got to his mother's city apartment, the less settled his stomach became.

It had been over two years since he'd last spoken with his mother, and those had been angry words. The role of dutiful Tallavan son wasn't natural to him. Not the Tallavan part, anyway. Soon after his brother's death, he'd conceded the need to sacrifice his work with the Marshals and tried to find a Tallavan wife that fit his mother's strictures. She didn't believe he'd really tried, convinced he was placing personal desires above familial duties, accusing him of sabotaging each potential relationship. In a furious confrontation, he'd told her he'd had enough. For all he cared, the estate could go to Aunt Callie and her heirs. His mother's face had been nearly purple with rage when she'd told him to leave. He was cut off. No longer a son in her eyes.

He'd also be introducing Adrianna. Her presence was a clear signpost he'd moved on with his life and didn't plan to marry a Tallavan first-family aristocrat. Still, his mother had to be mollified by his attempt to provide her an heir, despite the mess it had become.

He wanted his parents to like Adrianna. She was beautiful, intelligent, and confident, everything most Tallavan mothers desired in a daughter. The rumors surrounding Adrianna and himself would not faze his mother. Long ago, she'd learned that where her son was concerned, exaggeration ran rampant. However, she also knew that behind all the hyperbole there was an element of truth. He hoped his mother would accept Adrianna. Even more, he yearned for his mother to respect his—his what? Adrianna was more than his assistant now, but he couldn't call her his collared submissive to his mother.

His thoughts were interrupted when the lift reached his parents' floor. In just a few steps, Shane was knocking. He rolled his shoulders and gave Adrianna a forced smile just before the door opened.

"Shane!" His father backed up a step to allow them to enter and shut the door behind them. "Son, let me look at you." He held Shane at arm's length and then tugged him forward into a big hug. "So glad you're here."

The embrace went a long way to filling the void in Shane's heart. "It's good to be here, Dad. I've missed you." His father was just as he always had been, blue eyes alight with an inner kindness. A steadying presence in Shane's life. Relief eased the knot in his stomach.

His dad pulled back and placed a palm to Shane's cheek. "Your mother and I've missed you too." His eyes turned to Adrianna when he stepped away. "Who's this?" He reached out to her.

"Dad, this is Adrianna Pacquin, my assistant. Adrianna, my father, Pádraig," Shane watched, shifting from one foot to the other while his father greeted Adrianna. His mother had missed him? That was a positive sign, wasn't it? Still she hadn't tried to contact him.

"Hello, my dear." Pádraig's smile was warm, an expression of the kind-hearted father Shane loved.

Adrianna visibly relaxed at Pádraig's friendly greeting. "It's so good to meet you, sir."

"Please, no sir, call me Pádraig."

"Of course. And please call me Dria."

His father's nod of acceptance encompassed more than just calling her

Dria. He motioned them to follow him. "Come. Your mother is in the living room."

Shane straightened his shoulders before following his father, Adrianna at his side. His mother sat on an elegant camelback sofa, her slender figure swathed in a subdued lavender wrap dress that fell to her knees, her dark brown hair pulled back into a soft chignon. Gray streaked it; this sign that she was aging took Shane aback. She rose when they entered the room. Shane went to her, holding both hands out. His mother reached for them, taking them in her own hands. She kissed him on the cheek, offering him no more than good manners dictated. Her greeting was a far cry from the bear hugs she used to give him.

Her gaze wandered to Adrianna. "Who have you brought with you?"

"Mother, this is Adrianna Pacquin. Adrianna, my mother Breda Tiernan. Adrianna is my assistant."

While the two women shook hands, nerves itched along his spine, feathering across his chest.

Adrianna took the introduction to a more intimate level. "I've asked Shane's father to call me Dria. I hope you will as well."

"Thank you, my dear. Let's sit. Shane, join us on the sofa. Dria, if you'd like, you can wait in the library," his mother suggested in an imperious tone of voice.

Shane's jaw tensed, but he forced himself to remain calm. "Have a seat there." He pointed Adrianna to a chair, part of the sofa's seating arrangement. "She'll be staying with us, Mother."

His mother's eyes narrowed slightly. "Certainly."

When Adrianna had seated herself, Shane sat next to his father, his mother on the opposite end of the sofa.

"Your father tells me this unexpected visit is the result of your dealing with Ceana Kendrith. I'm happy you're once again taking your familial duties seriously, but Ceana Kendrith. Really? She made it clear before she'd have nothing to do with you, so it must be money she's after. What have you done to ruin your chances with her?" His mother's gaze wandered up and down Adrianna, leaving no doubt that she believed Adrianna was the cause of Shane's troubles.

Pádraig interceded with a gentle voice. "Breda, I told you this is not about Shane marrying Ceana Kendrith. Please let him explain."

Shane's heart swelled at the support his father never failed to grant him.

His mother raised an eyebrow at him. "Explain then."

ADRIANNA SAT BACK, silently listening to Shane while he talked with his parents. Even without her empathic senses, she wouldn't have missed the animosity Shane's mother directed her way. During Shane's interaction with his mother, Adrianna's muscles had tightened. Springing to his defense wouldn't help matters.

Shane was trying hard to keep his frustration in check. Not an easy task. Adrianna understood. This conflict was the root of the darkness he hid inside himself, of the anger he fought to control. His mother wasn't making it easy on him.

"Mother." Shane ducked his head, took a deep breath, and looked at Breda. "I regret the way we parted last time. I said things I shouldn't have. Things I didn't mean. Thomas's death affected all of us profoundly." He pressed his eyelids closed, bringing his hand to his face to pinch his nose. With a sigh, he opened his eyes to continue. "I should have taken more time before I jumped into wife hunting. I wasn't emotionally in a good place." His gaze dropped to stare at his index finger rubbing the top of his knee. "On top of..." He cleared his throat. "I was losing the career I loved. It felt like almost everything I held dear was being taken away from me." Another sigh escaped. "It's no wonder I was rejected on all sides. I don't doubt I acted like the beast I was labeled."

After several moments of expectant silence, Shane straightened his shoulders, pulling his hand back from his knee and fisting it. "I've had time to consider what happened and where to go from here." His head rose, and he looked straight into his mother's eyes. "One good thing came from all that. It helped me focus on what I did want, including what I wanted with you and Dad. I don't want to be banished from your lives."

Breda sat still through Shane's admission, hands clasped in her lap. When Shane spoke of losing everything he held dear, her eyes began to glisten. Adrianna could sense that Breda's resentment, much like Shane's anger, covered her own wounds. They had both been grieving, both afraid of losing something that was very important to them, and both struggling to do the right thing as they perceived it. A rupture in their relationship had been inevitable. Those unshed tears glistening in Breda's eyes were a sign that reconciliation was possible, if after this time apart, she was willing to compromise for her son's happiness. For Shane's sake, Adrianna hoped so.

Breda turned her head down and to the side away from Shane. Pádraig placed his hand over Breda's. "Son, we don't want you missing from our lives either. Do we, Breda?"

Breda lifted her head, her rapidly blinking eyes unable to hold back the small tear that slipped down her cheek. "Sha—" Her voice broke. "Shane. If I pushed too hard too soon, I apologize. I want you to be happy." More tears fell. "I love you." Pádraig handed her a handkerchief, which she used to dab her face. "We will find a solution we can both accept."

"I'm sorry I'm not Thomas," Shane said.

"No, you are not Thomas. There was only one Thomas, and I shouldn't have tried to force you into his mold."

Shane's countenance fell. He studied his hands, his shoulders slumping.

His mother reached across and clasped his hand. "No, Shane. I am just as proud of you as I was of Thomas. You were never second place in my heart. The two of you were different but equal. Never think you were second best."

Shane's eyes rose, his lips pressed together as though he were restraining all the emotion that threatened to burst from him. He gave a quick nod.

"So, tell me about Ceana Kendrith."

Shane sighed. In flat, unvarnished statements, he explained his plan for siring an heir and Ceana's role in it. When Breda had heard Shane out, she shook her head. "I wish you had talked to me before entering a contract with her. I would have told you it was an atrocious idea. She's a manipulative, greedy liar, and you would have tied yourself and me to her for years. Her demand for natural conception is a dead giveaway she was up to something. The possibility of a male child alone makes the stipulation ludicrous."

"She was up to something," Shane admitted. "Adrianna overheard the servants gossiping. Ceana's been taking morning-after pills to avoid pregnancy. I can't figure out why. And on top of that, yesterday she drugged me so I couldn't move but was physically aware of everything she did to me. I don't want to go into the details, but legally she assaulted me and could be charged."

Pádraig said, "I'd rather your mother not be subjected to what you told me over the phone either, Shane." With a look at Breda, he said, "I know. I know. You don't like me being protective. Trust me. It will only bring you grief."

"The contract can be voided because of the fraud. I don't want the scandal that pressing criminal assault charges would create," Shane said.

Breda's steely blue eyes turned from the battle of wills she engaged in with her husband. "I will contact my lawyers to get the ball moving on a civil complaint. I assume you've already filed a criminal complaint against Ceana?"

"Yes, I did that with the garda in Cahernamon while I was still at Maon's. Maon is already working to get a look at her finances and comm records. If she's hiding something, he'll find it."

"Excellent. Once we clear this matter up, we will discuss the proper way to engage a woman of good standing to carry an heir for the family."

Shane gave a nod of chagrin.

"It's time for a late lunch. Will the two of you join us? And plan to stay with us while you're here?" Breda asked.

Shane looked at Adrianna. "We'd be delighted."

Adrianna felt like one big happy smile. She was so pleased that Shane was resolving the conflict with his mother. Shane's life was looking better.

Pádraig's eyes met Adrianna's with an animated gleam when he offered her his hand to rise. "You must tell me how Shane has been treating you. I raised him to be a gentleman, and I would hate to hear he's slipping from his training." His gentle smile told Adrianna he wasn't seriously in doubt.

"From what I can see, he's the best of you both. I am blessed to know him."

"Perhaps you are both blessed." He gave her hand a soft pat.

Breda Tiernan was an intense woman. During the drive to the restaurant and while they ate, the focus of her attention rarely diverted to Shane or her husband. Adrianna responded as she imagined a planarian might while waiting under a magnifying glass, eyespots staring up as the scalpel descended. Breda's gaze was that piercing. Nothing escaped her notice, including the way Shane touched Adrianna's arm more than six times since they'd been seated. Breda must know that touch was an unconscious need for Shane. He loved to touch and be touched on the purely physical level, but it also offered him a sense of connection. So he'd been touching Adrianna, and Breda had noticed.

When the meal was finished but the desserts were yet to arrive, Breda turned to Adrianna. "Time for a visit to the women's room. Would you join me, Dria?" She didn't mean it as a request. Adrianna accepted immediately.

Breda pointed Adrianna to take a seat at the dressing table in the lounge of the restroom. Adrianna assured herself that no one was in the room before sitting.

Breda scrutinized her, looking neither pleased nor displeased. "You haven't known Shane long."

"No, not long." This was a little like answering Marshal Riordan's questions after Shane was attacked. Direct.

"May I be so pointed as to ask, what are your intentions toward my son?"

Definitely direct. How should she handle this? She began slowly, "He is my employer—"

Breda made a motion with her hand, waving aside Adrianna's words. "Yes, but you are also lovers."

Adrianna narrowed her eyes. "True. That is part of my employment contract."

Breda's response was sharp. "Don't play games with me. It is more than that, and we both know it."

Adrianna gave Breda a curt nod. "Yes, it is more than that. I love your son."

Breda lifted her chin, using silence to try to discompose Adrianna. "I see. Were you planning to parlay your contract into a permanent relationship with my son?"

Adrianna said, "No, ma'am. Before meeting your son, I had no such plan..."

Breda began to interrupt, but Adrianna continued in steady even tones. "And since then, I have made no such plan. I am fully aware that your permission is required for Shane to marry an off worlder, and that you will not give it while you remain without an heir. Shane will not disappoint you in that. Family is very important to him. I envy him his relationship with you and his father. It is something I no longer have. I would never force him to choose between his family and me."

Breda again attempted to speak.

"Please, hear me out. Secondary considerations make my remaining with Shane more than two years impossible. I must repay the debt I owe to the Opio Institute for the training I received. Shane told me he cannot afford to pay for more than this year and one additional year of my service, and I cannot pay off the loan without working. So you see; marriage or any other arrangement under such conditions is not an option."

"I see. Thank you, my dear, for being candid." Breda's features softened. "Yet you love my son."

"Yes. I do." Adrianna worked to control the strong emotions pushing past the surface. "He accepts me for who I am. Please understand. I can tell when someone is using me for their own purposes. Shane is different. When I am with him, I feel his care, his need to protect and honor me. I feel cherished, and that feeling... I don't think I could live without it. But I would do anything for him, including leaving him if it were the best thing."

Breda reached out and patted Adrianna's hand. "I understand, my dear. You are very much like Pádraig. He's devoted to making my life perfect. Shane, on the other hand, is more like me." Breda's gaze stared unfocused at her reflection in the mirror while she explained. "Tallav was founded as a matriarchy. Women in charge, resilient and creating a society based on female strengths. Our founders were such strong women, and yet they couldn't seem to imagine that strong women would bear strong sons. They saw only a future of strong daughters. We've created outlets, but it isn't enough for men like Shane." Her gaze sought Adrianna's. "I am glad he has found you."

"I am too," Adrianna responded, voice soft.

"You are an interesting young woman. I had you vetted by my legal team. To be honest, I couldn't believe anyone with your background could have amounted to much. Furzine isn't noted for producing strong, confident women. It's a male-dominated society in the worst patriarchal way. But you are the granddaughter of Élise Sauveterre. And although she is an off worlder, she is a woman of substance. As is your mother, who rebelled in her own way against the mores of her patriarchal society. You come from the right kind of women. If Shane had to fall in love with an off worlder, you are perhaps the ideal candidate."

"Thank you." What else could Adrianna say? She didn't really consider Furzine or Preatiens patriarchal societies, but she wouldn't contradict Shane's mother.

"He doesn't realize he loves you, you know. But it's clear to both his father and me." Pain welled up in her eyes. "Don't take him from us. Please."

Shaken by the power of the woman's emotions, Adrianna reached out and took her hand. "As I said, I would never force him to choose between his family and me."

Breda nodded, pulled her hand out from under Adrianna's, and patted it. "Thank you, my dear." She sat back and straightened her shoulders. "Come. Let us go back to the men."

While they wound their way to their table, Adrianna mused on life's vagaries. If she'd been born on Tallav, she and Shane would have no problem marrying. But then she might have been a completely different woman.

THE LAST SEVERAL days on Tallav had been interesting ones. Between becoming further acquainted with Shane's parents and spending more time with him, Adrianna had a better understanding of Shane. It had been a lot of fun practicing her weapons skills at the Marshals' firing and training range. He'd even been allowed to take her through the threat simulation course three times. After that, he'd presented her with her own weapon, an ankle holster, and a jacket with a concealed carry sleeve inside. She was set for Runner's Hub.

As the director strode into the conference room, Adrianna refocused her attention on the people sitting around the large table with her. This team would support them at Runner's Hub. The director greeted them and got the session underway. She was glad to be included at last. Shane had insisted.

"Good morning. Let's make this as quick as possible. No rehashing decisions already made unless there's some new aspect that changes the situation. Agreed?" The director looked around the table. "Good. Ms. Pacquin, glad you could join us. Everyone should have received the latest status updates. I want to remind you we have three objectives. The first, to remove Runner's Hub once again as an illegal human trafficking transshipping point. The second, prevent the Furzian Benefactor from gaining a foothold into the Preatien system. The third, to keep Ms. Pacquin safe and out of his hands." He waved his hand in her direction when he stated the last goal. "We'll start with the first. Shirley?"

"Yes, sir," Maon said. "As you read in the update, we believe we've found the means the Benefactor is using to blackmail Marge Boleo at Runner's Hub. He or his underlings now own majority stock in the company Astro Tex that provides the Hub with cheap fuel. Astro Tex has a monopoly on the raw resources and refineries that produce C-trol in the Hub's system. Continued purchase of the fuel is contingent on the Hub allowing illegal human trafficking to operate through it. Other sources are too far away to be cost-effective. We plan to move to take over the company using a private individual or in this case a consortium from Preatiens put together by Élise Sauveterre. Does anyone see any problems?"

The sector chief, John Hayden, shifted in his seat. "As I understand it, you intend this to be a stealth operation with the consortium buying up to twenty percent of stock from individual investors and thirty-five percent from Jason Holmes of Canthis. I guess my two concerns are even if you get Holmes to sell because of the child trafficking info you've dug up on his business, the investors will still need sixteen percent of the individually owned stock to manage a takeover. Also, what happens if the Benefactor discovers the takeover attempt and buys out the individual stockholders before we can?"

Maon nodded as though he'd expected just such a question. "The plan is to make an above-value offer to the individual stockholders contingent on them remaining silent. The bid will come from an investment firm located out of sector, making it harder for anyone here to find out about it.

It will also make it difficult to associate it with anyone on Preatiens. The move on Holmes won't be made until the investors already have sixteen percent of the stock."

"And you're sure you can guarantee his cooperation?" Hayden asked.

"Absolutely. Either way he turns, he's in hot water because the facts we will present him with are real. It will be his choice to face arrest for child trafficking or face the wrath of the Benefactor for selling him out. We're betting he won't want the Benefactor to find out about the child trafficking. A quick death being better than torture followed by death. Child trafficking is apparently anathema in the Benefactor's world of exploitation and depravity. With the Astro Tex Company in the hands of the Preatien consortium, fuel from the F8 system refineries will be available to the Hub with the concomitant incentives toward good behavior rather than bad."

Shane said, "Although the Benefactor will be led to believe that I'm the one holding the controlling interest in Astro Tex. I'll be demanding my cut of his operations through the Hub. He'll have to come to the Hub to meet with me."

"Does that satisfy you, John?" the director asked. Hayden pursed his lips and nodded. "Okay. Any questions about the second or third objectives? I assume that Élise Sauveterre is still involved in this part of the operation?"

Shane's response was brisk. "Yes, she is. She's agreed to meet the Benefactor on the Preatien space station. She's adamant about not allowing his shuttle to land on planet. As we've discussed, whatever he has planned, it involves Ms. Pacquin. She'll be with me on the Hub, and once the Benefactor has struck a deal with me over trafficking operations, I'm sure he'll demand her use against Sauveterre. Which I will grant, but only under the condition that Ms. Pacquin remain with me and travel aboard *Adrasteia*.

"I won't let her out of my sight. Letting him get his hands on her is out of the question. We can't be certain he'd take her to Preatiens, and even if he did, that's days she'd be in his hands."

"I understand your concerns, Tiernan," the director said. "We will do everything we can to keep Ms. Pacquin safe. You've established excellent pretexts for keeping her with you. The Benefactor will want to stay on your good side because of the fuel issue."

Shane nodded, his gaze focused on the table before him. "Yes, sir. As I said, the only way Ms. Pacquin will be going to Preatiens on the Benefactor's behest will be with me on board the *Adrasteia*. Otherwise, with your approval, I will end the operation."

The director eyed Shane. "If we weren't hoping to discover the details of the Benefactor's plans for Preatiens, she wouldn't even be going with you to the Hub. If you believe he's moving to take her, by all means, pull out. However, you and she knew from the start there would be a certain level of danger. We've put plans in place on Preatiens. If he takes her to Furzine, the marshals there will attempt to intercept him on the space station. Don't second-guess yourself now. You've covered all likely possibilities."

"Yes, sir."

The anxiety coming from Shane didn't lessen. Adrianna wanted to reach out and take his hand, but that wasn't something Ms. Pacquin would do. The possibilities they'd covered weren't the problem. The real worry Shane was struggling with was what they hadn't considered, something they'd missed.

"You've completed all the requirements we set to allow Ms. Pacquin's participation, so we're not going to rehash that now. Does anyone have any other concerns?" the director asked. "If not, then we'll adjourn. I expect any revisions to the op to be sent to all participants ASAP. Shirley, make sure you have ears on Tiernan and Ms. Pacquin at all times. I want a quick response if things go sideways."

"Yes, sir," Maon said.

"Good luck, Tiernan. Ms. Pacquin."

"Thank you, sir," Shane said. Adrianna nodded her agreement.

WITH ONE SHOULDER leaning against the wall in auxiliary command on the *Adrasteia*, Maon looked on while Shane entered navigation data into the flight computer and correlated it with status updates on the systems they would be visiting.

Shane turned, facing Maon. "You talked with Élise Sauveterre? She's moving ahead on buying up stock in Astro Tex?"

"Yes, she and a consortium of female heads of household on Preatiens are financing the takeover and have already engaged an investment firm from the Bing Lon Sector to act on their behalf. Last I knew they had eight percent of the individual stock purchased."

"Excellent. If her representative could meet us when we get to Canthis, that would be ideal. We could approach Jason Holmes with the child trafficking info and then hand off to the rep to finish the stock purchase. We'll be stopping on Asturnia for a half day. I'll comm you from there to see if that will work out before heading on to Canthis. Otherwise, I'll be directing him to make the sale when the rep approaches him. Get me the name of the rep too."

"Will do. The Marshals' ship providing you backup should be in system before you arrive at Runner's Hub. Their transponder is squawking Correggian transport B234L98D. Its validity will be hard to verify because of the conflict between the Correggians and Forplix, and it gives a good reason for them to pretend to be broken down. They have a dedicated comm set to your transmitter's hyperfrequency if you need them. You can also reach them on hpf CorreggianCantonMist."

"Okay. Thanks, Maon. Does Adrianna have all the info and documents we'll need?"

"Yes. I believe she's compiling a file for EBC storage for both of you."

Shane leaned back, lacing his hands behind his head. "The ever-efficient Ms. Pacquin."

"Yes, I really don't know how you got along without her. Take that back. I do know how you got along without her. You were an overworked, undersexed asshole."

"I wasn't that bad."

"Keep telling yourself that, but I'm beginning to see the guy who helped me water balloon the Quanthan Queen of Beers Bikini Team."

"Fuck. I'd forgotten about that. I don't know how we didn't get caught for that."

Maon raised an eyebrow and smirked. "We did. I smoothed things over with the spokesperson."

"What?" Shane couldn't help but laugh at the picture of his friend with the bikini team's watchdog. "That gigantic blonde muscle woman?"

"Yeah, she took me places." Maon let a lazy smile spread across his face as though even the memory brought him bliss. "Of course, I knew you had your eye on that tall black dude with the huge package."

Shane glared in mock anger. "I did not. As I recall, you were the one fixated on him. I was all about the little redhead."

"Did you ever connect with her?"

"I don't kiss and tell."

"Fuck's sake you don't." Maon shook his head. "Never mind. I'm just happy you're starting to have a little more fun in life again."

Shane frowned when reality reasserted itself. "Yeah, but I really need to get the Benefactor out of Dria's life before I spend too much time having fun."

"I'm with you," Maon said. "We're gonna take that bastard down a peg or two and take care of Dria."

"Yes. Yes, we are."

17

Shane had to admit that hiring Dria to be his assistant was turning out to be an excellent investment. She couldn't read his mind, but she could read his emotions. Every time he'd edged toward feeling frustrated, confused, or even bored, she'd stepped in with just the right information, comment, or means of escape. She made everything go smoother. He'd worked with a number of young marshals to give them field time with someone with experience. None had ever been half as useful as Dria. Plus, she didn't panic under fire. Maybe he could get the Service to underwrite the assistant portion of her contract. *Have to run that by Maon.*

"What's got you space brained?" Dria asked from behind him.

"Hmmm… Oh, nothing. Just thinking." He accepted the cup of café she'd brought him. The trip to Canthis had dragged. They were both eager to get started with the next part of Shane's plan. "The representative from Chin Tausu Gwohee Dasha… How do you say her name again?"

"Miáo Xiǎo Māo. And you can use the Standard translation of Chūnjì Guóhuì Tóuzī, Spring Investment Capitol."

"I probably should. Who knows what I'm really saying when I butcher the pronunciation. You know that's why I have you studying languages, don't you?"

Adrianna smirked. "Definitely use the Standard, and Miáo Xiǎo Māo advised me to call her Ms. Miáo. Then you only have to meow to say her name. Meeeooow." Adrianna giggled.

Shane set his cup down and snatched Adrianna onto his lap. "I'll give you something to laugh about." He tickled her until she was gasping for breath and then blew a big raspberry on her neck before releasing her. "What are you fooling around for? We have to leave for the shuttle in ten minutes."

"What was I thinking? I need to put the data cube for Holmes in my bag and grab my jacket while you finish your café. The high temperature in Century City on Canthis is supposed to be about seventeen degrees Celsius."

"Mmmm. I'll grab a jacket too."

THE TRIP by monorail to the city center and the walk to Jason Holmes's offices were uneventful. After a short wait, his receptionist announced them.

"Marshal Tiernan." Jason Holmes reached his hand out to take Shane's. "To what do I owe the pleasure of this visit?"

Shane shook the offered hand, noting that Holmes didn't look pleased to see him. Neither did he look apprehensive. *Interesting.* "Just here to conduct a little business. Let me introduce you to my assistant, Ms. Pacquin, and Ms. Miáo, a representative from Spring Investment Capitol."

"How do you do, ladies?" Holmes shook each of their hands, his face impassive.

"He's puzzled but not particularly anxious. No more than an unexpected visit from a marshal might cause," Adrianna subvocalized to Shane.

"Please have a seat." Holmes directed them to a sofa-and-chairs arrangement at the far end of his office where floor-to-ceiling windows looked out over the inner courtyard of the building. He settled his oversize bulk into a chair before asking, "How can I help you?"

"Is this office secure?" asked Shane.

"You mean can we be overheard or has it been swept for recording devices? Yes, it is secure. The only recording equipment is my own."

Shane spoke in a voice that brooked no opposition. "Please turn that off now."

"Very well. If you prefer." A small furrow appeared between Holmes's eyebrows.

Shane waited for Holmes to override the listening equipment in the room before continuing. "I'm here to bring to your attention a serious breach of Federation law. It's my understanding you run a service that connects young Canthian men and women with placement in brothels and sex training schools. Is that correct?" Shane asked, maintaining a piercing stare at Holmes.

"Yes, it is. But that's a legitimate business. Everything is aboveboard and fully compliant with the law." Holmes's right shoe flexed as though he was moving his toes up and down inside it.

"So you're stating that there is no illegal activity involved with your service?"

"No. None."

"I see. Then it will come to you as a complete surprise I have data that proves the opposite. That in fact, your company is illegally providing underage children. That, sir, is child trafficking, and it is very much illegal." Every part of Shane had gone flat and cold. This scum followed the letter of the law while living in a moral pigsty. Shane had no regret for applying the impetus that sent the man sprawling in his own filthy muck.

Holmes ran a hand over the stubble of his cropped iron-gray hair. Sweat beaded his forehead. "Absolutely not. We are very careful to verify the age of all the applicants who use our service."

"Apparently not careful enough. Ms. Pacquin, would you give Mr. Holmes the data cube?"

Adrianna complied.

"The cube has lists of names, ages, home addresses, and destinations of over three hundred underage children you have provided to a number of out-system brothels at Runner's Hub and a training school, the Wellington. A number of these children are now in protective custody, and they are willing to provide evidence against you and your company, Mr. Holmes."

Eyes glazing over while the information scrolled across his vidscreen, Holmes said, "This can't be. How did this happen?"

Shane said, "That really doesn't matter. It happened."

Holmes turned. His voice quavered. "Are you here to arrest me?"

"Yes. Unless you cooperate with me in an ongoing investigation. I've been empowered to offer you a deal, Mr. Holmes."

Holmes's hand trembled on the arm of his chair. "A deal?"

"This can all go away if you sign the paperwork Ms. Miáo has brought to transfer all stock you own in Astro Tex to me. You will be paid the current going rate for the stock. You will keep this transfer a secret. You will not give any information about it to other AstroTex stockholders. Is that clear?"

"I understand, but...he'll... I mean..."

"You have two options. Take this deal, or I arrest you on charges of child trafficking and hold an immediate press conference." Shane let his words hammer at Holmes.

Holmes slumped in his chair. "I'll sign," he said, his voice a sob.

Ms. Miáo placed a set of papers in front of him. "Please initial each page and sign where I have marked red X's. Please place your right index finger in the ident field. I'll be notarizing your signature, adding my fingerprint, and data scanning the documents. You'll receive a copy of the documents on cube. Please do not access the cube until the transfer becomes public."

Pasty-faced, Holmes complied, looking as though his life had drained from him. In a way, it had. His signature was a death sentence. The Benefactor would have him executed for betrayal. The alternative was torture and then death for making the Benefactor complicit in child trafficking. When she finished, Ms. Miáo handed him the data cube. It lay in his palm, as immobile as Holmes himself.

"Good-bye, Mr. Holmes." Shane didn't offer to shake hands before escorting the women to the reception area. "Your boss needs you, miss," he advised the receptionist. She rose from her desk and scurried into the office.

As they exited the building, Adrianna said, "I don't think he knew. He was surprised by the data."

"Whether he knew or not, he was dead the minute one child was sent on from Canthis and the Benefactor discovered it. Don't feel sorry for him. He made money sending young people to work in the worst brothels in the system. Places where their life expectancy is numbered in years, not decades."

"Yes, Sir. I understand." Adrianna didn't need the lecture, but it helped him release some of the pent-up anger dealing with Holmes had generated.

As they walked through the business district, Ms. Miáo came to a halt before a branch of the Federation First Universal Bank.

"This is my stop," she said.

Shane shook her hand. "Thank you, Ms. Miáo. You've helped us work toward slowing if not eliminating illegal human trafficking in this sector. Your discretion is appreciated."

"It was my pleasure, Marshal Tiernan. The world of finance doesn't offer many opportunities to be involved in a criminal sting." Her smile showed she'd enjoyed the adventure. "This takes the consortium over the fifty-percent mark, so you can proceed with any additional plans you have. SIC will file the Federation paperwork for the takeover immediately as well as notify the current board of directors."

"Thank you again, Ms. Miáo."

"You're welcome, Marshal. Safe journeys. Nice meeting you, Ms. Pacquin."

"You too. Safe journeys," Adrianna responded.

Shane felt the hunger pangs he'd been ignoring. "Let's grab a bite to eat, Dria. Then we'll head to Runner's Hub. It's a four-day trip. We'll arrive in the evening, so I'm thinking we should make a splashy entrance. What do you say, Pet?" He gave her a sinful grin.

"Oooh! Yes, Sir. Will I get to wear something fun?"

"Definitely fun for me." His eyebrow rose, and his lips curled into a smile wicked with possibilities.

ADRIANNA HAD BEEN SURPRISED by the outfit Shane had given her for disembarking at Runner's Hub. The demure flutter-sleeved empire-waist gown in light sage chiffon didn't adhere to his usual taste in play clothes—sensual, sexy, and very revealing. The dress was fully lined, and the bodice covered her entire bust. A large scarf in matching chiffon framed her face, falling to her fingertips and down her back. A sage and bronze beaded cap secured the scarf and held the attachment points for a veil of light sage crystals that covered her face below her eyes. The cap and a beaded band under her breasts were embroidered with darker vines and small yellow-orange sunburst flowers.

Shane had wound crystal yarn into her braid. Before he'd fastened the veil, he'd kissed her gently on the lips. "Very sweet," he'd said, but his darkened eyes had hinted at things he intended to do with her, which weren't sweet at all. Satisfied with Adrianna's attire, Shane had changed into brown leathers, a white shirt, and his bolo tie with his badge in plain view on his belt.

When he came into the *Adrasteia's* lounge, he held her ankle holster and firearm in his hand. "I want you to wear your gun. Pull your skirt up and let me attach it to your ankle." He strapped it on, positioning the gun on the inside of her ankle. "You are never to be without it while we're on Runner's Hub. Understood?"

"Yes, Sir. Understood."

He pulled a crystal-studded leash from his pocket and attached it to her collar. "*Are you ready?*" he subvocalized.

"*Yes, Sir,*" she subvocalized.

"Good. Remember, make full use of your empathic skills. While we are on Runner's Hub, you are free to look wherever you wish unless I say otherwise. Do not stare at anyone. Do not respond to anyone. If you need to bring something to my attention, subvocalize."

"Yes, Sir."

"If things go sideways, stay out of my line of fire. Use your own weapon if you have to. Remember, shoot to kill." He tilted her chin up with his finger. "I mean that, Adrianna. If you get yourself hurt trying to avoid hurting someone else, I will punish you."

"Yes, Sir." The heat in his eyes and voice made her stomach flutter. She tasted his fear for her and sensed the battle he fought between his need to protect her and to do his duty as a marshal. "I'll be fine."

Shane sighed. "Yes, you will." The reassurance was as much for himself as for her. "Let's go."

Life on Furzine hadn't prepared Adrianna for Runner's Hub. It was unlike any station or planet she'd ever visited. A cacophony of noises pummeled her ears from every direction. Her head spun. Her brain could not absorb the visual overload. Floods of people pushed and shoved. A rich man, stomach bulging out from his elaborate caftan, sauntered through the throng, surrounded by his bodyguards. A beggar, eyes rheumy and nose running, reached filthy hands out. Runners with packages slung in nets across their backs ran, dodging and weaving. From small rolling carts, merchants hawked wares: aromatic spiced meats in paper cones, animal fetishes hung from leather cords, and brilliant, colored scarves.

A thirty-foot walk along the dock was a clash of contradictions. One thing was universal—weapons. Nobody went unarmed here. Even the woman with a baby strapped to her chest had a huge firearm holstered at her side. Adrianna was glad Shane was in front, guiding her. Most people got out of his way at once. A few tried a faceoff with false bravado. His hard stare sent them slinking back.

If the sights, sounds, and pungent odors that swirled around Adrianna made it difficult to focus on any single thing, the rush of emotions made it doubly so. It was similar to one of the Benefactor's parties she'd attend as a teenager, but ten times heavier without the veneer of civility. Adrianna instinctively pulled her empathic senses in to protect herself while she did her best to make her shaking legs keep up with Shane. In the lift, Shane triggered the proper level and then hugged her to him, her back to his chest.

"Sorry for the rush. It's safest to clear the docks quickly."

"I can see why. I'm fine. But I had to restrict my empathic senses pretty hard." She allowed a tendril of her awareness to contact him. He was anxious. He didn't show it. At least he hadn't before she'd felt the apprehension seeping from him. There was a slight stiffness to his posture that wasn't usually there.

"Do what you have to do, Dria. You're the best judge of what you can and cannot handle."

"Thank you, Sir. It's going to be fine."

"Yes. It will. We're headed to level ten. It's restricted, so there won't be as many people." Shane squeezed her ribs just before the lift doors opened.

"Come, Pet." Shane led her along a quiet corridor past vidscreens displaying surreal landscapes on her left and a series of rooms on her right. A glance into an open door showed a small, dark chamber with comfortable seating. "Private meeting rooms for negotiating or getting acquainted before entering the main club."

Laughter sounded farther around the curve of the corridor, but before the laughing group came into view, Shane turned right at a T intersection. A huge dark-skinned man swathed in black leather, bald head shining and muscles bulging, stood in front of a double-hung ornate entry. He held out an ident pad, which Shane placed his palm on. Once Shane's identity had been logged, it was Adrianna's turn. The giant keyed the doors open without saying a word, his face impassive. Even his emotions were flat.

The quiet of the corridor became the churning noise and thumping beat of what passed for dance music on level ten. A mash of people writhed, grinding to the music while professional dancers did the same on a higher platform running along the inner curve of the room. Colored beams of light whipped across the dance floor, agitating an already frenetic mass of undulating limbs and torsos. The only steady but dim light came in splashes around the outer arc of the room where sleek bars serving expensive drinks alternated with seating areas with tall tables and stools. The dancing thrashed its way past where the club swerved out of sight. A short distance to the left, another set of ornate doors exited the area. Shane led her there.

If the dance club had been an overpowering chaos of sound, lights, and bodies, this next area was different but just as intense. Quiet music with a sensual throb floated in the air. Soft, plush rugs led to sumptuous sofas, chairs, and lounges. Pillows dotted the floor in easy reach. Once the doors closed behind them, the ambience in this space crept over Adrianna.

"This room is called the Salon. See anything you like?" Shane subvocalized.

Adrianna didn't respond while she scanned the groups of guests in various stages of undress, many engaging in sexual pleasures while others watched. The scene was decadent. Arousal vibrated at her core. There was no straight path. This room, too, stretched its way along the curve of the Hub. Shane took his time meandering, stopping to watch while three men came to completion, spurting cum across the chest and stomach of a small blonde woman. The lust and erotic sensations filling the room washed over

Adrianna, and her hips swayed. The sounds of moans, groans, and cries of ecstasy slunk along her spine. If Shane didn't do something soon, she'd be on her knees, begging him to make her come. She managed to follow until he came to a new set of double doors.

SHANE DIDN'T REQUIRE empathic skills to know Adrianna was aroused. The chiffon of her dress accentuated her sleek lines, floating with her movements. It had him clenching his fist to keep from sliding the fabric up her body. Covering her had been an inspiration. In the glut of scantily clad females, she stood out, an erotic gem waiting to be revealed. He wasn't the only person that wanted to touch her. Fingers had reached for the edge of her scarf, but those who wanted to see her would just have to follow them into something a little more dangerous. His gut relaxed when he entered the pain and pleasure club with Adrianna following obediently behind him. This was his venue, his playground. There were rules here that worked to his advantage to keep Adrianna safe. Even so, the Hub's clubs were a place to free-fall, to fulfill fantasies, and to contravene society's imperatives. The unwary got lost, never to be found. The danger kept many away. It drew others like moths too needy to worry about singed wings or a death spiral into the bright light. He'd never played here, and he wouldn't play long tonight. Just enough to display Adrianna fully and allow the right people to take notice. He'd worn his badge so none could miss that he was a marshal. Marge Boleo's security staff wouldn't miss that detail. He couldn't be certain about the Benefactor's people, but surely, here on the Hub, he didn't rely on men like the incompetents that had attempted to kidnap Adrianna.

A low throb of music, metallic and harsh, was punctuated by the crack of a whip. Shane found the open frame he needed halfway down the room. *Perfect.* Once again, he took a meandering path to reach his goal, using the time to gauge the participants and watchers. No one looked more interested than they should at his and Adrianna's arrival. He dumped his toy bag on the floor to claim the bondage structure and turned to Adrianna, staring deep into her eyes. "On your knees, Pet."

Adrianna dropped to her knees before him. His focus had become haphazard. The atmosphere of the room and Adrianna's swaying body were like a dial that had twisted his arousal into the red zone. Quick release would steady him, so he unlatched the crystal veil from one side of the headpiece she wore and let it fall along her cheek.

"Take my cock out and suck it."

Her fingers flew to his belt and freed his cock from his pants. His erection jerked when her tongue licked from its base to its tip, and then, wrapping it in her fingers, she plunged her mouth onto him, sucking him deep.

"Yes, Pet. Now all the way down."

Prickling pleasure threatened to overwhelm him, but he controlled himself, reaching out to move his hand under her scarf and hold her head while he thrust into her throat, moving in rhythm to the bass notes of the music that vibrated his core. He loved how she sucked cock. *Expert* barely described the level of skill she had. Watching her take his erection in and out through those firm, sweet lips, Shane added this moment to the memories he was storing of Adrianna. She swallowed around him, and the wave of his climax broke past the barriers of his control. One more swallow and he lost himself in a searing orgasm.

With breathing and heart rate in overdrive, he struggled to say, "Good girl." Adrianna licked him clean, settled him into his pants, and buckled his belt. When she'd finished, he drew the veil back across her flirtatious smile and latched it. "*You are beautiful, a mhuirnín,*" he subvocalized.

"Stand, Pet."

Adrianna rose, placing her hands behind her, partially hidden by the drape of the scarf down her back. "Turn the other direction," he said. When she stopped, Shane placed his hand on her cap, lifted it a bit, and pulled the scarf out from under it. With the scarf free, he replaced the cap. "Walk to the frame. Face away from me." His gaze followed her while she sauntered toward the frame. Her arms formed a V down to where her fingers meshed, emphasizing the sway of her hips. *Magnificent.* Inside his bag, he felt around for the ropes and spreader bar he would use.

He took his time lashing Adrianna's wrists to the top of the frame and her ankles to the spreader bar, using his peripheral vision to maintain his situational awareness. Her tiny movements caused the dress she wore to flutter, creating slight outlines, hints at the curves beneath. The flogger he now held would bring the perfect pink glow of warmth to her skin, but first he needed to remove that dress. When he smoothed his way up her backside to her shoulder, the feel of the silky cloth under his hand fed his urgency to get to the skin underneath. He unbuttoned the clasp, and when that side of the dress sagged, he undid the clasp on the other shoulder and pulled the center zipper down. The bodice slid to her waist. A quick tug brought it around her thighs. The superb swell of her ass required a caress, so he obliged, snuggling against her, biting the back of her neck when he did. Adrianna shivered, gasping with a squeak.

He chuckled. "Time for fun, Pet."

She rubbed her bottom into him, making his groin tingle even though he'd just come. *Provoking wench.*

He stepped back and brought the suede flogger into play, letting it do the work. The arc of her spine, when she stretched toward each impact, was pure poetry.

"Dance for me, Pet."

Pleasure throbbed through him, settling the return of an insistent yearning in his groin. *Fuck, she is incredible.* Whether he touched her with the flogger or not, she responded to the desire that roared through him, offering herself for his pleasure. The need to keep Adrianna safe helped him break his narrow focus on the dynamic that was forming between them in the scene. *Concentrate on the room around you!*

Time to switch floggers and move things along. The thuds from this heavier flogger would turn Adrianna into a begging mess. His favorite kind of disheveled woman. Before beginning, he scanned the room. No one was taking overt notice of them, but when he caught sight of a man leaned against the curve of the back wall, the man straightened and stared. Even if he hadn't been staring, the guy would have stood out in his plaid blue shirt and jeans.

Shane broke eye contact and began to slowly strike Adrianna with the new flogger, focusing on a specific spot on her back. Before changing his strike zone, he smacked or pinched her bottom. She claimed that strikes to her buns went straight to her clit, so he liked to oblige her. And he liked to turn her ass pink. Soon she was moaning, quivering after each strike.

"Please, Master."

"Please what, Pet?"

"More please, Master."

"My pleasure, Pet."

Shane increased the rhythm of his blows, keeping an eye on the man who was now strolling in their direction. He forced his body to remain relaxed even though anxiety started tap dancing in his gut. He let the hand holding the flogger drop to his side, and nuzzled into Adrianna, stroking her bright-pink ass cheeks. "You respond so well to a flogger, Pet. I love to watch you struggling for more. We're going one level higher, and I want you to give me everything you have. Can you do that?"

"Yes, Master. Everything. Just for you."

"Good girl." Shane gave a quick tug on her braid. He knelt beside his bag to return the flogger and pull out his stinger. The man, shorter than Shane but burlier, stopped near the side of the frame, watching them. Shane nodded to him, eyes narrowed. The man nodded back but didn't speak. Shane returned his attention to Adrianna, using the stinger with an economy of motion, allowing her to work through the pain before striking again. The rhythm of her breathing and the slackening of her muscle tone showed she was heading into subspace. Time to end this. He needed Adrianna on her feet and able to communicate. *"Breathe your way back, Adrianna,"* he subvocalized. He untied her from the spreader bar and massaged her legs and ankles. *"You with me?"*

"Yes, Sir. I'm with you," Adrianna subvocalized in response.

"Good girl. We have company. Pretend you're still out of it." Shane removed the ropes from her wrists and resettled the dress in place, fixing the clasps and zipper. An itch niggled in the center of his back where he was certain the stranger's eyes were focused. It took everything in him to ignore the man and that itch while he tended to Adrianna. He slung his bag over his shoulder after shoving the rope and stinger inside, and picked her up in his arms.

The man who'd been watching them stepped closer and said to Shane, "We need to talk. As soon as you're done..." He pointed at Adrianna.

"Sure. Come sit on that couch with us." Shane nodded toward an empty couch. Whoever the man was, the earring he wore hooked through one earlobe marked him as Hub security. It didn't appear that he worked for the Benefactor.

The cushions of the couch settled under Shane when he sat. He wrapped Adrianna in a blanket he'd grabbed. The man claimed the other end of the couch, his arm along the back, his shaggy blond head leaning against the cushions. Shane returned his attention to Adrianna. He combed his fingers through her hair, bringing a strand to his nose and breathing in deeply. *"Keep your eyes shut. Tell me what you sense from this guy."*

"Yes, Sir."

Shane waited, caressing her hip through the blanket.

"His primary emotions are curiosity and wariness. I don't sense any negative feelings toward us beyond worry we might cause him trouble."

Shane turned his head to the man. "Tiernan. Marshal Shane Tiernan. And you are?"

"Hugh Poulson. I work for the management here."

"The club or the Hub?" Shane asked, keeping his gaze fixed on Poulson.

"Yes. A bit of both." Poulson kept his own eyes trained on Shane. "Is this a personal visit or did you come to the Hub for business?"

Shane smirked. "A bit of both."

Polson's squinted at Shane. "We weren't informed you were coming. It's customary to give us a heads up when a marshal visits the Hub in his official capacity."

"It's personal business. Can you get me to Marge Boleo?"

With a probing look, Poulson asked, "Why?"

"Let's just say I have an offer for her. One way or another, she'll have to meet with me. I'd like it to be on friendly and mutually beneficial terms." Shane cocked an eyebrow.

Poulson pursed his lips, staring at Shane several moments before speaking. "I'll see what I can do. Where can I reach you?"

"Berth L51. I'll expect to hear from you by nine standard tomorrow."

"You will." Poulson got to his feet and sauntered away.

The citrusy scent of Adrianna's skin, mingled with the aroma of arousal that still dampened her pussy, reawakened Shane's cock. His dick was completely out of sync with Shane's need to leave as quickly as possible. "Time to wake up, Pet. We're returning to the ship where I can give you my undivided attention." He snapped his fingers by her ear. "Up. Now."

Her eyes shut, Adrianna stretched with a languorous arch to her back. Shane bent and bit her nipple through the dress. "Oh!" Adrianna's eyes opened, and her torso gave a much less graceful jerk.

"Do you need me to punish you to get you to move faster?" Shane's nostrils flared.

Lashes lowered, Adrianna's lips twitched when she responded, "Only if it pleases you, Master."

"It pleases me to get out of here." Shane stood, settling her on her feet before he picked up his bag, took her leash, and headed to the nearest exit to the outer corridor.

18

Marge Boleo's office was spare with a parsimony and neatness that fit her naval background. A former ship's captain in the Federation fleet, she ran the Hub like a military command. Starting out as a set of linked tankers providing fuel and an exchange point for those who didn't like Federation oversight, the Hub had grown to a huge cylindrical wheel. Multiple levels provided docking, warehouses, repair facilities, banking, trading, quarters, and pleasure. Boleo was the ninth person in a line that went back centuries to be responsible for the management of the Hub. All profits were shared by vested employees, but it wasn't a democracy.

Shane had read the report Maon had provided on Boleo. Early in her naval career, she'd been part of the team sent to secure a drifting cargo ship. When they'd gone aboard the derelict vessel, they found the holds full of the dead. Young people, even children, packed in, lying among the filth of their own excrement. The crew had abandoned the ship when life support had gone down and couldn't be fixed. Thousands of desperate kids coerced or manipulated into signing their future away, hoping for a better life, ended frozen, lifeless. The sight of five-, six-, and seven-year-olds huddled on a cargo bay floor would be something no one could ever forget.

Boleo looked up from her vidscreen when Shane and Adrianna entered her office. She rose and offered her hand, which Shane pressed firmly. "Marshal Tiernan. Please take a seat."

Shane directed Adrianna to sit beside him. She did, curling her legs next to her and leaning against him, her lavender shipsuit a striking contrast against his dark brown slacks.

Shane wasn't certain if he detected a hint of surprise in Boleo's face, but if he had, it was gone an instant later. "I don't believe we've met before, Marshal," she said.

"No, I never found it necessary to intervene in Hub affairs until now," Shane said.

Hands folded in her lap, Boleo began tapping her thumbs. She had to realize it would only be a matter of time before some representative of the Federation would show up to discuss her failure to uphold the agreement to stop illegal human trafficking through the Hub. Not all human trafficking was physically or circumstantially coercive. The Federation had developed regulations to eliminate the worst practices. Adrianna was an obvious beneficiary of those laws.

Politics and economics were on the Federation's side, something Boleo had appreciated in the past. From the files Shane had read on Boleo and the Hub, Boleo had made a point when taking over the Hub to wean it from accommodating those who broke Fed human trafficking laws. Ultimately, she had struck a deal with the Federation to block all illegal human trafficking. Since then, Hub profits had been up, but now, the Benefactor had forced her to renege on the pact with the Feds. That couldn't make her happy. It meant that the days of having a naval force routinely pop into the Hub with requests for its port entry and exit logs were about to return. Boleo was stuck between the Federation and the Benefactor. So far, the Benefactor was winning the tug-of-war.

"You've found a reason to intervene now?" she asked.

He expected her to play it cagey. "I'm sure you've been expecting a visit."

Her voice lowered into that dangerous zone that demanded respect. "What do you want?"

"No need to get defensive. We should work together."

She lifted her chin and tersely asked, "Well?"

"As I understand it, you have a fuel problem, and I'm here to pass on the good news that I'm looking into resolving it."

"What fuel problem is that?" she said.

She waited, studying him, a hint of curiosity mingling with her look of frustrated anger when he leaned in toward her. "Let me lay my cards fully on the table, Ms. Boleo. In my capacity as a special agent for the Marshals Service, I have investigated possible reasons for you to return to allowing illegal human trafficking through the Hub. I came to one conclusion. You're being held hostage to fuel prices. Specifically, that the primary source of your inexpensive fuel has been bought up by interests that wish you to turn a blind eye to their illegal human trafficking through the Hub."

Boleo pursed her lips.

"However, that interest failed to secure the company in question under his sole ownership. A partner was allowed to hold a considerable chunk of the investment. That stock and shares held by small investors has come into the possession of a new consortium."

Wary, Boleo said, "New consortium?"

Shane smirked. "The backers have empowered me to negotiate on their behalf."

Boleo's eyes narrowed. "I see. Why mince words, Marshal? You've managed to outflank the Benefactor, and now you want to capitalize on it. It won't work."

"Oh, but it will. His deal with you will remain the same. You'll continue to ignore human trafficking regulations. He'll be free to continue to supply the nasty underbelly of the sex trade industry with unsuspecting fodder." Shane dropped his hand to Adrianna's head, stroking her hair. She leaned into it, all feline appreciation.

Boleo smiled at him, but the expression was as false as her carefully controlled tone of voice. "Where do you get your cut?"

"I'll let Ms. Pacquin explain. She has a much better mind for figures." He looked down at Adrianna. "Tell her, Paquin."

When Adrianna moved her gaze from him to Boleo, she transformed from adoring submissive to calculating assistant. "We propose levying a fuel tax of five credits per metric ton. Five hundred thousand credits of the income produced per month will go to us. The big cargo haulers that use the Hub to evade Fed taxes will generate that amount by themselves.

Income generated by the small haulers and private ships would accrue to you once our minimum has been reached. In addition, we will supply fuel to the Hub at prices in line with sector averages. Of course, we are open to other suggestions, but however you decide to produce the income, we will expect payment of five hundred thousand credits on the first of each month into an account of our choosing."

Boleo stared at Adrianna, the content of her thoughts masked, but not for long. She began to tap her thumbs again and then snapped her focus to Shane. "I could always turn you in to the Marshals."

Shane smirked. "You could. But there are three good reasons why you won't. First, the consortium doesn't trace back to me, and I will deny everything I've just told you. Second, your customers won't look kindly on you turning informant for the Federation. Third, the Hub will receive credit for any amount the Benefactor pays me to maintain the Hub as a slaving route. I plan to charge him the full five hundred thousand. If he does, you'll pay nothing. The only real change for the Hub is that I will be pulling the strings, not the Benefactor."

A muscle in Boleo's jaw twitched. "I suppose I have no other option than to fall in line. At least for as long as the situation lasts. I wouldn't be so sanguine about the Benefactor's reaction. He's not going to take your interference well."

Shane waved his hand in dismissal. "He may not like the loss of control of the Hub's fuel, but he will like having a Tallavan marshal in his pocket."

Boleo's lip curled. "You're playing a dangerous game. Losers end up dead, frozen blips in the Hub's asteroid belt."

Shane bared his teeth. "I have no intention of losing."

She leaned back in her chair, crossing her arms with an ugly laugh. "I'm sure you don't. Now get the hell out of my office."

THE DAYS LEADING up to the Benefactor's arrival at the Hub seemed to go on forever. Boleo must have contacted the Benefactor the second he and Adrianna had left her office. Within the hour, Shane had received a summons from the crime lord, which he'd declined. Instead he demanded a face-to-face on the Hub. The worst possible scenarios had played in

Shane's mind on repeat. He'd probably lost weight. Eating had been nearly impossible with the way his stomach churned. He could handle dealing with the Benefactor. Fear for Adrianna's safety was the impetus behind the spike in his anxiety level.

Across from Shane, Hugh Poulson settled deeper into his leather armchair, taking a swig from the beer he was drinking. Once the Benefactor's ship had come through the hyperpulse point and entered the docking queue, Marge Boleo had given Shane access to a hospitality suite. When the ship docked, she'd insisted the Hub manager join them.

Until the Benefactor made a move or left the Hub, Shane and Adrianna would remain in the suite. She was curled up on a sofa at the far end of the long room, ostensibly napping with her head pillowed on the overstuffed arm. Shane had drawn a soft throw over her, which she'd pulled up under her chin.

After refilling his cup of café, Shane sat opposite Hugh.

Hugh tapped the arm of his chair. "How'd you do it?"

Shane raised an eyebrow.

"Put one over on the Benefactor? Not many with the balls to try."

Shane rubbed the back of his neck, glancing at the door to the suite. "Found a weakness. Exploited it."

"Yeah?"

Shane studied Hugh for a moment. "He left a sizable chunk of Astro Tex stock in Jason Holmes's name. Holmes was supplying kids for the Benefactor's school on Beta Tau for the sex market and the less pretty for other slaving venues. Most were of legal age, but we found proof some were underage."

Hugh grunted. "Leverage."

Shane nodded. "Yeah. Sell us the stock, or we go public about the child trafficking."

"Really. Boleo is adamantly against child trafficking through the Hub. Weird that the Benefactor opposes it too. He's a stickler about the age of consent."

Shane grimaced. "He's a sociopath. You can't make sense of a mind like that. To you and me, one day does not magically transform a fifteen-year-old child into a sixteen-year-old adult."

Hugh's lip curled. "Fuckin' creep. The boss will spit nails when she finds out underage children have been transshipped through the Hub in the last months. She had a hard sell when she wanted to sign the Fed human trafficking accord. Forged documents for underage kids was her biggest argument. Guess she was right. So what put you on the side of a sociopath? Not good enough bein' a Tallavan rich boy?"

Shane snorted. "Rich boy!"

"That ship of yours is fuckin' fine."

"Got it before my mom cut me off. I'm not rich. More of a pariah."

"Huh."

"After Boleo signed the accord, was there a lot of backlash?"

Hugh took a long swig from his bottle. "Some. A few ship captains didn't take the change well. Security had to use force to stop some crews trying to transfer people from one ship to another. Several pulled out of dock without notice, which is hell on the traffic lanes. No collisions though."

"That's not too bad." Shane glanced at the door to the suite.

"Yeah. The worst was a ship that left without detaching from the supply lines. Had fuel, water, and sewage all over the place. Shut down six of the berths adjacent to it."

"What a mess." Shane rubbed his hand up and down his thigh. His patience was wearing thin waiting for the Benefactor to arrive.

Hugh shifted in his chair and drained his beer. Shane checked the door again even though he knew Boleo would notify them when the Furzian was headed their way. Hugh's eyes went distant for a minute. "Marge says the Benefactor has left her office. She told him where to find you. He's on his way. He's not happy, but I guess that's to be expected. I can stay when he gets here."

"I'd appreciate it. I don't expect him to make any overt moves here. Extra muscle just in case can't hurt." Shane's shoulders had tightened at word that the Benefactor was coming. The room seemed to have shrunk. Even his shirt seemed smaller. Shane pulled on the cuffs to ease the chafing under his arms. Once the Benefactor found out Adrianna wouldn't be going with him, he might try to take her by force. Whether she was in his or Shane's custody shouldn't matter, but this fixation on marrying her was worrying.

Shane had half expected the Benefactor's underlings on the Hub to attempt to snatch her. Hugh had given Shane the names of several reliable men to act as backup guards. In the days since they'd docked, Shane had brought Adrianna with him out onto the station. But no one took the bait. Instead, the Benefactor had arrived in full panoply, asking where he could find them. It wasn't likely he'd try strong-arm tactics in front of a Tallavan marshal, but what if he did? This was the Hub, after all. *Fuck.*

"Sure. I'll stay. I assume the others are around?" Hugh bared his teeth in a smile.

"On the docks near the Benefactor's ship," Shane said. Hugh might relish a fight, but with Adrianna in the room, that was the last thing Shane wanted. They sat in silence until at last the suite's courtesy chime rang. Shane rose and hit the Open button on the door panel. The Benefactor stood outside.

"Come in, sir. I understand you wanted to speak with me." Shane forced himself to look directly into the man's flat gray eyes, barely avoiding curling his lip in disgust. His oversize presence was elegant in a charcoal bespoke suit. He evinced an aura of command, an expectation that once he spoke, his orders would be followed to the letter. Everything about him was manicured from the nails on his short, thick fingers to the shine on his expensive leather shoes. He moved with a grace unexpected from a man just this side of corpulent.

The Benefactor motioned for his protective detail to remain outside. "Thank you. Yes, I wanted to come and extend my gratitude to you for bringing an end to the heinous corruption that was infiltrating the business of some of my associates." He oozed sincerity. His manner made him seem more shocked older relative than sophisticated crime lord. How had he learned that Jason Holmes had facilitated child trafficking? One of Holmes's people must have leaked it. Holmes hadn't been arrested, so the knowledge wasn't public.

Rubbing his mouth, Shane moved toward the chairs he and Hugh had been sitting in. He hated being polite to the bastard. "Please, have a seat. May I get you something to drink? Or eat? We have a fully stocked bar and kitchen."

The Benefactor sat in the armchair Shane had been using. "No, thank you. I need no refreshments."

Hugh had already risen and waited at the far end of the room on the sofa with Adrianna. Shane took his chair.

The Benefactor spoke first. "I wanted to assure you personally that if I or any of my staff had discovered what Jason Holmes was doing, we would have crushed it at once and called in the authorities ourselves. Child trafficking is something I cannot and will not countenance. Children are like unripe fruit. One doesn't pluck and eat fruit until it is perfectly ripe." He pursed his lips and shook his head, jowls quivering.

"Adrianna has told me that children are special to you. She didn't believe you knew," Shane responded, his voice bland, requiring all his self-control to remain unperturbed. *Unripe fruit! What the fuck?*

The Benefactor looked past Shane to Adrianna's sleeping form. "Adrianna is the sweetest of girls. I do hope you've done nothing to corrupt her inner purity. I had hoped I would be allowed to speak with her privately." He turned his focus back to Shane. "She left Furzine so quickly I was unable to extend my condolences on the death of her father or offer her the assistance that would have kept her from the Opio Institute's doors."

"That will be up to Adrianna. First, let's talk business."

Shane wasn't certain, but it seemed a hint of anger flashed across the Benefactor's face.

"You've taken advantage of an error on my part." His lips pressed into a pouting grimace. "Those responsible have been admonished."

"My associates and I have agreed that for the sum of five hundred thousand credits per month, we will allow you to transship human cargo through the Hub. It will be an exclusive agreement. All others will be blocked."

The Benefactor turned his head slightly and squinted at Shane. "Hmm. And if I refuse to pay?"

"You may do so. However, in lieu of payment from you, the Hub will be paying us the five hundred thousand credits to obtain their fuel. Ms. Boleo will be allowed to reinstate the illegal human trafficking accord she signed with the Feds. We get paid no matter what." Shane forced a benign smile onto his lips.

"I've looked into you, Marshal. You've made quite a splash lately in the newsies. How do I know your undisciplined behavior won't cause me problems in the future?"

With a dismissive wave of his hand, Shane said, "That little contretemps was planned to gain your attention. I've been disciplined and will behave myself from now on."

The Benefactor made a delicate snort. "You'll pardon me if I don't take that on face value. However, for the moment, it seems you have me at a disadvantage."

Shane struggled to smile rather than sneer. "Don't think of it as a disadvantage so much as an opportunity to explore the benefits of having a Tallavan marshal as an ally."

The Benefactor eyed him, speculative. "Have your financial representative contact my first assistant with account details. Five hundred thousand credits will be dispersed to it immediately and in monthly increments. Meanwhile, if we are to be allies, there is something you can do for me."

"Excellent. What would that be?"

"Allow me to take Miss Pacquin to Preatiens with me for a meeting with her grandmother, Élise Sauveterre."

Shane's jaw set, muscles so tight he had to take a deep breath before he could speak. "No. Not possible. If you need her on Preatiens, she can go with me on the *Adrasteia*."

The Benefactor's laugh was arrogant. "How kind of you to offer to take her, but that really isn't necessary. She'll be perfectly safe with me. I will need to brief her on the negotiations I'm opening with her grandmother. She really needs to accompany me. You may tag along behind."

Shane forced himself to remain seated. "I won't allow her to go with you. You'll have to brief her here or on Preatiens once we arrive."

The Benefactor tipped his chin up. "May I speak with her?"

Shane flexed his fingers on the arms of his chair. "If she agrees, but before I wake her, I want to make it clear she is with me now. The attempts to take her stop. She doesn't need a man old enough to be her grandfather taking advantage of her."

The Benefactor's eyes narrowed, anger adding a bare undertone to his words when he said, "Marshal, I'm sure you can't mean to imply that I've done anything that would bring harm to Adrianna. I have had her best interests at heart since she was a little girl."

Shane clenched his fists to keep himself from taking physical action.

Don't let the bastard get to you. "If you truly cared about her, you'd leave her alone."

"Now who's speaking from self-interest, Marshal?" The Benefactor's lip curled. "Never mind." He waved his hand in the air. "May I speak with Adrianna?"

"I'll wake her and ask." Shane rose and walked to the end of the room.

"I'm awake," Adrianna subvocalized.

"You don't have to talk to him."

"Thank you. But I think it's better if I do."

Shane leaned over Adrianna and shook her shoulder. "Dria. Wake up, love." He waited while she sat up and stretched. "The Benefactor is here and would like to speak to you privately."

Adrianna looked where the Furzian sat waiting. "Okay. But please stay here."

"Hugh and I won't leave." It took everything Shane had to remain on the far side of the room rather than accompany Adrianna.

WHILE ADRIANNA WALKED toward the Benefactor, she reached out to him with her empathic senses. She felt a surface mixture of concern and good intent directed at her and anger aimed at Shane. She pulled back from the underlying black ooze that lay beneath. The crime lord's emotions were what she would expect if he were sincere. Maybe people with personality disorders didn't read empathically the way normal folks did. Were his feelings toward her real? Did sociopaths delude themselves?

The Benefactor rose, palms stretched toward Adrianna. "Adrianna, my dear. You look as lovely as ever."

Adrianna stopped short of his reach. "Thank you, sir. You are looking well yourself."

"Please, let's sit." He gestured toward the chair opposite his and then sat.

Adrianna perched on the edge with her hands folded in her lap. She would let him guide the conversation, so she remained silent.

"I have missed you, my dear." He smiled but grew more serious when Adrianna didn't match it with a smile of her own.

"I must apologize for the overzealousness of the two men I sent to invite you to come to Furzine. Force was never to be involved. I had hoped the return of your locket would demonstrate my sincerity of affection, and you would return to me. Ms. Heinrich was perhaps the wrong emissary."

He was lying. And yet there was no spike in the emotions that usually accompanied a lie.

"I have something important to ask you. As you probably know, your parents and I were planning for you and me to wed once you came of age."

Adrianna remained impassive, offering him no response on which to determine how she was receiving him.

He leaned in closer. "You left Furzine so quickly that I wasn't able to make my wishes known to you or to offer you my assistance on the death of your father. Certainly, a wedding at the time was out of the question. You needed time to grieve. I understood this, but I'm afraid others must have given you the wrong impression. For that, I'll be forever sorry. It has kept me from your side when you had most need of my comfort." He reached across the space between them and patted her hand.

Adrianna bit the inside of her cheek, drawing blood to keep from yanking her hand back. Gods, this polite persona he affected made him even more repulsive. He was like a perverse snake charmer, mesmerizing his subject so he could trap it in a woven basket and keep it forever. She would not become his prize, his trophy to be trotted out when and where he chose.

"I understand that your arrangement with the marshal is a practical one. You have debts to pay. However, it appalls me to see you submitting yourself to him when I want to put you on a pedestal for all to admire." The Benefactor paused and shook his head. "My wish to make you my wife has not waned over the years. I know I'm older than you, but I hope you'll appreciate that for the blessing it can be. I have a mature wisdom. Your every wish will be my command. I've built a special estate just for the two of us."

Adrianna dreaded where he was going, but there was no way of stopping him. She wanted to flinch back when he rose and knelt on one knee before her, amazed that with his girth he could do so without wobbling. "My dear, will you do me the honor of becoming my wife?" His gaze scanned her face expectantly.

Adrianna allowed her brow to furrow. "I'm sorry, but I cannot." Her ability to speak with calm precision surprised her. Inside she was screaming her refusal.

"My dear, have I not made it plain? I will pay all your debts. You need worry for nothing anymore. We will go to your grandmother on Preatiens and ask her blessing. I do not wish to cut you off from your family. I would hope to be welcomed into it."

Bile rose in Adrianna's throat, but she quickly swallowed, tasting the acid when it burned back down her throat. "I'm sorry. The problem is not money or family. I do not love you. I love another."

The Benefactor lumbered to his feet, staring at her; a thread of anger lashed across her senses. "My dear, what you feel is infatuation. It will dissipate, but the love that will grow between us will last a lifetime. I know you will come to love me as I love you when we spend more time together. You were meant to be mine."

Adrianna shook her head, wishing he would take no for an answer. "No no no. I cannot and will not marry you."

The Benefactor grimaced, his emotions taking a nasty turn that Adrianna recognized from her teenage years as the rage he had directed at those who hindered his plans or desires. That emotion had never been directed at her—until now. He lowered his voice, but the quieter tone was somehow more intimidating than if he'd yelled at her. "I hadn't wanted things to come to this, but you leave me no alternative." He reached into his pocket and pulled out an image card. Adrianna gasped and went pale when he showed it to her. His finger flicking through the images, he revealed picture after picture of Master Trey bound and bloodied. "It took several men to subdue him, but he is now in my custody. If you wish no harm to come to him, you will leave with me now. We will go to Preatiens, where you will ensure that your grandmother blesses our union and gives me access to Preatiens. Then you will go with me to Furzine where we will be married, and you will serve as my wife, my hostess, and my greatest treasure. Is that clear?"

Adrianna nodded. "Yes, sir." Nausea assaulted her. With a mental leap into the imaginary icy pool at her core, she blocked her empathic senses, trying to regain her equilibrium.

"You will tell the marshal you've decided to marry me after all. That life with me is better suited to you than to continue serving him. You will smile and act as though this is your greatest delight. You will make no mention of the good Master." He gripped her hand with a tight squeeze and drew her to her feet.

The Benefactor raised his voice. "Marshal, please join us for some happy news."

Shane stood and walked to the pair.

The Benefactor beamed at Adrianna, tightening his fingers. "Adrianna has graciously agreed to be my wife. Haven't you, my dear?"

"Yes." Adrianna managed a false smile, keeping focused on the Benefactor. "I'm sorry, Marshal Tiernan, but I will have to end our contract. You'll be reimbursed the full amount you paid. Please accept my apology. The Benefactor has reminded me of how frivolous I was to run away from the one person who has always tried to take care of me. We'll be going to Preatiens to get my grandmother's blessing and then celebrate our wedding on Furzine." She turned her eyes to Shane and nearly choked at the look of shock and hurt on his face.

"I may have said things that led you to think I was feeling something stronger than affection toward you. I'm deeply sorry for mistaking a girlish crush for something greater."

"Why would you go with him? I don't understand." Shane sounded bereft.

"It's for the best. We only had two years at the most." Adrianna wanted to reach out and touch Shane.

"I don't understand," Shane repeated. He moved his hand toward her. *"Why are you doing this?"* he subvocalized.

"I'm sorry. I never meant to hurt you," she said. *"He's got Master Trey. He showed me pictures of him bound and bleeding,"* she subvocalized.

"You don't have to do this, Dria. I'll find a way," Shane said aloud and then subvocally, *"Do not get on his ship."*

Adrianna shook her head. "No, it's what I want." One finger traced the collar around her neck. "I need to give this back to you."

Shane's hands fisted and released. "Dria…"

The Benefactor interrupted. "Marshal Tiernan, my security detail is outside. I prefer not to involve them, but I insist you accede to Ms. Pacquin's wishes. If I must, I can have you arrested. Marge Boleo will back me on this. Hub law is sacrosanct to her."

Shane's jaw clenched. With a mumble, he asked Adrianna to turn. His hands shook when he undid the lock on the collar. With one hand, he withdrew it while with the other he massaged the back of her neck. "Please don't go." He subvocalized, *"It's not necessary. We'll find Trey. I promise."*

"You can't promise that." Turning to the Benefactor, she said, "May we go now? Shane, please have my things sent to me on Furzine. My papers and such. Thank you." She made her way to the door with the Benefactor at her elbow. She turned one last time and looked at Shane, ensuring all her empathic senses were tightly contained in ice.

"Adrianna, don't go." He set his jaw and pressed his lips together. *"I won't let him take you to Furzine. I'll find a way to stop him."*

"Good-bye, Sir."

Shane's yell of anger was cut off when the door closed behind her.

THE BENEFACTOR and Adrianna had barely left the room before Shane was bellowing at Hugh. "Track them. Delay their takeoff."

"Already done," Hugh responded while he loped toward Shane. "Come with me to station ops." He led Shane through the back door of the suite to a staff lift.

A heavy weight crushed Shane's chest while he sprinted down the corridor. Adrianna in the Benefactor's hands terrified him. This shouldn't have happened. He had tried to cover every possible scenario that could lead to this result. All the fail-safes Shane had put into place to keep her from being grabbed had been subverted. When given the choice between harm coming to herself or a loved one, she'd delivered herself into that fuck's grasp. Shane had to stop them from leaving the Hub. If the Benefactor took her to Furzine instead of Preatiens, there would be no way Shane could take her back, no matter what the director believed the Furzian marshals could do. When he entered the lift that would take him to the station ops level, Shane slammed his hand into the back wall. "Fuck it! I should have taken Trey into protective custody."

"Explain," Hugh said.

"The Benefactor is holding Trey Johansson, the man who helped Dria escape Furzine and who is also her mentor. Dria would not have gone with the Benefactor under any other circumstances. Not after he tried kidnapping her and murdering me."

"He's not going to let Johansson go."

Frustration choked Shane. "She hasn't thought that far ahead. Her immediate response is always to rush to help. She doesn't think about her own safety."

The lift opened, and the men moved down the corridor and entered station ops. A wall of vidscreens showed views of ships in dock, the hyperpulse queues, and the hyperpulse point. The room hummed with the sound of voices busy conducting the Hub's business. The ops chief turned and addressed Hugh. "The Furzian ship has requested immediate departure, although the two passengers are not yet on board. A minor dock accident has stalled them, but that should clear in a few minutes. What are your instructions?"

Hugh said, "Delay them using any tactics available."

"They've requested hyperpulse transit to Preatiens. I haven't responded yet. I've got four large freighters waiting to join queue. I'll put them all through before responding to the Furzians. That should hold them in dock for an extra hour."

"Do it." Hugh turned to Shane. "What next?"

"Get me a connection to the Tallavan offices on Beta Tau. I need to speak to Marshal Riordan. If he's not available, tell them it's a level-five emergency. They need to find him and have him call me here. I also need a hyperfrequency connection to CorregianCantonMist."

Adrenaline was still pumping through Shane's system, and he wanted to do something. Sitting and waiting for the comm to Riordan to go through was eating him alive. He snatched up the headset when the operator informed him the call to the Tallavan ship waiting as backup had gone through.

"Captain, this is Marshal Shane Tiernan. New orders. Proceed to Preatiens immediately. Hub ops will give you immediate clearance to head straight to the hyperpulse point. Do not come into the station. I'll be flashing you complete orders before you leave the system."

Informed that Beta Tau was waiting, Shane quickly switched to the new frequency. "Riordan? I need you to determine the whereabouts of Trey Johansson. The Benefactor claims to be holding him and using him as a hostage to ensure Adrianna Pacquin's cooperation."

Riordan's response was quick and intuitive. "Is Adrianna with the Benefactor?"

"Yes, he's trying to leave the Hub right now to get to Preatiens with Adrianna on board. Find Trey and secure him. If you can get it done in the next hour, I intend to board the Benefactor's ship. If not, it's imperative that word not reach the Benefactor that you've rescued him. He'll bypass Preatien orbit and head to Furzine if he finds out. I'll be waiting to hear from you. Also, notify hpf CorregianCantonMist. They'll be arriving at Preatiens and will prepare a welcome for the Benefactor if he gets that far."

Shane returned his attention to the vidscreen showing the Benefactor's ship, *Beneficence*. It was still in dock. Another screen showed the Canton Mist headed toward the hyperpulse point. Even if the *Beneficence* undocked this instant, the *Canton Mist* would be well ahead of them. Excellent.

"Hugh." Shane crooked a finger and moved to a quiet spot in the room. "Can you prepare a boarding party? If word comes that Trey is safe, I want to be prepared to take that ship by force."

"I've already got security forces in place. However, we can't board the ship without justification. The Hub grants autonomy to all ships in dock," Hugh said.

"He's right." Both men turned to see Marge Boleo. "The protocols for boarding a ship docked at Runner's Hub are very restrictive. I'm sure you can imagine why, Marshal. Ms. Pacquin will have to make a direct request for aid to a Federation representative. If she asks you to get her out of there, we can board."

"Understood, ma'am."

Marge reached out and placed her hand on Shane's arm. "I'm sorry. My hands are tied. We'll do what we can. I warned you that the Benefactor wouldn't let things lie. He's always one step ahead."

Shane nodded. If Adrianna didn't want to leave the Benefactor, there was little anyone could do. They had to find Trey. With him safe, nothing would keep Adrianna at the Benefactor's side.

"Maybe, but he hasn't run into all the roadblocks we've set up for him. You might as well know now. The consortium holding majority stock in

Astro Tex is a group of women from Preatiens. They will expect you to reaffirm your agreement to the Fed human trafficking accord."

Her face flushed. "That is good news. So, the bribery scam...?"

"Cover to make the Benefactor believe I was his ally, so I could keep Ms. Pacquin with me. He plans to use her to gain entrance to Preatiens." Shane rubbed the ache in his jaw. Time was not on his side. "You'll excuse me; I need to prepare orders."

He chose the quickest, most direct route back to the *Adrasteia*, and while he brought the ship's engines online, he requested immediate access to the outgoing queue.

Gods, he wanted to lash out, hit something, tear something to pieces. Why did Adrianna have to be so fucking self-reliant? Why couldn't she let him handle getting Trey back safely? She'd handed herself over the Benefactor without a fight. His hands fisted at his sides. He waited, mired in dread, trying not to think about what the Benefactor would do to Adrianna in the six days it took to arrive at Preatiens.

As time ticked slowly by and the possibility that Adrianna could contact someone and request assistance diminished, his body remained frozen in the pilot's seat on the *Adrasteia's* bridge. He sat, his mind numb, watching the *Beneficence* pull out from dock and the station controller move it into the queue. It was ten hours from dock to hyperpulse point, but those extra hours were meaningless now. Once out of dock, the Benefactor's ship could exit via the hyperpulse point with or without the station's controller assisting. The *Canton Mist* was four hours ahead of them.

"*Adrasteia*, prepare to hand over control."

"Control is yours, station."

"*Adrasteia*, you are in queue. Hyperpulse point is 9.94 hours. You have a direct connection to Preatiens. Good luck, sir."

"Thank you, station."

As if on cue, another adrenaline spike hit him. "Fuck. Fuck. Fuck." He jumped from his seat, slid down the ladder, and rushed to his office. The *Canton Mist* was awaiting his orders. He'd also need to contact Riordan and coordinate with him, now that Adrianna was out of his reach until she reached Preatiens. "Fuck!"

19

A drianna had found it necessary to pull back, reforming her inner ice wall, excluding all outside emotional contact. Shane's reaction when she left the hospitality room was a crushing weight on her chest. Her mind reeled, slewing through a cacophony of pain, regret, and anger. The Benefactor's glee, dripping with caustic satisfaction, was apparent even with her empathic senses tightly controlled. Outward submission was paramount, but inside, she would grasp tight to her defiance. Inside, she would not quell her anger or submit to the Benefactor's plans. The first notes of Sibelius's "Lemminkäinen's Return" came to her. The martial music fused her emotions into a singular focus of resistance. No more hiding behind her ice wall. She would become ice itself, an ice warrior to take the fight to the enemy.

With her inner defenses secure, Adrianna focused on where the Benefactor was taking her. They were on the docks, a path clearing before them as the Benefactor's security muscled their way through. A large access port loomed ahead, leading to a warm, carpeted passageway. The size of the ship allowed it to claim this luxurious berth. No cold flexible tube. Her eyebrows lifted slightly when she entered. It was built and decorated with sophisticated grace rather than the ostentation found in the Benefactor's official residence on Furzine.

"You're surprised, my dear. The palace was designed for the citizens. I can't abide the gaudy glitz. In my private spaces, I prefer elegance and refinement. A purity of line, color, and style. That's also what I find so attractive in you."

Adrianna looked at him, choosing to ignore his compliment. "May I see my quarters?"

"Certainly, my dear. I thought you might wish a quick tour to accustom yourself to the ship. It's my primary mode of travel off Furzine, and I expect you will accompany me from time to time." He gave her a patronizing smile. "I'm sure the excitement has tired you, so perhaps it's best if you went to rest in your quarters."

Adrianna scowled at him. "Thank you."

"Here we are. You'll find a full wardrobe provided for you. My quarters are the second door down the passageway. Your bath is here, and this door leads to our shared sitting room. Join me there for a light supper at half twenty. Dress will be informal tonight, but in the future you will dress more formally. I'll leave you to your repose." He approached her and moved in to place a kiss on her cheek, which Adrianna avoided. With a tsk, he stepped to the door. "Rest well." The door closed behind him.

Adrianna resisted the urge to lie on the bed and cry. Ice warriors didn't cry. Probably couldn't cry. How do you cry when you're frozen? *Stop rambling.* Adrianna sat looking around the room. A vanity with mirror, clothes cupboards, and drawers lined the walls. The Spartan lines, a necessity on a space-going vehicle, were softened by the pastel blues, lavenders, and greens used throughout. A light floral fragrance added to the room's ventilation was an additional feminine touch.

No vid or audio pickup points were apparent. Better to assume they were there. To her surprise, no one had checked her for weapons. The gun Shane gave her was still in the holster on her ankle, hidden by her boot. Somehow, she needed to keep it concealed until they arrived at Preatiens. Rest first. If he was watching her, he'd expect her to be tired. She'd give him what he wanted—naive, malleable Dria, the bubbly little girl who always did as she was told. After setting the bed alarm to give her plenty of time to dress later, she lay on top of the coverlet, tucked her hands under her chin, and shut her eyes.

When the alarm woke her, Adrianna was surprised she'd slept. The rest had done her good and fortunately hadn't given her that muddled feeling that midday naps often brought. *Time to start operation featherhead.* After freshening up in the bathroom, she sat at the vanity, found a brush in a drawer, and brushed out her hair, choosing to leave it down rather than braid it.

Beautiful clothes packed three large cupboards. "How pretty." Sighing over some, squealing over others, she held items against her body, examining herself in the cupboard mirror. She contemplated every dress, blouse, shirt, skirt, and pair of slacks. "Goodness! So much to choose from." *The Benefactor had damn well better be watching.* Once more sorting through the hanging clothes, she placed outfits on the bed, the overstuffed chair anchored in the corner, and the vanity. Then she went to the cupboard with the shoe bins and went through each bin, pulling out shoes and matching them to the outfits. Finished, she had a pile of discarded shoes heaped next to the cupboard. "Oh gosh! Now I have to put these all away."

This better work. On the floor next to the pile of shoes, she pulled off her boots, making sure to loosen the ankle holster and leave it behind. Then she began to put shoes away, grabbing handfuls to pile in front of her and opening bins. In one handful, she grabbed the boot with her gun and surreptitiously transferred it to a dress boot. After she finished putting all the shoes away, she hoped that anyone who searched her things would look only at the clothes she'd worn before boarding and skip the dress boots that had been provided to her.

With the gun hidden, she went about selecting an outfit for supper. "The red or the dark blue? Hmmmm. Maybe I should just go with the pink." She tittered. "No, the blue will make me look more sophisticated." The clock on the bed said she had ten minutes to finish getting ready. She put on a perfect performance, dithering and hurrying to clean up, put the dark blue outfit on, and touch up her makeup. Ready, she took a deep breath and opened the door to the sitting room.

When she entered the room, the Benefactor rose from a dark red leather armchair, his arms outstretched in greeting.

"My dear, please come in. I promise I won't bite. We got off wrong-footed. Let's begin anew." False benevolence curled around him. "Such a beauty. You light up every room you enter." He motioned her toward a small table set for two. "Please, let's talk while we eat."

Adrianna allowed him to seat her. "Thank you, sir."

As he took his own seat, the Benefactor said, "My dear, you must call me Franklin. My given name is Franklin Stanton. We will wed soon, and such formality is not acceptable between husband and wife."

"Yes, sir...Franklin." Eyes fixated on her plate, she stirred the rice dish with her fork, unable to take a bite, uncertain she'd be able to swallow.

"Don't be afraid, Adrianna. Your impurity has not dimmed my love for you."

She jerked her eyes up, widening them when she ascertained his sincerity.

"I can see that your inner purity is unsullied. You've been blemished on the outside, but it is a small crack that can be repaired. I will restore you to your former self. A surgeon shall once again make you an untouched beauty. It will be as though you are sixteen once again. You will be my treasure as I've always planned."

Adrianna's grip tightened around her fork. Her skin crawled as though a thousand insects skittered over her. *What the hell?* He was planning to repair her? She would never be sixteen again. He was delusional if he thought she was anything like the naive girl she'd been five years ago. But that was the problem, wasn't it? He was delusional, and she must play her assigned role for all she was worth to keep the truth from confronting him. She forced herself to eat.

When she'd finished the last bite, the Benefactor reached across and took her hand. "Come with me. I have something to share with you in the bedroom."

Adrianna swallowed hard, glancing from one side to the other. "I-I'm not sure that..."

"Your hesitance is admirable, my dear. I will not use you tonight if that is what you fear. No, tonight I've planned something that will show you what a kind and gentle lover I can be. Tonight, you will be the audience, a voyeur into my world." He pulled on her hand. "Come now."

Adrianna stumbled after him. The food in her stomach threatened to rise and stain the Benefactor's exquisite carpeting. Inside his room, a girl sat nude on the bed, legs curled beside her, hair in a long demure braid trailing down her chest. *Gods, the girl is almost my twin.*

"Reentha, greet my wife-to-be. She will be viewing our activities."

"Hello, mistress."

If Adrianna could flee, she would, but where could she go on this ship? Sensors would find her even if she hid. With her arms tightly wrapped around her midsection, which still cramped, she acknowledged the girl with a nod.

"Please sit, Adrianna." The Benefactor motioned to a straight-back chair that had been positioned facing the bed, four feet distant. When he sat, the side of the bed sank beneath his bulk. The luxurious coverings had been pulled back, folded neatly on a bench at the foot of the bed. White sheets and a bank of white pillows remained.

"Reentha has been my companion for this trip." He stroked the girl's foot. "Tonight and in the coming nights, I will teach you what pleases me. Reentha is already well versed in pleasuring me. I will use her to show you how to satisfy me. I want nothing to detract from the first time I take you as my bride-to-be. Everything will be perfect. You will be perfect. I long for that moment, but of course, it must wait until your imperfection has been repaired."

Adrianna was staggered by the enormity of his madness. He planned to have sex in front of her so she could learn how to please him in bed? At least he didn't have plans to have sex with her until his surgeon had created a new hymen for her. *Merde*, she was going to have to sit here night after night, enduring this bizarre performance. The girl sat in placid silence. Was she drugged?

"How old is Reentha?" Adrianna asked.

The Benefactor smiled the benevolent smile that made Adrianna want to grind her teeth. "Ah. Do I detect jealousy? Never fear, my dear. You are so much more than Reentha could ever hope to be. She is sixteen. The age I believe, and in which Federation law concurs, that she has attained the maturity to consent. She came to me on her birthday, her day of perfection. It was my pleasure to take her perfection and bring it to full flower with the act of love. But she is like a hothouse flower that withers far too quickly. You, my dear, are nothing like that. Once we are wed, the marital state will preserve your perfection for a lifetime."

He stood and walked to Adrianna. "All this talk of perfection has stirred me." His hand reached out and took Adrianna's, positioning her palm over his erection. "This is what thoughts of your perfection do to me.

But for now I must sate myself on another. Watch closely, Adrianna. I do not want our first joining marred by punishment. The ritual of a perfect joining must be followed exactly."

Adrianna's whole body trembled. When at last he dropped her hand and began removing his clothing, she clenched her arms tightly around herself. Squeezing her eyes tight was an impossibility. How was she going to endure days of this?

IT HAD BEEN a long ten hours while the Benefactor's ship made its way to the Hub's hyperpulse point. Shane's body was a wreck from the fatigue and pain of muscles that had remained tense through long hours while he considered and rejected various scenarios for keeping Adrianna from leaving the Hub's system with the Benefactor. When the *Beneficence* finally winked away, Shane plunged into a dark void. His connection to the station controller faded away. A dull roaring filled his ears. The ship's oxygen levels must have dropped because his lungs couldn't fill with enough air while he gasped to breathe. His hands and feet were weights attached to deadened, lifeless limbs. His mind narrowed tightly into one trickling stream of thought. *I could lose her. I could lose her. I could lose her. No. Please, no. No. No.*

Like clockwork, the stress nanites in his system made adjustments. His pulse slowed. His breathing steadied. His hearing came back. With the return of his normal body functions, he mentally quashed his fear. *The worst has happened. Fuck. It wasn't supposed to.*

He'd been so fucking sure. Maon had tried to tell him. Even the director had reminded him there was a strong possibility Adrianna could be taken. *You're a fucking stellar idiot!* Shane hadn't believed the contingency plans he'd made for Preatiens would ever be necessary. Now, they were the point of hope he relied on. After Preatiens, she'd be taken to Furzine, and he wouldn't think about that. Or that Adrianna was now at the Benefactor's mercy.

If only Dria was as good at following orders as Adrianna. *Fuck.* She took care of everyone else. Why couldn't she let him take care of her? Why couldn't she trust him to get Trey back alive? *Because she's Dria.* If she thought she could help, she'd plunge right in. She was fearless and almost too smart for her own good. She scooped up knowledge by the shovelful, and without personal experience relied on her "experts" to work her way out of tight spots. How many times had he heard her quote the advice of her governess, her defense instructor, or Master Trey? The fact that she'd been successful so far didn't reassure Shane. There was nothing he could do now but wait. He sat in the pilot's seat, waiting for the station controller to initiate the *Adrasteia's* entrance into the Hub's hyperpulse point, his whole body straining to be gone. He'd done everything possible until he arrived in the Preatiens system.

He listened as the controller said, *"Initiating hyperpulse entry in three, two, one..."*

Shane slowly exhaled. He really should go to bed. He had six and a half days before docking at the Preatien space station. His feet like boulders, he trudged into his quarters, stripped, stowed his clothes, and climbed into bed. His hand on autopilot, he switched on the safety field. And laid there. His mind looping through the last day made it impossible to relax. Without chemical inducement, the sleep he needed wouldn't come. His thoughts were full of Adrianna while his body longed to feel her snuggled tight in his arms.

He switched off the safety field, dragged himself out of bed, and slumped his way to the med clinic. He ran a finger over the bottles and vials in the med cabinet, trying to remember where to find the Snooze Quik. It took his brain a moment to realize the cabinet had been organized. Bottles together. Vials together. Tubes in neat rows. And everything in alphabetical order. Dria's handiwork. *Fuck.*

With a dose of the sleeping aid in his hand, he went to the galley, pulled a bottle of water from the cooler, and took the pill. That should put him out for at least eight hours. He'd have to figure out how he would fill the other 148 hours when he woke. Back in bed, it wasn't long before he fell into a deep, dreamless sleep.

~

Three Days Later

In the three days since the *Adrasteia* entered hyperspace, Shane had poured over the schematics of the Preatien space station. He hadn't found a better location for the meeting between the Benefactor and Élise Sauveterre than the one he'd proposed before the *Canton Mist* left the Hub. The conference room of the Preatien Commercial Alliance was built with up-to-date security features including a hidden doorway for armed security to use, vid and audio surveillance, and signal dampers. No one could listen in from the outside, but even better, the Benefactor could not communicate with his own forces. It wouldn't matter whether he brought Adrianna with him, once he'd entered that room. Élise Sauveterre could request to visit her granddaughter, and the ship's captain would be hard-pressed to deny her.

As long as the Benefactor believed he had Trey Johansson in his custody, he would not hesitate to make the meeting with Élise Sauveterre. Six days was more than enough time for the marshals to find Trey, but the real trick was recovering him without the Benefactor finding out. It frustrated Shane that he wasn't part of planning that operation. With Trey safe, the *Beneficence* could be locked into dock and boarded if need be. Shane did not want both Adrianna and the Benefactor to be on board if that happened. Ideally, Adrianna would be in the conference room where Shane could assure her safety. He'd also avoid the sticky situation of boarding and searching a designated diplomatic ship. Not that he'd let that stop him.

Shane ran his hands over his face and shook his head. The details were solidly fixed in his brain, and no matter how he looked at things, he couldn't tease out any other options that gave them a better chance at securing Adrianna safely. He stood, flexing cramped muscles. Going over his plan repeatedly was doing him no good. He stripped while he walked to his bedroom, tossing his clothes in the laundry bin and donning workout clothes.

It had been days since he'd worked out, so he pulled a jump rope from a gym cupboard. He jumped with a steady running motion, arms and legs moving smoothly. Tight muscles relaxed when they warmed up, but his mind was far from steady. His attempts to focus on the exercising were unsuccessful. Instead, he found his thoughts returning repeatedly to Adrianna.

He'd never been lonely in his life despite the extended time he'd spent alone on the *Adrasteia*. At least that was what he'd always told himself. Now, every place on board reminded him of Dria. Even here in the gym, images of working out together or of him teaching her defensive fighting techniques assailed him. Or images of sex. They must have had sex in every room and compartment.

A thought struck him. The rope curled on the floor when he stopped jumping and stood silently. Dria had become a part of him. A part now amputated. His priority list had re-sorted itself, and now she was at the top, number one. More important than the *Adrasteia*. More important than the Marshal Service. More important than his family. More important than anything, and he had to do something to keep her. If he had to, he'd sell the *Adrasteia*, pay off her debts, and take a marshal position on planet somewhere. If that didn't work out, he could always join a local police force. A smile spread across his face, and he resumed jumping rope. He had a plan. Once he got her away from the Benefactor, she'd be his forever. He'd never allow the Benefactor or anyone else to come between them. Together they would deal with whatever the Benefactor did to her. Shane prayed that her training and ability to distance herself from what was physically happening to her would limit any harm. With hands tight on the handles of the jump rope and knuckles white, he increased his pace, jumping until his heart was hammering and he couldn't lift his legs.

ADRIANNA DRESSED CAREFULLY in one of the long dresses the Benefactor had provided for her. The ship would dock in less than an hour, and the Benefactor had directed her to be dressed and ready to go. A meeting had already been arranged with her grandmother. They were to meet her on station. It was none too soon. Another night spent watching the Benefactor ritually fuck Reentha would have driven Adrianna to use her pistol on herself or to shoot the Benefactor. She couldn't allow the Benefactor to take her to Furzine, and she couldn't allow him to kill Master Trey. If only the marshals had found and rescued him. They hadn't. The Benefactor had shown her a live vid feed of Master Trey just this morning. The gun Shane had given her was snugged into its holster in her boot, ready to be used. How she would use it was still to be determined.

When she entered the main lounge, she heard the Benefactor saying, "Beta Tau. Excellent. And the *Fantasy* is standing by at hyperpoint gamma?"

"Yes sir. They will enter hyperspace one hour and twenty-eight minutes from now," the Benefactor's aide responded.

"Excellent." The Benefactor turned to Adrianna. "My dear. You look beautiful. Your grandmother will be so pleased to see what a lovely young woman you have become." He took her arm, ushering her to the ship's exit. "Come. Let's be off."

The Benefactor's head of security, Torbold, had positioned guards along the route the Benefactor would take to his meeting with Élise Sauveterre. Torbold lost the argument to take security into the meeting room before he even made it. The Benefactor insisted on looking as peaceable as possible. So no guards with him. Just a future son-in-law visiting his bride-to-be's grandmother for the first time. Torbold himself accompanied them, taking up position outside the conference room once Adrianna and the Benefactor had entered.

~

THE MOMENT THE *ADRASTEIA* DOCKED, Shane joined the marshal waiting for him dockside. "Report."

"The Benefactor and Ms. Pacquin are inside the meeting room, as is Ms. Sauveterre. The Benefactor's security chief and about a dozen of his guards have taken up positions along the route from his ship to the conference room."

"Are our people in position?" Shane asked.

"Yes, sir. We're waiting for word that Trey Johansson has been recovered."

"Gods, this is cutting things fine."

drianna waited while the door to the meeting room was opened by a representative of the Preatien Commercial Alliance resplendent in a navy-blue coat with the PCA logo. The Benefactor gestured for her to enter and then followed her. Across the featureless room, a woman rose from behind a bland wooden conference table and came forward to greet them. She was tall with an erect carriage and grave expression, which the short, severe cut of her steel-gray hair did nothing to soften. Bright green eyes fastened on the Benefactor when she held out her hand to welcome him.

"Hello. I'm Élise Sauveterre," she said, looking down her nose at him.

"Franklin Stanton at your service." The Benefactor bowed and attempted to bring her hand to his lips to kiss. Sauveterre forcefully denied him by pulling it away with a sharp motion.

She turned to Adrianna and said, "And you are little Dria all grown up." She took Adrianna's hands and looked her over before placing a kiss on both of Adrianna's cheeks.

"It's good to meet you, Mémé."

"Come, let's sit and get to know one another. I'm afraid this conference room is rather austere." Sauveterre gestured to the table and seated herself on the far side again.

The Benefactor assisted Adrianna into a chair, then selected one next to her and opposite Sauveterre. Adrianna bit the inside of her cheek to keep her lip from curling. The reality was this was a business meeting between the Benefactor and her grandmother. Adrianna was a bargaining chip. It was getting harder to keep her true emotions from showing on her face. They were, however, on full display to her grandmother's empathic ability. The Benefactor was a shrewd man. Did he think Mémé wouldn't discern them? Another of his delusions? Maybe it didn't matter to him and whatever he wanted from her grandmother. Shane had thought the Benefactor wanted Adrianna to use against her grandmother, and there seemed to be some truth to that. Whatever he was up to right now was secondary to his fixation on Adrianna and her "perfection." No one outside his inner circle would have ever believed he had this weird fetish for sixteen-year-old virgins. With a shake, Adrianna made herself listen to the conversation.

"I felt it my duty, when I was finally able to extract Dria from the arrangement she had made with Marshal Tiernan, to bring her to you to show you she was safe and sound."

"I appreciate that, Franklin. May I call you Franklin?"

"Yes, please do. I have additional news that makes our speaking on terms of familiarity even more proper."

"Oh?" Sauveterre raised an eyebrow.

"Yes." The Benefactor took Adrianna's hand and held it with his on top of the table. She clamped her teeth together to hold in a sound of disgust and prevent herself from wrenching it away. Instead, she sat rigidly beside him. "Adrianna has agreed to make me the happiest of men and become my wife. I know this is a surprise, but you are fully able to see with your special abilities that I am quite sincere in my admiration and love for this delightful girl."

"Yes, I do see your sincerity of affection. Have your affections been engaged as well, Adrianna?" Sauveterre asked.

"Mémé, I admit at first I did not wish to marry Franklin. I even ran away from him. But I've since discovered that he's more than I ever saw before. He asked me to marry him, and I knew that it was the right time to say yes." It was impossible to smile without grimacing, so Adrianna didn't even attempt it.

"I see," Sauveterre responded.

The Benefactor looked at Adrianna with eyes bright and beady like a magpie absorbed in the shiny bits and pieces collected in its nest. When his gaze left her, Adrianna closed her eyes, releasing the barest of sighs before opening them again.

"We have come to ask for your permission to marry in the hopes that, in granting it, you will also grant us the right to set up a home on Preatiens. A place that can be a home away from home for when Adrianna wants to spend time with her family. I'm sure she'll want to make regular visits." The Benefactor lifted his eyes to the ceiling as though some idyllic vid of the future played there. With a sigh, he regarded Sauveterre. "I'd also like to offer, in the way of a wedding gift, to establish a new visitor's center in Preatien orbit, with all the income going to an account solely in Adrianna's name."

"I see. Well, you do have big plans, don't you, Franklin?" Sauveterre said. Adrianna admired the control her grandmother maintained at the Benefactor's outrageous suggestion.

"Nothing is too good for my own sweet Dria." He squeezed Adrianna's hand. "I do hope I haven't overstepped, but the Fantasy Resort is already on its way here and should arrive in the next hour or so. The ship will establish permanent orbit once it receives coordinates from the station master." He reached into his jacket and pulled out a document. "Here is the ship title, which you can see is prepared to be transferred into Dria's name as soon as we are officially married. I hope to have the center fully functional on that date." He gave Adrianna a beneficent smile and patted her hand.

"Well, that does present a difficulty, Franklin. You are of course correct to infer that I care about my granddaughter's well-being. However, you are sadly mistaken if you believe that concern could coerce me into agreeing to allow you a foothold in Preatien space."

The Benefactor leaned forward, clearing his throat as though to begin speaking.

One slender finger rose to forestall him. "Franklin, you've told me your plans; now let me explain how I see matters. Adrianna is certainly free to marry anyone she pleases. I will not stand in the way of her heart's desire. It is rare for a Preatien woman to marry off planet and forgo the protections of living on Preatiens, but Adrianna isn't typical in many ways.

"However, it is a long-standing rule of law that Preatiens decline off worlders any form of permanent status in system. Once Adrianna marries you, she will become an off worlder. Your visitor's center must leave Preatien space as soon as it arrives, or we will be forced to seize it. You will not be allowed to purchase or build a residence on Preatiens."

"But surely your granddaughter deserves special consideration." The Benefactor's voice grew hard.

"I will grant her special consideration. The consideration to return with me down world and leave off this foolish notion of marrying you. I do not know what you have done to make her submit to your plans, but I know it is not love that keeps her at your side." Sauveterre turned to Adrianna. "Will you leave with me, Dria?"

"I cannot, Mémé."

"Very well." She rose and tapped the hidden door, which opened to allow her through.

"Fucking cunt!" the Benefactor said, thrusting Adrianna's hand away from him and slapping the table. "I will not let that old woman stymie me. There has to be another way."

Shane had taken up position down the corridor from the conference room. The Benefactor's security must know the *Adrasteia* had docked and he was on station, so it made sense to let them see him. He was counting on them thinking he was alone. Why would they think otherwise? While he waited, he reviewed the setup, looking for flaws in the positioning of the marshals and the Preatien security police. The locations of all the players were no longer a guess. Decisions had been made and executed. What would be, would be. The Benefactor's head of security was stationed beside the conference room door. Once the Benefactor had passed through that door and it had locked behind him, his security was effectively blocked from intervening in anything that took place in the room. If necessary, the marshals could use the room's hidden door to take control of the Benefactor.

The hope was news of Trey's rescue would reach them in time for Élise Sauveterre to reveal that covertly to Adrianna. With that knowledge, Adrianna would surely leave with her grandmother. But the news hadn't come yet, and time was running out. When the message came that Sauveterre was standing and leaving the conference room without Adrianna, Shane had to take action.

He walked sedately toward the conference room door where the Benefactor's security chief stood watching him. Shane maintained eye contact when he took up position on the opposite side of the conference room door. He didn't allow any reaction to show when he was notified that the marshal communications officer was patching his EBC into the feed from the operation on Beta Tau to rescue Trey.

"*On three. One, two, three.*" A loud *thud* was followed by the sounds of wood splintering and metal buckling. Shane heard a *clunk* and then a hissing sound. They were using gas.

"*Clear.*"

"*Clear.*"

Nothing else was communicated for a long stretch of seconds.

"*All targets down and immobilized. Johannsson is here. Send in the med tech. He's down from the gas and looks like he's been beaten.*"

Shane took a satisfied breath. The security chief's eyes flickered. He knew. Shane smiled ferociously and launched himself at the man, who turned and attempted to open the door. With a shove, Shane pushed him into the door, struggling to secure both arms and cuff him. The man kicked back with one booted foot, striking Shane in the shin. Shane grunted at the pain but didn't release his hold. With the hall filling with marshals and security police, the security chief yelled, "They have Johannsson." Another marshal helped Shane push the still-struggling man to the floor, where a third marshal clamped plasti-steel cuffs on him.

INSIDE THE MEETING room, the Benefactor's manners did not desert him even though he was angry. When he took the back of Adrianna's chair to assist her in rising and returning to his ship, he was halted by her bending over and fiddling with her boot. "My dear, let us go."

You can do this. She straightened. He pulled out her chair and then turned toward the door, waiting with crooked elbow for her to take his arm. When she didn't, he looked back. Adrianna pushed the chair aside and stood facing him, a gun held in both hands pointed at his chest. She would not allow the thumping of her heart or the steady drip, drip, drip of apprehension to shake her.

"Dria, what are you doing?" he asked. It was one of the few times that Adrianna had ever seen him look startled.

"I'm not going with you." She held the gun steady. "I do not wish to be your wife. I have never wished to be your wife. If you try to compel me to leave with you, I will shoot you. This gun may look small, but its electro-charged bullets are just as capable of killing you as a larger caliber if I hit your heart or head. I've become quite a good shot, and at this range I won't miss."

"My dear, you cannot mean this. You are not yourself. Your grandmother's rejection has agitated you. Hand me the gun. I only desire to comfort and care for you." He reached out to take it.

Adrianna moved back. "I am not distraught. My grandmother has acted exactly as I would have in her place." She bit the words out, hoping to break through his delusion.

The Benefactor reeled a step and shook his head. "You have forgotten someone." His voice was menacing. His hand jerked forward. "Stop this nonsense and give me the gun."

"No, you are going to go to comm your men on Beta Tau and order them to release Master Trey. When I have been assured he is free and safe, I will allow you to return to your ship."

"Adrianna, you must—"

Muffled thumps sounded on the door. Adrianna backed away. Outside, sounds of a scuffle were punctuated by a man's voice shouting, "They have Johannsson!" Men poured through the main and hidden doors, pointing drawn weapons, aiming them at her.

Over bellows from the Benefactor demanding to the meaning of the interruption, Shane said, "Put the gun down, Dria. You're safe now."

Shane was behind a marshal who stood, weapon pointed at her. The gun fell from her fingers as though it were too hot to touch. "Shane!" She would have run to him if the Benefactor hadn't been between them.

The crime lord was gesticulating wildly, his face flushed. "Do you know who I am? I am the Benefactor of Furzine. This is a diplomatic mission to Preatiens. I want all your names." He reached into the inner pocket of his jacket to remove something.

Every marshal in the room drew his gun, aiming at the Benefactor. "Remove your hand from your pocket and place both of your hands on your head," a marshal ordered.

The Benefactor complied. One marshal rushed to secure the crime lord in handcuffs while the other removed a small recording device from the Benefactor's pocket. Once he was cuffed, he was frisked for weapons. None were found.

Shane went to Adrianna and scooped her into his arms. Tremors overtook her while Shane muttered soothing sounds, his lips pressed to the top of her head.

"A mhuirnín! It's okay. You're safe, *a chroí*. I'm here. It's all over, a ghrá."

"I couldn't leave with him. I just couldn't."

"Of course not, a ghrá geal." Shane soothed.

"But he'll kill Master Trey." Sobs overtook her.

"Trey is safe, a mhuirnín. Riordan found him and rescued him."

Adrianna pulled back, face streaming with tears, and looked into Shane's eyes, searching the blue depths. Everything was fine.

Behind him, the Benefactor, shaking with fury, returned to shouting demands and threats. "I will not be treated in this manner. I am the Benefactor of Furzine. You will unhand me, or I will see that charges are filed against you for false arrest."

Shane kissed the top of Adrianna's head. "I need to deal with this, a ghrá. Sit here." Adrianna sat in the chair he pulled out for her and worked at settling her breathing. He gestured for another marshal to come over. "Would you take her statement, please?"

She watched Shane walk to the Benefactor. With his hands cuffed in front of him, the Benefactor was still managing to gesticulate wildly.

"You!" He waved his fists at Shane. "This man tried to extort money from me. He's facilitating illegal human trafficking through the Hub. Arrest him!"

Shane smirked. "Sorry. Not happening. I've been operating with the full approval of the Director of the Marshals."

The Benefactor sputtered. "Fucking bastard." He brought his hands up and pointed a puffy finger at Shane. "You above all should know that you cannot place me under arrest. In the first place, I have done nothing wrong.

In the second place, I have diplomatic immunity as the Furzine head of state. Release me this instant!" The last words were more snarl than speech.

"Ma'am?" the marshal taking Adrianna's statement said.

"Hmmm?" Adrianna pulled her eyes away from the scene between Shane and the Benefactor.

"I'm Marshal Collins. I need to ask you some questions."

"Yes. Of course." Adrianna's response was automatic. Her mind continued to stray toward Shane and the Benefactor. "He's taking the cuffs off him!"

"Yes, ma'am. He's the head of state for Furzine and has diplomatic immunity."

"But he kidnapped Master Trey and was dealing in illegal human trafficking through the Hub."

"You and I know that's true, but we don't have any evidence against him."

"What do you mean no evidence?" Adrianna was having a hard time believing what the marshal was saying. Had she gone through all this, not to mention what Master Trey had gone through, for the Benefactor to walk away? "I can testify that he showed me that picture of Master Trey and told me he had taken him hostage."

"I'm sorry to say, that isn't enough. The men we arrested for the kidnapping have already confessed that they acted alone for their own purposes. As for the illegal human trafficking, Marshal Tiernan knew that catching him red-handed was virtually impossible. He covers his tracks that well. The goal was to stop the business, not put the Benefactor in prison." With a look of sympathy, Collins said, "Sorry, ma'am."

"That's not right." She exhaled.

"No, ma'am, it's not, but it's the way it is. I need to ask you some questions about how you came to be with the Benefactor and what happened in this room."

"Certainly," she said, watching Preatien security move in and place their own cuffs on the Benefactor. Shane followed them as they maneuvered the Benefactor, still yelling threats, out of the room.

Collins said, "Looks like the Preatiens are going to hold the Benefactor."

Adrianna leaned forward. "Does that mean they'll charge him with a crime?"

Collins shook his head. "I wouldn't think so. Spaceports have dual jurisdictions, Fed and planetary. Depends on which side of customs you're on. We're on the Fed side right now. Usually planetary security wouldn't make arrests here without the approval of a Fed representative. Tiernan must have okayed it. I don't know why, but I'm sure there's a good reason. It would be a black mark on a marshal's career to detain the Benefactor without substantial guarantee the arrest would lead to conviction. Planetary security isn't part of the Fed system. They can get away with it, especially here on Preatiens."

Adrianna shuddered. "The Benefactor is repulsive. The universe would be a better place if they locked him away in a dark hole where he could harm no one again."

Collins nodded. "I totally agree. Why don't we get back to your statement? First, tell me from the moment you left with the Benefactor at Runner's Hub, everything that happened."

"Sure." She wrinkled her brow. "But first can I ask that someone check on a girl onboard the *Beneficence*? Her name is Reentha. She's been serving the Benefactor sexually, and I'm not sure if she's doing so of her own free will. She looked drugged to me."

"Yes. I'll make sure that happens. If she chooses to leave, we'll assist her." Collins signaled another marshal to join him.

21

S   hane had never been so glad to get away from someone as he was when he left the Benefactor harassing the Preatien security police. They'd concluded they should hold him and his detained staff while they verified his status, giving the marshals the opportunity to obtain a warrant to board and search the Fantasy Resort when it made orbit. The Fed judge was happy to authorize the warrant on the basis of the underage trafficking by the Benefactor's agent, Jason Holmes. The marshals would be weeks going over the Fantasy with a fine-tooth comb. Marshal Collins messaged Shane that Adrianna was waiting at the little café where the marshals had gone to celebrate.

When he arrived, the restaurant was packed with people. He looked around for Adrianna, finally spotting her at a table surrounded by marshals and Preatien security police. While he approached, he noted some unabashed flirting in progress by several of the males at the table, all directed at Adrianna.

"Excuse me, gentlemen." Shane pressed his way next to Adrianna's chair. "Adrianna, are these gentlemen bothering you?" he asked, looking down at her, trying to keep his emotions in check. The jealousy squeezing his gut probably resembled a clashing cymbal to her empathic senses.

"No, Sir. Nothing can bother me now you're here." Adrianna looked straight up at him to show him her sincerity, then lowered her eyes submissively.

Shane broke out in a wide grin. "That's my girl!"

One marshal punched a police officer in the arm. "I told you she was taken."

The marshal seated next to Adrianna rose. "Here, Tiernan, take a seat."

"No, sit back down, Jim. I think Ms. Pacquin and I need to go over her statement in detail now that I'm free." Several of the marshals responded to Shane's grin with grins of their own. He was free and not just in the mundane sense of being off duty. "Thank you, gentlemen, for all your help. I deeply appreciate it because Adrianna is—well, as someone once told me —she's special." He beamed down at Adrianna, who had looked up at him. Her soft smile beckoned him, so he placed a gentle kiss on her lips before taking her hand and pulling her up. "Let's go, a ghrá."

The moment the lift doors closed, Adrianna and Shane melted together in a tight embrace. Wrapped in his solid strength, Adrianna allowed the emotions she'd held back to break free. Every part of her shook. "I was so afraid."

Somehow, though her voice was a mixture of whisper and sob, Shane understood her words. "Me too." He snuggled her in closer to him.

Shane's palm rose to cradle her head, his face buried in her hair. "Did he touch you?" His arms and chest tensed when he asked the question.

"No. He didn't," she said. His taut muscles softened, and then he squeezed her tighter. With a muffled squeak, she thumped a hand against his back. "Can't breathe."

Shane loosened his hold. "Sorry. I'm just so..." He swallowed. "I'm so glad you're safe."

Adrianna took her turn to squeeze him tight. "There's so much I need to tell you, but right now, I want to forget all that. I just want you to hold me."

The lift bell gave a ding. They'd arrived at the level where the *Adrasteia* was docked. Shane released her, but he claimed her hand when they exited to the concourse.

"Your grandmother has invited us for supper. We're to meet her at her shuttle," Shane informed Adrianna while they walked toward the *Adrasteia's* access port. "She's a formidable woman."

I don't want to talk about my grandmother. Not right now. Once again things were lined up and right in Adrianna's world. Walking with Shane. Talking with him. Being with him was like coming home.

"I would expect any female relation of yours to be no less. You, *a ghrá*, are formidable." Shane glanced down at her with a heat in his eyes that sent a flash of need caroming through her. Underneath the passion, Adrianna sensed his need to reassert his control. To reassert that she was his and his alone.

"If you are going to say things I can't understand, I'm going to do the same to you, *mon bel homme*." Adrianna puckered her lips into a provocative pout.

"I know what that means." He chuckled. "*Mé a fháil fós a spank tú.*"

"Did you just say you were going to spank me?" Adrianna arched an eyebrow at him.

"Only if you're very good," he responded, arching an eyebrow in return.

Relief and happiness emanated from Shane. Inside Adrianna, those same emotions percolated like bubbles, a giddy froth that overflowed. With a whoop, she threw herself at him, nearly knocking him off his feet in her attempt to smother him in a ferocious hug. Instead of falling, he pulled her up, pushed her legs to wrap his waist, and trotted the last stretch to the *Adrasteia's* port. When they entered *Adrasteia's* foyer, he took her mouth in a harsh, claiming kiss, tongue tangling with hers, finishing by biting her lower lip and holding on to it when he drew away. "You're mine, Adrianna. Mine." An invisible collar tightened around her throat, secure and immovable.

THE CITRUSY LEMON fragrance that was pure Adrianna intoxicated Shane as much as the pressure of her soft curves molded tight against him did. She was here. In his arms. His. He was throbbing with an ache he had to grit his teeth to surmount. But he would not spoil the most significant event of his life by rushing. The mewling sound she made when he released her was evidence of her own consuming need.

"Adrianna, go wait in the gym." Her instantaneous reaction—her change in posture, breathing pattern, even the muscles of her face—transformed her to a fully submitted woman, his woman.

"Yes, Master." She went immediately to the ladder that would take her to the lower level and the gym.

Shane fisted both hands. No questions. Pure obedience. The gratification he derived from that one simple act was so intense he stood still to relish its potency until his cock reminded him that more pleasure awaited on the deck below. In his quarters, he stripped and selected the rope he would use tonight from his toy cupboard. Luck had been with him when he'd found the lemon-yellow *kinshthan* rope in the Hub's dockside bazaar. He would use the bright skeins of rope to bind his own personal sunbeam, keeping her with him to light his life. He was turning into a romantic sot. He didn't care. The rope was in lengths perfect for creating a corset and leg and arm ties for Adrianna. The need to run his hands over her soft arms and thighs continued to hammer at him. He slid rather than climbed down the ladder to the lower level.

The door opened. He took in the sight of her, his gaze caressing what he would soon feel beneath his fingers. She awaited him exactly as he expected to find her, on her knees, legs spread, eyes lowered. Her nipples were already beaded up and her lips the slightest bit pursed, an attempt to keep from smiling. *So fucking beautiful.*

"Go ahead and smile, *a gréine.* My sunshine." He stood before her, pulling her face tightly against him so her cheek rested against his abdomen and his erection was pinned under her jawline. While his hand stroked the silky sheen of tresses tumbling around her shoulders, he said, "The last seven days have been hellish, Adrianna. For both of us. We've been living by other people's rules. I'm done with that. We're going to start living by our own rules. Starting now. Rule number one, you are mine." He anchored his fingers in her hair, tilting her head so they looked in each other's eyes. "Stand."

Adrianna stood, her body slipping up along his, her skin skimming against him. Eyes shut, he brought his forehead down to hers, inhaling the scent of sunshine until it permeated his senses. "Mine," he whispered and claimed her mouth, his tongue stroking her bottom lip before he nibbled at it. "Mine," he said again.

With a little hitch in her breathing, she said, "Yours, Master. Only yours." Her murmured response soothed the possessive need that was like a fist squeezing his heart.

A smile broke across his face when he ended the kiss. "I've got a present for you. Would you like it now?"

"Yes, Master. Thank you, Master." An eager shine glistened in her eyes.

"First things first. You will stand here at rest, eyes closed." It was a pity to cover those expressive green jewels, but seeing them when she first saw his gift was a moment he wouldn't miss. From the duffel bag he'd brought with him, he pulled out a blindfold. She bit her lip when he placed it across her head.

He chuckled. "This will keep you from peeking until I'm ready for you to see your present," he said while he secured the blindfold. "Someday we'll have to play find the cock." He brought his hand to her breast and squeezed. "Not now."

The quick intake of Adrianna's breath when he took the new rope and ran it over her body was but the first of the hisses and gasps to follow. "You make the most erotic sounds, Adrianna." He pinched her nipple and elicited a husky groan. "Fucking sexy."

He slapped the rope across her stomach. "The rope feels good, doesn't it? Especially when you know you'll be helpless, completely dependent on my will alone. Do you love the rope, Adrianna?"

Her chest rose and fell in fervent response. "Yes, Sir. I love the rope. Please tie me with it. It's a lovely present."

Shane's whole body became lighter as though the gravity in the room had been altered. "It's my pleasure to tie you, Adrianna, but the rope isn't your present. It is new. Bright yellow. Like you, my sunshine. But you'll have to wait a bit longer for your present." He pinched her bottom. Her squeal of protest added to his enjoyment.

Years of practice helped his fingers fly while he tied her into a rope corset. He wound the rope around her torso, crossing it between her breasts. The silky heat of her skin intensified his need to surround her, cover her, merge with her.

Touches weren't enough. He bent, using his lips to nibble along her inner thighs when he brought the rope through her crotch. *Tastes so fucking good.* Adrianna swayed a little, so he steadied her.

"Steady, Adrianna. I'll have you fixed up soon, so you won't have to rely on those poor shaky legs." His laugh was partly due to her response and partly due to the titillating thoughts coursing through his mind.

"Yes, Sir." Adrianna's smile was broad, trusting, an encouragement all by itself. He loved that she couldn't see what he would do next, and reveled in the tension.

She was so beautiful. Completely his. It overwhelmed him. If only he could connect himself to her and never release her. To let the sensation he now knew was love radiate out from his soul and envelop them in an impenetrable field that preserved this moment forever. Joy flooded him. It wasn't an emotion he had any familiarity with in the last few years. He communicated it to Adrianna without words, an intimate perception of his heart. That she returned his love was evident in every response she made to him. Under his control, she melted, and he intended to melt into her.

He moved to view her backside, reaching out to graze a hand over her bottom. "There it is again. That glorious ass of yours. Bend over, Adrianna." When she complied, he steadied her. He stepped back, skimming her curves with an adoring gaze. With her bent over before him, the yellow rope nestled beside the dark curls on either side of her pussy acted as guiding lines. If he stayed between them, he would find her ultimate treasure. *Magnificent.* He smoothed his fingers along the cleft of her ass, straying to brush the hair between her legs. "You are stunning, a ghrá."

On his knees, he put an arm around her and rubbed his cheek against her bottom, embracing the torment it caused his aching cock. Even with the stubble of his beard scruffing her tender skin, Adrianna pushed back into the sensation. Gods, she was perfect. He kissed her hip and stood. "You may straighten."

With slow movements, he encircled one of Adrianna's wrists and pulled her arm out straight, admiring the graceful sweep of her bicep. *So strong. So lovely.* He gently massaged her from her shoulder to fingertips before nuzzling his nose into the soft hair of her armpit, inhaling deeply the scent that was pure Adrianna. A quiver ran through her, transferring to his fingers, which trembled against her satiny skin.

Along her inner arm, Shane placed kisses, tiny licks, and gentle nibbles, tasting her salty sweetness until he reached her wrist, where he sucked. Her head fell limp to the side while she succumbed to his sensual attack. He continued the swirling of his tongue in a spiral toward the center of her palm, and then he took each of her fingers briefly into his mouth before biting her thumb. Her gasp of pleasure made his erection jerk. Her tang cajoled him, tempting him to sample her more intimate flavors.

"You taste wonderful, a ghrá. I could spend hours eating you up." He grinned when she groaned in response. With deft hands, he applied a hanging wrist shackle to that arm and repeated his attentions to the other arm before shackling it. "Hold on to the knots on your palm." He checked their placement. "Good."

With two more ropes, he tied shackles to her ankles, running his hands up and down her legs before reaching through to pinch the bottom of one ass cheek. "Stay there. Don't move." He watched for a minute while she waited patiently, her fingers twitching ever so slightly. Another powerful surge of emotion poured from his chest out to the tips of his extremities, including his cock. Soon he would wrap himself around her, plunge into her warmth, and never release her. It was more than an urge to mark her as his. He wanted to show her with all his physical being that he loved her, a deep and true love that would abide and withstand the trials of fate. He exhaled and returned to his preparation.

From inside the duffel, he pulled a ten-centimeter-wide black leather belt, strapped it on, and attached short ties to D-rings on each side. He made a quick check that the safety cabinet was fully stocked and extracted one additional item from the duffel before storing it. With all the equipment stored, the gym was now bare save for Adrianna and himself. Her hand grasped in his, he led her to the middle of the room and removed her blindfold. His mouth dry, his stomach an empty pit, he stared down into her eyes. Her flashing green gaze, open, honest, trusting, reassured him.

"Adrianna, when you left the Hub with the Benefactor, you had me remove my collar from your neck. Rule number one, you are mine." He brought what he was holding from behind his back. Adrianna gasped. "This is not the same collar. When I bought this, years ago, it was with the woman who would be my wife in mind."

"It's beautiful." Adrianna reached out to trace a finger along the curve of the platinum collar and touch the large emerald-cut yellow diamond set horizontally at the center front. "This must be worth a fortune!"

"At the time, I had plenty of money. It's been my dream to put it around the neck of the woman I would spend my life with. You are that woman. Adrianna. Dria. I want to spend every day, every hour, every minute with you. There is no forever without you in it. You've brought light into my life that's let me see what's truly important. I know I told you being together permanently was impossible, but I've found a way. Will you be mine forever, Dria? I love you. I will always love you. I want to be with you. To be your Master. Will you wear this collar knowing it means we'll always be together?"

Adrianna looked deeply into Shane's eyes when she responded. "Yes, I accept your collar." Her eyes blazed. "I love you. I think I loved you almost from the first time I saw you. I will follow you wherever you go. Rule number one. I am yours, and I promise to submit to all the rules you set for our life together. Please, be my Master forever."

Shane gently placed the collar around Adrianna's neck, snapping the ends together and depressing a stud that chemically fused them. He brought his hands to her shoulders, grasping her with fingers firm with dominance, possession, and protection. "You are mine, Adrianna."

"I'm yours, Master."

Even while she was speaking the words, Shane was moving to take her mouth, to kiss her with the slow, gentle intensity of someone who had a lifetime of kisses to enjoy.

ADRIANNA WASN'T SURE she ever needed to breathe again if Shane kept kissing her like this. She was his. Not for one or two years. For always. She placed her hands on his chest. His skin was warm. She slid her hands, encircling his neck, placing her thumbs over his pulse points, feeling the vibrant throb of life in him. Her fingers slid through his hair, curling and tugging. She clung to him, to his heat, his strength, his passion. Fused to him, to the powerful force that was Shane, body and soul, she lingered in the timeless moment of the kiss, finally bringing one hand forward to stroke her knuckles along his jawline. When Shane broke the kiss, he pulled back, looking into her eyes, his purely wicked smile flashing down at her. *Oh my. He has plans.*

She watched his muscles ripple across his back and shoulders while, without saying a word, Shane connected tethers anchored high on opposite sides of the room to each of her wrist shackles. His erection stood out, the tip brushing against her when he moved past her. Her breasts and her sex were heavy with need, longing for him to touch, to stroke, to pinch, to fill her.

He pressed a control on his belt, and weight fell away when the buoyancy she associated with low or null gravity took effect. She laughed. They'd tried this before. It hadn't worked out well. They'd ended up on the floor, gravity restored, Shane holding her in place on her knees while he took her from behind. That experience taught her to remain still. Any motion on her part might send her floating off in a direction Shane didn't wish.

He latched his hands to her waist and pushed off with the right amount of force to cause them to float slowly up to the ceiling. Legs wrapped around her to hold her to him, Shane shortened the tethers that held her arms. The press of his cock against her, the tip nestling against the edge of her breasts distracted her from the work he was doing. If he'd move up higher, she could swipe that plump head and get a taste of the precum leaving a wet gloss on her skin. She whimpered when he released his legs.

He ran his tongue over her ear and whispered, "That should keep you in place."

She shuddered, the motion moving her toward the ceiling. The tethers stopped her momentum, sending her downward. She might go up and down, but a short distance either way.

He grinned while he moved with her, fingers clamped tight on her waist. "I love to hold on to you, but I'm going to need my hands for other things. Wrap your legs around my waist and hold them there. Don't let go."

Oh, I won't. Shane snug between her thighs was in the perfect place for him to be. She tipped her pelvis forward to grind against his cock, but he rotated to face away from her. Not what she was expecting, but the sensation on the insides of her legs was wonderful. Now if only he would turn back around and move between her legs in a more stimulating way. Her feet jerked when he tied the shackles on her ankles together. Such tugs always heightened her arousal, but impatience was coloring the experience differently. She wanted him. Now.

He turned around to face her again, kissed her fiercely, and growled one word, "Soon." With the short straps attached to his belt, he tied himself to her on either side of her corset.

He had her right where he wanted. No bouncing into walls this time. No drifting apart. Tied together, the heat of his body, the crinkly texture of his chest hair, the hard rod that pushed against her pussy fired her arousal to a fever pitch. He was like an arrow poised on the bow, awaiting the moment it was set free to fly toward the target. She was the target.

Eyes boring into her, he said, "Rule number two, always be honest with each other. That means no meaningful secrets. No lies. The truth spoken in love won't sever our connection." He tugged on the straps binding them together. "Lies and keeping secrets will."

"Yes." Her mind was foggy with lust, but she fought to concentrate. She nodded. "Yes, Master. Rule number two, always be honest with each other."

His eyes were dilated, a rim of blue showing around the hungering dark of his pupils. "The truth is…I honestly want to make love to you right now."

"Yes, please." With that breathy response, she let desire completely claim her, letting herself drown in the sensations of his hands and fingers brushing her skin, positioning her limbs, and grasping her with assured skill. The smell she always associated with sex, the earthy scent of leather and aroused man mingled in an erotic bouquet like a fine wine's, filling her nostrils with an essence that was purely Shane. His erection pulsed between them. He took it in hand, positioned them, and began slowly entering her, inching in slightly, withdrawing, and then pushing a little farther. It was maddening. It wasn't enough.

"All of you. Please." Why delay the consummation of the connection they had already made when his collar had fused around her neck? They needed to be one body, one mind, one heart. *Please. Now.*

At last, he pushed his way to her core, pulled out, and thrust with long strokes, his rhythm even and slow, moving deep, kissing her with mimicking thrusts of his tongue. There was no stretching sensation. It was as though her body engulfed him. His hard length filled her, completed her. She shuddered from a surfeit of physical and emotional elation.

She tipped her head back, heaving a soft cry of satisfaction. When she brought her mouth back to his, she pushed her tongue past his lips, and he sucked it in. His spicy taste was an aphrodisiac intensifying her arousal. His calloused hands skimmed up and down her back, fueling her ardor with their rough tenderness. She couldn't clutch his ass the way he was clutching hers, but she could clasp his hips with her legs, absorbing the sensation of his muscles flexing against her inner thighs, and dig her heels into his perfectly toned backside.

Shane was everywhere, filling up her entire world. He nibbled over to her ear, down her neck, and on to her breast. At the moment he took her nipple into his mouth, a rippling effect zipped down to her clit. "Aughhh," she cried.

Shane chuckled around his mouthful and moved to suck in her other breast. Joy bubbled inside her, an effect caused by the rush of his delight over her empathic senses. The euphoria of spirit and body spiraled higher, rapidly moving her toward climax.

"Master, may I come? Please, I need to come."

"Fuck yes."

Three more strokes touched her core, and Adrianna hit the pinnacle, ecstasy washing through her. Her body shook, and her lungs drew ragged breaths while the intoxication of her release thundered through her. Shane had increased his thrusting rhythm. She closed her eyes, dissolving into the sensation of floating while the man she was tied to pummeled her with his cock.

He moved from her breast to the side of her neck, the muscles throughout his body growing rigid. He ground his pelvis so that the base of his cock rubbed against her clit each time he pushed deep inside her. Another climax loomed. Shane pulled her tightly to him, arms cinched around her, shaking, panting, his release bursting from him while he cried her name, and when he relaxed, his satisfied groans were accompanied by words of love and adulation. Adrianna exploded in a second deeper orgasm, her inner walls locking on Shane in spasm after spasm, her cries mingling with his.

Wrapped up in each other, they floated, sweat slicking their bodies, and panted for air. Shane stroked her skin with the tips of his fingers. He gently kissed her. "Rule number three, we make love often."

He smiled against her lips when she repeated, "Rule number three, we make love often." He held her tight and continued to kiss her, smiling between each one. When Shane had recovered, he began the process of getting them grounded. While he loosened the tethers holding her wrists, he glanced up, his eyes glowing.

"You keep looking at me like that, and I may need to go another round," Shane said.

"Would that be so bad?" Her words drifted out from the pool of contentment where she floated.

He grinned, a rakish tilt to his smile. "Not at all. But we do need to get cleaned up for our visit to your grandmother. Remember?"

Adrianna sighed and wriggled so her nipples brushed against his chest. "I suppose so."

Shane pinched her bottom and kissed her, restoring gravity to the room while he did so. He ended the kiss when his feet touched the ground, Adrianna hanging on to his neck. He lowered her to the floor and knelt to remove the shackles from her feet and wrists. "Wear the harness under your clothes."

"Yes, Master." Adrianna flexed, the tug of the rope rubbing against her skin.

"Go clean up and be sure to wipe the harness down. It's kinshthan. It doesn't absorb fluids, so you can take a shower without worrying about getting it wet."

"Yes, Master." She stood and went to the door. Before she left, she turned. "I love you, Master. For always."

22

S hane shifted to get a better look at Adrianna's face while he sat next
to her on the couch in *Adrasteia's* lounge, his arm around her shoulders. She'd overcome the trauma of her time spent on the Benefactor's ship admirably. She was made of sturdy stuff. The Benefactor's
refusal to participate in child trafficking made some sense when she'd told
Shane about the Furzian's purity fetish. As much sense as you could
ascribe to a sociopath.

The trip from Preatiens to Tallav was drawing to a close. The healing
they'd found in each other's arms would help them face the challenges to
come on Tallav. When Adrianna giggled, he brought his attention back to
the vid they were watching.

The vids and still images Mémé Sauveterre had given Adrianna
included vids sent by her mother to Preatiens, vids of Adrianna when she
was still a child. While they watched, Adrianna had reminisced about her
childhood. The bleak impression he'd developed of her early years hadn't
been as true as he'd thought. Her parents had loved her, which these vids
of birthdays and trips to the seashore evidenced. His favorite had to be the
vid where little Adrianna had buried her father in the sand and then
dumped a bucket of seawater over his face. The vid was shaky because her
mother couldn't keep from laughing. A triumphant Adrianna had

squealed, followed by gales of giggles while her father sputtered and squirmed his way out of the sand.

"That's the last," Adrianna said.

This was what Shane's future was about—Adrianna and children of their own, making sweet memories. When he'd told her of his plans to sell the *Adrasteia* to pay her bills so they could settle somewhere and marry, she'd accepted it without reservations. He'd been afraid she'd try to talk him out of it, but she hadn't.

The time they'd spent with Mémé Sauveterre on her shuttle had gone well. She'd made it clear she thoroughly approved of Shane and had invited them to visit her. It was good Adrianna had family to support her. If only the news he intended to marry Adrianna went over as well with his parents as it had with Mémé Sauveterre.

Shane nuzzled above her ear. "You were adorable. Still are." He tickled the top of her ear with his tongue.

Adrianna squirmed with a laugh. "Don't start something we don't have time to finish."

"Oh, we have time. We won't dock for another thirty minutes." Before she could respond, he flipped her to her knees on the deck. "Mmmm. Did you wear this easy-access skirt just to tease me?"

"I was thinking more invitation," Adrianna responded.

"Invitation accepted." Shane slapped her bottom, followed by a groan, and three more slaps.

MAON WAS WAITING for them on dockside when they scrambled through the entry tube. His broad smile was followed up with bear hugs for each of them.

"Shit, I'm glad you're back. You worried the crap out of me," Maon said when he released Shane.

Shane pulled Adrianna to his side and kissed the top of her head. "Me too, Maon. Me too."

"I have good news. Car's over there." Maon pointed to the parking lot on the right.

"You got a close spot, or is there other good news?"

Maon waved his hand, slinging Shane's remark away. "Ceana has capitulated. I promised your mother I'd let her explain the details, but she said I could tell you there was nothing to worry about."

Shane restrained the whoop that bubbled up, replacing it with a wide smile. "Excellent news. I assume you found incriminating evidence."

"Assume all you want. My lips are sealed." Maon zipped his fingers across his lips.

"You spend too much time with small children."

"I have no idea what you're talking about. Come on. Stop dawdling. The director wants to see you right away. You too, Adrianna."

"Let's not keep him waiting," Shane said.

When they arrived at the car, Maon opened the back door for Adrianna while Shane climbed in the passenger seat. Once inside, Maon worked his way through spaceport parking to the main road back to Cahernamon.

"Where's the triple threat?" Shane asked.

Maon grinned. "Back home with Mommy. She and her mom are on vacation right now. I'm not sure they intend to get any farther than the pool."

Shane laughed. "Which you don't mind at all."

Maon let a pained expression slide onto his face. "Not when I'm there."

"Fuck. You didn't have to be here to pick us up."

"You owe me one." Maon chuckled. "Nah. I had to be here anyway. Another case. Which reminds me. I have the latest news on the Benefactor."

Shane turned at the waist, focusing on Maon. "Yeah?"

"The visitor's center he tried to establish in Preatien orbit was exactly what we thought it would be. Lots of levels of family fun, water park, amusement park, shopping, massive adventure maze. A wonderful friendly place."

"And?"

Maon's cheerful, bubbly voice dropped. "Private owner member level with adult-only amenities, fine dining, shows, dancing, vanilla sex. But below that a level for those looking for the outré. They specialized in entertainment that makes the Whip Hand look like a kiddie show."

"Damn," Adrianna said.

Shane looked over his shoulder at her and grimaced before turning his gaze back to Maon.

Maon nodded. "Yeah. Not pretty. Preatiens is seizing it. Don't know what they'll do with it. They won't be keeping it in orbit, though. The Benefactor must not know the Feds have cracked Vorlooph encryption, or he wouldn't have used it to block unauthorized access to his data. The investigation team was able to access all the files and data they found on the *Fantasy*. We got a complete list of Preatien officials and bigwigs he was planning to co-opt and the methods they intended to use. There's been a spate of strongly influenced retirements."

Shane looked out of the car, his arm along the window's edge, his finger tapping the door. Apartment complexes flashed by while they made their way to the city center to the complex of government office buildings. How many men and women on Tallav had sexual proclivities they hid? He'd learned firsthand what it was like to be a societal outcast. He turned to look back at Maon.

"Preatiens isn't a sexually open society," he said.

"No," Maon said. "But in some cases the motivation was greed, power. Anything that could leave them open to blackmail. He already had a few Preatien citizens in his pocket. Their job was to introduce new members to their exclusive club."

"Better to be open about things," Shane said.

"You are so right." Maon steered the car toward the building entrance. "And here we are. If you want, I'll take your bags to your car."

Shane opened the door. "Thanks. You remember the key code?"

Maon tapped his forehead. "Locked inside."

Adrianna had exited the car and was standing next to Shane. She bent down and said, "Thanks, Maon."

"Stop by Ettington if you have time. I know my wife, Selina, is dying to meet you."

"We'll try. Soon," Shane said. He slammed the door shut and guided Adrianna with a hand on her back to the entrance of the Marshals Head-quarters.

EXITING THE LIFT, Adrianna recognized the same receptionist from her last visit. Derek quickly ushered them to the director's office. When he opened the door and announced them, he raised his eyebrows and gave Adrianna an I-know-something-you-don't-know smile.

She studied the family pictures displayed on the light wooden shelves on the wall behind the director's desk when she settled into the seat offered her. She noted that the youngest son in the family portrait was Derek. Two sons and one daughter with the director's dark-headed, square-jawed rugged good looks, two daughters, and one son with his wife's sandy-haired, slender frame. Shane sat in the chair next to Adrianna and took her hand in his.

His hands clasped in front of him, elbows on the arms of his chair, the director said, "Adrianna, I want to express the Marshals Service and my personal appreciation for your assistance in bringing a successful conclusion to the operation you recently took part in. Your willingness to put yourself in harm's way has not gone unnoticed."

Adrianna resisted the impulse to fidget. "Thank you, sir. I'm not sure I was ever truly in harm's way, but I will admit spending time with the Benefactor is a 'pleasure' I'd gladly forego."

"Fortunately, that's something you shouldn't ever have to do. I've read the official reports submitted by the marshals involved in the operation, and they've expressed admiration for the way you handled yourself throughout." He motioned toward Shane when he said, "You probably know that Marshal Tiernan has requested additional training for you, and I'm happy to expedite that. You weren't initially hired by the service, but you've turned out to be quite an asset to Marshal Tiernan and the service."

"Thank you, sir." Her cheeks pinked at the praise. She returned the squeeze Shane gave her hand.

The director smiled and rubbed his hands together. "As for you, Tiernan. You've handled this operation well. Not that I expected any less from you. You've done exemplary work as the supervisory special agent for organized crime in this sector. There's an opening in the organized crime section here at headquarters for an assistant section chief, and I'd like you to consider applying for that position."

"Thank you, Sir. I'd be honored to hold such a position." Shane shifted in his seat. "It's always been my goal to make the Marshals Service a career. However, my priorities have changed recently. I will be applying for a change of position, but it will have to be off world. Adrianna and I will be marrying, and I will need to live off Tallav. I'm hoping my mother will sanction the marriage, and I'll be able to remain with the Marshals. If she doesn't, I still intend to marry Adrianna." Shane gave Adrianna a solemn look before returning his gaze to the director.

The director's brow furrowed. "I see. Well, I can't blame you. Adrianna is a fine young woman. Congratulations to both of you."

"Thank you, sir. Our next stop is a visit to my mother's estate. Once I know my mother's intentions, I'll file formal paperwork with workforce management." Shane stood and offered his hand to the director.

"I'll be waiting to hear from you. But no matter the outcome, I'm sure we can find you something that will make the most of your talents," the director said.

WHEN THEY REACHED the outskirts of Cahernamon, Shane drove around a curve, laughing when Adrianna punched his arm.

"You've got something up your sleeve. Don't deny it." His nonchalant act interspersed with quick gleaming glances would have given him away even if his emotions hadn't.

Shane waggled his eyebrows at her. "What if I do?"

Oh yes. He had a surprise for her. "You're not going to tell me, are you?"

Shane shook his head with a smirk, looking entirely too pleased with himself. "You won't have long to wait."

She squinted at him. "But it's twenty hours by car to Gleann Millis."

"Yes, it is. You won't have to wait that long." He continued to glance at her while he monitored the road, chuckling when she threw her hands up and released an exasperated sigh. "We're almost there." He turned onto a long road that led toward several large buildings.

As they drew closer, Adrianna said, "A shuttle port? We're going to fly?"

With a broad smile, Shane nodded. "It is faster. My mother keeps shuttles hangared here in the city and at Gleann Millis. You'll be able to see more of the countryside than you can from a road."

Adrianna looked at him, eyes bright, a grin matching his stretching from ear to ear.

A shuttle and pilot were waiting for them in front of the hangar. As soon as they'd buckled in and taken off, Adrianna plastered herself to the window by her seat. Shane removed his seat belt to scoot next to her, placing his hand on her waist and his chin on her shoulder to look out with her. He supplied commentary, asking the pilot to slow or circle when they approached something of particular interest.

When low clouds blocked their view, they settled back, holding hands. Adrianna rested her head on Shane's shoulder. Silence was like a warm blanket enfolding them in a space they alone shared. Her connection with Shane was strong. It was as though, when he'd fused the collar she wore, he'd fused them together as well. An hour later, the clouds had dissipated, and a spectacular site stretched for miles below them.

She looked down at the rainbow-colored hills below her, glancing back at Shane to share her wonder. "I've never seen anything like this."

"It's a Tallavan legend that when the original settlers of Tallav looked down on their new planet, they saw these rainbow hills and knew they'd found their pot of gold, Tallav itself."

"I think they were right." She continued to press her nose to the shuttle window. "What a glorious place to live. I wish we could stay."

"Dria." Shane waited until Adrianna turned to look at him. "I found my pot of gold when I found you. The setting of our life isn't as important as the people we live it with."

Adrianna snuggled into his chest. "You're absolutely right."

Soon after, the clouds returned, blocking their view. Shane nuzzled his face into her hair, letting the sunny citrus smell permeate his senses. She had fallen asleep, breathing in a steady rhythm. He relaxed into the peace of holding her.

Before landing the shuttle at the Gleann Millis shuttle port, Shane woke her and had the pilot make a wide loop to show her the portion of the estate with the family residence and estate buildings. After climbing down from the shuttle, he drew Adrianna to where two large black horses stood waiting before an open cart. Shane helped her up to a seat on the front bench and then helped the pilot load their luggage into the bed at the back of the cart. Once he'd joined her, Shane took the reins and drove toward a lane lined with a hedgerow and tall trees.

"I asked Ned, our overseer, to have the cart waiting for us. It's a bit of whimsy my family maintains. Whenever possible, we arrive by horse cart when we've been away for a long time. It's meant to help us return to the quiet rhythm of the land."

Adrianna hugged his arm. "That's lovely."

"My great-grandmother had the trees planted along this lane to shade the drive. My mother hates that they block the view up to the house, but Father has managed to keep her from cutting them down."

"What do you think?" she asked.

"I like them. You'll see when we come out at the end, the house pops into view, and it's just there. This old stone castle house. You only get that surprise from this lane with the trees hiding the view."

As they made the turn that brought the house into view, Shane looked at Adrianna. "Well?"

"It's magical," she said, her eyes round. "I feel transported to another time."

Shane's smile held a wistful note. "It does feel like time has passed it by."

ADRIANNA TRAILED behind Shane when he entered the family lounge. The comfortable, lived-in room had large windows looking out over a vista of meadows with horses grazing in the distance. Pádraig rose to greet them with a smile and hug for each.

"Your mother is in the midst of a conference comm. She said we should eat lunch without her. She wants to speak with you, Shane, after you've eaten." Shane's father led them to a windowed alcove off the lounge where platters of thick crusty bread, slices of grilled chicken, and a variety of cheese slices waited to be turned into sandwiches. Vegetable sticks, a fruit compote, and iced tea completed the meal's offerings.

While they ate, Pádraig recounted recent events at Gleann Millis, seeming to understand that Shane was in no mood to talk. Adrianna filled in the gaps in the conversation with comments and questions.

Between the two of them, they allowed Shane to retreat into his own thoughts.

When lunch finished, Shane went to his mother's office. Pádraig offered to take Adrianna on a tour of the stables, which she accepted. She was glad to have the distraction even while her concern followed Shane.

"Have you ever ridden before?" Pádraig asked while he walked with her to the stables.

"No, I haven't." A slight breeze ruffled her hair, and the scent of fresh-mown grass tickled her nose.

"We'll have to get you started soon." When they entered the stables, he said, "Most of the horses have been turned out to pasture already." A black mare whickered when he approached her stall. "This is Ebony Miss." Pádraig reached out to pet the horse. "She's got an appointment with the farrier. Don't you, sweet girl?"

Adrianna looked up tentatively at the tall horse. "She's beautiful. May I pet her?"

"Yes. Of course."

She stroked Ebony Miss's white blaze, delighted when the horse bumped her hand for more when she stopped.

"We keep draft horses and sport horses. Ebony Miss is the dam of the two horses that drew your cart yesterday."

Adrianna cooed sweet nothings at Ebony Miss while she petted her. "So Shane grew up riding?"

"Oh yes. I don't think there's a spot on the whole estate Shane hasn't seen on horseback. He and his brother, Thomas, spent weeks roughing it. Come, let's head on out and see who they've got in the training yard."

The more she saw of Gleann Millis, the more Adrianna understood how much Shane was giving up to be with her. She'd always believed that people were more important than things, but she hadn't had many things worth holding on to. Gleann Millis was a place to cherish. When Shane had collared her, she'd sensed his sincerity when he'd told her there was no forever without her in it. Since they'd arrived at Gleann Millis, Shane had been quiet, struggling with the sadness of knowing his children would never experience the home he loved as he had. Adrianna resolved that wherever they settled, she and Shane would build a life of equal substance to the one his ancestors had built at Gleann Millis.

~

SHANE HAD LEFT his mother's study, pausing in the hallway to wipe the moisture from his eyes. Now he needed to find Adrianna. The stables. His father had taken her to the stables.

Adrianna and his father were leaning against a fence, watching the trainer work a chestnut gelding. While Shane walked toward them, she turned to face him with an expectant look, a smile quivering at the corners of her mouth. His father turned and beamed at him, knowing the news he was bringing Adrianna.

"Dria, I have good news."

His father grasped Shane's shoulder. "I'll leave you to tell Dria. When you're ready, come up to the house."

Shane nodded and then took Adrianna's hand. "Come. Let's go somewhere we can sit and talk." Without another word, he led Adrianna to the path that wound its way down to a small wooded area near a stream. Overhead the leaves rustled and birds chirped. One larger mottled brown bird must have felt they'd invaded its space because it screeched at them, hopping from branch to branch until they left its territory.

Adrianna laughed when he brought her to the base of a stout tree, a thick rope ladder dangling from above. When her head tilted back to look up at the platform ensconced in the leafy branches, she said, "Your tree house!"

"Yep. This is the ladder to mine." He pointed on a little farther to another large tree. "Thomas's tree house is there."

"Are we going up?"

"Of course." Hands on the rungs, he followed her up. "You may be the first girl who's ever been up here."

"I'm honored."

As they reached the platform, Shane took her in his arms and kissed her. With her held tight, he let love flow from his eyes while he looked deep into her flashing green ones. "I love you, a mhuirnín. You are my heart, my sunshine, and my love. I want you to live life with me, to bear my children, to grow old with me."

Adrianna returned his gaze with equal intensity. "That sounds perfect. I love you, Shane Tiernan, and I would gladly spend forever with you."

He brought his hand to her cheek, stroking the smooth skin, overwhelmed at the fervency of her emotional response. Empathic senses were not required to feel the love that flowed from Adrianna's eyes straight to his heart.

He claimed her lips, finding an outlet for the exhilaration that brimmed over inside him. He poured all his love into that kiss. It was true Adrianna could sense his emotions, but with this kiss, he showed her the staggering depths of his love for her. When he at last broke the kiss, Adrianna swayed against him.

"Your mother sanctioned the marriage?" she asked, breathless.

"No." He rushed to explain. "She would have, but she's found another solution. Come sit while I tell you." He helped her perch with dangling feet on the edge of the tree-house floor.

With a deep breath, he began. "My mother has worked a miracle." Adrianna sucked in her own breath and held it, eyes wide when Shane said, "I don't have to enter into any more contracts to sire an heir."

She turned, bending one knee so she could sit facing Shane. "How is that possible?"

Shane shifted to face her. "My mother has made you her ward and heir." He nodded when her eyebrows rose. "I know. I didn't think such a thing was possible. She more or less strong-armed the governing council into accepting it. It was a trade-off. She agreed not to pursue a legal matter that would create an enormous scandal and give ammunition to the men's rights movement. They agreed to let her adopt you as her heir."

Her voice soft, Adrianna said, "Wow. I don't know what to say."

Shane couldn't contain the grin that burst across his face. "It gets better. The legal matter is tied up in the fraud Ceana committed against me."

"Ceana?" A small furrow appeared like a question mark between her eyes.

Shane drew his finger down the side of her face. "Yeah. Maon and I couldn't figure out why she would do something against her own interest. She needed the money that my child would bring her. As it turns out, someone had already paid her off to keep me from fathering an heir."

Adrianna's eyebrows rose. "Who would pay her to do that?"

Shane reached out and took her hand. "My aunt. She's been trying for the last few years to get me declared legally unsuitable to be a breeder, removing me from my mother's line of descent. My mother had managed to block her. When my aunt heard I was looking for a woman to bear me a child, she got desperate. She arranged for Ceana to accept my contract and take the after pills to keep from getting pregnant."

Shane placed a finger under Adrianna's chin and pushed up to close her mouth, open from when her jaw had dropped.

"Remember the man in the audience at the Whip Hand? The one you pointed out to me?" Shane drew her hand to his mouth and kissed the back.

Adrianna sighed. "Yes."

As he spoke, Shane stroked her hand with his cheek. "He was a man my aunt hired to watch me and gather evidence of my unsuitability to breed. He'd made an illegal hidden vid of our suspension and the scene between Trey, Randolph, and me. Tying up a naked woman would definitely make my aunt's case. Must have followed me quite a while. Until you"—he brought her fingers to his lips—"I hadn't played in public in a long, long time."

"How did your mother stop her?"

A wicked smile lit Shane's face. "Ceana blew it. I guess I should be thankful she spiked me and assaulted me. She must have thought she could get away with it because she'd seen the vid my aunt had. Probably wanted to administer a little personal justice as well."

Adrianna's nostrils flared. "Bitch!"

Shane released her hand to caress Adrianna's cheek. "Well, once Maon got on Ceana's trail, he found out that my aunt was paying her large sums of money. It all sort of snowballed from there. Members of the council got involved, and a deal was struck. It didn't hurt that about the same time I'd been declared a local hero for leading the team that stopped illegal human trafficking through the Hub."

Adrianna stared into Shane's eyes. "Amazing. All because two sisters fell out years ago."

Caught in Adrianna's gaze, Shane leaned forward. "Yeah, I can't be happy about that, but I am happy about how all this mess has worked out for us. With you as my mother's heir, I don't have to rush to have a girl." He grinned wickedly. "Although there will be pressure on you to reproduce as soon as possible."

"I think I could work that out. I have someone in mind that would make a great father." She grinned in return.

Shane scooted back and pulled her on top of his chest when he lay back against the wooden boards of the tree-house floor. Hands in her hair, he prepared to kiss her when Adrianna said, "But won't you still have to quit the Marshals?"

"Not if we don't marry."

"I see." Her forehead wrinkled, and she blinked down at him.

"Is that a problem? Because when our children are of age, I can marry and remain a marshal."

Her face smoothed. "Your collar is all the commitment I need. But there is this tiny bit of traditionalist in me. Marriage is more than just commitment to each other. It's commitment to our children too. But, I know you will be every bit as dedicated to our children with or without marriage."

"Absolutely. You and our children will be the center of my world. Nothing, even the Marshals, will come between us."

Shane's eyes darkened. "Adrianna Pacquin, will you do me the honor of becoming my wife?"

A wicked need to tease him bubbled inside her. Through smirking lips, she said, "I'm not sure I can handle such a long engagement. I could meet some other handsome marshal between now and then. I'll have to think about that…"

"Adrianna." Shane looked up at her sternly.

"Yes, Master." Her gaze fluttered from his lips to his eyes and back again.

"You will marry me when the time comes, Adrianna."

Adrianna bit her lip. "Yes. Master. Of course, Master. Anything you say, Master." She giggled when Shane rolled her over and pinned her to the tree-house floor.

"Be quiet, Adrianna. I'm going to kiss you now."

~

Discover more of Cailin's sci-fi romance on her website at
https://cailinbriste.com

Subscribe to her newsletters for monthly updates on her releases, sales, and events.
https://cailinbriste.com/cailins-newsletter-sign-up/

Read on for an excerpt from *Maon: Marshal of Tallav* book #2 in this series.

MAON: MARSHAL OF TALLAV EXCERPT

Space travel held no appeal for Selina. The CEO of the sector's leading fashion house, she'd accepted it as the necessity it was, but she'd be glad to get her feet on solid ground again. Her nose alone told her she wasn't there yet. The air filtration system on the Beta Tau station did a better job than most at removing the metallic tang of C-trol, the fuel ships ran on in hyper-space that permeated all space stations. A harsh aftertaste still clung in silvered wisps to the more mundane odors of fried foods and roasting meats that tempted travelers to part with credits before heading down world or returning to space. No, she wasn't there yet.

The strap of the portfolio slung over her shoulder slipped. A nudge and it was back in place. A trio of vacationers passed her, their excitement palpable in the pitch and volume of their voices. They hadn't noticed Selina, but who would? Hidden inside the drab, shapeless dress that constituted her armor against amorous attentions, she was perfectly content to be overlooked. No one would credit the truth. She was on her way to the Whip Hand to meet the owner and notorious sadist Randolph Meryon. The drawings she carried in her portfolio were the first install-ment of a trade she'd made. He would become her mentor while she explored sexual domination, and she would design exclusive apparel for his staff.

The underlying frisson of unease that always attended her in space was sliding up and down her spine. But the churning in her stomach, while she walked along the companionway from the private ship docks, wasn't caused by her fear of space. Her father's death over a year ago had cemented a number of things in her mind. One was the need to acquire a husband. Knowledge that she was on the marriage market would set in motion the machinations of the aristocratic mamas of Tallav—some because of her wealth and others for the connection. She wrinkled her nose. *Not going that route.*

Her Domme lessons with Randolph were the initial step in a concise plan to find her perfect husband. Emphasis on *her*. Implementing that plan was the root of her anxiety, akin to the strain of her first business negotiation for the House of Shirley.

A couple, the woman tipping along in platform heels, were cuddling and cooing while they walked toward Selina. She averted her face, seeing but not really taking in the concourse bar she was approaching. Then her gaze met a stranger's, and for an interminable moment, his eyes ensnared hers. She blinked, and the spell was broken. His lips moved in a smirk while he continued to stare at her.

Damn playboy.

When she yanked her head away, the oversize art case slipped down her arm, the strap tangling in her long dark hair. Rather than stop to fix the problem, she kept walking while struggling to release the strands that were pulling painfully on her scalp. Portfolio back in position, she sped up.

That man was the exact opposite of her ideal mate, although he was Tallavan. The string tie he wore made his Tallavan citizenship a possibility, but the badge clipped to his belt settled it. He was a Tallavan marshal. Despite his tousled sandy-brown locks that were made to comb through and pull, he wouldn't make the cut on her very exacting list of requirements. Even before he'd smirked at her, it was apparent he was a player. He'd been sitting still on a bar stool, but swagger oozed from his pores. His navy-blue eyes were full of a boldness that reached out to her and offered her more fun than she could imagine.

What the heck are you thinking, Selina? He's a snack and nothing more.

For her steady diet, she needed something less attractive, less powerful, and much more malleable. Truly malleable, not just a man who played the role to catch a Tallavan aristocrat and then left their children to nannies and tutors to raise while they flitted from event to event gambling and whoring.

The deal with Randolph couldn't have come at a better time. With his mentoring, she'd learn to recognize a submissive personality along with discovering where her preference for control would lead in the bedroom. Today was her first session. They'd had several long discussions via comm, focusing on the types of play she was interested in. Sensation play had been at the top of her to-do list. She wasn't attracted to bondage or the delivery of pain except where it enhanced the upward spiral of sexual need. Randolph had convinced her that a whip in clever hands was the perfect tool to heighten arousal.

She'd find out tonight. He required all dominants he mentored to assume the submissive role initially. To understand what you were dishing out, you had to experience it. The thought of his whip was adding its own provocation to her case of nerves. Allowing someone to use a whip on her wasn't her idea of pleasure. He'd said the effective use of a whip was more mental than physical. She could attest to that. Her mind was on full dread overload.

Steady on. You've input your destination. Now grab hold of the hyperstrand and don't let go.

Gods, she was exhorting herself with space metaphors. Maybe that was appropriate. She sure had her emotional teeth gritted like she did every time she stepped on a shuttle to head into space.

The shuttle docks were on the bottom level of the space station. Once she exited the lift and passed through entry control, she palmed the pass she'd been given. Berth 21 was to her left. Departure was close, so she hurried to the entry port. A quick scan showed three empty spots, all in the rear of the transport. With a nod to the passenger seated in the window seat, she slid into the aisle seat across from the other two vacant places. After receiving the assent of the gentleman next to her, she handed him her portfolio to slide against the shuttle wall. It fit below the large view window. Most travelers looked forward to the spectacular sight of Beta Tau while spiraling around the planet toward the spaceport. Funny how from such a great height the shifting reds, pinks, browns, and oranges of the desert planet's sands were awe inspiring, while down planet they were a nuisance to overcome.

A quick mental check of shuttle departures on her Electronic Biological CoServer showed the shuttle should start disconnecting from dock in about a minute. Where were the last two passengers? She leaned out of her seat to try to see the entry port. *Good.* Someone else was making their way on board. She settled back, and as did every other passenger who was ready to get going, she watched the pair of men amble down the aisle. The man in the lead was tall and dark. And oh sweet petunias, he was a Tallavan marshal. When they drew closer, a second marshal appeared, and a cocky half smile flashed when his gaze met hers. Again. The playboy. Selina dropped her gaze to her lap and tried to ignore the banter between the men while they settled into the two seats across the narrow aisle from hers.

"Take the window," the darker headed of the two said.

"Sure." The playboy slid past the other marshal to sit in the window seat. "Are we going straight to the club?"

"No. You eager for Randolph's challenge?"

"Eager to collect the prize."

Selina resisted the urge to stare across the aisle. Had she really heard the name Randolph?

"I don't think I'll ever get why you accept his challenges."

The playboy responded, "That isn't dropping the subject, but I'll answer you. Why does Ray Nox climb the mountains on Tallav's moon? Because they, in all their airless, soaring height, are there, a challenge to conquer. Randolph challenges, and I conquer."

"I still don't get it. But I don't get Ray Nox either."

"And you never will," said the playboy. "Just as I'll never get why you spend so much time tying women up in intricate rope creations."

Selina straightened in her seat, realizing she'd been leaning toward the pair. They couldn't be going to the Whip Hand. Could they? Clubs abounded on Beta Tau, but then they'd mentioned the name Randolph.

The tall, dark marshal grunted. "Randolph said if I can work out my Ball of Beauties, he might use it as the Whip Hand's ball drop on New Year's Eve. Put up Earth's ball drop on live vid and drop our own at the same time."

"You should think of another name. Ball of Beauties sounds dumb."

"Yeah. I'll work on that. But can you imagine crystal-studded harnesses and lights…"

The playboy laughed. "I can see you're getting transported to your happy place. So why not go straight to the club?"

"I brought special equipment in my baggage. We'll have to stop at the hotel first and wait for it to be delivered. You can spend the time checking out the staff."

"Heh."

Selina turned her head to look out the shuttle window, one finger tapping on her leg. *Damn.* Just what she didn't need. Tallavan aristocrats catching sight of her at the Whip Hand. The gossip would rabbit through the upper echelons of society, contradicting the asexual persona she presented to the world. The men had said they weren't going straight to the club like she was. If they were meeting Randolph, it would be after her appointment with him. She ought to be gone before they arrived. Randolph would help. He knew her preference for absolute privacy. Besides, she'd be masked. Stepping outside her comfort zone was giving her a case of the jitters. She took a deep breath and released it. *You're Selina Shirley. You can handle anything.*

Maon fiddled with the glass in his hand. From his perch at the end of the space-station bar where he sat waiting for Shane to meet him, he could observe everyone entering the companionway from the private ship docks on this side of the station. The usual eye candy passed him, rushing to explore as much as they could of the pleasures that awaited them on Beta Tau. Shane was due in on the *Adrasteia*. Maon didn't envy Shane much, but the *Adrasteia* was one sweet little craft.

"Refill?" asked the bartender.

"Yeah. But no alcohol. Something fruity."

When the bartender returned with his drink, Maon noticed a Tallavan woman heading his way. He should know her name, but it wasn't coming to him. Definitely a prude. Wearing some misshapen, baggy sack of a dress. Nice legs, but they'd look better in heels rather than the flats she wore. Shirley. That's who she was. He'd heard something about her taking over her mother's fashion house. Fuck's sake. If that was her sense of style, they'd be out of business soon.

He eyed her when she passed him, and their gazes met for a moment. He acknowledged her with a smirk. The portfolio she carried slipped, and she struggled to keep it from falling, her long sable hair snagging in the strap. Her head remained down while she swept from view. Maon chuckled.

"Are you harassing passersby again?"

"Shane!" Maon stood and grasped his friend's outstretched hand. "I can't help being devastatingly good-looking. The bane of my existence. Females dropping at my feet."

"Some bane. You up for fun?" Shane focused on the people walking past the open bar. "Randolph told me he's got the subs I need and plans for you. You're not gonna let him stretch your balls again?" He centered his bright blue gaze on Maon, one eyebrow arched.

Maon grinned. "He tries. Never wins. I have balls of steel."

"Brains of mush."

"You're jealous." Maon winked at a pretty girl passing by, letting his tousled good looks and crooked smile work their magic. One thing Beta Tau had in abundance—women, all shapes and sizes ready to have fun. And he was here to make their dreams come true.

Shane glanced at Maon and looked away in disdain. "What? Jealous! You get one girl as a prize. I've already got eight waiting on me."

"What do you do with them? Tie 'em up." Maon shook his head and paid the bartender. Both men headed toward the lift to take them to the shuttle docks. Shane seemed, as usual, oblivious to the undisguised interest the two handsome Tallavan marshals received while they strode down the companionway. Maon noticed, enjoying the attention, a slight exaggeration to his swagger while he winked and appreciated the varied reactions to his flirting. Yes, this trip was what he needed after a long stint of ferrying prisoners around the sector.

Having the owner of the top kink club on Beta Tau as one of your best friends was a definite benefit. The twins Randolph had offered as prizes on Maon's last vacation had fueled his fantasy life for months, fantasies Maon had amped up by adding in a hot Domme to put the girls through their paces. Randolph never set him up with a Domme. The prizes for winning Randolph's challenges were always subs. Not that many Dommes were willing to offer a session as a prize. Randolph said he'd never found the right one for Maon. Maybe this time.

Maon's one slim thread of hope for a long-term relationship was to find a Domme who could accept him as the switch he was and keep his cock in line. He didn't know which was harder, but combined, his requirements made that thread whisper thin. Which was why he'd stopped worrying about it. *If you can't have apple cobbler, eat the peach pie.* He was dedicated to peach pie.

Shane interrupted Maon's reverie. "You don't have to accept Randolph's challenges. They're only going to get worse. He's a sadist. He likes rigging you up and seeing you suffer. One of you has to say it's time to stop."

Maon pressed his lips together. "That won't be me. He knows I won't step back, so he'll have to be the one to call it quits. Talk to him. Not me."

"Fuck it. You—"

"No. He hasn't done me permanent damage, and he won't. Drop it. We're here to have fun, not fight."

Shane sighed, nodding. "I am going to talk to him."

"Good luck with that."

Both men showed their badges to bypass the entry control line and obtain shuttle passes. The attendant directed them to the last two open seats at the back of the shuttle. It wasn't until Maon neared the last row that he noticed the Tallavan frump he'd spotted from the bar. Up close she was quite pretty. Why the hell was she hiding in those awful clothes? He winked and flashed his panty-melting half smile and waited for her reaction. She focused her gaze on her lap, pretending to ignore him, but Maon could tell she was affected because of the muscle that twitched in her jaw. He annoyed her. Time to stop, then. He didn't like making women angry. He slid into the window seat and dropped her from his mind.

Purchase Maon: Marshal of Tallav, Book #2
https://books2read.com/maon

ALSO BY CAILIN

A Thief in Love Suspense Romance Series

It Takes a Cat Burglar

How to Steal the Pharaoh's Jewels

A Touch of Greed

Sons of Tallav

Maon: Marshal of Tallav

Rand: Son of Tallav

Trey: Son of Tallav

ABOUT CAILIN BRISTE

Cailin Briste is a USA Today Bestselling author who writes erotic, science fiction, suspense, and fantasy romance. She and her husband are vagabonds, living in an RV named Floyd pulled by a beautiful monster of a truck, Fiona.

Her Sons of Tallav series is set in a sector of Federation space far off the beaten path. The Tallavan marshals are tasked with keeping the peace while coming to terms with the matriarchal system of their home planet, Tallav. Tricky because each is heavily involved in the BDSM lifestyle.

A Thief in Love Suspense Romance series, begins with a cat burglar who steals priceless art and antiquities from other thieves. Sebastian is a Robin Hood character whose Maid Marion is his equal on the rooftops of their futuristic city. Each book in the series focuses on a member of his crew.

The Guardians of the Vale series, starting with *A Prince of Her Own*, will be published sometime in the future.

Subscribe to her newsletter at http://cailinbriste.com/cailins-newsletter-sign-up/ for information about her latest releases, exclusive giveaways, and special prices.

www.ingramcontent.com/pod-product-compliance
Lightning Source LLC
Chambersburg PA
CBHW021220250626
47155CB00008B/2893